murder
at the
conspiracy
convention
and
other
american
absurdities

murder at the conspiracy convention and other american absurdities

paul krassner

Introduction by **george carlin**

BARRICADE BOOKS • FORT LEE, NJ

Published by Barricade Books Inc.
185 Bridge Plaza North
Suite 308-A
Fort Lee, NJ 07024
www.barricadebooks.com

Design and typesetting by Sam Sheng, CompuDesign

Library of Congress Cataloging-in-Publication Data

Krassner, Paul.
    Murder at the conspiracy convention and other American
absurdities / Paul Krassner with an introduction by George Carlin.
        p. cm.
        ISBN 1-56980-231-9 (pbk. : alk. paper)
            1. United States–Politics and government—1989–   2. United
States—Social conditions—1980–   3. United States—Social life and
customs—1971–   4. Popular culture—United States—History—
20th century.   5. Political culture—United States—History—20th
century.

E839.5 .K73 2002
973.92—dc21

                                                            2002016396

First Printing

Manufactured in Canada

contents

Introduction by George Carlin   xiii

Foreword by Paul Krassner   xv

THE FEDERAL BUREAU OF INTIMIDATION

Me and the FBI   3

John Lennon and the FBI   6

NOW AND THEN

The Sexual Revolution   15

Dirty Underwear at Disney World   18

Moments of Cringe   21

A COUPLE OF SUBCULTURES

Evolution for the Hell of It   27

Life Among the Neo-Pagans   31

THREE FACES OF EVIL

Charlie Manson's Image   37

Timothy McVeigh's Body Count   40

The Devil in Me   42

THE WHITE HOUSE SCANDAL

The Memoirs of Monica Lewinsky   47

President Clinton's Private Confession   51

Kenneth Starr Meets JonBenet Ramsey   55

CAMPAIGN IN THE ASS

Dan Rather, Harry Shearer and Me   59
We Shall Overlap   61
An Election Carol   69
Bush Whacked   72

SEVERAL DEAD FRIENDS

Waiting for Shepherd   77
Saint Abortionist   80
A Game of Mind Tennis With Timothy Leary 84
Allen Ginsberg's Last Laugh   94
Anita and the Blow-Up Doll   99
Further Weirdness With Terence McKenna   109
Remembering John Lilly   119

CELEBRITY CULTURE

Country Joe McDonald Wore Khakis   125
Steve Allen and Lucille Ball   127
A Letter to Hunter Thompson   131
Worship at the Celebrity of Your Choice   135
The House That Frank Destroyed   143

THE WAR ON NON-CORPORATE DRUGS

The Pied Piper of Hemp   147
Checkmating With Pawns   154
Ask Your Doctor   157
An Interview With Chiquita Banana   160
How Sinsemilla Came to America   163
Ritalin Wars   167
Plan Humboldt   170
False Alarm   173
Who Killed Peter McWilliams?   176

THE PENIS MONOLOGUES

The Missing Episode of *Seinfeld*   185

Pissing Contest   188

COUNTERCULTURAL ICONS

The Persecution of Lenny Bruce   193

Steal This Abbie   201

Jerry Garcia and His Magic Shield   214

The Evolution of Just Plain Ram Dass   225

Kesey's Last Prank   239

DEFYING CONVENTIONS

Jealousy at the Swingers Convention   261

Murder at the Conspiracy Convention   276

My Cannabis Cup Runneth Over   323

This one is for Robert Anton Wilson—guerrilla ontologist, part-time post-modernist, Damned Old Crank, my weirdest friend and favorite philosopher.

Also By the Author

- *How a Satirical Editor Became a Yippie Conspirator in Ten Easy Years*
  - *Tales of Tongue Fu*
  - *The Best of* The Realist
- *Confessions of a Raving, Unconfined Nut: Misadventures in the Counter-Culture*
  - *The Winner of the Slow Bicycle Race: The Satirical Writings of Paul Krassner*
    - *Impolite Interviews*
  - *Sex, Drugs and the Twinkie Murders: 40 Years of Countercultural Journalism*
    - *Pot Stories for the Soul*
    - *Psychedelic Trips for the Mind*
  - *Magic Mushrooms and Other Highs: From Toad Slime to Ecstasy*

*"Let me issue and control a nation's money,
and I care not who writes its laws."*

—*Meyer Rothschild*

*"I guess I'm just an old mad scientist at bottom. Give me an
underground laboratory, half a dozen atom smashers, and a
beautiful girl in a diaphanous veil waiting to be turned into a
chimpanzee, and I care not who writes the nation's laws."*

—*S. J. Perelman*

Portions of "Irony Lives!," "Kesey's Last Prank" and "My Cannabis Cup Runneth Over" were published in the *L.A. Weekly*.

"Me and the FBI," "An Election Carol," "Worship at the Celebrity of Your Choice" and "Checkmating With Pawns" were published in the *Los Angeles Times*.

"John Lennon and the FBI" was published in *In These Times*.

"The Sexual Revolution," "Dirty Underwear at Disney World," "Moments of Cringe," "Evolution for the Hell of It," "Life Among the Neo-Pagans," "Charlie Manson's Image," "Timothy McVeigh's Body Count," "The Devil in Me," "Bush Whacked," "Further Weirdness With Terence McKenna," "Remembering John Lilly," "Steve Allen and Lucille Ball," "A Letter to Hunter Thompson," "The Pied Piper of Hemp," "Ask Your Doctor," "An Interview With Chiquita Banana," "How Sinsemilla Came to America," "Ritalin Wars," "Plan Humboldt," "False Alarm," "Who Killed Peter McWilliams?," "The Persecution of Lenny Bruce," "Steal This Abbie," "Jerry Garcia and His Magic Shield," "The Evolution of Just Plain Ram Dass," "Kesey's Last Prank," "Murder at the Conspiracy Convention" and "My Cannabis Cup Runneth Over" were published in *High Times*.

"The Memoirs of Monica Lewinsky," "President Clinton's Private Confession," "Kenneth Starr Meets JonBenet Ramsey," "Saint Abortionist," "A Game of Mind Tennis With Timothy Leary," "Allen Ginsberg's Last Laugh" and "Country Joe McDonald Wore Khakis" were published in *The Realist*.

"Dan Rather, Harry Shearer and Me" was published in *Funny Times*.

"We Shall Overlap" was published in *George*.

"Waiting for Shepherd," "Pissing Contest" and "Jealousy at the Swingers Convention" were published in *Playboy*.

"Anita and the Blow-Up Doll" was published in *Tikkun*.

"The House That Frank Destroyed" was published in the *Desert Post Weekly*.

"The Missing Episode of *Seinfeld*" was published in *Penthouse*.

introduction

George Carlin

Funnier than Danny Kaye, more powerful than Jerry Lewis, as important as acid. That was Paul Krassner to me during the 1960s. I'll explain.

As America entered the Magic Decade, I was leading a double life. I had been a rule-bender and law-breaker since first grade. A highly developed disregard for authority got me kicked out of three schools, the altar boys, the choir, summer camp, the Boy Scouts and the Air Force. I didn't trust the police or the government, and I didn't like bosses of any kind. I had become a pot smoker at 13 (1950), an unheard-of act in an old-fashioned Irish neighborhood. It managed to get me through my teens.

But my career goals had a different flavor. From the earliest age, I had wanted to be a comedian—like Danny Kaye or Jerry Lewis. It was an understandable goal for someone who didn't quite fit in, but it was a decidedly mainstream dream. To get ahead, it required playing by the rules and pleasing the public, mostly on their own terms.

So that's what I did. My affection for pot continued and my disregard for standard values increased, but they lagged behind my need to succeed. The Playboy Club, Merv Griffin, Ed Sullivan and the Copacabana were all part of a path I found uncomfortable but necessary during the early 1960s.

But as the decade churned along and the country changed, I did too. Despite working in "establishment" settings, as a veteran malcontent I found myself hanging out in coffee houses and folk clubs with others who were out-of-step people who fell somewhere between beatnik and hippie. Hair got longer, clothes got stranger, music got better.

It became more of a strain for me to work for straight audiences. I took acid and mescaline. My sense of being on the outside intensified. I changed.

All through this period I was sustained and motivated by *The Realist*, Paul Krassner's incredible magazine of satire, revolution and just plain disrespect. It arrived every month, and with it, a fresh supply of inspiration. I can't overstate how important it was to me at the time. It allowed me to see that others who disagreed with the American consensus were busy expressing those feelings and using risky humor to do so.

Paul's own writing, in particular, seemed daring and adventurous to me; it took big chances and made important arguments in relentlessly funny ways. I felt, down deep, that maybe I had some of that in me, too; that maybe I could be using my skills to better express my beliefs. *The Realist* was the inspiration that kept pushing me to the next level; there was no way I could continue reading it and remain the same.

My changes took a year or two and, as the '70s rolled into view, I found my comic voice, just as *The Realist* found countless rich targets in Nixon, Agnew, Kissinger, and the many Republican criminals who paraded through our lives. Not even disco could dim Paul's light, and in subsequent years it has grown only brighter, as these pages and his earlier books will attest.

Readers of *Playboy, High Times,* the *L.A. Weekly* and the *Los Angeles Times* all have benefited from his informed sense of outrage, his intelligent dissent and his ever-lively spirit of civic mischief. The fun and laughs are simply bonuses. You will find them all present in this collection of reminiscences, reportage, illuminations, fantasies and just plain hallucinations.

By the way, I still have my collection of *The Realist* from the '60s and '70s. I keep them in a cheap plastic, red-white-and-blue, American-flag shoulder bag inscribed on the side, "1968 Democratic National Convention." I wasn't there—I was represented by Paul Krassner.

Foreword: Irony Lives!

It was ironic that *Vanity Fair* editor Graydon Carter and *Time* magazine contributor Roger Rosenblatt got into a fistfight over which one had been the first to declare "the end of the Age of Irony." Both, of course, were referring to history's latest dividing line, the day of those terrorist attacks in New York and Washington.

So, I guess it's appropriate for me to mention here that everything in this book was written *before* September 11, 2001, except for "Remembering John Lilly," "The House That Frank Destroyed," "My Cannabis Cup Runneth Over," "Kesey's Last Prank" and George Carlin's introduction.

Even Carlin, who ordinarily doesn't do topical material, found it necessary to insert a bit of war humor into his HBO performance because you have to acknowledge "the elephant in your living room."

Lane Sarasohn, an editor of *Ironic Times*—an online weekly which satirizes the news, always leading off with apocryphal headlines marching along a ticker—got caught on the cusp. On Monday, September 10, the new edition came out, and this was one of the jokes on the ticker: "Taliban: 'No more Mr. Nice Guys. . . .'"

Sarasohn told me that, in the wake of the utter devastation committed the next day by suicide pilots and their hijacker crews, the editors decided to excise that particular joke from their Web site. Otherwise, since the Taliban had been sheltering Osama bin Laden—CIA Frankenstein monster turned into "prime suspect"—that headline could have been perceived as insensitive.

What made the reference sardonic in the first place was that— having just put eight aid workers on trial for attempting to convert

Muslims to Christianity, a crime punishable by death—the fundamentalist Taliban ruling party in Afghanistan had not exactly been Mr. Nice Guys *previously*. They gave fanatics a bad name, and when it came to human rights, they made China look positively angelic.

Under Taliban theocracy, females were not allowed to appear in public without being covered from head to toe. They were forbidden to leave the house without being accompanied by a male family member. They were not permitted to attend school. They couldn't be treated by a male doctor, nor were they allowed to practice medicine. Or *any* profession. No education was allowed. Music was banned. So were movies and radio and television. And laughter itself.

Men could go to prison for shaving their beard or just trimming it. Indoor games like chess and outdoor sports like soccer were forbidden. Taliban zealots destroyed a gigantic statue of Buddha, and they deemed it compulsory for all non-Muslim inhabitants of Afghanistan to wear a piece of cloth attached to their pocket to indicate that they were not Muslims. Shades of Nazi Germany.

And yet, on May 17, 2001, the United States government presented the Taliban rulers with $43 million of *our* money. Hey, wasn't the American Revolution supposed to be about taxation without representation? And I'll bet that darned old Taliban didn't even have to submit a business plan. Five days later, syndicated columnist Robert Sheer wrote:

"Enslave your girls and women, harbor anti-U.S. terrorists, destroy every vestige of civilization in your homeland, and the Bush administration will embrace you. All that matters is that you line up as an ally in the drug war. The gift, announced by Secretary of State Colin Powell, in addition to recent aid, makes the U.S. the main sponsor of the Taliban and rewards that 'rogue regime' for declaring that opium growing is against the will of God.

"Never mind that Osama bin Laden still operates the leading anti-American terror operation from his base in Afghanistan, from which, among other crimes, he launched two bloody attacks on American embassies in Africa in 1998. Sadly, the Bush administration is cozying up to the Taliban regime at a time when the United Nations, at U.S. insistence, imposes sanctions on Afghanistan because the Kabul government will not turn over bin Laden. The war on drugs has become our own fanatics' obsession and easily trumps all other concerns.

"Most of the farmers who grew the poppies will now confront starvation. That's because the Afghan economy has been ruined by the religious extremism of the Taliban, making the attraction of opium as a previously tolerated quick cash crop overwhelming. For that reason, the opium ban will not last unless the U.S. is willing to pour far larger amounts of money into underwriting the Afghan economy.

"As the DEA's Steven Casteel admitted, 'The bad side of the ban is that it's bringing their country . . . to economic ruin.' Nor did he hold out much hope for Afghan farmers growing other crops such as wheat, which require a vast infrastructure to supply water and fertilizer that no longer exists in that devastated country. There's little doubt that the Taliban will turn once again to the easily taxed cash crop of opium in order to stay in power."

It's bad enough that the United States helped sponsor state-sponsored terrorism against itself, but on top of that, American taxpayers didn't get any refunds this time.

In the days after 9/11, I read the newspapers, listened to the radio and channel surfed, from CNN (with their "America's New War" logo reassuring viewers that it wasn't a rerun) to MTV (where one of the Beastie Boys advised, "The last thing the terrorists want is for us to work together"). Then I checked the Internet—especially alternative sources and the foreign press—to see what was left out of American mainstream media.

On the Fox News Network, Edward Peck, former ambassador to Iraq, was an unusually outspoken guest. He said the terrorists acted as they did, not because America was "a freedom-loving country," but because they felt the U.S. had long been treating them the same way— "bombing Iraq for the last 10 years whenever they felt like it, and acting with disregard for the lives of their citizens."

The anchor asked, "When has America ever done something so preposterous?"

Peck responded, "We've invaded and attacked many countries. Take Panama. Take Haiti. Take Cambodia. . . ."

He was cut off and dismissed.

Back in May 1996, on *60 Minutes*, Lesley Stahl confronted UN Ambassador Madeleine Albright: "We have heard that a half-million children have died [because of sanctions against Iraq]. I mean, that's more children than died in Hiroshima and, you know, is the price worth it?"

"I think this is a very hard choice," Albright replied, "but the price— we think the price is worth it."

None of this provides one nano-iota of solace for the mass anguish experienced by shell-shocked America and beyond. So much human suffering, for the sake of our nation's karma.

In the face of all the platitudes and rhetoric from politicians, professors and pundits—those who speak of unspeakable horror and then, when thanked by their TV host, reply, "My pleasure"—the original impact of this tragedy was summed up concisely by a teenager who was interviewed by Tom Brokaw on NBC. That sorrowful Tuesday, she was awakened by her mother and brought into the living room to see what was happening on television. "I was like *Whoa!*" she recalled. And then she added, "It will probably be in the history books."

Meanwhile, *Ironic Times* decided to run a best-of edition for the week beginning September 17—"something that will hopefully cheer you up," subscribers were notified, "and give us time to cheer up as well." An editor, Matt Neuman, told me, "Were we publishing a regular edition, our ticker might start: 'Bin Laden cancels all public appearances. . . .'"

Who knows, by the time you read this, bin Laden may already have been taken out, and I don't mean to dinner and a movie. The air is filled with a mixture of testosterone and saccharine. But if you put your ear to ground zero, you can hear the sound of paradigms shifting gears all over the place.

• • •

What do George W. Bush and Osama bin Laden have in common? They both believe that God is on their side. Ultimately, the war is a competition between Jehovah and Allah. Bush proclaimed, "God is not neutral," which is the antithesis of my own spiritual path—that God *is* neutral—but I've learned that whatever people believe works for them.

Everybody perceives every occurrence through their own subjective filters, yet how incredibly cruel of televangelists Jerry Falwell and Pat Robertson to agree on TV about the terrorist attacks:

"God continues to lift the curtain and allow the enemies of America to give us probably what we deserve. The abortionists have got to bear some burden for this because God will not be mocked. And when we destroy 40 million little innocent babies, we make God mad. I really believe that the pagans, and the abortionists, and the feminists, and the gays and the lesbians who are actively trying to make that an alternative lifestyle, the ACLU, People for the American Way—all of them who have tried to secularize America—I point the finger in their face and say, 'You helped this happen.'"

This pious pair became such pathetic parodies of their own fundamentalist agenda that at first I thought it was a hoax, despite the fact that the quote was published in *The Washington Post*. Afghanistan has its insane zealots, and we have ours.

If the universe is infinite, then the trajectories that connect with the universe are also infinite. My own personal idol is a *papier-mâché* Donald Duck with eight arms. He has alternate names: Shiva Duck or Donald Sutra.

As an absurdist and an atheist, I realized that the most absurd thing I could do would be to develop an intimate relationship with the God I don't believe in. And so we're in constant dialogue. For example, in my capacity as a stand-up satirist, every time I perform, before I go onstage I pray, "Please, God, help me do a good show." And then I always hear the voice of God, booming out: "*Shut up, you superstitious fool!*" It restores my sense of false humility.

On September 11th, I asked God, "How could you let this happen?" And God answered, "Don't blame me, I just make the laws, like gravity. Would you rather I control everything and *not* let you have free will?"

● ● ●

In 1968, while speaking at an Unbirthday Party for Lyndon Johnson held during the Democratic convention in Chicago, I revealed to the audience the true story of a journalist who had once interviewed LBJ. After the formal question-and-answer session, the president, referring to the Vietnam War, told him, "What the Communists are really saying is 'Fuck you, Lyndon Johnson,' and nobody says 'Fuck you, Lyndon Johnson' and gets away with it."

"Well," I continued, "when I count three, we're all gonna say it— *and we're gonna get away with it*! Are you ready? One . . . two . . . three . . . " And, from the Yippies and Mobilization-Against-the-War and the Clean-for-Genes, it came at me like an audio tidal wave—thousands of voices shouting in unison: "*Fuck you, Lyndon Johnson!*"—a mass catharsis reverberating from the rafters.

And now, 33 years later, while emceeing a rally in October on Day 5 of the Retaliation—symbolized by CNN's change of logo to "America Strikes Back"—I felt a powerful sense of continuity. The rally, held at Masonic Auditorium in San Francisco, starred Ralph Nader, making a stop on his "People Have the Power" grassroots-organizing tour.

I introduced former stand-up comic and teacher Tom Ammiano, the openly gay president of the San Francisco Board of Supervisors. "You all know me," he began, "I'm the president you can believe when I say, 'I didn't sleep with that woman.'"

The event was originally supposed to be about corporate domination generally and about the energy crisis specifically—promoting public power and solar power—but the international situation had intervened, and Nader had morphed from a consumer advocate into an antiwar leader.

The missing link was provided by Medea Benjamin—founder of the human rights organization Global Exchange and Green Party candidate for U.S. senator from California in 2000—who asked the audience, "What one word can sum up the real reason why we're in Afghanistan?" And they shouted back in unison—"*Oil!*"—aware that the U.S. government had been negotiating to build oil pipelines running beneath the Caspian Sea through Afghanistan.

And then there was Nader, who noted that Bush's campaign slogan, "I trust the people, not the government," utterly reeks with irony. "Truth is the first casualty of a nation in crisis," Nader said, stressing the importance of guarding our freedom. "Americans must be vigilant about attacks on civil liberties in the wake of the terrorist attacks."

Nader insisted that the "inhumane and criminal" terrorists be brought to justice, but advocated an end to the bombing. He posed a question to the audience: "How many of you, since September 11th, have wanted to express an opinion that was something other than the thought-police stampede?"

To all those who raised their hands, he advised, "If you feel yourself inhibited, that's the moment to break out and make yourself known. Otherwise, your silence is allowing suppression of the Constitution." The prolonged standing ovation Nader received was indicative of the burgeoning peace movement, with teach-ins at college campuses and, in effect, on the Internet.

My role was to provide comic relief. Comedy is supposed to be tragedy plus time, but we were still in the throes of an intensifying tragedy, so I was somewhat apprehensive. Two hours before going onstage, I had watched Bush's press conference, and now, at the risk of committing comedic treason, I felt compelled to report my own version, but this audience responded enthusiastically.

"Bush explained that simultaneously dropping bombs and food on Afghanistan is just an example of compassionate conservatism," I said. "He also divulged that the ABM treaty had an expiration date in tiny print. And he pointed out that the United States gave $43 million to the Taliban because they're a faith-based organization."

I told the audience that ABC News correspondent Cokie Roberts had been asked if there was any opposition to the war. "None that matters," she replied. Hissing and boos. "Well," I said, "would you all care to join me in saying 'Fuck you, Cokie Roberts' when I count three? Okay, one . . . two . . . three . . . " And it came at me like an audio tidal wave—2,500 voices shouting in unison: "*Fuck you, Cokie Roberts!*" It was a moment of *déjà vu* supreme.

• • •

In December 2000, newly appointed President Bush had stated, "If this were a dictatorship, it'd be a heck of a lot easier, just so long as I'm the dictator," and now it seemed that his wish was coming true.

The invasion of America was the mother of all conspiracies. Immediately there were those who began spinning scenarios of an inside job, an American version of the Reichstag Fire, carried out in order to justify the rise of a police state in the guise of security procedures. In any case, political opportunism has been providing the same results.

On Halloween of 2001, I was a panelist at a taping of a TV series, *The Conspiracy Zone*, and the plot behind the terrorists was certainly a topic of conversation in the greenroom—"Do you think this is the endgame?" someone asked—but the official subject that evening would be the assassination of Robert Kennedy in 1968.

On the program, hosted by former *Saturday Night Live* cast member Kevin Nealon, I mentioned that Kennedy had once been on the *Tonight* show, telling Johnny Carson that cigarettes kill more people than marijuana, and I speculated that Sirhan Sirhan was a hired gun for the tobacco companies. On a more literal note, I talked about the ballistics inconsistency; a total of 10 bullets were found, though Sirhan's gun could hold only eight.

And I discussed the fact that, during his trial, psychiatrist Bernard Diamond used post-hypnotic suggestion to program Sirhan into climbing the bars of his cell like a monkey; in the book *RFK Must Die*, Robert Kaiser—who was there—wrote: "Sirhan had no idea what he was doing up on the top of the bars. When he finally discovered that climbing was not his own idea, but Dr. Diamond's, he was struck with the plausibility of the idea that perhaps he had been programmed by someone else, in like manner, to kill Kennedy. . . ."

(On November 26, 2001, the *Wall Street Journal* published an article about Osama bin Laden's network, including this: "In May 1993, three months after the bombing [of the World Trade Center parking garage], Sheik Omar [Abdel Rahman, the blind iman now in prison for orchestrating that crime] was speaking with one of his disciples at his Jersey City, N.J., apartment when the man asked whether it would be acceptable in Islam to bomb the FBI's Manhattan headquarters. 'Slow down; slow down a little bit,' the sheik cautioned, whispering for fear the FBI was bugging his apartment—which it was. 'The one who killed Kennedy was trained for three years.' It was never made clear in later court testimony which assassination the sheik was talking about.")

There were two others beside myself on that TV panel, plus a separate segment with a dentist who practices hypnosis.

One panelist was Michael Ruppert, a former member of the Los Angeles Police Department, Narcotics Division, who became a prolific conspiracy researcher. Off camera, I asked him what the turning point had been for him. He said that it was when his fiancée, a CIA operative, tried to involve him in drug smuggling, and he refused. He worked on Ross Perot's 1992 presidential campaign, and CamNet cable network captured him crying when Perot dropped out of the race. Ruppert and I are both columnists for *High Times* magazine but, he told me, "I don't smoke grass."

The other panelist was scheduled to be former Nixon speechwriter and now bespectacled, drone-voiced TV personality Ben Stein, but he cancelled out at the last minute. Ann Coulter, former Justice Department attorney and Senate aide, now a professional reactionary and Stepford pundit, was at the studio for a subsequent taping about secret societies, and she was drafted into taking Stein's place.

Two days after the terrorist attacks, she had written in *National Review Online*, "We should invade their countries, kill their leaders and convert them to Christianity." The Web site refused to run her follow-up column, which is syndicated, because it included a reference to "suspicious-looking swarthy males." She publicly dissed *National Review*—which had received "a lot of complaints" from sponsors and readers—so her column was dropped, and the magazine dumped her as a contributing editor.

A frequent guest on talk shows, from *Rivera Live* to *Larry King Live*, Coulter is recognizable by her long blonde hair and short black skirt. The taping of *The Conspiracy Zone* was slightly delayed because she was still in the makeup room.

"It takes a long time to turn Ben Stein into Ann Coulter," I explained.

During a break in the show, I suggested to her that the labels "conservative" and "liberal" had become obsolescent.

For instance, Senator Bob Barr blocked information on how many votes a medical-marijuana referendum in Washington, D.C., received, yet he also criticized the increasing invasions of privacy being voted into law as security measures.

Also, anti-ERA activist Phyllis Schlafly wrote: "The current attempt to inflict Americans with the burden of having to carry a national ID card is a thoroughly un-American idea. Totalitarian governments keep their subjects under constant police surveillance by the technique of requiring everyone to carry 'papers' that must be presented to any government functionary on demand."

I asked Coulter what she thought might be appropriate substitute labels for conservatives and liberals.

"Americans and cowards," she said.

"Yikes," I said.

After she was fired, Coulter went on *Politically Incorrect*, accusing *National Review* of censorship and calling the editors "just girly-boys." Host Bill Maher had gotten in trouble himself on the September 17th program when he said, ironically enough, "*We* have been the cowards, lobbing cruise missiles from 2,000 miles away—*that's* cowardly. Staying in the airplane when it hits the building, say what you want about it, it's not cowardly."

In Houston, a conservative—I mean American—talk-show host, Dan Patrick, went on the air and urged listeners to call FedEx and Sears, demanding that they stop advertising on the program. Calls started coming in—50 the next day—many from people who didn't even know the name of the show or what they were offended by.

FedEx and Sears pulled their commercials, Disney Chairman Michael Eisner indicated his disapproval to ABC, 17 affiliates cancelled the program, White House Press Secretary Ari Fleischer weighed in—"It's a reminder to all Americans that they need to watch what they say, watch what they do"—and Maher issued a written apology, then apologized on his own show and wherever else he could, on six syndicated radio talk shows including Howard Stern, and on TV from Bill O'Reilly to Jay Leno.

"Maher should resign," wrote Victor Navasky in the liberal—I mean cowardly—magazine, *The Nation*, "not for what he said but for flying under false colors. You can't have a show called *Politically Incorrect* and then abjectly apologize for not being PC."

As for Ann Coulter, he wrote, "Now there are two possibilities here: One is that *National Review* fired her because they didn't like what she said. The other is that *National Review* fired her because by saying what too many *National Review* readers believe, she embarrassed the home team. Solution: After Maher apologizes for apologizing and resigns, *Politically Incorrect* should hire the truly politically incorrect Coulter."

There she could present a televised basketball game between the swarthy males and the girly-boys, rooting for neither team to win.

• • •

Larry King wanted to know what it would be like after September 11th. He asked Dr. Andrew Weil if bulimics started throwing up more often. And he asked Bill Maher how soon it would be all right to be funny again—"One month? Two months?"

Actually, Maher was funny six days later, when—referring to the arrest of *West Wing* creator Aaron Sorkin—he questioned the priorities of a country in which a band of terrorists elude airport security but not a Hollywood producer carrying "funny mushrooms."

Chris Wright wrote in the *Boston Phoenix* that some of those who were employees at the twin towers "reportedly made light of the situation by reeling off the flights of stairs they were descending as if they were counting down to the New Year: '10, 9, 8, 7 . . .'"

Rescue workers digging through the rubble for clues and body parts indulged in humor so dark that it bonded them, like asking a fellow worker, "Hey, can you give me a hand?"

The Haslam Septic Service in Ellsworth, Maine, placed a message on its tanker saying that the company "will haul sewage waste from almost anybody, but we won't take any shit from bin Laden."

When the late-night TV talk-show hosts started being funny again, much of the humor was in the context of demonizing bin Laden.

Jay Leno: "More and more facts coming out about Osama bin Laden. You know, he never sleeps in the same place two nights in a row, just like Clinton." And: "The leaders of the Taliban said today that killing bin Laden won't solve the problem. But, you know, it couldn't hurt." And: "We are getting more and more insight into the life of Osama bin Laden. Today the Saudi Arabian ambassador to the United States said that bin Laden had an unhappy childhood growing up, 52 brothers and sisters. You think his childhood was unhappy, wait 'til we deliver his mid-life crisis." And: "This Osama bin Laden guy, spoiled rich kid worth $300 million. I have three words for this guy: Anna Nicole Smith. We send her over there, she'll get his money, he'll be dead in a week."

For a while, Leno stopped shaking hands with audience members. "They were still digging bodies out of the World Trade Center, and we didn't want to look like we were having too much fun," he said. "Some thought I stopped shaking hands for security reasons. No. The audience is searched when they enter. We were just trying to say, 'We'll be silly but also respectful.'"

David Letterman referred to bin Laden as "a little weasel" and "a boob." After letters containing anthrax had been sent to NBC News anchor Tom Brokaw and ABC News anchor Peter Jennings, Letterman announced: "CBS News finally received anthrax in the mail. As usual, we're number three." When CBS News anchor Dan Rather was a guest on the show, he broke down and started crying while reciting the lyrics of "America the Beautiful," then apologized because he was supposed to be a professional, and Letterman said, "Sure you're a professional, but Good Christ, man, you're also a human being," and the audience applauded in agreement.

Jon Stewart sobbed uncontrollably his first night back on *The Daily Show*, but eventually he returned to normality: "If the events of September 11th have proven anything, it's that the terrorists can attack us, but they can't take away what makes us Americans—our freedoms, our liberty, our civil rights. No, only Attorney General John Ashcroft can do that."

On *Saturday Night Live*, Darrell Hammond played Dick Cheney delivering a message from his secure hideout—a cave in Kandahar.

Harry Shearer, on his weekly radio program *Le Show*, did the voice of George W. telling his father about his crusade to stamp out global terrorism: "I found my mission. I haven't been this focused and this determined since the fourth time I quit drinking." In his own voice, Shearer says, "It's like the war on drugs. It's a totally metaphorical war in which some people get killed. I expect the Partnership for a Terrorist Free America to start soon."

The first joke I saw on the Internet was one day after the terrorist attacks: "What is the capital of Afghanistan?" Answer: "Kaboom!"

Online humor magazines became delayed flights of fancy.

The Onion suspended publication and waited two weeks before it ran headlines like: "Rest of Country Temporarily Feels Deep Affection for New York," "President Urges Calm, Restraint Among Nation's Ballad Singers," "U.S. Vows to Defeat Whoever It Is We're at War With," "Hijackers Surprised to Find Selves in Hell" and "UN Study Shows Two-Thirds of World Could Use Benefit Concert."

Modern Humorist waited one week, then posted a list of "New Entertainment Guidelines for a Changed America," such as, "Comedy about violent Islamic extremists should not impugn all of the innocent violent extremists of other faiths," and, "Any stand-up comic who does a routine about airplanes is to be accompanied onstage by a federal marshal."

Indeed, stand-up comics walked a fine line.

In New York on September 29, Gilbert Gottfried began, "Tonight I'm going to perform under my Muslim name, Hasn't bin Laid," and got a big laugh, but when he closed with, "I have to catch a flight to Los Angeles, I can't get a direct flight, they said they have to stop at the Empire State Building first," the audience booed.

Mort Sahl found that the audience applauded his setups—"Isn't the president a great leader? What about that speech he made on the state of the union?"—until he got to his punch lines: "He's doing so well it makes you embarrassed that he wasn't actually elected. . . . Bush wants to be the education president. Yeah, and now he's being home-schooled by Condoleezza Rice. . . . They said if you hear anybody say anything that sounds disloyal, you should report them to the Office of Homeland Security. What a great way to get even with your parents."

Will Durst: "One problem is Americans can't even conceive of suicide terrorists. 'Well, how do they get paid? Is it a union gig? Obviously, they don't have a decent dental plan.'"

Colin Quinn: "I'm not trying to start trouble here, but what was that about authorities saying there was 'a 100 percent chance of retaliation' by Osama bin Laden? If it's 100 percent, it's not a *chance*."

Chris Rock envisioned "a 50-pound bag of food falling on some poor, starving *40-pound* Afghan"—a joke which came true a month later when a civilian was killed by a 1,200-pound bundle of humanitarian supplies dropped by parachute and crushing her house in Afghanistan.

Middle Eastern comedians had a special burden to bear: In New York, Hood Qa'Im-maqami temporarily suspended his usual opening line where he bestows the audience with "an offering from Allah" and then lifts his shirt to show sticks of dynamite strapped to his chest. Instead he announced, "I'm from Iran, which means for the next year or so, I'll be Italian." In Los Angeles, another Iranian-American comic, Maz Jobrani, talked about his Mideastern friends who are "changing their names to Tony, trying to pass as Italians." And Ahmed Ahmed, an Arab-American comedian: "I was asked at the airport whether I packed my bags myself. I said yes, and they arrested me."

A few syndicated comic strips got into the act.

Garry Trudeau's *Doonesbury* portrayed the irony of an African-American airline passenger who finds himself profiling as dangerous an Arab-American passenger. Trudeau revealed the ulterior motive of a woman at the WTC site who hopes to pick up a firefighter. And he showed President Bush thanking the terrorists for their attacks, which opened the way for his domestic agenda—corporate tax cuts, missile defense, oil drilling in Alaska and subsidies for the power industry.

Nicole Hollander's *Sylvia* had a woman telling a private detective, "The only way I can explain it is that there was a lot going on. First the war, and then the anthrax scare. So it was weeks before I noticed some of my civil liberties were missing. Please get them back." He replies, "Sure, sweetheart, but remember, the impossible takes a little longer."

Editorial cartoonist Jimmy Margulies dealt with that same theme in the form of Attorney General John Ashcroft's department-store ad: "Ashcroft's, since 2001, Fabulous Holiday Savings!"—showing the Bill of Rights "Reduced 60%."

Aaron McGruder's *The Boondocks* was most radical, with angry black preadolescent Huey Freeman calling the FBI: "I know of several Americans who have helped train and finance Osama bin Laden . . . the first one is Reagan, that's R-e-a-g . . . "; saying grace at Thanksgiving dinner: "We are thankful that *our* leader isn't the spoiled son of a powerful politician from a wealthy oil family who is supported by religious fundamentalists, operates through clandestine organizations, has no respect for the democratic electoral process, bombs innocents and uses war to deny people their civil liberties"; and being misunderstood when he calls the FBI to see how the war's going: "Oh, no, I'm sorry. I meant the war on drugs. I mean the government has spent a fortune, thrown countless people in jail, invaded a country—I figure we're gonna win that one any day now, right?"

Get Fuzzy by Darby Conley has a main character Rob and his talking dog Satchel who both donated blood to the Red Cross. *Non Sequitur* by Wiley Miller depicted a dog moving its bowels on the curb as a woman tells her husband, "It seems like no matter where I go, some ordinary sight or smell of the city will trigger my thoughts of the terrorists." And Scott Adams dropped from *Dilbert* any strips about the fictional Elbonians threatening to bomb their neighboring Kneebonians, because "Now the thought of a bearded man in a robe holding a nuclear device just doesn't seem funny."

The DVD version of the movie *E.T.* has been sanitized to avoid the possibility of upsetting children. A line of dialogue—"You look like a terrorist"—has been replaced, and government agents' guns have been digitally replaced with walkie-talkies.

An episode of *Seinfeld*, in which George Costanza's fiancée dies from licking cheap wedding-invitation envelopes, has been pulled from syndication for fear that it might upset viewers concerned about anthrax-tainted mail.

Britain's Sky Satellite service ran an episode of *The Simpsons* where Lisa is worried about her genes—that she'll grow up as stupid as Homer—but a scene was edited out where Lisa, Bart and Homer are watching a TV show called *When Buildings Collapse*, and the announcer says, "Man has always loved his buildings, but what happens when the buildings say '*No more!*'"—followed by a montage of crashing buildings and Bart's remark, "The best part was when the buildings collapsed."

In Ireland, TV superimposed the subtitle "This is not a Hollywood movie" on shots of the suicide planes ramming the World Trade Center.

On Comedy Central's British sitcom, *Absolutely Fabulous*, a character, upon seeing a sculpture of Buddha, said, "Better not let the Taliban know it's there," followed by a laugh track.

A rock radio network issued a suggested list of records *not* to play, including Alanis Morissette's "Isn't It Ironic?" Scott Ian, lead singer of the band Anthrax, started taking Cipro, an antibiotic used to treat anthrax, vowing, "I will not die an ironic death."

Unintentional irony ruled.

A member of al-Qaeda, who had been arrested in a global drug-trade probe, became an informant to avoid jail time and tried to provide the FBI with information on Arab terrorists in Boston before 9/11, but they were more interested in his knowledge of heroin being brought there from Afghanistan. However, the FBI did contact several psychics, who had worked with U.S. intelligence at the Stanford Research Institute until 1995 as "remote viewers," in the hope that they would be able to foresee terrorist attacks.

And, on the same day that Bush urged Americans to "Get on board, do your business around the country, fly and enjoy America's great destination spots, get down to Disney World," the Pentagon confirmed a new aspect of the nation's air defense system, which gives two generals authority to order the military to shoot down commercial airliners in "extraordinary circumstances" when people on the ground are endangered.

In December 2001, when I performed at the Santa Barbara Humanists Winter Solstice Banquet, I described how, while eating in a restaurant, the waitress asked if everything was okay, and I replied, "The food is delicious, but my knee hurts and I'm concerned about creeping fascism." I concluded, "Former president George Bush said, 'Read my lips,' and now his son George W. is saying, 'Read *Mein Kampf.*'"

Several years ago, satirical folksinger Tom Lehrer said that satire died when Henry Kissinger was awarded the Nobel Peace Prize. And now it turns out that it was Andrew Coyne who first declared—on September 12 in Canada's *National Post*—that "the Age of Irony died yesterday." *Vanity Fair* editor Graydon Carter admitted that what *he* had actually said was "the end of the Age of Ironing," and that he currently wears his shirts straight from the dryer.

And now here's my personal salute to the rebirth of irony.

This occurred at Copia, a new food, wine and arts museum in Napa, California. The Catholic League of Religious and Civil Rights denounced an exhibit there by Spanish artist Antoni Miralda. It featured 35 miniature ceramic figurines—all in the act of defecation, to represent the cycle of eating and fertilization of the earth—including Popeye, Laurel and Hardy, Fidel Castro, Santa Claus, the pope, nuns and angels. However, a Copia spokesperson explained that such figurines are rooted in Catholic Catalonian peasant tradition dating back to the 1800s, and that one is typically placed in a nativity scene to bring families prosperity and good health, though it is unlikely to be their most recent figurine, a squatting Osama bin Laden.

The spokesperson, incidentally, was my daughter Holly.

• • •

On September 10, 2001, I mailed copies of the manuscript of *Murder at the Conspiracy Convention and Other American Absurdities* to several publishers. The rejections were all complimentary but . . .

- "Your anecdotes are always delightful and your satire never gets stale, but I'm afraid this strikes me as too much of a miscellany for us to publish successfully."
- "I'm going to have to pass on this project. I think there is a lot of charming and interesting material here, but unfortunately I think it would be almost impossible to sell."
- "As a long time admirer of your work, I'm very sorry to be coming back to you without an offer. We've had a hard time pub-

lishing collections in the past, and I fear that the changes in the bookselling climate would make this even harder."

And so it's poetic irony—and immensely appropriate—that *Murder at the Conspiracy Convention* is being brought to you by an independent publisher, Barricade Books, which is run by my friend and mentor, Lyle Stuart, who published my first book 40 years ago.

I hope you enjoy reading this book as much as I enjoyed plagiarizing it. But if you don't, just remember, you'll only be helping the terrorists to win.

Paul Krassner
January 2002
Desert Hot Springs, California

the federal
bureau of
intimidation

me and the FBI

My high school didn't have a baseball team, but the local American Legion post wanted to cosponsor a team with a local automobile dealer, so I tried out and made the team. I was the only one who brought a shoehorn to all the games to help me put on my spiked shoes. My parents brought a pitcher of orange juice for the team.

Every Sunday morning I became a living parody of a Norman Rockwell painting on the cover of the *Saturday Evening Post*. I wore my uniform with the American Legion logo on the front and "Universal Cars—Sales & Service" on the back, riding my bicycle on my newspaper route, with my dog Skippy in the basket. I wanted to be a G-man—an FBI agent—when I grew up. I was such an idealistic kid. But things change, and I would become disillusioned.

Frank Sinatra was my role model as a preadolescent because he made a 10-minute-film, *The House I Live In*. The lyrics of the title song inspired my patriotism: "All races, all religions, that's America to me. . . . The right to speak my mind out, that's America to me."

In school I had to write a report on a political candidate. I chose Vito Marcantonio, who was running for mayor of New York. I didn't know anything about him except that Sinatra was supporting his campaign and sang at a fundraiser. Marcantonio was running on the American Labor Party ticket, but my teacher called him a communist, got very agitated and phoned my parents.

At home I learned that the Constitution didn't guarantee the separation of politics and culture. One of my favorite songs, "But Not for Me," included the phrase, "More clouds of grey than any Russian play could guarantee," but on the radio I heard an altered version: "More clouds of grey than any *Broadway* play could guarantee." The Cold War was on.

Flash ahead to October 1968. A man in New York City has been reading a profile of me in *Life* magazine. Now he sits down at his typewriter, trying to choose every word carefully as he composes a letter to the editor on plain stationery:

"Your recent issue, which devoted three pages to the aggrandizement of underground editor Paul Krassner, was too, too much. You must be hard up for material. Am I asking the impossible by requesting that Krassner and his ilk be left in the sewers where they belong? That a national magazine of your fine reputation (till now that is) would waste time and effort on the cuckoo editor of an unimportant, smutty little rag is incomprehensible to me. Gentlemen, you must be aware that *The Realist* is nothing more than blatant obscenity. . . . To classify Krassner as some sort of 'social rebel' is far too cute. He's a nut, a raving, unconfined nut . . . "

The letter was signed "Howard Rasmussen, Brooklyn College, School of General Studies." That was the pseudonym of an FBI agent, and his letter was for Cointelpro, the FBI's counterintelligence program. Before mailing it to the magazine, he was required to send a copy to FBI headquarters in Washington, along with a memo requesting permission because "the *Life* article was favorable to Krassner."

The return memo—approved by J. Edgar Hoover's top two assistants, Kartha DeLoach and William Sullivan—stated: "Authority is granted to send [the] letter, signed with a fictitious name. . . . Krassner is the editor of *The Realist* and is one of the moving forces behind the Youth International Party, commonly known as the Yippies. . . . This letter could, if printed by *Life*, call attention to the unsavory character of Krassner."

In 1969, the FBI attempt to assassinate my character escalated to a more literal approach. I discovered this, not in my Cointelpro file, but as part of a separate project calculated to cause rifts between the Jewish and black communities. The FBI produced a wanted poster featuring a large swastika. In the four square spaces of the swastika were photos of Yippie leaders Abbie Hoffman and Jerry Rubin, SDS (Students for a Democratic Society) leader Mark Rudd and me.

Under the headline—"Lampshades! Lampshades! Lampshades! Lampshades!"—the copy stated that "the only solution to Negro problems in America would be the *elimination* of the Jews. May we suggest the following order of elimination? (After all, we've been this way before.)" There followed this list:

"*All Jews connected with the Establishment. *All Jews connected with Jews connected with the Establishment. *All Jews connected with those immediately above. *All Jews except those in the Movement. *All Jews in the Movement except those who dye their skins black. *All Jews. (Look out, Abbie, Jerry, Mark and Paul!)"

The flyer was approved, once again, by DeLoach and Sullivan:

"Authority is granted to prepare and distribute on an anonymous basis to selected individuals and organizations in the New Left the leaflet submitted. . . . Assure that all necessary precautions are taken to protect the Bureau as the source of these leaflets [which] suggest facetiously the elimination of these leaders [to] create further ill feeling between the New Left and the black nationalist movement. . . ."

And, of course, if some overly militant black had obtained that flyer and "eliminated" one of those "New Left leaders who are Jewish," the FBI's bureaucratic ass would be covered: "We *said* it was a facetious suggestion, didn't we?"

Now, a few decades later, the FBI is in disarray. And, rather than song lyrics being censored, the White House Office of National Drug Control Policy has budgeted $195 million for five years of an anti-drug media campaign, including $800,000 to *NSYNC's Web site management team, Music Vision, so that the popular group can instill in youth the notion that "mind reading, scary movies and hand puppets" are anti-drug measures. But mind reading isn't anti-drug; mind control is.

The Vietnam War has evolved into the Drug War, and the military-industrial complex has become the prison-industrial complex. In the United States of Marketing, patriotism has been replaced by consumerism. *Adbusters* magazine is distributing flags with the 50 stars replaced by 50 megacorporate logos.

The paradox of America is that, while the nation seethes with corruption, we still have the freedom to expose that corruption. It's a start.

john lennon and the FBI

No wonder Mae Brussell was so excited. The attempted burglary of Democratic headquarters at the Watergate Hotel in Washington, D.C., on June 17, 1972, had suddenly brought her eight and a half years of dedicated conspiracy research to an astounding climax. She recognized names, *modus operandi* and patterns of cover-up. She could trace linear connections leading inevitably from the assassination of John F. Kennedy to the Watergate break-in.

Three weeks later—while Richard Nixon was pressing for the postponement of an investigation until after the election, and the mainstream press was still referring to the incident as a "caper" and a "third-rate burglary"—Brussell completed a long article for my magazine, *The Realist*, revealing the conspiracy and delineating the players, from the burglars all the way up to FBI Director L. Patrick Gray, Attorney General John Mitchell and President Nixon himself.

Brussell documented the details of a plot so insidious and yet so logical that we naively believed her article could actually forestall Nixon's reelection. The typesetter even wrote "Bravo!" at the end of her manuscript. However, instead of my usual credit arrangement, the printer insisted on $5,000 cash in advance before that issue could go to press. I didn't have the money, and I had no idea how I would get it, but as I left the printing plant, I was filled with an inexplicable sense of confidence.

When I got home, the phone rang. It was Yoko Ono. She and John Lennon were visiting San Francisco, and they invited me to lunch. The Nixon administration had been trying to deport Lennon, ostensibly for an old marijuana bust in England, but really because they wanted to prevent him from performing free for protesters at the Republican convention that summer, which would have attracted several thousand young people who were for the music and against the war.

I brought the galleys of Mae's article to the restaurant. Her account of the government's motivation and methodology provided a context for the harassment of John and Yoko. When I mentioned my printer's ultimatum, no persuasion was necessary; they immediately took me to a local branch of their bank and withdrew $5,000 cash.

This occurred so *precisely* when I needed the money that my personal boundaries of coincidence were stretched to infinity. I could rationalize my ass off—after all, John and Yoko had been driving across the country, and they just *happened* to arrive at the particular moment of my need—but the timing was so exquisite that, for me, coincidence and mysticism became the same process.

• • •

When Jon Wiener was writing a biography of John Lennon, *Come Together*, he tried to obtain Lennon's FBI files, but some 200 documents were withheld because, it was alleged, their release would endanger national security. What little Wiener managed to obtain included pages that were fully blacked out. After a 14-year legal battle that ended up at the Supreme Court, the FBI agreed to release all but 10 documents and to pay $204,000 to the ACLU for court costs and attorney fees.

Now, Wiener's *Gimme Some Truth* tells the story of that struggle. His book—dedicated to Mark Rosenbaum and Dan Marmalefsky, the lawyers who paved the path to that victory—chronicles Lennon's legal commitment to test the political potential of rock music, and documents the government's illegal commitment to stop him.

Before Wiener met with the ACLU attorneys, their main concern was his agenda. "Was I some kind of obsessed fan? Or perhaps a burned-out hippie, living in the past? Or a conspiracy buff, eager to prove Reagan had ordered Lennon's assassination?" They were relieved to find that he was a history professor seeking the Lennon files as part of his research on the American past.

The ACLU strategy would be to show that Lennon was subject to surveillance as part of an effort to monitor political opponents of the Nixon administration, rather than because he was the subject of a legitimate law-enforcement investigation.

The government claimed they were investigating Lennon because of his involvement with the Election Year Strategy Information Center (EYSIC)—an organization dedicated to defeating Nixon, led by two members of the Chicago 7, Jerry Rubin and Rennie Davis—to which Lennon had contributed $75,000. FBI files indicate that EYSIC disbanded on March 1, 1972, yet 27 documents postdated that event.

"So this has nothing to do with a continuing investigation of a relationship between John Lennon and EYSIC," argued the ACLU. In fact, those documents "don't concern themselves with enforcement of the Anti-Riot Act, they concern themselves with statements being made at INS hearings . . . and 'how can we get John Lennon out of the country before the Republican convention?'"

Vincent Schiano, the INS chief trial attorney in charge of deporting Lennon, had orchestrated the deportation cases of such biggies as mob boss Carlo Gambino, happy hooker Xaviera Hollander, former Nazi Hermine Braunsteiner Ryan and IRA revolutionary Joe Cahill. *Rolling Stone* reported that, after the Lennon case, Schiano left the INS, protesting that he was given carte blanche in the Lennon case but was given no power to go after former Nazis.

Ten days after Lennon's visa was revoked, the New York FBI office sent an urgent teletype to J. Edgar Hoover, reporting that Lennon had won a delay in his deportation, that he would "fight a narcotics conviction in England," and that if he "wins overthrow of British narcotic conviction, INS will reconsider their attempts to deport Lennon."

Hoover died in May 1972, a month after he sent a letter to H.R. Haldeman at the White House about this "former member of the Beatles singing group," warning of his "avowed intention to engage in disruptive activities surrounding RNC [Republican National Convention in Miami]." The entire text was withheld, but since Haldeman was Nixon's chief of staff, this letter would have served as blatant proof that the investigation of Lennon was totally political.

For 14 years, the FBI withheld four lines of another document: "For information of Bureau, NYCPD [New York City Police Department] narcotics division is aware of subject's recent use of narcotics and are attempting to obtain enough information to arrest both subject and wife Yoko based on PD investigation." Lennon told me how strangers kept trying to give him drugs.

In July 1972, the Miami office of the FBI was contacted by the New York office: "Miami should note that Lennon is reportedly a 'heavy user of narcotics'. . . . This information should be emphasized to local Law

Enforcement Agencies covering MIREP [FBI code for the convention], with regards to subject being arrested if at all possible on possession of narcotics charges."

The FBI even printed a flyer for distribution to local law-enforcement agencies in Miami to facilitate the arrest of Lennon. However, the flyer featured a photo of a Lower East Side musician, David Peel, with a speech balloon announcing his new record, "The Pope Smokes Dope."

In September 1972, the government declassified secrets of H-bomb design, but still kept dozens of pages in the Lennon files confidential, stored in locked containers inside locked strong rooms within secure buildings in fenced facilities patrolled by armed guards.

In December 1971, a month after Nixon had been reelected, the Lennon files ended. The FBI had inserted an asterisk adjacent to the symbol number on many documents whenever "the source of the information was not a person but an illegal investigative technique." This whole case was, in Jon Wiener's words, a "rock 'n' roll Watergate."

• • •

Yoko Ono and John Lennon spent that weekend at my home—situated on a cliff overlooking an almost deserted beach—in Watsonville, south of San Francisco. They loved being so close to the ocean. In the afternoon I asked them to smoke their cigarettes outside, but in the evening we smoked a combination of marijuana and opium, sitting on pillows in front of the fireplace, sipping tea and munching cookies.

At one point, I referred to Mae Brussell as a saint.

"She's *not* a saint," John said. "*You're* not a saint. *I'm* not a saint. *Yoko's* not a saint. *Nobody's* a saint."

We talked about the Charles Manson case, which I had been investigating. Lennon was bemused by the way Manson had associated himself with Beatles songs.

"Look," John said, "would you kindly inform Manson that it was *Paul* [McCartney] who wrote 'Helter Skelter,' not me."

Yoko said, "No, please *don't* tell him. We don't want to have *any* communication with Manson."

"It's all right," John said, "he doesn't have to know the message came from *us.*"

"It's getting chilly in here," Yoko said. "Would you put another cookie in the fireplace?"

We talked about Mae's theory that the deaths of musicians such as

Jimi Hendrix, Janis Joplin, Jim Morrison and Otis Redding had actually been political assassinations because those performers served as role models, surfing on the crest of youth rebellion.

"No, no," Lennon argued, "they were already headed in a self-destructive direction." A few months later, he would remind me of that conversation and add, "Listen, if anything happens to Yoko and me, it was *not* an accident." Such was the level of his understandable paranoia. For now, though, we were simply stoned in Watsonville, discussing conspiracy theory, safe at my oasis.

Lennon was absentmindedly holding on to the joint.

I asked, "Do the British use that expression, 'to *bogart* a joint,' or is that only an American term, you know, derived from the image of a cigarette dangling from Humphrey Bogart's lower lip?"

"In England," he replied, with an inimitable sly expression, "if you remind somebody else to pass a joint, you lose your own turn."

•   •   •

A few months previously—in early March 1972—a paid FBI informant, Julie Maynard, traveled from Madison, Wisconsin, with a local activist, Jane Hopper, to meet with antiwar-movement leaders in New York City. Here's an excerpt from Julie's FBI report on Jane:

"She went over to Rex Weiner's house. He is the editor of the *New York Ace* which is an up-and-coming underground paper. He seems to be an old political hand. He was very glad to see us and proposed a party that night at his newspaper office to welcome us to New York. The party started at about 9 p.m., so Hopper had time to go eat at Tom Forcade's house. He lives in a real dump. . . . He has no legitimate phone. To call out he taps into a Hungarian person's phone.

"There is a girl there named Linda who acts as a servant for Tom and [his roommate] Frank. Linda's parrot interjects 'Right on' whenever the conversation gets rousing. Tom is trying to train it to say 'Eat shit' whenever he argues with anyone, but the bird now says it to him whenever he sees him. The cage is surrounded by small objects that Tom has thrown in response. From there Hopper went to the party. She was introduced to the elite of the radical left. . . ."

This document had been blacked out in its entirety, not because Tom Forcade tried to teach a parrot to say "Eat shit," but presumably because the report concluded with a crucial piece of information—John Lennon had announced that he would come to the convention *only if it was peaceful*—thus contradicting the FBI's justification for investigating him.

This report from FBI informant Julie Maynard was filed 10 days after Hoover's warning to Nixon of Lennon's "avowed intention to engage in disruptive activities." Moreover, in May 1971, a confidential FBI document about Lennon's appearance on the Dick Cavett show reported that "Lennon declared he would not participate in antiwar activities at the Republican National Convention."

Other released documents reveal such endangerments to national security as "Mike Drobenare is using his parents' car again," "Alex is still in NYC and is growing a full beard," and "Yoko can't even remain on key."

For the first time in 14 years, Yoko Ono commented publicly on the FBI files. "I was there," she told the *Minneapolis Star-Tribune*. "I knew all that, John was not being Communist or being violent or anything like that. It was obvious to all of us. It was kind of surprising, I think. We were being bugged, so we knew they were after us. I think it's nice that they're releasing [the files] now. It's due to the fact that the then-government and the now-government are totally different."

And now, if you'll excuse me, I have to put another cookie in the fireplace.

now and then

the sexual revolution

So who's to say what constitutes art?

Recently, at the Gagosian Gallery in Los Angeles, Vanessa Beecroft presented a performance piece consisting of two dozen naked women. These models wore only platinum-blond wigs, shoes and white body paint. Their job was simply to stay in place for three solid hours—first standing up (in concentric circles), then sitting, and then lying down.

Beecroft is an Italian-born New York artist who likes to challenge the notion of traditional artwork by using living forms, dressed and undressed, rather than using paint or clay. She has exhibited her work at the Whitney Museum of American Art, the Guggenheim in New York and the Museum of Contemporary Art in San Diego.

Her credentials aside, I experienced a major flashback.

In 1970, at the Gallery of Erotic Art, a private gallery on Manhattan's Upper West Side—in an entirely dark room except for a bed lit from within by colored light—the artist's naked wife performed an "erotic dance." That is to say, she lay on her back on the bed, one hand on her breast, the other hand masturbating with sensual grace.

Yes, the Sexual Revolution had already become chic. It was, oh, so fashionable. Just another modern trend. Ah, but what a time it had been. This was before AIDS, before the right-wing mindset would finally approve of sex education because it could now be associated with the fear of death instead of pleasure for its own sake.

And, sure, that woman who publicly masturbated at an art gallery in 1970 may have devolved and split into 24 naked but non-masturbating women exhibiting themselves at an art gallery in 2001, but the socially acceptable voyeurism of the visitors encircling the naked ladies at both events provided a sense of continuity.

When I was growing up, it was a cheap thrill merely to get a quick glimpse of a girl's bra strap through the sleeve of her blouse. And although Ed Sullivan wouldn't permit the bottom half of Elvis Presley to be seen undulating on his TV show, young children across the country were practicing pelvic movements with their hula hoops which could bring a blush to the face of Elvis himself.

But who could have predicted that, in the beginning of this century, an Earth, Wind and Fire concert tour would be sponsored by Viagra; Bob Dole would be paid to watch a Britney Spears rock video and tell his penis—I mean his dog—"Easy, boy"; and the network news would feature a commercial showing a car bursting through a barrier labeled Erectile Dysfunction? Why, back in the '60s, we achieved our hard-ons the old-fashioned way. We earned them.

On December 31, 1966, the Sexual Freedom League invited me to its New Year's Eve Orgy in San Francisco. The party was for couples only, so I went with my friend Margo St. James. She was a member of the Psychedelic Rangers, who snuck around late at night painting fire hydrants in Day-Glo colors. She was also a former prostitute and was now wearing one of her Christmas gifts, a brand-new nun's habit. Little did the cab driver know. He presented her with a rose.

After we were admitted to the orgy site, Margo, who had dinner guests that evening, gave me the rose and returned home. The party was in a large theatrical studio, with 150 people dancing in the nude. Behind the closed curtain on the stage, there were 15 small mattresses for those who wished to indulge in sex.

A few loners stood around backstage, playing with themselves as they ogled couples playing with each other. I sat on a chair out front, feeling mighty conspicuous because I was fully dressed, sniffing my rose. Then a naked girl who had been dancing sat down next to me.

"Those guys out there," she complained, "they shouldn't just automatically assume that they're going to have intercourse with their dance partner of the moment."

"But," I asked naively, "in effect, aren't you cockteasing?"

"No," she replied. "It's okay to hug when you're dancing close, but if a guy starts to kiss me or put his tongue in my ear, I tell him not to. Or if he begins to get an erection, then I tell him we'd better stop dancing. It's only fair. You have to draw the line somewhere."

At 11 p.m., a League official announced that somebody had been smoking an illegal substance, and since the orgy, albeit legal, was particularly vulnerable to a visit from the police, the smoker was endangering the other guests and should kindly leave.

Three-quarters of the partygoers left. By then I had taken off all my clothes so that I could blend in with the crowd. After midnight, comedian Professor Irwin Corey arrived in his tuxedo, resembling a horny penguin as he tried to mount a naked lady.

The girl sitting next to me started stroking my knee. This was a dream come true, yet I didn't quite know how to react.

"You're very neighborly," I said.

At 2 a.m., we went onstage and started making what looked like love on one of those small mattresses. Suddenly the curtain opened. They were closing the theater, and there we were, fucking our brains out right there on the stage. I looked up at a man who was sweeping the near-empty auditorium.

Eagerly, I asked, "Did we get the part?"

dirty underwear at disney world

Lately, more and more often, I find myself becoming unable to tell the difference between the news and a parody of the news. The other day, for example, I thought I was watching a *Saturday Night Live* sketch, but it turned out to be an actual hair-removal competition on a depilatory infomercial.

Then I received an e-mail requesting "any information on coir pith and its uses, spent mushroom waste and its uses, and poultry droppings and its uses. I would also be interested to know from anyone who would be commercially interested in the same. . . ." I thought for sure this was a scatological-joke spam, but it turned out to be a sincere inquiry from an international list-serve for environmental journalists.

And so, in June 2001, when I heard that the workers who play characters such as Mickey Mouse and Cinderella at Walt Disney World had won the right to wear clean underwear, I was positive that I was in on the early tremors of an urban legend with negative brand-name placement. But no, it was in reality a dispatch from Associated Press. There had been nearly two months of negotiations between Disney and the Teamsters union. Donald Duck and Goofy—who had become close friends on the picket line—could now celebrate their victory.

It seems that, previously, all the Disney characters would turn in their undergarments with the rest of their costumes each night before going home. This ritual would be completed the next day, when they would pick up a different set of undergarments, supposedly laundered with hot water, but workers complained about stained or smelly undergarments, and there were several characters at the Magic Kingdom who found themselves infested with scabies and pubic lice. I could hardly wait to see the animated version of *that* scene.

Well, now the situation is different. Now each worker will be assigned individual underwear. Now they'll have the option of taking their underwear home—neatly wrapped in a package or worn under their street clothes—and washing it themselves. But what intrigued me was the reason behind this imbroglio. Many of the characters are required to wear Disney-issued jockstraps, tights or bike shorts underneath their costumes, simply because regular underwear bunches up and is noticeable.

It was just such paranoid prudishness, perfectly epitomized by the notion of a politically correct crotch, that first inspired me to publish the Disneyland Memorial Orgy in 1967 in *The Realist*. After all, the magazine's official mission statement was, "Irreverence is our only sacred cow." Walt Disney's death had occurred a few years after *Time* magazine's famous "God Is Dead" cover story, and it occurred to me that Disney had indeed served as God to that whole stable of imaginary characters now mourning in a state of suspended animation.

Disney had been *their* Creator and had repressed all their baser instincts, but now that he had departed they could finally shed their cumulative inhibitions and participate together in a Roman binge, signifying the crumbling of an empire. I contacted Wally Wood, who had illustrated the first piece I sold to *Mad* magazine. Without mentioning any specific details, I explained my general vision of a memorial orgy at Disneyland. He accepted the assignment and presented me with a magnificently degenerate montage.

Pluto was pissing on a portrait of Mickey Mouse, while the real bedraggled Mickey was shooting up heroin with a hypodermic needle. His nephews were jerking off as they watched Goofy fucking Minnie Mouse on a combination bed and cash register. The beams shining out from the Magic Castle were actually dollar signs. Dumbo was simultaneously flying and shitting on an infuriated Donald Duck. Huey, Dewey and Louie were peeking at Daisy Duck's asshole as she watched the Seven Dwarfs groping Snow White. The prince was snatching a glance at Cinderella's snatch while trying a glass slipper on her foot. The Three Little Pigs were humping each other in a daisy chain. Jiminy Cricket leered as Tinker Bell did a striptease and Pinocchio's nose got longer.

This centerspread became so popular that I decided to publish it as a poster, which sold several thousand copies. I learned that the Disney people had considered a lawsuit, but took no action against me, realizing that it would only cause them further embarrassment. Besides, they knew I had no assets.

Disney's own finances aren't doing too well these days. In June 2001—on the same day as that AP report about dirty underwear—the Business section of the *Los Angeles Times* published a story about the Disney corporation's offer of a voluntary separation program to 4,000 employees, 3,000 of whom agreed to accept the package. The remaining number of employees would be dismissed, losing their jobs by the end of July. Which meant that 1,000 Disney employees would be given pink slips that summer. And, of course, when they got home, they would all have to wash those pink slips themselves.

moments of cringe

One reason for the popularity of those so-called reality-television shows—
Jerry Springer, Tom Green, Survivor, Spy TV, Jackass—is that they make
you cringe. You want to look away, but at the same time you're riveted
to the action, so you just surrender. You watch and you wince. And
you're glad that it's not *you* up there on the screen.

But we all have our own private moments of cringe. The earliest one
I recall is when I read *The Catcher in the Rye*. My adolescent mind identified so strongly with the alienated protagonist, teenaged Holden
Caulfield, that I actually wrote to the author, J.D. Salinger, asking permission to use his character in a novel that I planned to write. Of course,
he completely ignored my request. It was an eloquent Zen message.

I still blush with embarrassment at how incredibly naive I had been,
but at least I didn't place myself in a dangerous position, like the time
I sold 12 hits of acid for $50 to someone I didn't really know. It's a few
decades later now, yet I continue to cringe at the way my life would have
changed if he had been an undercover narc. Retroactively, I berate myself
for such stupidity. Apparently, I was more afraid of being rude than of
being busted.

Some moments of cringe are unintentionally cruel. At a party where
the guests were evenly divided between African-Americans and Caucasians,
we were all smoking pot in the kitchen and joking about hackneyed racial
stereotypes—eating watermelon, tap dancing, having giant penises—and
everyone was laughing good-naturedly.

In the hallway, I passed a black man who said, "Hey, Paul."

"I don't remember your name," I pretended. "You all look alike."

I expected him to laugh, but he reacted as if I had punched him in the solar plexus with all my might. And, in effect, I had.

"Yeah," he replied, slowly and bitterly, "we all *do* look alike."

Immediately I realized that he had just arrived at the party and wasn't in on the gag. I wasn't used to hurting people, and I've never stopped feeling awful about that encounter.

Other moments of cringe are simply absurd. Once I had an appointment to interview comedian Jonathan Winters. He answered the doorbell, I introduced myself, and while we were shaking hands his elbow kept banging against the door. He didn't think that the electric charge shooting from his funny bone was so funny.

As a stand-up comic myself, I never did the exact same show twice—I had a powerful resistance to memorizing material—but when I was invited to perform in an off-Broadway review, the producers expected me to do the identical act every night. I cringed with discomfort. During rehearsals, I felt so uneasy repeating my lines word for word, as though I were a tape recorder, that I could only do it by standing with my back to the imaginary audience. I was kicked out of the cast.

Much later in my comedic career, I was asked to serve as the opening act for a singer named Tonio K. at the Roxy in Hollywood. Usually I performed in theaters rather than nightclubs, but this was a favor Tonio's manager requested on the day of the show. Evangelical scandals had been heavy in the news, so I talked about that.

"Jack Kemp is announcing his withdrawal from the presidential race, because he got caught in a motel room with Jimmy Swaggart, where he was learning the missionary position."

No response.

"Bob Dylan became a born-again Christian, but now he's going back to his Hebraic roots. He's currently in a halfway house for secular humanism."

Silence.

"John DeLorean is another born-again Christian. He now lays out his lines of cocaine in the form of a cross."

Deeper silence.

"Pat Robertson wants prayer in the schools, but maybe pregnant young girls will pray for safe abortions."

Open hostility.

I cringe in retrospect. A few days after that fiasco, I found out that Tonio K. was a born-again Christian, and so was his audience.

Conversely, a moment of cringe had occurred in 1976, when an audience *did* laugh but not when they were supposed to. It was at a five-day symposium, "The American Hero: Myths and Media," in Sun Valley, Idaho. There were pop-cultural heroes all over the place, including Tom Laughlin (*Billy Jack*), Lindsay Wagner (*The Bionic Woman*), radical attorney William Kunstler, feminist Kate Millett and even LSD cheerleader Timothy Leary. I delivered the keynote address at the Sun Valley Opera House.

Having just covered the Patty Hearst trial, she was still on my mind. I described her as "a victim, then a hero, then a villain, and now she's a celebrity but not a personality." Previously, I had written an imaginary interview with Patty for *Crawdaddy* magazine—implying that the kidnapping had been orchestrated by her father and the FBI—and then I perceived the trial as if that interview had been satirical prophecy.

Now I was telling this audience what I must have hypnotized myself into believing was true. I explained that Patty Hearst's parents had arranged for her to be kidnapped in order to extricate Patty from her engagement to marry her pot-dealing boyfriend. I reminded the audience that if this seemed far-fetched, it was only in keeping with the family tradition, since William Randolph Hearst had once started a war in Cuba to build up circulation for his newspaper.

I was being serious, but the audience laughed—and woke me up. I suddenly realized that I had lost my sense of empathy, forgetting that one person's logic is another person's humor. Although I had been fortunate enough to experience my original awakening when I was just a little kid—that instant epiphany when you know in your guts that life will never be the same—I always have to *keep on* waking up. Which was the lesson of that particular moment of cringe.

Meanwhile, we've gone from reading about the fear of rats in George Orwell's *1984* to watching folks voluntarily *eating* rats on reality television. Is that progress or what?

a couple of
subcultures

evolution for the hell of it

Here I am, a professional skeptic among 700 true believers ($435 each, plus airfare, hotel and meals) at the three-day Prophets Conference, a neo-New Age event being held in December 2000 at a glitzy hotel in Palm Springs, California.

Exploring the prophet motive, my focus is on three particular presenters, though I give honorable mention to the woman selling angel harps—"Angels bless each harp," she explains, "and every harp has its very own angel"—and to the man selling vibrational healing sound bowls, who warns, "Don't place your head inside the crystal bowl while I'm playing it."

• • •

John Mack—professor of psychiatry at Harvard Medical School, whose specialty is clients who have been abducted by aliens. He not only believes all their anecdotes, he eagerly extrapolates on them.

"The standard abduction scenario involves taking someone into a spaceship, the probing and reproductive agenda, the creation of hybrids in this very traumatic way," he says, "but whether that can be thought about literally in our three-dimensional reality, I'm not sure. But my emphasis has been different. We need to put more emphasis on the evolution of the *relationship* with the alien beings.

"They are cold, they don't have any interest—we're just property to them—they are harvesting eggs or sperm. This is just business—they are indifferent to our feelings—and yet if you stay with the experiences, go into the depth of it, they discover that they have a profound relationship with one or more of these beings, and they may find they have a mate on the other side that they're parenting with, that these hybrids *need* some kind of nurturing—they're like failure-to-thrive babies when they don't have human connection and love, so they will create parenting partners. The need of these beings for some kind of combined human-alien presence is an important dimension of this."

Later, I suggest to Dr. Mack that repressed childhood rape might be a basis of these stories.

"The whole sexual abuse thing," he responds. "I call it the Anything-But Syndrome. Any explanation, no matter how bizarre, is preferable and gets more currency in the mainstream media than the fact that these are serious and important reports of people having powerful experiences. It seems a kind of desperate way to reach us and to bring about an awakening. It is intrusive, but," he quips, "this is an outreach program from the cosmos for the spiritually impaired."

• • •

Jean Houston—powerful performer, a combination of Marianne Williamson and Elayne Boosler, mixing evangelism with entertainment. Her father wrote jokes for Bob Hope and created the classic "Who's on First?" routine for Abbott and Costello. Like a stand-up comic, she peppers her lecture with impressions of the Dalai Lama, Judy Garland and her Airedale trying to sing in tune.

"We are now living in the most interesting time in history," she declares. "I realize other times thought they were it. They're wrong. This is it. The only expected is the unexpected, everything it was isn't anymore, and everything that isn't is coming to be. Ours is an era of quantum change, probably the most radical deconstruction and reconstruction that the world has ever seen, and we are the ones who carry on.

"You are here because you've refused to believe that chaos has to lead to chaos and breakdown to catastrophe. You know that you all sitting here have the power to direct the process along lines very different from those that the prophets of gloom proclaim as inevitable. You are providing another kind of prophecy and another order of manifestation."

Later, I tell her that I'm a skeptic, and she advises me to read her new book, *Jump Time*. In the paper that morning, there's a report that Hillary Clinton will receive an $8-million advance for her memoir. Jean Houston had gained notoriety—and lost her PBS show—when it was reported that she had served as an unofficial spiritual adviser to the then-First Lady.

"Four years ago," she says, "I was supposed to be the guru of Hillary Clinton and the spook in the White House. None of this happened. I did not download Mrs. Roosevelt from the cosmos for Hillary Clinton. That never happened. That was a made-up story. However, now that she has $8 million . . . "

•   •   •

Robert Anton Wilson—now in a wheelchair because of post-polio syndrome. In 1959, I published this prolific author's first article, "The Semantics of God," in *The Realist*, where he asserted, "The Believer had better face himself and ask squarely: Do I literally believe 'God' has a penis? If the answer is no, then it seems only logical to drop the ridiculous practice of referring to 'God' as 'He.'"

Now he greets me, "How're you doing?"

"Still skeptical after all these years," I reply. "How're *you* doing?"

"Still open-minded after all these years."

"There was a friend of mine who swears to God," he tells the audience, "he swears by all the Gods that writers believe in—and most writers don't believe in any God except their own creative unconscious—but he swears he was in Philadelphia when Eleanor Roosevelt introduced Marian Anderson at a concert."

Anderson was an African-American operatic star who had been banned from singing in Constitution Hall by the Daughters of the American Revolution because of her race.

"Eleanor Roosevelt was sort of like Hillary Rodham Clinton to the *n*th degree," he continues. "She was the most controversial First Lady we ever had. Anyway, she was introducing Marian Anderson when somebody—some lowbrow, loud-mouthed, redneck, right wing, fascist, Ku Klux Klan son-of-a-bitch motherfucker—crept into the audience and yelled out, '*Marian Anderson sucks cock!*' And there was a deathly silence. Nobody knew what to do about this character. And Eleanor leaned forward to the microphone and said, 'Nonetheless . . . ' And went on with her introduction. That's the way Hillary should've handled all of Bill's extracurricular activities."

Wilson turns out to be the irreverent bad boy at this oh-so-polite conference.

"I started out to be an engineer," he says, "and I was quite horrified to find out that, according to modern science, the universe doesn't have any color. Color is created by our brains from light waves bouncing off things. The universe doesn't have any temperature, either, below the molecular level. And, learning this scientific model of a colorless, tem-peratureless world, I just couldn't believe in it, and yet it works. At the same time I'm seeing colors, I'm experiencing sensations, and I didn't solve this until I became a pothead. Well, that was when I was young. I haven't smoked pot in about 12 . . . hours, and I want you to know it's great to be clean."

Wilson began smoking pot in 1955. He is the author of 32 books. He does six drafts of everything he writes, alternating between straight and stoned, the final draft always while stoned.

"Reality," he continues, "depends on what part of the world your nervous system is keyed to pick up, depending on what species you are. Then within your species it depends on your cultural reality tunnel. And it depends on your own personal experiences, your own life history and reality tunnel. Ergo, there are as many realities as there are sentient beings, so when people start arguing about who's got the right reality, I think they're a couple of hundred years behind the times and they haven't smoked enough weed yet. Everybody's reality is equally real. Some realities, of course, make more problems for us than others."

•   •   •

Well, I've tried to keep an open mind, and in the process I've been converted. My chakras have been balanced, my inner child has been lib-erated, and I am now more spiritual than thou. *Hallelujah*! Yes, I too have become, in the words of Jean Houston, "a steward of the solar system."

Also, there's a reason I've never been abducted by aliens. It's because I sleep on my stomach. According to the Center for UFO Studies in Chicago, the most effective thing you can do to *avoid* being abducted by aliens is "sleeping on your stomach." So from now on I'm sleeping on my back. And then those big-eyed alien rascals will have to turn me over if they wish to endow me with one of their famous anal probes. I can hardly wait.

Nonetheless . . .

life among the
neo-pagans

In the summer of 1997, I performed at the 17th annual Starwood Neo-Pagan Festival in Sherman, New York—Amish country on the border near Ohio and Pennsylvania. This event—a female-oriented celebration of the sensual and the spiritual—took place on private campgrounds, where clothing was optional. Many women were bare-breasted, and several men and women walked around fully naked, a practice known as the "sky clad" experience.

Instead of camping out, I stayed at a nearby bed-and-breakfast place. Downstairs in the living room, I asked a woman—falsely assuming that she was the proprietor—where the key would be left if I came back late at night.

"I don't know," she replied. "I'm here for the festival."

"Oh. In what capacity?"

"I'm in the craft."

"Which craft?"

"That's right," she said.

She has been a Wiccan for 20 years, but now she complained, "Witchcraft has become trendy. I mean, ever since *Buffy the Vampire Slayer* . . . "

On Merchants Row, there was an inviting banner over one of the booths: "Stop by for a Spell."

A positive perspective on witchcraft was one of the themes at this Neo-Pagan Festival, along with such workshops as "Privacy Rights and Drug Policy," "Cultivating Consciousness in Your Child," "Live Meditations in Drumming and Dance," "The Supreme Court and the

Free Exercise of Religion," "A Procession to Honor the Earth Goddess," "Safer Sex," and "Dark Ecstasy: The Ritual Use of Pleasure, Pain and Sensory Deprivation as Psychedelic Experience."

When I walked on to the outdoor stage, my opening line was: "I'm gonna start with two words that have been *thought* year after year at these festivals, but which have never actually been uttered out loud, and those two words are, 'Nice tits.'"

The audience hesitated a second, because in that context this could be a politically incorrect observation—I had deliberately taken that chance—but then they laughed and applauded, because they knew it was true.

I was invited back to perform at Starwood again in the summer of 1998. The previous month, two Amish men had been arrested for distributing cocaine they bought from a biker gang, the Pagans, one of whose members was a police informer.

The two men were from a particularly conservative Amish sect, where not only electricity and tractors were forbidden, but even zippers. Did those tempting zippers on the Pagans' leather motorcycle jackets serve as a gateway drug to cocaine?

Speaking of illegal drugs, at the festival I came across the only individual I've ever met who has actually hallucinated on toad slime. I pictured him as a young lad with a tadpole in his pocket, and now as a grown man with a frog in his pocket.

I also met Reverend Ivan Stang, leader of the infamous Church of the SubGenius. He talked about "how to milk the Internet for all it's worth, and get away with murder, before the Conspiracy figures out how to spoil it for us."

But Stang was in deep embarrassment mode, since this was only a couple of weeks after the failure of his widely circulated prediction that, on July 5th at 7 a.m., Pleasure Saucers would descend to Earth as part of the great "Rupture" and take away all those SubGeniuses who had paid $30 for the privilege.

The festival climaxed with a tremendous, 50-foot-diameter, 25-foot-high bonfire, constructed during the week with the aid of a derrick. On Saturday night, several dancers with torches ritualistically teased the pyramid of logs, encircled at a distance by 2,000 enthusiasts, although one impatient woman yelled, "Just *do* it!" The neo-pagans danced and pranced and cavorted around the bonfire late into the night.

My own personal highlight was when a beautiful woman named Pearl approached me. She was in the process of transforming her breasts from fetish to functional by nursing a baby that had been conceived there the year before.

During that festival, she had walked in on my performance, bare-breasted, at the precise moment that I uttered the words, "Nice tits." She assumed that I was referring specifically to her and was flattered, so now I didn't have the heart to disillusion her. But I did write about it in my *High Times* column, "Brain Damage Control," ending with this sentence: "I hope she doesn't read this."

Furthermore, at the 20th annual Starwood Festival in 2000, I found myself in front of a microphone on that same stage, and I told that story. Pearl was in the audience, and she was laughing heartily. This time, though, when I said, "Nice tits," I added, "Okay, *every*body," and the words came booming back at me: '*Nice tits!*'"

And later, as I was leaving the stage, Pearl called out, "Nice dick!" I was fully dressed, but it didn't matter. This was a perfect example of tit for tat. Or dick for tit.

My old friend Steve Gaskin and I were staying at a bed-and-breakfast house where there were angels all over the place. Stuffed angels, plastic angels, plaster-of-paris angels, embroidered angels, stained-glass angels, *papier-mâché* angels, teddy bear angels and origami angels. There were angel dolls and angel paintings and angel sculptures and even an angel mobile hanging from a ceiling.

In the bathroom, there was an angel tissue-dispenser and an angel night-light. In the hallway, there was a pile of *Angels on Earth* magazines. In my room, on the bureau, there was a copy of *Whispers From Heaven*, featuring such articles as "Feeding Angels," "When Angels Kiss" and "Rescued By Angels: The Amazing Story of a Kidnapping Survivor."

Gaskin's room had a door that led to the roof, and the first night we sat out there and smoked a joint. The next day there was a note taped to the door: "The roof is to be used only as a fire escape. Please use the patio." The next night we smoked a joint in my room. And the next day there was a *No Smoking* sign on the inside of my door, and the electric fan was on, aimed toward the now-open window.

At breakfast the next morning, I was just about to apologize to the kindly Christian woman whose home this was, explaining that a doctor had recommended marijuana for my arthritis, but *she* apologized *to me* because she hadn't told me in advance that smoking wasn't allowed.

"Some people are allergic to cigarette smoke," she explained, and I almost blurted out, "That wasn't tobacco, that was pot."

I hope she doesn't read this.

three faces
of evil

charlie manson's image

Proud to be a hippie and wearing my new yellow leather fringe jacket for the first time, I was on my way to the original Woodstock Festival along with half a million others on a musical pilgrimage. At the same time, newspapers were headlining the murder in Beverly Hills of Sharon Tate, the actress wife of director Roman Polanski, their unborn baby and a few friends.

The killers turned out to be members of the Charles Manson family, the ultimate perversion of a hippie commune. Manson was portrayed by the media as a hippie cult leader, and the counterculture became a dangerous enemy. Hitchhikers were shunned. Communes were raided. In the public's mind, flower children had grown poisonous thorns.

But Manson was raised behind bars. His *real* family included con artists, pimps, drug dealers, thieves, muggers, rapists and murderers. He had known only power relationships in an army of control junkies. Charlie was America's own Frankenstein monster, a logical product of the prison system—racist, paranoid and violent—even if hippie astrologers thought his fate had been predetermined because he was a triple Scorpio.

In August 1969, he sent his brainwashed family off to slay whoever was at the Tate home: the pregnant Sharon; hair stylist and drug dealer to the stars Jay Sebring; would-be screenwriter Voytek Frykowski; and his girlfriend, coffee heiress Abigail Folger. The next night, Manson accompanied the killers to supermarket mogul Leno LaBianca and his wife.

And what a well-programmed family they were. A prison psychiatrist at San Quentin told me of an incident he had observed during Manson's trial. An inmate had said to Manson, "Look, I don't wanna know about your theories on race, I don't wanna hear anything about religion, I just wanna know one thing. How'd you get them girls to obey you like that?"

"I got a knack," Charlie replied.

His "knack" was combining LSD and mescaline with singalongs and games accompanying his perversion of techniques he'd learned in prison—encounter sessions, Scientology auditing, post-hypnotic suggestion, geographical isolation, subliminal motivation, transactional analysis, verbal probing and the sexual longevity that he had practiced upon himself for all those years in the privacy of his cell.

Hal Lipset, San Francisco's renowned private investigator, informed me that not only did the Los Angeles Police Department seize pornographic films and videotapes they found in Roman Polanski's loft, but also that certain LAPD officers were *selling* them. Lipset had talked with one police source who told him exactly which porno flicks were available, a total of seven hours' worth for a quarter-million dollars.

Lipset began reciting a litany of those private porn flicks. There was Greg Bautzer, an attorney for Howard Hughes, with Jane Wyman, the ex-wife of Ronald Reagan, who was governor of California at the time of the murders. There was Cass Elliot in an orgy with Yul Brynner, Peter Sellers and Warren Beatty, the same trio who, with John Phillips, had offered a $25,000 reward for the capture of the killers. There was Sharon Tate with Dean Martin. There was Sharon with Steve McQueen. And there she was with two black bisexual men.

"The cops weren't too happy about *that* one," Lipset recalled.

The murders were intended to imply that the victims had been selected at random, but I had always felt that Manson and his killers had some connection with them before the murders took place. I finally tracked down a reporter who told me that when she was hanging around with Los Angeles police, they showed her a porn video of Susan Atkins, one of Charlie's devils, with Voytek Frykowski, one of the victims, even though, according to legend, the executioners and the victims had never met until the night of the massacre.

But apparently the reporter mentioned the wrong victim, because when I wrote to Manson and asked directly, "Did Susan sleep with Frykowski?" he answered, "You are ill advised and misled. Sebring done Susan's hair and I think he sucked one or two of her dicks. I'm not sure who she was walking out from her stars and cages, that girl *loves* dick, you know what I mean, hon. Yul Brynner, Peter Sellers . . . "

I continued to correspond with Charlie. He has become a cultural icon. There are songs about him. In surfer jargon, Manson means a crazy, reckless surfer. For comedians, Manson is a generic joke reference. In 1992, I asked him how he felt about that.

He replied, "I don't know what a generic joke is. I think I know what that means. That means you talk bad about Reagan or Bush. I've always ran poker games and whores and crime. I'm a crook. You make the reality in court and press. I just ride and play the cards that were pushed on me to play. Mass killer. It's a job, what can I say."

I interviewed Preston Guillory, a former deputy sheriff. "A few weeks prior to the arrests at the Spahn Ranch raid," he said, "we were told that we were not to arrest Manson or any of his followers. The reason he was left on the street was because our department thought that he was going to launch an attack on the Black Panthers."

And so it was that racism in the Sheriff's Department inadvertently turned them into collaborators in a mass murder. Yet Charles Manson is the only face you'll see glaring at you from some rebellious teenager's T-shirt. Because the killers left clues to imply that the victims had been slain by black militants, the media continue to imply that Manson's only motive was to start a race war.

However, on the evening of Friday, August 9, 1969, just a few hours before the slaughter took place, Joel Rostau, the boyfriend of Jay Sebring's receptionist and an intermediary in a cocaine ring, visited Sebring and Frykowski at the Tate house, to deliver mescaline and cocaine. During the Manson trial, several associates of Sebring were murdered, including Rostau, whose body was found in the trunk of a car in New York.

Charles Manson's brainwashed family unknowingly served as a hit squad for organized crime figures that he had met in prison. Three decades later, Manson continues to be a symbol for the end of the '60s. One thing is certain, though. Charlie was never a hippie. Recently, *Variety*, the bible of show biz, reported that prosecutor Vincent Bugliosi's 1975 book about the Manson family, *Helter Skelter*, has been bought by, appropriately enough, Propaganda Films.

timothy mcveigh's body count

During the Vietnam War, there developed a horrible ritual that was broadcast across the nation on the TV news—every Thursday, for some reason. It was the body count. So many "American dead"; so many "Vietnamese dead"; so many "Enemy dead." Just abstract numbers, functioning to hide the utter futility of it all. U.S. military intervention killed three million Vietnamese, as well as 60,000 Americans.

One Thursday, my four-year-old daughter Holly was sitting on my lap as I watched Walter Cronkite deliver the CBS News. When Cronkite came to the body count that evening, Holly asked, "Is that happening in our universe?"

I experienced a flashback to that moment when it was disclosed that Timothy McVeigh had referred to the slaughtered children in the bombed Oklahoma City's Murrah Federal Building as "collateral damage," a concept he had learned as a soldier fighting in the Gulf War to make the world safe for oil magnates. On one hand, his utterance referred to legalized evil. On the other hand, it was an expression of the darkest possible humor, satirizing American chauvinism.

In a strange way, it reminded me of Lenny Bruce in 1962, addressing the audience with a German accent:

"My name is Adolf Eichmann. And the Jews came every day to what they thought would be fun in the showers. People say I should have been hung. *Nein*. Do you recognize the whore in the middle of you—that you would have done the same if you were there yourselves? My defense: I was a soldier. I saw the end of a conscientious day's effort. I watched through the portholes. I saw every Jew burned and turned into soap. . . ."

And so it came to pass that McVeigh—perhaps this was the only positive remnant of his legacy—inadvertently forced us to come to grips with the realization that the grief of families on the other side of the globe matched the grief of families in Oklahoma City.

His attorneys have clung to his defense with a sense of identification that could be diagnosed as Reverse Stockholm Syndrome. It is an ethical disease of the profession that certainly affected O.J. Simpson's dream team. More recently, a lawyer for the man who killed Madalyn Murray O'Hair, her son and granddaughter, insisted that they had all committed suicide. And, presumably, buried themselves.

But the inhumanity epitomized by McVeigh transcends military action. Citizens do it all the time. For example, the Partnership for a Drug-Free America is sponsored by the pharmaceutical, alcohol and tobacco industries. From 1970 to 1998, the revenue of major pharmaceutical companies more than quadrupled to $81 billion. Pfizer alone has a $290-billion market capitalization; the entire pharmaceutical industry has a $500-billion capitalization. In 1999, 100,000 people died from prescription drugs. Alcohol killed 150,000. And 450,000 died from smoking cigarettes.

All collateral damage.

As long as any government can arbitrarily decide which drugs are legal and which drugs are illegal, then everyone who is behind bars for a nonviolent drug offense is a political prisoner of the war on drugs. That is, the war on *some* people who use *some* drugs. Sometimes.

In the book *Trust Us, We're Experts*, John Stauber and Sheldon Rampton report that in the early 1990s, tobacco companies paid $156,000 to 13 academic scientists to write letters to influential medical journals, arguing the tobacco industry's case. One biostatistician was paid $10,000 for an eight-paragraph letter published in the *Journal of the American Medical Association*. Was he morally any better than Timothy McVeigh? At least McVeigh acted out of principle, albeit the ultimate perversion of principle.

Timothy McVeigh is gone, but the malady lingers on—people somehow robotized out of their innate compassion.

And every day continues to be Thursday.

the devil in me

When I moved from Venice Beach to Desert Hot Springs—from one California extreme to the other, from the ocean to the desert—I thought that I would keep a low profile. But when I was invited to speak at a local decriminalization-of-marijuana rally, I couldn't say no. A month later, a woman who organizes events at the Miracle Springs Hotel and had heard my first comedy CD, *We Have Ways of Making You Laugh*, invited me to perform at the Chamber of Commerce annual installation banquet.

It seems the city had adopted a new slogan, "Clearly Above the Rest," and so the theme of that dinner would be heaven. There would be blue sky above the tables. The servers would be dressed as angels. The stage would be a cottony white cloud, enhanced by a fog machine. There would be a blond angel onstage, and she would be playing the harp. At 7 p.m., the salad would be served.

At precisely 7:15, a clatter of pots and pans would be heard, and then I would be thrown out of the kitchen, right into this heavenly ballroom. Oh, yes, and I would be dressed as the devil. Now the devil is not merely a metaphor. According to a recent poll, one out of every four Americans believes in the devil literally.

At first I resisted. Although I've been performing stand-up for decades, I never played a character before—but I surrendered to the challenge. I rented a devil's costume—black shirt with everything else red: pants, bowtie, jacket, cape, tail and horns—with a silver three-prong pitchfork. I pulled the hair hanging on my forehead into a pointy widow's peak. Yes, I was the personification of evil. Try putting *that* on your résumé.

Then I began to get into the role. My favorite song became the Rolling Stones' "Sympathy for the Devil," with "That Old Devil Moon" as runner-up. I resented it whenever there was a negative reference to the devil—I mean to me—in the media. I began to remember a lifetime of movies about myself. *The Devil and Daniel Webster. Rosemary's Baby. The Exorcist. The Devil's Advocate. Devil in a Blue Dress.* And, of course, *The Devil in Miss Jones.* How could I forget that? It was the second porn flick, after *Deep Throat*, to infiltrate mainstream awareness.

On the night of the event, I changed into my devil's costume in a bathroom at the hotel. When I looked in the mirror and said—to the image of Satan!—"Please, God, help me do a good show," it felt as if, for just that instant, God and Satan were in total harmony.

Then, in the corridor, I overheard a woman say to her companion, "Right now, I would sell my soul for a massage." I absolutely could not resist this opportunity. I walked behind her, tapped her on the shoulder and said, "Just sign right here." Her reaction was a rare and precious moment to be preserved in amber for posterity.

My appearance was preceded by the high school ROTC presenting colors, the pledge of allegiance, the national anthem, and a nondenominational religious invocation: "God bless Desert Hot Springs, especially the Chamber of Commerce. . . ." After I burst through the swinging doors, I announced that I was originally kicked out of heaven but now I was being kicked *into* heaven. I explained that I was fulfilling an equal-time requirement, that this was a cultural exchange, and that the new city slogan should have been "It's Hotter Than Hell Here."

Then I proceeded to conduct a one-devil roast of local leaders in the audience whose eternal souls I had previously purchased, revealing how I had kept my part of each deal. As promised, I got the president of the Chamber of Commerce reelected; I got a green card for the police chief's undocumented Mexican nanny; I got $200,000 for the city manager's marketing plan.

And I saved the mayor for last. An appeals court decision had ruled that the city would have to pay $3 million to real-estate developers who had unsuccessfully attempted a low-income housing project called Silver Sage. "It sounds like a brand of marijuana," I remarked. I disclosed that, in order to raise such a large sum of money, I had arranged for the mayor to run a meth lab, hidden behind a popular restaurant.

"The devil made me say that," I explained. "I mean I made myself say it. That's the trouble with people. They should take responsibility for themselves instead of blaming me all the time. What am I, the all-purpose scapegoat for everybody else's evil?"

The whole time I was up there, that angelic harpist remained sitting in her chair facing sideways on the stage behind me. At one point I turned around, jabbed my pitchfork toward her, and asked if I could use her harp to slice my deviled eggs. Finally, when my 15 minutes of infamy were up, I departed, telling the audience, "I'm gonna go home and smoke some devil's weed now."

Postscript: In order to avoid paying $3 million to those real-estate developers, the city of Desert Hot Springs has declared bankruptcy. Presumably, their new slogan will be changed to "Clearly Above the Credit Limit."

the white
house scandal

the memoirs of monica lewinsky

The following is an exclusive sneak preview of an autobiography by Monica S. Lewinsky, titled Going Down in History. *The manuscript in progress was leaked to* The Realist *by, of course, a reliable source.*

I am not an airhead. I'm a victim, partly of my own making. And, mostly, I'm a political pawn of the spin-doctors. There are several books being written about the White House scandal, but only a few individuals know what really happened, and only I know who I really am, which is why I have decided to write this book. I would write it even if I didn't need the money for legal expenses. My life may be ruined—at least my reputation will be forever tainted—but the truth must be told.

I don't like being a one-dimensional symbol. If anybody were to take a free-association test, the psychiatrist would say, "Monica Lewinsky," and the patient would immediately respond, "Oral sex." Maybe soon my name will be in a crossword puzzle—eight letters across—and the answer will be "Fellatio." This country was originally founded by puritans and pioneers, and I feel trapped between those two forces.

Back home in Brentwood, I've been listening to talk radio a lot. Ronn Owens on KABC had listeners phone in with nothing but jokes about me for a solid hour. First he warned the audience that if they were easily offended, they should tune out. I have never felt so objectified in my life, and yet at the same time I found the program quite riveting.

The best call came from a nine-year-old who said, "Bill Clinton violated the Eleventh Commandment: Thou shalt not put thy rod in thy staff." The worst call came from a man who asked, "What do the Titanic and Monica Lewinsky have in common?" The answer was, "They both have dead seamen [semen] floating in the hull."

And remember that ridiculous rumor—the one Lucianne Goldberg *admitted* she made up in order to get attention from the press—that I kept a dress stained with Clinton's dried ejaculation as a souvenir? Well, Jonathan Brandmeier on KLSX invited listeners to call in and suggest euphemisms for presidential sperm. My favorite was "Bubba butter." Apparently, my role is to serve as a vehicle for the destruction of taboos.

I have also become an automatic comedy reference. So, to Jay Leno, David Letterman and Conan O'Brien, I'm very useful in punchlines. To *Saturday Night Live*, I'm just a character in their sketches, and never without that beret from my famous hugging-Bill TV footage. But I did think it was hilarious to cast John Goodman in drag as Linda Tripp. That cheered me up. I've been simultaneously depressed, scared and, strangely enough, exhilarated.

As an instant celebrity, I've learned that everybody—Democrats, Republicans, men, women, the other interns—they always see everybody else through their own subjective eyes. Like, for a manufacturer of novelty items, I was simply a disembodied inspiration for the marketing of "Presidential Kneepads." And for *Penthouse* magazine, I would only be their next notorious masturbation enhancer.

In the eyes of the media—from NBC News to *Dateline*, from CBS News to *Sixty Minutes*, from ABC News to *Nightline*, from *Time* magazine to *People*, from *The New York Times* to the *National Enquirer*, from *The Washington Post* to the *Globe*—I am purely a commodity. Naturally, I believe in the First Amendment, so I'm against censorship. All I'm saying is that while America is achieving adolescence publicly, the tabloids have won the war.

The battleground is like an ongoing contemporary Shakespearean tragicomedy, but there is no script, there is no producer, there is no director. There is only the process of everyone's karma interacting. I recall the words of Terence McKenna when he was a guest lecturer at Lewis & Clark. He said, "Chaos is the tail that wags the dog."

Damage control is the name of the game. It was Dick Morris who advised Clinton to get a dog. Buddy, huh? They should've named him Photo-Op. It was also Dick Morris who suggested taping that ostensibly candid scene of the First Couple dancing on the beach. And I would bet my entire book advance that both Hillary and Bill *knew ahead of time* that Dick Morris was going to release a trial balloon that *if* the

rumor about Hillary being a lesbian were true, *then* it would be perfectly reasonable that her husband would need to seek sexual gratifi-
cation elsewhere.

In fact, the reason I think that Clinton's approval ratings have been
so high is because people can *identify* with him fooling around. I mean,
when Jimmy Carter admitted that he had lust in his heart, it was the
adultery vote that helped get him elected. And that was only lust in his
heart. But Bill Clinton is a full-time *activist*.

I've been reading a book, *Spin Cycle* by Howard Kurtz, and there's
a story in there about that time in 1996 when the president said he
"might like to date" a shapely, 500-year-old mummy whose remains were
on display at the National Geographic Society. Later, chatting after a few
cocktails, Press Secretary Mike McCurry told a dozen journalists on the
press plane that he could understand Clinton's remark. "Compared to
that mummy he's been fucking," McCurry chuckled, "why not?"

Without bothering to mention that it was off the record, McCurry
assumed his joke wouldn't be reported, and it wasn't until that book.
Washington is a very cynical place. Everything is stated carefully and
deliberately, with the *intention* that it will be repeated. When McCurry
told the *Chicago Tribune* in an interview that Clinton's relationship with
me could turn out to have been "complicated," it was no slip of the
tongue. He was fully aware that his observation would appear in print.

Unlike Richard Nixon, who never dreamed that *his* words would be
published in a book, *Abuse of Power, The New Nixon Oval Office Tapes*:
"Bob [Haldeman], please get me the names of the Jews, you know, the
big Jewish contributors to the Democrats. Could we please investigate
some of the cocksuckers?" Well, my mom is a member of the Book of
the Month Club, and in their brochure they printed it c*cks*ck*rs."
Anyway, that's how everybody thinks of *me* now. I'm America's official
c*cks*ck*r laureate.

The image of me on my knees giving head to the president has
become a cultural icon. The irony is that *it never happened*. When Wolf
Blitzer of CNN asked Clinton at a press conference what he would like
to say to me, Clinton smiled and said, "That's good, that's good." It
was extremely ironic, because that's *exactly* what I *imagined* he *did* say
to me: "That's good, that's good." And I replied, "I gave you a blowjob,
but I didn't swallow." He started laughing hysterically, just like that time
he did with Boris Yeltsin. Bill liked my sense of humor. That's why we
went from flirtation to friendship.

However, the reason I visited the White House 37 times was not for Bill—it was to be with Hillary—*she* was the one who desired me physically. The rumor about her being a lesbian was *true*. And so my relationship with Bill *was* complicated. He just acted as a middleman for Hillary. Now he's telling the truth when he denies having an affair with me, *and* at the same time he's taking the fall for her. In that sense, he's an incredibly loyal husband. Despite what the public may think, Bill is absolutely devoted to Hillary.

Everyone is watching so closely for him to commit the next indiscretion, but it would have to be with somebody he can *totally* trust, who could suck the dick of the leader of the Western World and *not* confide to a friend, or to somebody who *pretended* to be a friend. So, for a while, Bill is left with only Buddy's tongue for sexual companionship. But at least Buddy won't lick and tell. And if I know my president, while Buddy is pleasuring him, Clinton will fantasize that it's a female dog.

president clinton's private confession

The following is an exclusive transcript of a closed-door, secretly taped prayer breakfast that Bill Clinton hosted for a group of religious leaders after the impeachment trial failed to remove him from office.

Gentlemen and lady—I guess you must be the Episcopalian, ma'am— thank you all for being here. It's too bad Reverend Moon isn't among you, or he could perform a mass impeachment of all the senators who swore under oath that they would be impartial. But seriously, this morning I want to begin with an epiphany I had, one that truly humbled me. Strangely enough, it happened while I was watching Roseanne interviewing Paula Jones and, as my mother used to say, curiosity got the best of me.

Ms. Jones was telling Roseanne about the first time she saw me in that hotel. She was working at the courtesy booth for the governors' conference. She described me as funny looking, the way my hair was styled, being overweight, how my suit was out of fashion and didn't fit. So, she was sitting at the registration desk with her girlfriend, pointing at me and giggling. Somehow, I perceived her through the filter of arrogance that people with power develop, and I assumed she was giving me a come-hither look. That simple misperception is what triggered this whole long ordeal. I took her willingness for granted.

It was different with Monica Lewinsky, though. I mean, when she flashed the strap of her thong underwear, it made my heart go *thump*, and, you know, I'm a prisoner in the White House, I can't go to a motel, but Monica just appeared like a gift from heaven, and I succumbed to temptation. I was fully cognizant that this was a very delicate situation— I even asked for *permission* to kiss her—and yet I blocked out my own foresight. Way back in college, when I tried to avoid military service, I was already thinking ahead to campaigning for president, but now I found myself ignoring the certainty that Monica would never be able to keep our relationship a secret.

I certainly didn't consider the possibility that she would become so seriously involved with me. It was embarrassing to hear the tape that Linda Tripp made, where Monica told her what she had said to me on the phone: "I love you, Butthead." I remember thinking when it happened, "Hey, I'm the president of the United States, you can't call me Butthead." However, I immediately decided to treat the situation with humor. But she hung up before I could say, "I love you, Beavis."

Surprisingly, I was *not* embarrassed about the infamous cigar incident. I felt that it had been an act of restraint from *actual* intercourse. Kind of tender and playful. Now, if it had been a Cuban cigar, *that* would have been illegal. But this was not the sort of intimacy that I would have felt comfortable performing with the First Lady. Hillary and I are really close, but, as I'm sure you understand, no cigar.

For her, the most revealing thing in *The Starr Report* is Monica's fantasy about our being together more often when I'm out of office, where she quotes me as saying, "I might be alone in three years." Hillary was furious, not only because it had provided a young intern with false encouragement, but also because it implied that Hillary and I don't have sex, and she felt it divulged our agreement that if we were to separate, it would not occur before we left the White House.

For me, the most revealing section of the report is Monica's testimony that I jokingly said, "Well, what are we going to do when I'm 75 and I have to pee 25 times a day?" True, I did say that, but I wasn't joking. It was my fear of old age that kept drawing me to Monica. She was my direct link to youth. So I was being quite literal about peeing 25 times a day when I'm 75. Hell, I drink at least eight glasses of water a day *now*—just like I'm supposed to, for my health—but then I have to *pee* at least eight times a day. Ironically, I've read that if you have to pee more than eight times in 24 hours, it's a symptom of overactive bladder.

Indeed, irony has permeated this scandal from beginning to end. It was ironic that my sexual appetite helped put me in office—the Gennifer

Flowers allegation originally placed me in the media spotlight—and it was also my sexual appetite that almost tossed me out of that same office. And it's ironic that, although Kathleen Willey *enjoyed* our brief encounter, to prove it we would have had to resort to testimony by her confidant, Linda Tripp.

Now, there are things that I've done as president of which I'm *truly* ashamed. Even before my inauguration, I made it a point to stop in Arkansas to oversee the execution of a mentally retarded prisoner. At his last meal, he said he'd wait to have his dessert, a slice of pecan pie, until after the execution; that's how much he understood what was going on. I'm ashamed of *under*protecting the rights of gays and *over*protecting children from the Internet. I'm ashamed of being *against* medical marijuana and *for* requiring a urine test as a prerequisite to obtaining a driver's license. I'm ashamed of bombing Iraq, Afghanistan and Sudan. I'm ashamed of *in*creasing the military budget and *de*creasing the welfare budget. I'm ashamed of dropping cluster bombs and continuing to plant land mines.

But the Republicans didn't dare attack me for any of those positions because they are all *their* positions, too.

But I'll tell you how I survived this past year, how I maintained such high approval ratings, while Newt Gingrich and Bob Livingston fell by the wayside. How I managed, in short, to remain president. It was partly the state of the economy, and it was partly the state of the culture. Pornography is a $20 billion-a-year business in this country. Steven Spielberg told me that's more than Hollywood's entire domestic box-office receipts. Because that's what the American public *wants*. And the TV networks exploit that fact. Harry Thomasen told me it's why sweeps weeks are always so raunchy. So, then, what I did wasn't considered such a big deal after all.

Mainly, though, I have survived because, one sunny afternoon, Monica was positioning herself on the carpet under my desk in the Oval Office while I was on the phone with Benjamin Netanyahu. I was telling him about that time Monica was performing oral sex on me while Yasser Arafat was waiting in the Rose Garden for our appointment. I *didn't* tell Netanyahu that she was just about to perform the same act on me while I was on the phone with *him*. Anyway, at that point, Monica found a big old dusty Mason jar under my desk. There was a label on the side which read, "Property of Ronald Reagan." That Mason jar was filled with Teflon, and I have rubbed it on myself every day since.

I began my talk this morning with an epiphany, and I'd like to end with another. This epiphany also occurred while I was watching television—*Larry King Live*—and, once again, Paula Jones was the guest. At one point she said, "I've never voted in my life." I was astounded. Then she added, "I'm so apolitical, it's unreal." And I realized what an incredibly great country America really is, that somebody who was just a plain citizen, who was never even *interested* in politics—somebody who had never even *voted* for a president—had nearly succeeded in toppling one.

Well, this has been a catharsis for me. I just want to say once more how much I appreciate your presence here. And finally I would like to share with you a little witticism that Hillary came up with last night, an idea for what my epitaph should be: "Here lies Bill Clinton, but that depends on what you mean by lies." Isn't she wonderful?

Oh, and one more thing. Now listen carefully. I did *not* have sexual assault with that woman, Ms. Broaddrick. I'll be honest with you, it may have been *rough* sex, but it was totally consensual.

That, I can guarantee. God bless you.

Kenneth Starr has accepted an invitation from the Boulder, Colorado Chamber of Commerce to serve as an independent prosecutor in the JonBenet Ramsey murder case.

"I am just as surprised as you are," he announced at a press conference. "Actually, I thought I had retired from this business, but I just couldn't refuse. You know, I worked for a while investigating pedophiles, and I came to realize that a grown man who is capable of having sex with young children is also capable of killing them. It's simply a matter of degree."

"Sir," a reporter from the *San Francisco Chronicle* asked, "are you saying that you believe a pedophile was responsible for JonBenet's death?"

"It's too early to tell."

"But," a reporter from *The New York Times* asked, "since DNA—so far, unidentified DNA—was found on Ms. Ramsey's underpants, wouldn't it be a foregone conclusion that the murderer was a pedophile?"

"Not necessarily. It could be two separate individuals. Now, this is purely hypothetical, of course, but say the father could be a pedophile, and the mother could be a murderer."

"Judge," a *Los Angeles Times* reporter said, "you issued that extremely graphic *Starr Report* after the Clinton investigation. Will you issue a similar report about JonBenet?"

"I can't answer that yet. I just don't want to have a premature ejaculation at this stage of the game."

The *Washington Post* correspondent followed up, sarcastically: "Well, will there be any leaks, like there were to the White House press corps?"

"I'm sorry, I don't accept the premise of your question. Next?"

And a gossip columnist for the *National Enquirer* stood up to ask, "What was the result of your original investigation of pedophiles?"

"Oh, that. Well, after six months, it turned out that every single member of the pedophile chat room was an undercover officer posing as a pedophile."

"Sir—"

"Thank you, all. I look forward to our next meeting."

campaign in
the ass

dan rather, harry shearer and me

As I entered the lobby of a hotel in Philadelphia, where the Republican National Convention was taking place, I saw my old friend and fellow satirist, Harry Shearer, checking in.

We were both there to participate in the Shadow Convention, organized by columnist Arianna Huffington in conjunction with a coalition of progressive organizations—including Common Cause, the Lindesmith Center Drug Policy Foundation and the National Campaign for Jobs and Income Support—to explore three basic issues ignored by the major political parties: campaign finance reform; poverty and the wealth gap; and the failed drug war.

Naturally, Harry and I shared a joint to celebrate that failure as well as to toast our reunion.

Being incurable media junkies, we took a cab to the four airplane-hangar-sized, inflated pavilions that served as working space for newspaper and magazine journalists as well as Radio Row and Internet Alley. TV news personalities Sam Donaldson and Tom Brokaw were there, engaging in a fierce battle of dueling smirks. Shearer, a master impressionist, does a great Donaldson and Brokaw as well as a score of politicians and several voices on *The Simpsons*. In fact, he called my hotel room in the concierge's voice to ask if my water was all right.

The media pavilions were adjacent to the convention, reeking with buzz words. The naming rights for the site had been purchased by a cable company, so that the marquee of the First Union Center proclaimed it as the "Comstat Republican Convention." Everything was for sale at this event. There was a fundraising golf game where each one of the 18 holes had been purchased by various multinational corporations.

So there we were, paying a visit to the United States of Advertising. Even our taxi receipt provided ad space for CBS News, with a photo of Dan Rather under the slogan, "Experience You Can Trust," which Harry stated in a perfect rendition of Rather's precisely clipped style of speech. I mentioned that Rather, anchoring the convention from a sky booth, had referred to "*Sixty Minutes* man Ed Bradley" reporting from the floor.

"That's racism," Harry observed. "He would never refer to Morley Safer like that."

We proceeded to compare our respective encounters with Dan Rather. When the Museum of Radio and Television honored Rather, he personally invited Shearer to attend. Harry wanted to talk about issues, but Dan wanted to discuss *Spinal Tap*.

As for me, I had recently been invited to perform at the 135th anniversary of *The Nation* magazine. It was held at the posh University Club in New York City. I wore jeans, a red Bread & Roses T-shirt and a tuxedo jacket, but the gatekeeper informed me that I didn't quite meet their dress code.

"But I'm an entertainer," I explained, "and this is my costume."

He then instructed me to go around the corner, through the employees' entrance, past the kitchen and up the elevator to the ballroom where the $600-a-plate dinner would be. Milling around were liberal celebrities—Phil Donahue, Nora Ephron, Harry Belafonte, Jules Feiffer and, sitting at a $1,000-a-plate table, Dan Rather himself.

"Mr. Rather," I said from the dais, "you ended your broadcast the other night by saying, 'If you like the CBS News, be sure to tell your neighbors,' and I just wanted to take this opportunity to tell you personally that I went around recommending your newscast to my neighbors, but they kept chasing me away because they mistook me for a census taker."

Dan Rather has very good posture, which he maintains even when he laughs.

we shall overlap

In the '60s, "We shall overcome" became the musical mantra of the civil rights struggle. But, in Philadelphia in 2000, the phrase was co-opted by George W. Bush in his acceptance speech. Such incongruity inspired my Presidential Campaign Academy Awards—the Kafkas—published in the *Los Angeles Times* and leading off with: "The Roseanne Multiple Personality Award goes to Eddie Murphy for his magnificent portrayal of all five African-American delegates at the Republican convention."

In 1968, during the protests outside the Democratic convention, Hugh Hefner was walking home to his Playboy Mansion in Chicago when he got whacked on the butt by a police billy club for no particular reason. This year, his Playboy Mansion in Los Angeles was considered an inappropriate venue for a Latino Democratic fundraiser because Party officials were afraid that their Gore infomercial at Staples Center might be tainted by the image of stapled centerfolds. This time, Hefner—a contributor to the Democrats—was *really* radicalized.

In August 1968, a couple of weeks before the Democratic convention took place in Chicago, Abbie Hoffman, Jerry Rubin and I—cofounders of the Yippies (Youth International Party)—met with Tom Hayden—representing Mobe (New Mobilization to End the War in Vietnam)—in order to establish communication lines between the Yippies and the Mobes. We decided to buy some walkie-talkies. We were standing in an open field in Grant Park. Several yards away, a ridiculously obvious undercover cop was pretending to read a newspaper. Whenever we moved, he would move along with us, remaining several yards away.

A few months previously, Yippie leaders had gone to Chicago and were in the office of Mayor Richard Daley's assistant, David Stahl. To loosen the tension, I explained to him, "We're here to get a permit for the revolution." "Come on," he said, "what are you guys really planning to do at the convention?" I asked, "Didn't you see *Wild in the Streets?*" In that youth-cult movie, teenagers put LSD into the water supply, lowered the voting age to 14 and took over the government.

"*Wild in the Streets?*" Stahl repeated. "We've seen *Battle of Algiers*." In *that* movie, a guerrilla hides a bomb under her *chador*, plants it in an ice-cream parlor and the camera pans around to show the innocent faces of children who are about to be blown up. What was to happen with the Chicago police, then, would be a clash between *our* mythology and *their* mythology. The violence reached a peak on the third day of the convention, during speeches in Grant Park. The *Chicago Tribune* later reported that Bob Pierson—a police provocateur posing as a biker and acting as Rubin's bodyguard—was "in the group which lowered an American flag"—the incident which set off what *The Walker Report: Rights in Conflict* would describe as "a police riot."

Pierson wrote in *Official Detective* magazine: "One thing we were to do was defile the flag. The American flag in the park was taken down, then rehung upside down. After this had been photographed, a group of us, including me, were ordered to pull it down and destroy it, then to run up the black flag of the Vietcong. I joined in the chants and taunts against the police and provoked them into hitting me with their clubs. They didn't know who I was, but they did know that I had called them names and struck them with one or more weapons."

And so, when the Democrats returned to the scene of the crime and brought their convention to Chicago again in 1996, that scraping sound you heard was philosopher Herbert Marcuse twisting in his grave as the term he coined—"repressive tolerance"—came to life in the form of a lottery for would-be demonstrators—from Psychologists for Quality to the Lesbian Avengers—seeking government-sanctioned time slots in a location where delegates wouldn't hear them. This was the ultimate trivialization of protest. No wonder the National Space Society yielded its hour to a marijuana-rights group.

In an officially approved, fenced-off site opposite the Hilton Hotel facing Grant Park—where in '68 the whole world was watching as sadistic police turned a peaceful rally into a brutal riot—now, *nobody* was listening as an individual spoke about the injustice of the legal system: "I would like to share with you another experience. . . ." He was supposed to be followed by the American Art Party, which, like several other groups, didn't bother to show up.

But then came the most successful demonstration, to honor the work of the late comedian, John Belushi, with a postage stamp. *Chicago Sun-Times* columnist [and now Roger Ebert's movie-review partner] Richard Roeper led 200 spectators in a chant: "Give him a damn stamp!" There were two prototypes, but Belushi as one of the Blues Brothers was deemed more popular by the crowd than Belushi in his *Saturday Night Live* bumblebee costume. Democracy in action.

● ● ●

In 1968, the Yippies decided to nominate a pig named Pigasus for president. When William Burroughs learned of this plan, he said, "It would be more interesting if you ran a tape recorder." When Chicago authorities learned of this plan, they put an armed guard on the pig in the zoo. Meanwhile, a certain competitiveness developed between Abbie and Jerry. Abbie bought a pig, but Jerry thought it wasn't big enough, mean enough or ugly enough, so he bought a bigger, meaner, uglier pig, which was released at City Hall and seized by Chicago police.

In 2000, an animal-rights activist wearing a seven-foot tall pig costume (with a small, battery-operated fan built into the head) prepared for the protests against the World Bank and the IMF in Washington, D.C., by obtaining a truckful of manure—the kind you use for dumping in front of a building—from Police Department horse stables. At the Republican convention, he conducted another manure dumping and was arrested for "transporting a material intended to be used to create a public nuisance." At the Democratic convention in Los Angeles, he dumped four tons of manure in front of convention headquarters at the Wilshire Grand Hotel. Before he was cited for misdemeanor vandalism, police questioned him for two hours.

"C'mon, Lefty, you better sing to us, or you're goin' up the river! Now, for the last time, who'd you buy that shit from?"

● ● ●

During the Vietnam War, at first peace demonstrators were virtually all white—later, "No Vietnamese ever called me nigger" became a black slogan—but in 2000, the demonstrations were multiethnic. Back then, organized labor originally had an adversarial relationship with protesters—later, "No Vietnamese ever froze my wages" became a working-class slogan—but now, with some Big Labor exceptions, union members were out in the streets with them. Ebony and Ivory Meets Teamsters and Turtles.

Tom Hayden, then a California state senator, had been observing the new breed of young activists. "One difference I see with '68," he told me, "is that back then you had a war and a draft that forced people to pay attention. What is extraordinary about the new movement is how they are motivated by idealism and moral rage—like the early SDS. If they connect with the broad constituencies of 'at-risk youth' and their families around the issues of 'jobs, not jails,' and if they also connect with labor around the working poor and immigrants, we will see great swelling of social action like we haven't seen since back then."

Philadelphia used to be known as the City of Brotherly Love. Now it's called the place that loves you back. And Los Angeles, of course, is the city that cheats on you. Prior to the conventions in 2000, although police in Philly and L.A. didn't see *Battle of Algiers*, they *were* shown a 10-minute video featuring WTO protesters in Seattle smashing Starbucks windows. Consequently, in a somewhat unusual process, the California Highway Patrol requested $1 million in convention "security equipment" for the L.A. Police Department, which was in total embarrassment mode because of a scandal-in-progress at the Rampart station involving the planting of false evidence, the selling of narcotics and the murder of innocent civilians.

Hayden theorized that they didn't have enough nerve to ask the City Council for pepper spray ($125,000) and a paper shredder ($2,400), so instead tried to sneak those purchases through the legislature. "Can you imagine," he asked, "at this point in the Rampart [police corruption] crisis, showing up on your budget with pepper spray? And a paper shredder? For a police force under scrutiny for framing people?"

Things evolve. Vietnam has become Colombia. Woodstock Nation has become Hip-Hop Nation. Leadership is no longer dominated by white males. Abbie Hoffman and Jerry Rubin have been replaced by Lisa Fithian and Margaret Prescod (who is black). Not only is there a strong sense of continuity, there's also a specific linear connection. Fithian—an organizer of the Direct Action Network—had worked with Hoffman on his Save the St. Lawrence River project, and in 1984-5 he hired her as a guide on a tour of Nicaragua he arranged. Clients included feminist Betty Friedan, New York Senator Israel Ruiz and *New York Post* reporter Fred Dicker. It was there that Abbie, his wife Johanna Lawrenson, Lisa Fithian and Al Giordano (a fellow tour guide, now editor of *Narco News*), concocted a plan for the People's Peace Corps—brigades to work at the camps in Nicaragua, to build clinics and bring medicines.

Along with everything else, technology has evolved, changing the nature of protest: Walkie-talkies have been replaced by cell phones; organizing once done with messy mimeograph machines is now accomplished via the Internet—quicker, cheaper and way more widespread; and demonstrators are now well armed—with information. The '60s Bread & Puppet Theater has given way to individual artists whose puppets have been confiscated as weapons. "Hey, Hey! Ho, ho! LBJ has got to go!" now ends, "HMO has got to go!"

The Yippies have become the Ruckus Society, and its leader, John Sellers, was arrested by 35 officers while walking down a Philadelphia street. His cell phone and Swiss Army knife were confiscated as "instruments of crime." He was charged with aggravated assault on a cop, but that was dropped and he was instead charged with a misdemeanor. His bail was initially set at a million dollars—for a misdemeanor—and later reduced to $100,000.

"It was like a bad SWAT movie," Sellers recalls.

In 1968, the Vietnam war was the main target of demonstrators, but in 2000, R2K and D2K—the networks planning protests respectively at the Republican and Democratic conventions—served as umbrella organizations for a dazzling myriad of causes, including reproductive rights, child support, corporate globalization, capital punishment, racism, sexism, wages for housewives, universal health care, nuclear abolition, welfare issues, media monopoly, gay rights, three-strikes laws, rainforests, wetlands, militarism, veterans' benefits, AIDS, immigration, disability rights, starvation, breastfeeding rights and genetic engineering. The unsung theme song of this movement has evolved into "We shall overlap."

• • •

The name of the game in the summer of 2000 was alternative conventions.

There was the Homeless Convention, bringing together homeless activists at the Dome Village, a homeless enclave led by Ted Hayes, who stressed the need for nonviolent dialogue, only to be injured by a rubber bullet when he got caught in the middle of police overreaction in their zeal to shield delegates from protesters. Tom Hayden's son, Troy, was also injured by a rubber bullet as he was leaning over Ted Hayes trying to protect him.

And there was the Anarchists Convention, held in a warehouse. Anarchists had become generic scapegoats. They think of themselves as "people, not legally bound, watching out for each other." But you could watch as police at a demonstration would target anyone dressed in black clothing, because that's what anarchists always wear. Instead of political vandalism, however, a group from the Bay Area arranged to feed homeless people near Staples Center. "It's our obligation as anarchists," explained one, "to look after those communities that the state fails to look after."

The People's Convention—run by earnest socialists and communists whose anti-capitalist outrage permeated the sparsely filled auditorium—took place at Belmont High School. Just as a session on police brutality was about to begin, a pair of cops strolled into the auditorium. They were asked to leave. "Sorry," it was explained, "we don't allow any weapons at our meetings." They left, and the audience laughed and applauded. This event was budgeted at $8,000, and there was resentment expressed that its thunder was being stolen by the Shadow Convention, budgeted at $500,000.

Philanthropist George Soros had funded the Shadow Convention with $100,000 on the bipartisan proviso that it be held in both Philadelphia and Los Angeles. I was invited to participate in the Rapid Response panel, whereby journalists and satirists would react in real time to the speeches being delivered at the official conventions. At the University of Pennsylvania's Annenberg School for Communication, there were two giant screens on the stage of the 950-seat auditorium, and the idea was to provide commentary as if we were watching—and reacting—in our own living rooms.

When Dick Cheney said, "We will never see one [Al Gore] without thinking of the other [Bill Clinton]," what pleasure it gave me to observe publicly that the GOP's underlying campaign theme would be to stress the notion that Clinton, Gore and Monica Lewinsky had indulged in a threesome.

I was most moved at the Shadow Convention by the transformative experience of Arianna Huffington's 11-year-old daughter, Christina. On the day when the war on drugs was examined, she was horrified to learn of the blatant unfairness of mandatory-minimum sentencing. She could identify with the utter inhumanity of law enforcers snatching parents away from their children for growing medical marijuana. To Christina, "Just say no" has become, in the words of Timothy Leary, "Just say know."

I was happy to see a few old friends from the '60s who were fellow participants at the Shadow Conventions. In Philadelphia, it was Reverend Howard Moody of Judson Memorial Church in New York City. We— the Christian minister and the professed atheist—had both run underground abortion referral services while that particular form of surgery was still illegal. In Los Angeles, I reunited with Ram Dass. He and I had shared some memorable psychedelic journeys. Now in a wheelchair after a stroke, his Zen spirit remains high.

I also saw Tom Hayden both at the Shadow Convention and in the street at a rally in Santa Monica supporting striking members of the Hotel and Restaurant Employees Union. Somebody was trying to engage him in "radical nostalgia." Another demonstration, denouncing slave labor, was taking place a few blocks away in front of the Gap, where I encountered another old friend, Jeff Cohen, founder of FAIR (Fairness and Accuracy in Reporting) and commentator on the Fox network's *News Watch*; he had been told by CNN that he's too controversial for them. He was now campaigning for inclusion of third-party candidates in the presidential debates.

Although the Republican ticket of Bush-Cheney was the darling of oil tycoons, on the first day of the Democratic convention, police attacked a peaceful afternoon march to protest Al Gore's involvement with Occidental Petroleum (his family owns half a million in stock, inherited from his father) and the company's intentions to drill oil from the sacred land of the indigenous U'wa people in Colombia.

That evening, while lame-duck President Clinton was speaking to delegates of the Democratic machine, Rage Against the Machine was performing in the designated protest pit, known as "the Gaza strip," across the street from Staples Center, protected by 14-foot chain-link fencing. The cops wore earplugs.

The concert climaxed with the band's song "Freedom" and a vision of 8,000 citizens giving the finger to Staples Center and chanting in unison, "Fuck you, I won't do what you tell me!" Police dispersed the crowd—using tear-gas pellets, flash grenades, rubber bullets and bean-bag bullets—indiscriminately rather than singling out obvious trouble-makers. Inside Staples Center, the sound of "76 Trombones" drowned out the noise from outside.

There may not have been as much overt police violence toward protesters at this Democratic convention as there was at the one in Chicago, but in Los Angeles there was more covert police violence toward the

First Amendment. Based on an anonymous tip that there was a bomb in a van, at 4:30 p.m. police detained its owners and blocked the Independent Media Center's parking lot, eliminating their broadcast capabilities in the process.

Fifteen minutes later, based on another anonymous tip that there was a bomb in the parking lot of the Shadow Convention, 700 people were ejected from the auditorium at Patriotic Hall. It took three hours for the bomb squad to arrive, so the Rapid Response panel was moved onto a truck. There, Arianna Huffington stood between panelists Gore Vidal and Christopher Hitchens like a neo-populist sandwich, while a phalanx of 100 riot police looked on. An officer announced, "If you don't move, we'll use tear gas." When they refused to move, the cops told them that they could go back inside.

Amidst all the violence in the streets, I had escaped unscathed until the final night of the Democratic convention, when—in the most calculated kiss since Michael Jackson and Lisa Marie at the MTV awards— Al and Tipper Gore smooched heavily, as if to say, "We don't need no steenkin' interns!" Roseanne was on the Rapid Response panel that night. When she announced her candidacy for president even though she had never voted, the audience booed. So, what happened to me might merely have been her displaced hostility, but I'm sure it was because she had read my Kafka Awards in the *Los Angeles Times*. When we were introduced, one of Roseanne's personalities beat me to a bloody pulp.

an election carol

Martin Scrooge, great-grandson of the legendary Ebenezer Scrooge, may be the CEO of a multinational corporation—Octopus & Illuminati, the ultimate merger—but, like any ordinary American citizen, he had trouble sleeping the other night. He was at the height of REM, in the middle of a pleasant dream, romping in the woods with his dog Snippy, when he was suddenly awakened by an ethereal figure standing at his bedside.

"Who are you?" asked the startled Scrooge. "And what do you want?"

"I am the Ghost of Election Past. And I'm just doing my job. I'm supposed to remind you of the presidential election of 1960. As you know, John F. Kennedy reportedly won by fraudulent methods. Do you realize what that means? If Richard Nixon had won as he should have, then JFK would be alive today, and there would have been no Watergate scandal."

"Well, you can't change the past."

"Tell me about it. I live with a profound sense of futility every day."

"What you need is a good antidepressant. Ask your spin doctor."

• • •

Scrooge had gone back to sleep when, once again, he was suddenly awakened by another ethereal figure standing at his bedside.

"Don't tell me," said Scrooge. "Let me guess. You must be the Ghost of Election Present."

"Oh, God, am I that obvious?"

"Are you kidding? You're absolutely transparent."

"Well, I'm totally discombobulated. Everything is in litigation. In Florida, there are ballot counters who have filed lawsuits because they developed carpal tunnel syndrome. In Washington, the Supreme Court is going to decide whether pregnant chads are entitled to partial-birth abortions."

"Calm down now, you'll be all right."

"That's easy for you to say—you're just hallucinating—but me, I'm stuck on the cusp between real life and showbiz. This is all actually happening, yet at the same time it's all one big sitcom. George W. Bush is George Costanza in that episode of *Seinfeld* where he acts as if he works at this company; only now the stress has resulted in boils all over Bush's face, and each one is covered with a Band-Aid. Whereas, Al Gore is Bill Murray in that movie *Bob* where he unremittingly stalks his psychiatrist; only now Gore is stalking an entire focus group."

"Speaking of shrinks, I think you ought to get help from one yourself."

"Listen, you'd be going nuts if you couldn't tell the difference between reality and satire anymore. Satire has been nipping at the heels of reality for the past few decades, but I can tell you the precise moment that reality finally overtook satire. It happened in Cuba, when Fidel Castro offered to come to the United States and oversee the election recounts. And we've received similar offers: from Jerry Adams in Ireland and Nelson Mandela in South Africa; from Jimmy Carter in Georgia and Larry Flynt in Los Angeles. But one thing is certain. Whoever becomes president will think that he deserves it."

"Do me a favor, will you? Let me go back to sleep. I have to take a meeting with the Ghost of Election Future. It's already on my to-do list."

• • •

Right on schedule, the Ghost of Election Future arrived at Scrooge's bedside.

"Greetings," said Scrooge. "Strange, isn't it, how things evolve? Traditionally, I would have been influenced by the visits of you Election Ghosts, and consequently I would abandon greed for compassion. But it's different now that trickle-down greed affects stockholders who welcome the downsizing of employees because it means more profits. And it's also different now that government-by-bipartisan-bribery has become such an open secret. There has been a severe case of role reversal, and now *I'm* the one who's influencing *you*. So tell me, because I find these charades, oh, so very entertaining, what do you foresee will occur in the 2004 election?"

The ghost of Election Future sighed deeply, as though participating in a presidential candidates' debate, and then began:

"Okay, I'll skip the part about who the candidates will be—you can decide that for yourself—and I'll cut right to the chase. New York Senator Hillary Rodham Clinton will lead a crusade to eliminate the Electoral College, but her proposed law will lose in the popular vote. The drug war will become a huge campaign issue. Medical-marijuana protesters will carry placards insisting, 'States' Rights—Not Just for Racists Anymore!' Other demonstrators will have signs demanding, 'End Corporate Welfare Now!' Police on horseback will be chanting, 'Whose streets? *Our* streets!' There will be several new third parties, from the Anarchist Party to the Lawyers Party, but the Greens will remain the most prominent. And the slogan of Democrats and liberals will be 'A vote for Ralph Nader is a vote for John McCain.'"

bush whacked

When Dan Quayle endorsed George W. Bush during the presidential campaign, he also passed the torch to Bush to replace Quayle as America's generic dumb-guy icon, easy-joke reference. But I'll get back to that.

There was this awful tragedy that occurred in Egypt. After an earthquake, a whole family was trapped under the rubble. The husband survived only by drinking his own urine, but his mother, his wife and his daughter all refused to drink *their* own urine—the taboo was *that* powerful—and so he had to witness them die, one by one. His daughter's last words were, "I want a Pepsi."

Yet, in Japan, there is a Buddhist monk who drinks his own urine to maintain his health, and he has a huge cult following. In India, there are Hindus who drink their own urine in order to reach a higher plateau in their spiritual quest. And the prime minister of India once proudly told Barbara Walters—on *my* TV set in *my* living room—that he drank his own urine. I finally decided to try it myself, and I'll be glad to share what I learned, and save you the trouble of drinking *your* own urine.

Drinking your own urine does *not* raise you to a higher plateau in your spiritual quest. It's the *decision* to drink your own urine that does the trick. Once you decide to drink your own urine, you're halfway there. If you're able to transcend that taboo in your mind—a taboo that you learned in your crib before you ever learned the English language—then it's merely a matter of taste. Mmmm, a little salty, perhaps. So that's the secret: Transcending a taboo frees you from a lifetime of conditioning and opens up your psyche.

Urine is in the news a lot these days in the context of drug testing in the workplace. But there are mail-order companies that sell drug-free powdered urine. You simply pour the yellow powder into a glass and add warm water, stirring it with a teaspoon. Then transfer the resulting liquid into a condom and use that to pass your drug test. Or bring it with you with your résumé on your first job interview and *really* make a good impression on your boss-to-be.

Now, remember when former mayor Marion Barry got caught buying crack from his former mistress in a bugged hotel room? Standing in front of a one-way mirror so that the camera in the adjoining room could get a proper angle, he lit up the pipe, simultaneously getting high and busted. Before going to prison, he was put on probation and had to take a drug test every week, so he sent away for a large supply of drug-free powdered urine.

Well, when the media inferred from President Bush's refusal to answer questions about his having been a cocaine user during his fraternity days at Yale, he panicked, thinking that there might *still* be traces of cocaine in his system. So, since he and Vice President Dick Cheney had promised to be first in the line of White House employees to take a drug test, Bush sent away for some of that powdered urine.

When the package arrived in the mail, he opened it and poured the yellow powder into a glass.

And then he *peed* in it.

And then he drank it.

And nothing happened.

several dead
friends

waiting for shepherd

One night Jean Shepherd instructed his listeners: "Okay, open the window, put your radio on the window sill, and turn the volume way down." Then you could barely hear him whispering, "Now, when I count to three, turn the volume all the way up. One, two, three . . . " I was a rebellious adolescent and gleefully followed his instructions. Everything became quiet. Suddenly he shouted, "*You filthy pragmatist*!!!" Shepherd had "hurled an epithet." And, with all our help, it reverberated around the whole neighborhood. What a fine cheap thrill that was. What a strange sense of invisible community.

• • •

Jean Shepherd, who died in October 1999 at age 78, was a frequent contributor to *Playboy*, an author (*In God We Trust, All Others Pay Cash*—an actual sign he'd seen near a cash register—and *Wanda Hickey's Night of Golden Memories and Other Disasters*)—his work appeared on PBS, and his boyhood memories of Christmas graced the big screen. But it was his radio program on WOR in New York City, starting in the 1950s, five nights a week from midnight to 5:30, that kept me awake and stimulated my imagination.

He would free-associate with humor and style, totally scriptless, spinning stories—playing all the characters—and commenting on social issues, accompanying himself on a kazoo, intertwining his enthusiastic tales with jazz records like Bessie Smith singing "Empty Bed Blues." He would constantly explore his own motives, trying to extend those motives to understand why other people did the things they do. This was my *real* education, and I treasured it.

Sometimes I would doze off, only to wake up at 3 a.m. and hear Shepherd discussing how you would explain to a Martian the purpose of an amusement park. Or how you think your life is going to change for the better when you buy a new pair of jeans. Or describing his friend who could taste an ice cube and tell you the exact make and model of the refrigerator it had come from and what year that refrigerator had been manufactured.

My idea of a hot date in those days was to find a girl and lie in bed with her all night listening to Shepherd.

"One of the secret desires that all kids have," he would be saying in his charismatic Indiana twang, "is to be invisible and to, you know, to sneak somehow, nobody would see you, see. And, well, of course, not only kids want to do that. But this is a kid thing and leads to all kinds of things. For example, there used to be a thing advertised in the back of *Popular Mechanics* and also *Boy's Life* when I was a kid, and it said, 'See-Through X-Ray Eyes.' Ever seen that thing? It said, 'See through bones,' and it shows a hand that says, 'Look through and see your very own bones. This see-through X-ray eye device enables you to see through anything at will. Send 10 cents to Johnson & Johnson.'

"And about three months later, this thing came back, this little round tube, you know. And it's got what looks like frosted glass or something on the end of it, see. And the instructions came with it, a little smudgy piece of paper that showed a kid, you know, looking through this thing, holding his hand up, and you can see the bones. And it says the see-through X-ray eye device is very simply worked. It is worked by placing it to your eye, as shown in Diagram A, and then holding your hand up to the light, as shown by Diagram B. Then, if the light is properly adjusted, one will see the bones through the eyepiece marked C in Diagram D.

"I've been had. All my life I'm going to walk around seeing the bones of my left hand and my right hand, nothing but the bones in my mitt. It does *not* look through flowered print dresses. So, kids, don't believe everything you see. Don't believe every ad you read."

One time, he called for a "milling" of his listeners across the street from the burned-out Wanamaker's department-store building, to take place on a certain day and time. Police came upon that scene, but nobody among this horde of citizen stragglers would reveal *why* they were congregated there. One cop complained, "This is like trying to break up a pack of friendly dogs." Finally someone spilled the beans, the dirty snitch, and police began to herd those who were milling around into an empty parking lot, asking passersby, "Are you waiting for Shepherd?" Of course, he didn't show up. He never said he would.

Indeed, one of the basic threads that ran through his show was the concept that everybody is waiting for something. In that context, I once asked Shepherd what *he* was waiting for. He replied, "I don't think anybody is waiting seriously for anything concrete. I think everybody's waiting for something—and I say that in capital letters: SOMETHING—it's what Samuel Beckett was saying in *Waiting for Godot*. I don't know what I'm waiting for. I don't think you know what *you're* waiting for."

● ● ●

Somebody in my own apartment building had opened the window and put his radio on the window sill, and I tried to determine from which apartment I had heard Shepherd hurl that epithet: *"You filthy pragmatist!!!"* It turned out to be a 17-year-old bursting with acne and spouting fascist rhetoric. My neighbor was a teenaged Nazi. And he liked Shepherd the most when he would read aloud from the German philosopher, Nietzsche. This made me realize that everyone listened to Jean Shepherd through their own individual filters; that everything in life is perceived through a totally subjective lens. This was the greatest lesson of my unofficial education.

saint abortionist

Several decades ago, while Robert Spencer was in high school, his father, a district attorney, had a case brought to him by a renowned minister whose daughter was getting bizarre threatening letters. The elder Spencer suggested that the minister get samples of her handwriting, and it became clear that she had written the letters to herself. An investigation brought out the fact that she was pregnant and didn't want to be. The minister blew his brains out.

Young Spencer never forgot that incident. He went to medical school and became a general physician in Ashland, Pennsylvania. He served as an Army doctor in World War I, then became a pathologist at a hospital in Ashland. He won the town's respect for descending into coal-mining shafts after an accident, later aiding miners to obtain Workmen's Compensation for lung disease. Eventually he began performing abortions, though it was still an illegal surgery.

At a time when 5,000 women were killed each year by back-alley abortionists charging as much as $1,500, Dr. Spencer performed extremely cautious operations at low cost, sometimes for as little as $5 and never more than $100. He built facilities at his clinic for African-American patients who were not allowed to obtain overnight lodgings elsewhere in town. His reputation spread across the nation by word of mouth, and he became known as the Saint.

The citizens of Ashland didn't merely tolerate his presence; the local economy *depended* on him. Merchants had become accustomed to the extra business that a steady stream of patients brought to the hotel, the restaurant, and the dress shop. In 1962, when an article in *Look* magazine stated, "There is no such thing as a 'good' abortionist—all of them are in business strictly for the money," I decided to ask Dr. Spencer for an interview, promising that I would go to prison sooner than reveal his identity. He was a subscriber to *The Realist* and agreed to do the interview.

During the five-hour bus ride from New York City to Ashland, lugging my huge Webcor tape recorder, I could only imagine the emotions that a pregnant woman must have felt on her way to Dr. Spencer. There, she would see how the walls of his office were decorated with those folksy sayings that tourists like to buy. A placard on the ceiling over his operating table advised, "Keep calm."

He was the cheerful personification of an old-fashioned family doctor. He used folksy expressions like "by golly," and he rarely said the word "pregnant." Rather, he would say, "She was *that* way, and she came to me for help." Over a few decades he had performed 27,006 illegal operations, including some for priests who "had gotten their housekeepers in trouble." Here's an excerpt from the interview:

Q. "You've violated the law 27,006 times—how have you gotten away with it?"

A. "Well, I don't know."

Q. "I mean you're not in jail."

A. "No, that's true. And I haven't any doubt the country's known about me because, heavens, I've had people from practically every state in the union."

Q. "You mean you can't explain it to yourself, why you're free?"

A. "No, I don't know exactly why that is at all."

Q. "Have police come to you for professional services?"

A. "Oh, yes, I've had police in here, too. I've helped them out. I've helped a hell of a lot of police out. I've helped a lot of FBI men out. They would be here, and they had me a little bit scared—I didn't know whether they were just in to get me or not."

Q. "What would you say is the most significant lesson you've learned in all your years as a practicing abortionist?"

A. "You've got to be careful. That's the most important thing. And you've got to be cocksure that everything's removed. And even the uterus speaks to you and tells you. I could be blind. You see, this is an operation no eye sees. You go by the sense of feel and touch. And hearing. The voice of the uterus . . . "

After my interview with this unidentified "humane abortionist" was published, I began to get phone calls from scared females—from teenagers to middle-aged—all, including a nurse, in desperate search of a safe abortion. It was preposterous that they should have to resort to seeking out the editor of a satirical magazine, but their quest so far had been futile, and they simply didn't know where else to turn.

With Dr. Spencer's permission, I referred them to him. At first there were only a few calls a week, then several every day. I had never intended to become an underground abortion referral service, but I wasn't going to stop just because in the next issue of *The Realist*, I would be publishing an interview with somebody else.

In January 1966, state police raided Dr. Spencer's clinic and arrested him. He remained out of jail only by the grace of political pressure, but he was finally forced to retire from his practice. I continued mine, however—the only alternative would have been to say no to those asking for help—and I began referring women to other physicians that Dr. Spencer had recommended.

Occasionally I would be offered money by a patient, but I never accepted anything. And whenever doctors offered me a kickback, I not only turned them down but also insisted that they give a discount for the same amount to those patients referred by me.

I continued to carry on my underground abortion referral service. Each time, though, I would flash on the notion that this was my *own* mother asking for help, and that she was pregnant with *me*. I would try to identify with the fetus that was going to be aborted even while I was serving as a conduit to the performance of that very abortion. Every day I would think about the possibility of having never existed, and I would only appreciate being alive all the more.

Pretending to be the fetus was just a way of focusing on my role as a referral service. I didn't want it to become so casual that I would grow unaware of the implications. By personalizing it, I had to accept my own responsibility for each soul whose potential I was helping to destroy. That was about as mystical as I got.

Maybe I was simply projecting my own ego. In any case, by the time these women came to me for help, they had *already* made up their minds. This was not some abstract cause for peace on the other side of the globe; these were actual individuals in real distress right now in front of me, and I just couldn't ignore them. So I made a choice to abort myself every time. Throughout the '60s this was my fetal yoga.

Dr. Spencer died in January 1969. He would have been 80 years old that March.

In September 1969, I was subpoenaed to appear before a Grand Jury investigating criminal charges against abortionists. I refused to testify. District Attorney (now Judge) Burton Roberts threatened me with prison if I didn't reveal the names of doctors who performed abortions. I still refused.

Then he promised that I would be granted immunity from prosecution if I cooperated with the Grand Jury. Extending his hand as a gesture of trust, he warned me that his investigators had uncovered one particular abortionist's financial records, revealing all the money I had supposedly received, thereby proving that I had been engaged in a criminal conspiracy for profit.

"That's not true," I said, declining to shake hands with him. I realized that if I *had* ever accepted any money, I would now have no way of knowing that he was totally bluffing.

At this point, attorney Gerald Lefcourt (later president of the National Association of Criminal Defense Lawyers) filed a suit on my behalf, challenging the constitutionality of the abortion law. He pointed out that the district attorney had no power to investigate the violation of an unconstitutional law, and therefore he could not force me to testify.

I became the only plaintiff in the first lawsuit to declare the abortion laws unconstitutional in New York State. Later, various women's groups joined the suit, and ultimately the New York legislature repealed the criminal sanctions against abortion, prior to the Supreme Court decision in Roe vs. Wade.

Dr. Spencer would have been gratified. His decades of dedication had not been in vain.

```
        a game of mind
   tennis with timothy
               leary
```

This dialogue with the ailing Timothy Leary was taped in September 1995,
several months before he died. There was a cartoon—Gary Larson's "The Far
Side"—on his living room wall, depicting some cryonic heads in a freezer;
a careless janitor has just knocked the plug out, and they will all melt. Leary
had seriously considered having his own head posthumously frozen.

"So, Tim, here's a toast to 30 years of friendship."

"And still counting. We've been playing mind tennis for 30 years.
Isn't that great?"

"The one thing in countless conversations we've had that sticks out
in my mind is something you once said, that no matter what scientists
do—they can decodify the DNA code, layer after layer—but underneath
it all, there's still that mystery. And I've enjoyed playing with the mystery.
Are you any closer to understanding the mystery, or further from it?"

"Well, Paul, I watch words now. It's an obsession. I learned it from
Marshall McLuhan, of course. A terrible vice. Had it for years, but not
actually telling people about it. I watch the words that people use. The
medium is the message, you recall. The brain creates the realities she
wants. When we see the prisms of these words that come through, we
can understand. Do I understand the mystery?"

"I guess the ultimate mystery is inconceivable by definition. But have
you come any closer to understanding it?"

"Understand? Stand under! I'm overstood, I'm understood."

"The older I get, the deeper the mystery becomes."

"The faster."

"Let's get to a specific mystery. The mystery of you. Because everybody sees you through their own perceptions. How do you think you have been most misunderstood?"

"Well, everyone gets the Timothy Leary they deserve. Everyone has their point of view. And everyone's point of view is absolutely valid for them. To track me, you have to keep moving the camera, or you'll have just one tunnel point of view. Sermonizing there. Don't impale yourself on your point of view."

"Some people know you only through that '60s slogan, 'Turn on, tune in, drop out.' I think a lot of people don't really understand what you meant by dropping out."

"Everybody understood. Just look at the source."

"All right, here's words. Fifteen years ago at a futurist conference, you called yourself a Neo-Technological Pagan. What did you mean by that?"

"*Neo* has all the connotations of the futurist stuff that's coming along. *Technological* denotes using machines, using electricity or light to create reality. There are two kinds of technology. The machine—diesel, oil, metal, industrial technology. And then the Neo-Technology, which uses light. Electricity. Photons. Electrons. *Pagan* is great. I love the word. Pagan is basically humanist. I grew up in a Catholic zone, and pagan was the worst thing you could say. Of course, I'd never met a pagan in Springfield, Massachusetts, going to a Catholic school. 'Where do these pagans hang out? I want to be one.'"

"Was there any specific thing that made you turn from Catholicism?"

"Yeah, there was a period, I know exactly what it was, I was 15 or 16, I was being sexually molested in my high school and actually seduced by a wonderful sexy girl, much more experienced than I. And, *whew*! She opened it up! The great mystery of sex. *Wow*! At that time I was going routinely to confession on Saturday afternoon. But I had a date with Rosemary that night. Sitting there in the dark church. Then you go in and say, 'Bless me, father, for I have sinned.' Absolutely, totally hypocritical! They want you to confess and repent while I have every intention in the world of being seduced by this girl tonight."

"The glands overshadowed the philosophy."

"The glands? Shit, Paul, that statement is very mechanical."

"I'm a recovering romantic."

"Because you used the word *glands*? Glands are very interesting. People don't talk about glands very much."

"Talk about machines, then. What's the relationship you see between acid and technology?"

"Well, LSD is one of the many drugs which are based on neuroactive plants. Peyote and grain on rye. Those crazed experiences which happened in the Middle Ages, what did they call them? 'The madness of crowds,' simply because of some plant they had chewed. The point is that the human brain is equipped with these receptor sites for various kinds of vegetables that alter consciousness. So our brains evolving over 50 million years have these receptor sites.

"The reason why certain people like to take these drugs is because these receptor sites activate pleasure centers. Now this was not a mistake. The DNA didn't fuck up. The devil didn't do it. There was obviously some reason for those receptor sites that would get you off on peyote, psilocybin. And there are dozens of compelling receptor sites and drugs we don't even know about."

"In the changing counterculture, then, do you see a continuity from psychoactive drugs to cyberspace?"

"Of course. It's a fact. Every generation developed a new counterculture. In the Roaring '20s, jazz, liquor. In the '60s, the hippies with psychedelics."

"The counterculture now, it's not either/or, it's not necessarily drugs *or* computers. I'm sure some do them simultaneously. But how do you think that the drug experience has changed the computer experience?"

"I did not imply that you can't do both. The brain is equipped to be altered by these receptor sites. So we can see these receptor sites overwhelm the mind. The word-processing system. Then suddenly you can take psychedelic plants that put you in different places. I'm being too technical. But there's an analogy between receptor sites for marijuana and for LSD or opium which activate the brain and the way we can boot up different areas of our computers.

"Back in the 1960s we didn't know much about the brain. I was saying back in 1968, 'You have to go out of your mind to use your head.' But head simply is an old-fashioned way of saying brain. We didn't know about brain-receptor sites. But now, we can use bio-chemicals to boot up the kind of altered realities you want in your brain. So you smoke marijuana because it gets you in a mellow mood. Grass is good for the appetite. That's operating your brain. But now it's specific: 'Use your head by *operating* your brain.' That's the new concept. Use your head! That's hot. Operate your brain because the brain designs realities."

"Do you see a connection between the war on drugs and the attempt to censor the Internet?"

"Oh, absolutely, yes. The censors want to control. We have to have people to impose to keep any society going. I don't knock rules, rituals. We have to have them. The controllers censor anything that gives the power to change reality to the individual. You can't have *that* happen."

"My theory is that the UFO sightings and all the people who claim to have been abducted by aliens, that this is really just a cover-up for secret government experiments in mind control."

"That's a very popular theory, Paul. I get like 10 mimeograph letters a day about UFOs and the government. Boy, the governments are really fucking busy, trying to program our minds."

"And of course those U.N. soldiers in Bosnia can hardly wait to get back in their black helicopters so they can attack Michigan and Arizona."

"I'm happy about UFO rumors. I'm glad because at least people are doing something on their own. The 60-year-old farm wife in Dakota thinks she's been taken up and serially raped by UFO people. *Wow!* They came all the way from another planet a thousand light years away to get this lovely grandmother and pull her socks off and have an orgy with her. *Wow!*"

"Or at least an anal probe. To your knowledge, is the government still doing experiments in mind control? We know they used to, with the MK-Ultra program and all. Do you know if they're still at it? I can't imagine they would've stopped."

"G. Gordon Liddy would give you the current CIA line. Liddy says, 'Yes, it is true. When we learned that the Chinese Communists were using LSD, the CIA naturally cornered the whole world market for Sandoz LSD. They didn't realize that LSD comes in a millionth of a gram. The CIA found LSD to be unpredictable.' Well, no shit, Gordon! Can you name one accurate CIA prediction? The fall of the Shah? The rise of the Ayatollah?"

"What did you think of Liddy getting that free speech award from the National Association of Talk Show Hosts after he said that if the ATF comes after you, they're wearing bulletproof vests so you should aim for the head or groin?"

"That's pure Liddy. He's basically a romantic comedian."

"When you were debating him, if you had listened to his advice retroactively when he led the raid on Millbrook [16 years previously], then later you would've been onstage debating yourself, because he would've been shot in the head and groin by somebody, if his advice had been followed."

"He was a government agent entering our bedroom at midnight. We had every right to shoot him. But I've never owned a weapon in my life. And I have no intention of owning a weapon, although I was a master sharpshooter at West Point on both the Garand, the Springfield rifle and the machine gun. I was a Howitzer expert. I know how to operate these lethal gadgets, but I have never had and never will have a gun around."

"But when you escaped from prison, you said, 'Arm yourselves and shoot to live. To shoot a genocidal robot policeman in the defense of life is a sacred act.'"

"Yeah! I also said, 'I'm armed and dangerous.' I got that directly from Angela Davis. I thought it was just funny to say that."

"I thought it was the party line from the Weather Underground."

"Well, yeah, I had a lot of arguments with Bernadine Dohrn."

"They had their own rhetoric. She even praised Charles Manson."

"The Weather Underground was amusing. They were brilliant, brilliant, Jewish, Chicago kids. They had class and dash and flash and smash. Bernadine was praising Manson for sticking a fork in a victim's stomach. She was just being naughty."

"She was obviously violating a taboo. What are the taboos that are waiting to be violated today?"

"There is one taboo, the oldest and the most powerful—I've been writing and thinking about it for 30 years—the concept of *death* is something that people do not want to face. The doctors and the priests and the politicians have made it into something terrible, terrible, terrible. You're a victim! If you accept the notion of death, you've signed up to be the ultimate victim."

"Is that why you announced publicly that you have inoperable prostate cancer? Friends knew it but—"

"I actually have been planning my terminal graduation party for like 20 years. Of course, I'm a follower of Socrates, who was one of the greatest counterculture comic philosophers in history. He took hemlock."

"The Hemlock Society was named after that."

"I've been a member of the Hemlock Society for many years. They talk about self-deliverance. That's the biggest decision you can make. You couldn't choose how and when and with whom you were *born*."

"Although there are people who say you can."

"All right, well, go for it. But for those of us who don't have that option—"

"Ram Dass even once said that a fetus that gets aborted knew it didn't want to be born so it chose parents who wouldn't carry it to term."

"Richard's so politically correct. Isn't that fabulous?"

"Are you planning to do what Aldous Huxley did, which was to make the journey on acid?"

"That's an option, yeah."

"Do you believe in any kind of afterlife?"

"Well, I have left an enormous archive covering 60 years of writing, around 300 audio-videos. It's being stored away. And I belong to two cryonic groups, so I have the option of freezing my brain."

"By afterlife, I didn't mean the products of your consciousness so much as your consciousness itself."

"My consciousness is a product of my brain. How can I know about my mind until I express thought?"

"Obviously there are people who believe in the standard heaven and hell and purgatory. I'm assuming that you don't believe in *that* kind of afterlife."

"They're useful metaphors. I must be in purgatory now, huh? Occasionally I have a pop of heaven. That's not a bad metaphor. Of course we realize that hell is totally self-induced."

"On Earth, you mean."

"Well, wherever you are. What do *you* think about that, Paul? Do you believe in life after death and all that? What's your theory?"

"That you are eaten by worms and just disappear, or you're cremated and your ashes—"

"Wait, now, Paul, you have your choice of being eaten by worms or barbecued. Or you can be frozen. You don't have to be eaten by worms. You don't have to be microwaved. I'm going to leave some drops of my blood, which has my DNA, in a lot of places. I'll leave my brain with them. Why not try all these things? Not that I *care*, Paul, believe me. I have no desperate desire to come back to planet Earth.

"I think that I have lived one of the most incredibly funny, interesting lives. I'm fascinated to see what's gonna happen in the next steps. But I have no desire to come back. Most nonscientists don't realize that in scientific experiments you learn more from your mistakes. So I hope that I will leave a track record of making blunders about the most important thing in life. How to preserve your DNA. I hope someone will learn from my mistakes."

"Are there regrets that you have? Things that you would've done differently, knowing what you know now?"

"I'd play the whole game differently, sure. About a third of the things I've done have been absolutely stupid, vulgar and gross. About a third have been just banal. But a third have been brilliant. Like baseball, one out of three, you lead the league. M.V.P. Most Valuable Philosopher."

"When I first met you in 1965, you were talking about baseball—and games in general—as a metaphor. How would you describe your game in life? It's been a conscious game. You didn't just fall into a pinball machine and get knocked around. Although that happened, too."

"Well, I identified with Socrates at a very young age. The aim in human life is to find out about yourself and know who you are. The purpose in life is to discover yourself."

"With these big media mergers going on now, giants, Time-Warner-Turner here, Disney-Capital Cities-ABC there, how do you think the individual can fight that best?"

"Why fight it? Like Southern Pacific merges with Pennsylvania Railroad, so what?"

"But you said before, they're trying to control, so aren't they trying to control the information?"

"You can't control information if it's packaged in light. In photons and electrons. You simply can't control digital messages. *Zoom*, I can go to my Web site and put some stuff up there. Immediately my messages are accessed by people around the world. Not just now but later. The nice thing about cyber communication is that counterculture philosophers who learn about technology can work together, can be faster than committees, politicians and the like.

"So I have great confidence. You have to learn to play their game. That's why I went to West Point and that's why I went to the Jesuit school, and learned enough so I could play that mind-fuck game. I understood. And I moved on."

"Do you mean you knew before you went to West Point, before you went to Jesuit school, that you wanted to learn their tools?"

"I didn't want to go to either. My parents insisted on that."

"But you went with that attitude."

"Yeah. They took me around to about 10 Catholic universities and colleges in New England. None of them would accept me because of my high school track record. I was the editor of the newspaper in high school, and I made it a scandal sheet exposing the principal. I had a great uncle who was a big shot in the Catholic Church. He had pull in the Vatican, and he pulled some strings so I got into a Jesuit school. I just watched, repelled but fascinated."

"I don't believe in reincarnation, but if I did, I would think I knew you in a previous life. But that's only a metaphor, I don't believe in it. Do you believe in that concept?"

"In the time of Emerson, the 1830s, there was a counterculture very similar to ours. Self-reliance. Individuality. Emerson took drugs with David Thoreau. Margaret Fuller went to Italy and got the drugs. Later William James started another counterculture at Harvard. Same thing. Nitrous oxide. Hashish. *The Varieties of Religious Experience.*"

"Well, have the medical people given you a prognosis on *this* life, of how many years you have left?"

"I'm 75, and I've smoked and lived an active life but not the most healthy life. So my prognosis would be like two to five years. Jeez, I'll be 80 then."

"Are there specific things that you want to accomplish during this period?"

"Our World Wide Web site is a big thing. We are putting books up there on the screen. You can actually play or perform my books. You read the first page and my notes. And you can revise my text. We call them living books. As many versions as there are people that want to perform 'book' with me. True freedom of the press! The average person can't publish a book. This way they can."

"Do you think it's destiny or chance that one becomes in a leadership position? A change agent, as you call it?"

"Well, destiny implies that you were created that way. No, I think that the individual person has a lot to do with it. Thousands of decisions you make growing up in high school and college to get to a point where you have constructed your reality. You can be a judge or—"

"A defendant."

"I think one of the good side effects of the Simpson trial is that people understand how totally evil lawyers are."

"You mean defense lawyers *and* prosecutors?"

"Yes."

"A friend of mine was scheduled to be on jury duty, and they asked him what he thought of prosecutors, and he said, 'Cops in suits.' Are you optimistic about the future, even though there's creeping fascism?"

"The future is measured in terms of individual liberation. You have politicians. And the military people want to hurt other people. That's all about control. They have to devise excuses for victimizing people. I do think that the new generations growing up now use electronic media. A 12-year-old kid now, in Tokyo or in Paris or here, can move more stuff around on-screen. She is exposed to more R.P.M., Realities Per Minute! A thousand times more than her great grandfather. There's gonna be a big change.

"The greatest thing that's happening now is the World Wide Web. Sign-ups zoom up like *this*. The telephone is the connection. *The modem is the message!* You can explore around. If you're a left-handed, dyslexic, Lithuanian lesbian, you can get in touch with people in Yugoslavia or China who are left-handed, dyslexic lesbians. It's great! It's gonna break down barriers, create new language. More and more graphic language. And neon grammatics. Anything that's in print will be in neon."

"Well, that really brings us full cycle. We started talking about words, and now they've become neonized."

"Consider, Paul, death with dignity, dying with elegance. It's wonderful to see it happening. I talk about orchestrating, managing and directing my death as a celebration of a wonderful life! That touched a lot of people. They say, 'My father went through this whole thing. He wanted to die.' Amazing."

"So the response has been that people are glad to know that they aren't the only ones who are thinking about death?"

"Yeah. People are thinking about dying with class but were afraid to talk about it."

"What do you want your epitaph to be?"

"What do *you* think? You write it."

"Here lies Timothy Leary. A pioneer of inner space. And an Irish leprechaun to the end."

"Irish leprechaun! You're being racist! Can't I be a Jewish leprechaun? What is this Irish leprechaun shit?"

"Okay. Here lies Timothy Leary, a pioneer of inner space, and a Jewish leprechaun to the end."

Although Leary had decided in 1988 to have his head frozen posthumously, he became disillusioned with cryonics officials shortly before his death and changed his mind.

"They have no sense of humor," he said. "I was worried I would wake up in 50 years surrounded by people with clipboards."

Instead he chose to be cremated and have a small portion of his ashes rocketed into outer space to orbit the Earth. I asked him if the remainder of his ashes could be mixed with marijuana and rolled into joints so that his friends and family could smoke him.

"Yeah," he replied. "Just don't bogart me."

Our paths had often crossed—at civil rights marches, antiwar rallies, marijuana smoke-ins, environmental demonstrations—and he was always on the front lines, especially when it came to gay rights. Long before Ellen came out on a sitcom, Allen came out in the streets.

In March 1968, the Yippies held a press conference in New York to announce plans to protest the Vietnam War at the Democratic convention in Chicago. I was one of the speakers. When I mentioned that, in peace candidate Eugene McCarthy's Clean-for-Gene presidential campaign, "Allen Ginsberg wouldn't even be allowed to ring anybody's doorbell unless he agreed to shave off his beard," a reporter asked me, "Would you cut your hair if it would end the war?"

Before I could answer, Ginsberg himself popped up like a Zen-master-Jack-in-the-box, his index finger waving in the air. He asked the reporter, "Would you let your hair *grow* if it would end the war?"

Later, Yippie leaders held an impromptu competition to follow up that line of questioning, concerned with exactly how open to self-sacrifice one might become in the pursuit of peace. Ginsberg's fellow poet, Ed Sanders, was unanimously declared the winner, with this criterion: "Would you suck off a terminal leper if it would end the war?"

Over the decades, Ginsberg and I had shared many a stage at benefits for various causes, but in 1988 we were both booked for a paying gig at Lincoln Center, along with New Age musician Philip Glass and performance artist Karen Finley, whose reputation for shoving a sweet potato up her ass preceded her appearance. My opening line was, "Allen Ginsberg is very disappointed. He thought that Karen Finley was gonna shove a sweet potato up *his* ass."

I could hear Ginsberg's laughter reverberating from backstage like a Tibetan gong. When we embraced, he said, "How did you *know*?"

Ginsberg once asked his father if life was worth living. His father answered, "It depends on the liver." This was a touch of inadvertent prophecy; Allen died of liver cancer on April 5, 1997. But he had indeed lived his life to the hilt and beyond, balancing with dignity and grace on the cusp between rationalism and mysticism, one individual, with curiosity and compassion for all.

On April 7, Michael Krasny hosted a memorial for Ginsberg on his radio program, *Forum*, over KQED-FM in San Francisco. The panel included novelist/Prankster Ken Kesey, poet/publisher Lawrence Ferlinghetti, Digger/actor Peter Coyote and me. The following is excerpted from that conference call.

Kesey: I was at a party one time when I first knew Ginsberg, and he was standing by himself over by the fireplace, with a wine glass in his hand, and people milling around, and finally some young girl sort of broke off from the rest of the crowd and approached him and said, "I can't talk to you—you're a legend." And he said, "Yes, but I'm a friendly legend."

Ferlinghetti: He lived so many flames. Today the youth, like the 20-year-olds, are really turned on to Ginsberg and the Beat poets, but the thing they're turned on to is the apolitical part. One forgets how political the Beats were in the '50s, which was the Eisenhower and McCarthy era. And that's a flame that seems to be flickering these days.

Kesey: He was a great warrior. I think that's more important than his poetry. In fact, in later times, I haven't read much of his poetry at all, because the warrior aspect of Ginsberg has loomed much larger. When we went to the Vietnam Day parade up in Berkeley [1965], they had been interviewing the Hells Angels [motorcycle gang]—all the Hells Angels were gonna come out and oppose the opposers—they were gonna come out and start a riot, is what it was.

So Allen asked me to take him up there, to where the Angels hung out in this big white house in Oakland, and we went in there, and here's all these big brutes holding their beer cans, with their beer bellies and their beards, and Ginsberg goes right in and starts talking to them. And you look around, here are these great-big, mean-looking guys wearing swastikas, pretty soon Ginsberg has just charmed the hell out of 'em, until there's *not* gonna be a riot.

He took himself into that—they marveled at him. It was the courage, again, the courage of this man to come into this situation and defuse it.

Krassner: I knew Allen more as a researcher and an activist than as a poet. In fact, in 1984, at the Naropa Institute in Boulder, at the 25th anniversary of Jack Kerouac's *On the Road*, Abbie Hoffman was saying how much he and other political activists like Ed Sanders were influenced by *Howl*, and Ginsberg dismissed his own poem as "a whole boat-load of sentimental bullshit." But, as a researcher, he had meticulously acquired files on everything that the CIA ever did, and I'm happy that these are included in his archives [at Stanford University].

The one image I have of him from Chicago in 1968, when we were holding our Yippie counter-convention—as opposed to the Democratic "convention of death," as we called it—the police were in Lincoln Park teargassing and clubbing people, and Ginsberg sat in the middle of it like some kind of stoned Buddha, chanting *Om* over and over again, and people gathered around him, and he led them out of the park, and it created a kind of mystical force field, so that the cops just ignored them, and he was like the Pied Piper of Peacemaking.

Allen just articulated the consciousness of people who knew that the mainstream culture was a sado-masochistic bizarre mess.

Krasny: What do you do with the kind of bizarre mess that some people would claim is characteristic of Ginsberg in the wake of his death, all the NAMBLA [North American Man/Boy Love Association] stuff, and his apparently not only supporting that organization, but also expressing favor where little boys are concerned, sexually, and also using drugs somewhat recklessly and excessively as some attribute him to do?

Krassner: Well, that's the risk of free will. Allen has always admitted, you know, he would go to a poetry reading and say he was hoping to meet a young boy there. He was honest about his perversion of pedophilia, if that's what it was, but it may have been just a fantasy. He was for dialogue, and he was nonviolent, so it's just interesting as to what he considered the age of consent. A few months ago he told me it was 18.

Coyote: (*chuckling*) It's just so funny. I mean, as a father of two kids, I'm *repulsed* by the idea of pedophilia, but you know, by the same token, it's Allen. It probably wasn't easy being Allen. It's easier to be some of us than others of us, and I think that Allen's great courage was to be unequivocally who he was. And when he went to Cuba and announced that he wanted to have oral sex with Che Guevara, it actually was to

Castro's detriment, in my mind, that he threatened to lock him up, or threw him out.

The thing that Allen represented to me was more than the Beats, more than anything else—I harken back to Gary Snyder's great phrase, "the great underground," which he calls the tradition, coming from the Paleolithic shamans on up to the present—the tradition of yogans and healers and midwives and poets and artists and people who stand for archaic, earth-centered values, life-supporting values. It's like a great river that kind of surfaces in various cultures all around the world at different times. It's quenchless, transcendentalist for just one little rivulet of it. And Allen was a great prophet of it.

Kesey: When we [Merry Pranksters] went to see Leary at Millbrook, Ginsberg was on the bus, and we had pulled over somewhere, and he was up immediately, sweeping the stuff out of the bus with a little broom, and Cassady at the wheel said, "Looky there, it's our Jewish mother." And he was the Jewish mother, in some way, to a whole literary movement. He did all he could to help all of his friends get into print, all the time. He was a great benefactor to this art, and worked very, very hard to have his friends have as much fame as he did.

We had a poetry festival some years ago up here in Oregon, and the way we were doing it, during the day we had a stage outside of our basketball court, and we had headliners that were gonna be on that night, and during the day people read poetry and we judged it, and they were gonna be the people that read with Ginsberg, and during the day all the people in the field outside gradually trickled into the basketball court, like 3,000 people in there, and we were gonna charge them $5 apiece, but they were already in. Allen said, "Let me see what I can do." And he got up there with his harmonium, and he began, *Om, Om.* Pretty soon he had 'em all *Om, Oming,* and he just gave a gesture like that, stood up, walked out, and 3,000 people walked out with him, so we were able to charge 'em money.

Krassner: We've been praising Allen so much, but I'll give you one little revealing story. On one hand, he was a pacifist. I remember when he first started taking LSD, and he thought that world peace would come about if only John F. Kennedy and Nikita Krushchev would take acid together. And yet, I remember a scene—this was in the early '70s—Ken Kesey and I and my daughter Holly, who was a young girl then, were visiting William Burroughs in New York, and he had this huge loft, and a cat, and a lot of cardboard boxes, and he was wearing a suit and tie and high-top red sneakers.

We all decided to visit Ginsberg in the hospital—he'd had a stroke, and part of his face was paralyzed—he was in bed there, and I introduced him to my daughter, and he graciously struggled to sit up and shake hands with her, but he was kind of weak and deep in some kind of medication, and he blurted out—what they would call in psychiatry a "primary process"—he blurted out, "Henry Kissinger should have his head chopped off!" It was some kind of Ginsbergian Tourettes' syndrome.

Krasny: There's been a lot of solemn talk, so I'm glad you added that note of levity. Ginsberg would want, I think, a discussion about his life to be infused with a lot of humor and satire, don't you think?

Krassner: Oh, absolutely. You can't take yourself too seriously if you're walking around with an Uncle Sam hat and Mahatma Gandhi pajamas, chanting "The war is over" when the war was at its height. But that act inspired Phil Ochs to write his song, "The War Is Over," and to organize rallies in Los Angeles and New York on the theme of "The war is over."

Coyote: I think that Ginsberg represented an enlarged notion of sanity—which is not to say it's not without contradictions, which is not to say it's not as stained and tattered as anything else. You may not like the fact that Gandhi tested his celibacy by lying naked with young girls, or that Freud was shooting cocaine while he was working out his psychotherapy theories, or that Martin Luther King had sex with women outside of marriage, but to me what these facts do is reinforce the humanity of the person in question and remind us that we don't have to be perfect to make contributions, that we can struggle against the dark or the undeveloped sides of our nature and still make a contribution, and I think that's kind of the beacon Allen is. The thrust and underpinnings of his life were fundamentally sane in every venue. That's really what I respect him most for.

Ferlinghetti: I think maybe you could say Allen started out mad and became *saner* all his life, and he then became more quietus, I think, in his last years, and this was an influence of Buddhism, I believe. He died as a Buddhist, he didn't want any life-support systems. There were Buddhists around him at all-night vigils the last two nights, and he died the way he wanted to die.

Kesey: Ginsberg had a terrific laugh. I was just trying to think, what am I gonna miss most? Even in the most serious moments, this thing would bubble up and bark forth, his eyes twinkling. It was a great laugh, and I'm gonna miss him.

Exactly five weeks before Sunday, December 27, 1998—the day that Anita Hoffman had chosen to die—she was talking on the phone about a blow-up doll that she and her husband, Abbie, had once bought as a present for me. That was almost three decades ago. The blow-up doll never arrived, and Anita now found it necessary to reassure me that they really had ordered it. Their gift may have been a gag, but it wasn't a hoax.

"We were probably the only ones that happened to," she said.

"Oh, no," I replied, "I think they probably screwed everybody. No one *ever* received their blow-up doll, but they were all too embarrassed to report it to the Better Business Bureau."

My missing blow-up doll was just another loose end from Anita's past. She was in the process of tidying up her life before taking it. Three of my closest friends had ended their lives too early—satirist Lenny Bruce in the '60s, folksinger Phil Ochs in the '70s and revolutionist Abbie Hoffman in the '80s—and I was deeply saddened each time, but it was different with Anita.

"There's no despair here," she said. "I'm happier than I've ever been. I'm really looking forward to my death."

She had been suffering from breast cancer, which metastasized to her hips. In September she e-mailed:

"I've been very ill. Too sick to sit at computer, thus off-line for several weeks. Today felt like sitting here and catching up. I'm undergoing radiation treatment. The cancer in my spinal column is affecting my spinal cord, and thus weakening my right leg. I can't walk so good. Use cane. Bedridden. Anyway the radiation is in hope of stopping that encroachment."

She spent her time on the Internet, watching television and reading *The New York Times*, which didn't carry program listings for California, so I got her a subscription to *TV Guide*.

"I must admit," she said, "that I'm hypnotized anew by the visual medium."

But now she was paralyzed from the waist down and had been informed that she had two months to live. "Maybe four," she said, "but, you know, I've always been a pessimist." So here she was, at the age of 56, in an altered state bordering on ecstasy from painkilling drugs—morphine, Marinol, marijuana—combined with the self-empowerment of orchestrating her own departure.

• • •

Whenever Abbie got in trouble, Anita immediately got on the phone to contact lawyers—and journalists.

"Hi," she would begin each call, "this is Anita Hoffman—Abbie's wife. . . ."

That was her role, and she played it with diligence. She would have preferred a simpler lifestyle, but Abbie functioned as a community organizer, and Anita was his willing helpmate. Whether bailing him out of jail or bringing him to a hospital after he was beaten by cops at a demonstration, she was always there for him, planning and participating in guerrilla theater events, from showering $1 bills on the Stock Exchange to levitating the Pentagon.

Abbie provided an adventurous vehicle for the radical consciousness that Anita had already been exercising before they met. She had become politicized simply by reading between the lines of *The New York Times*. With a master's degree in psychology, she had intended to get a Ph.D. but dropped out because she was so upset about the Vietnam War. She began working for the New York Civil Liberties Union but quit her job, afraid, ironically, that she wouldn't get promoted because of sexism. This was in 1967.

She met Abbie—who also had a master's in psychology—when she went to volunteer at Liberty House, a store he founded as an outlet for items crafted by poor people in the South. That same evening, Anita and Abbie had their first date. She put on the Beatles' "Revolver" album, and while they were dancing she told him that she wasn't a good dancer but that she *was* a good kisser. Abbie stayed the night.

Soon after, they got married in Central Park in an alternative ceremony. Without telling her, Abbie had leaked an invitation to the press, and a photo of their wedding appeared in *Time* magazine, where they were identified only as "a hippie couple." Anita wore dark glasses because she didn't want to be recognized by her parents.

She had taken her vows with Abbie, and now she was also married to the media.

There was, for example, the fake orgy that took place in their apartment. In order to build up interest in the exorcism of the Pentagon, Abbie had invented an imaginary drug, LACE—supposedly a combination of LSD and DMSO—which, when applied to the skin, would be absorbed into the bloodstream to act as an instant aphrodisiac. It was to be sprayed on the National Guard and the military police at the Pentagon so that they would literally make love, not war. Now who wouldn't want to go to Washington and witness *that*?

Actually, LACE was "Shapiro's Disappero," a novelty item from Taiwan that leaves a purple stain, then disappears. A press conference was called to demonstrate the effect of LACE on three hippie couples. Mattresses were spread across the Hoffmans' living room floor for the couples to have sex on after being sprayed with LACE from squirt guns, while the journalists would dutifully take notes. For some reason, Abbie wasn't even there, leaving the shy Anita to host this bizarre prank.

Originally, I was supposed to be there as a reporter who got accidentally sprayed with LACE. To my surprise, I would put down my notebook, take off my clothes and start making love with a beautiful redhead who had also been accidentally sprayed. I was looking forward to this combination media event and blind date. Even though the Sexual Revolution was at its height, there was something exciting about knowing in advance that I was guaranteed to get laid, although I felt guilty about attempting to trick fellow reporters.

But there was a scheduling conflict. I was already committed to speak at a literary conference at the University of Iowa on that same day. So Abbie assigned me to go to a farm in Iowa and purchase some cornmeal, which would be used to encircle the Pentagon as a pre-levitation rite. I was a rationalist, but it was hard to say no to Abbie.

In Iowa, novelist Robert Stone drove me to a farm.

"I'd like to buy some cornmeal to go."

"Coarse or fine?" the farmer asked.

I looked at Stone. He shrugged. "Since it's for a magic ritual," he said, "I would definitely recommend coarse."

"Coarse, please," I said to the farmer.

"How many pounds?"

"Thirteen, please."

The farmer smiled and said there would be no charge. And I flew back to New York with a 13-pound sack of coarse cornmeal properly stored in the overhead compartment.

Meanwhile, there were stories about LACE in the *New York Post*, the *New York Daily News* and *Time* magazine, as well as the wire services, perpetuating the promise that three gallons of LACE would be brought to Washington, along with a supply of plastic water pistols.

The hippie who substituted for me in that ostensibly accidental sexual encounter with the beautiful redhead at the LACE press conference ended up living with her. Even though I had never met her, I was jealous. Somehow I felt cheated out of a romance.

"You really should have a steady girlfriend," Anita teased.

Abbie and Anita had an open marriage, but only Abbie acted on it. He was insatiable. He occasionally stopped by my loft on Avenue A with his latest lust object for a matinee performance. I would be at my desk, writing something for *The Realist* or on the phone, and they would be screwing away in my bed.

Abbie obviously wanted his trysts to be kept secret. Yet, since he and Anita were my friends individually and as a pair, I felt conflicted—strangely disloyal—as though I were part of a conspiracy to keep the truth from her.

●   ●   ●

Two days before Thanksgiving 1998, Anita moved from Petaluma to San Francisco.

"Goodbye, room," she said to her little cottage. "Thanks for giving me cancer."

Her immobility had prevented her from seeing the sky, but her friend Cindy Palmer was living at a house in San Francisco owned by her daughter, actress Wynona Rider, and offered the master bedroom to Anita. The plan was to have a steady stream of visitors there. Poet Diane Di Prima, for instance, might be coming over to read some Buddhist death prayers.

Timothy Leary had been Anita's role model during the final months of his life, except that, unlike him, she would not be seeing groupies or reporters. Leary had said, "You couldn't choose how and when and with whom you were *born*, but you can take charge of your own death," and now that's precisely what Anita was doing.

"I'm in total hostess mode," she said, joyfully. "I'm on automatic party time."

My wife Nancy and I flew to San Francisco in early December to visit her. Steve Wasserman, a friend and editor of the *Los Angeles Times Sunday Book Review*, arranged to be on the same flight. He had once edited the *Times'* Sunday Opinion section, but moved to New York to escape the pain of an unrequited crush on Anita. Now he was going to see her for the last time.

My friend Julius picked us up at the airport. We brought him a red Buddha candle and a 1999 calendar. For Anita we brought a multicolored mushroom candle, a CD—Krishna Das' "Pilgrim Heart"—and a bag of cookies. At her bedside, I panicked at the possibility that I had given Julius the candle intended for Anita, which would mean that the one she was now unwrapping would have the calendar for a year in which she would be dead. What could have been an unintentional sick joke didn't occur, though, and the relief was worth the tension.

Anita was living her fantasy. She could not only see the sky but also the San Francisco Bay and the Golden Gate Bridge. Alcatraz Island was included in the view, though not from the angle of her bed, and she preferred it that way.

Her appetite was ravenous, and her humor was dark. After devouring a pastrami sandwich, she remarked, "I better brush my teeth, I don't want to get gum pockets." Someone was bringing over "pineapple-coconut ice cream to die for," and Anita responded, "I guess I'm ready for that." And when we were talking about an upcoming movie, she said, "I'm sure we'll all be going to see that—oops."

In this frame of mind, she would act on an impulse immediately because, as she explained, "I'll never have a chance to do it again." And so she asked for a photo that was on a bookshelf. The rest of us in the room assumed that perhaps she was going to share a memory, but instead she simply ripped the photo in four pieces and tossed them in the trash. Who was in that photo and why she tore it up remain a mystery.

The question rose, since Anita was so euphoric, why not continue living? But her euphoria came from knowing exactly when there would be closure. Of course, Anita's family—her mother, her sister and her son—were not quite so elated. Nevertheless, she wanted them to be at her bedside "to comfort each other."

• • •

After the debacle at the Chicago convention, Mayor Richard Daley's office produced a documentary, *What Trees Do They Plant?*—asserting that reporters were accidentally beaten by police because their credentials were hidden in their jacket pockets. Even if that were true, it only indicated that the cops did in fact attack at random, but the truth was that clubbings took place as a *result* of being shown press cards. Notebooks were seized, cameras were smashed, film was thrown into the lake.

When this anti-protesters documentary appeared on network TV, the Yippies managed to get rebuttal time. Abbie asked me to write a script. At one point, I included this line: "It is not that we hate America, it is that we feel the American dream has been betrayed."

"But we *do* hate America," Anita scolded me.

"No, we hate what America has *become*."

We argued, but they finally agreed with me, and the line stayed. Indeed, at the Chicago conspiracy trial, Abbie repeated that line in his final statement. Moreover, when Anita gave birth to a baby in 1971, he was named america—with a lower case *a* "because we didn't want to be pretentious," she explained. "We chose that name because he was our vision of what the country could be." While america went to school, he was called Alan, though he would later reclaim his name and his heritage (as opposed to Wavy Gravy's son, Howdy Do-Good, who legally changed his name to Jordan Romney on his 13th birthday).

When Abbie went on the lam to avoid serving time for a cocaine bust, he and Anita had already separated, but she continued to be supportive, even after he met Johanna Lawrenson while on the lam and she became his "running mate."

Anita wrote to him, "I needed to live desperately, separately now from you in order to become a separate person. Do you understand?"

Now on her own, she founded a self-help center for mothers and children who were receiving public assistance. When a collection of Abbie's correspondence with Anita, *To America With Love: Letters From the Underground*, was published, she gave me an inscribed copy of the book, and she made sure that Abbie, still a fugitive, mailed me *his* inscription on a yellow Post-It from wherever he was.

•　•　•

In the final weeks of Anita's life, members of her extended family visited her in San Francisco.

Yippie organizers Stew and Judy Albert flew in from Portland, Oregon. They had a reunion with Anita and Rosemary Leary, whom they had last seen 20 years ago, when they were all tripping on the beach in Algeria. Anita had been there trying to renew an alliance between the Yippies and the Black Panthers, but she found Eldridge Cleaver so authoritarian and misogynistic that, afraid for her safety, she climbed out a window to escape. Now they were laughing about it over an afternoon snack of matzohs and jam.

Sam and Walli Leff, Yippie archivists and the cornerstone of Abbie's overground support system, flew in from New York. At Anita's request, they brought from Zabar's delicatessen a carton (packed with dry ice and properly stored in the overhead compartment) containing kippered salmon, sliced sturgeon, smoked sable, herring in cream sauce, herring in wine sauce, whitefish, Jewish rye bread with caraway seeds, coleslaw, potato salad, Russian coffee cake—and they all had a lovely picnic in her bedroom.

Ron Turner, publisher of Last Gasp Comics, brought a whole case of grape soda and promised to deliver a video of *A Bug's Life*.

Janeane Garofalo—who had successfully sought to portray Anita in Robert Greenwald's unreleased film biography of Abbie, *Steal This Movie*, for which Anita was a consultant—came to visit her fading prototype. They had met during the filming. She called Anita "a very, very bright woman who definitely marched to the beat of her own drummer. She was very dynamic. When she walked into the room, you knew she was there." Garofalo said the whole experience reinforced her desire "to live a very Berkeley life wherever I am."

Anita felt she had to warn certain visiting friends—Martin and Susan Carey from Woodstock; Nancy Kurshan from Chicago (who ran the Yippies' New York office and was Jerry Rubin's girlfriend)—that they would not be portrayed in the movie.

"The film makes it seem as though Stew and Judy were the only other Yippies and our best friends," she told me. "Everything other people did, such as donate their kid's bar mitzvah money (the Careys) or forward underground mail, is credited to Stew and Judy. When I mentioned the paucity of other characters, Robert replied that on a low-budget film we just can't afford a lot of major players. This is Hollywood."

Robin Williams learned about Anita's situation from his costar in *Good Will Hunting*, Matt Damon, who had been told about it by his girlfriend, Wynona Rider. Williams had never met Anita, but he called and offered to pay a visit, in keeping with his benign case of Patch Adams syndrome. After all, if Patch could travel to Trinidad to entertain murderers who would be hanged three days later, why shouldn't it be appropriate for Robin to make Anita laugh on Christmas day? Anita hesitated—"I've never really been a fan of his work"—then invited him to come.

Jay Levin—who had been a reporter for the *New York Post* assigned to cover the Yippies, then became a Yippie himself, and years later launched the *L.A. Weekly*—was also there, and described Williams as "an incredibly funny human being." He did conversational shtick for a solid hour, and Anita became an instant fan.

Wavy Gravy, the socially active countercultural clown, originally met Anita at Liberty House in 1967, when she and Abbie were busy stringing love beads. Now Wavy came to her bedside holding a stiff, knotted, leather dog leash, leading a large rubber fish named Saul Bass. Anita wanted to touch it, but Wavy wouldn't let her.

"No," he said, "you don't know where this fish has been. People try to kiss him all the time, but he's been out sniffing a lot of dogs' asses."

Wavy sang a plaintive song, "She Carries Me to the Other Side," while Anita sat in bed wearing his red plastic clown's nose.

•   •   •

On February 14, 1969, I was a guest on the *Tonight Show*—host Orson Bean, substituting for Johnny Carson, had invited me—and naturally I ingested a tab of LSD for the occasion. I was wearing a black Mexican hat that Abbie had given me and a bright orange shirt that Anita had embroidered with an Aztec Indian design of an owl.

They and many other Yippies had spent the previous day rolling thousands of joints, wrapping each one in a flyer wishing the recipient a Happy Valentine's Day and containing facts about marijuana. Over 200,000 pot busts were made the previous year, and Mayor John Lindsay had just petitioned Governor Nelson Rockefeller to raise the penalty for possession from one year to four.

The Valentine joints were sent anonymously to various mailing lists—such as teachers and journalists—plus an individual in the phone book solely because his name was Peter Pot. The whole project was financed by Jimi Hendrix. One newscaster who displayed a joint was visited by a pair of narcotics agents on camera while he was still delivering the news. It was a TV first.

Without revealing the culprits, I discussed this political prank on the *Tonight Show*, and Anita would later recount it in *Trashing*, a fictionalized account of the Yippies, under the pseudonym Ann Fettamen. "There was no way of knowing how many people got high on Halloween [sic]," she wrote, "but we knew it was the busiest night in the history of the Narcotics Division."

The next day I was visited by a pair of narcotics agents who had seen me on TV. I told them that the Mafia must have sent out all those marijuana joints in order to discredit the Yippies.

And, although I was the one who had been tripping on acid, it was a viewer who wrote to NBC complaining that I had worn a shirt with the internal diagram of a uterus.

•   •   •

Anita was efficient in death as in life, taking care of business right to the end. And so it was that I received a refund from *TV Guide* for the unused portion of her subscription. Details, details . . .

At 10 p.m. on Saturday, December 26, she ingested a cocktail that had previously been provided by a compassionate doctor. That she would administer her own deliverance in such a way had been kept secret from almost everyone. Not even the hospice volunteers knew. On Sunday, at 4:15 p.m., Anita accomplished her goal. She died in peace and serenity, believing in the continuation of her consciousness.

"I know I'm not enlightened," she had said, "so I'll probably have to come back."

In her latter years, Anita had become intrigued by the twin towers of mysticism and conspiracy. She read books and magazine articles about those subjects, and loved to listen to Art Bell's late-night radio show. She believed that there is life on other planets and accepted the notion of certain UFO aficionados that extraterrestrials have been making a movie of the earth's progress.

Her last words to me were, "I hope I remember to ask to see that movie."

•   •   •

"Somehow, Abbie will see the movie," Anita had said—referring to *Steal This Movie*, in which she appears briefly in a courtroom scene. "He was the love of my life," she added. "One of the best things about dying is that I'll be able to say hello to him again."

Meanwhile, she continued to serve as the keeper of Abbie's image. She wrote a letter to the editor of the *Los Angeles Times Sunday Book*

Review, which had stopped printing such correspondence several weeks earlier, but she called Steve Wasserman and told him that she was dying— yes, she played the death card—and he published her letter:

"Abbie's legend has a life of its own by now and is surely beyond correction, but I can't help sending in a small correction to J. Hoberman's otherwise fine review of *Steal This Dream* and four other books about the '60s counterculture. Contrary to the quotation from one observer, Abbie Hoffman did not ingest LSD 'like corn flakes' every morning. I would estimate he took LSD about four times a year for three years during the late '60s.

"Also, Abbie never took acid or any other psychedelic during the Chicago conspiracy trial. It was Paul Krassner who was on acid during his testimony in that trial. Abbie and I were furious and didn't speak to Krassner for several years thereafter. I think it's important to be accurate about this for the sake of young people who may be influenced. I continue to believe that psychedelics are a useful tool or sacrament for special occasions."

Actually, it was not several years, but 10 months, that Anita and Abbie didn't speak to me, although it *seemed* like several years. It was after our reconciliation—when I still didn't have a steady girlfriend— that they had ordered a blow-up doll for me, the one that never arrived. But it really was the thought that counted.

further weirdness with terence mckenna

The first thing you notice about the naked men and women soaking in the outdoor hot springs overlooking the Pacific Ocean is that they all seem to maintain excellent eye contact while engaging in casual conversation.

They have come to the Esalen Institute—a New Age human-potential resort in Big Sur, California—to participate in various weekend workshops. The group in this particular tub includes Terence McKenna, who will be conducting a workshop titled "Pushing the Envelope." With his curly brown hair and beard, a twinkle in his eye and a lilt to his voice, he could easily pass for a leprechaun.

"I'm convinced," he is saying, "that probably for most people, the most important thing in a workshop situation is nothing that I will say or do, but whom you might meet here."

Of course, those who are at Esalen for McKenna's workshop have come mainly to meet *him*. He is a psychedelic adventurer and a visionary author—his books include *True Hallucinations, Food of the Gods* and *The Archaic Revival*—and he serves as a missing link between botany and technology.

He took his first acid trip in the '60s when he was a student, majoring in shamanism and the conservation of natural resources at UC-Berkeley, where he became active in the free speech and antiwar movements. He was influenced by Aldous Huxley, Timothy Leary and Ram Dass, and became a countercultural icon himself.

He handles that role with intelligence, grace and humor. In person, he is spontaneously charming and effortlessly witty. He loves language, and though he is glib without being speedy, he chooses his words carefully. He communicates with the precision of an architect and the passion of a poet, speaking in a friendly, entertaining twang. He is, in short, a Mr. Rogers for grown-ups, and the neighborhood he welcomes you to explore is your own inner space.

A woman approaches our hot tub from the walkway to tell McKenna that it's time for his massage. When he rises from his sitting position in the water, I can't help but notice that not only is he fairly well hung, but also that he's much too tall to be a leprechaun.

I continue to soak for a while, replaying in my mind the incident that had brought me here. I had been arrested for possession of psilocybin in San Francisco, handcuffed behind my back, and my Miranda rights were not only read to me, but I later had to sign a form affirming so. My heart pounding fast and my mouth terminally dry, I tried to keep my balance on the cusp between reality and unreality.

The cop's question—"So you like mushrooms, huh?"—was asked with such archetypal hostility that it kept reverberating inside my head over and over again. *So you like mushrooms, huh?* It was not as though I had done anything which might harm another human being. This was simply an authority figure's need to control. But control what? My pleasure? Or was it deeper than that?

This need to understand the basis of my plight became the impetus for my decision to meet Terence McKenna. He was, after all, the Head Mushroom Guru. I contacted McKenna in Hawaii, where he lived in happy isolation. "My Web site is on a machine in the Bronx," he said, "although I administer it from the big island." However, he was coming to the mainland, and he invited me to his workshop at Esalen.

We met on a Friday evening in the dining room, just as a fellow sitting next to him was leaving the table.

"If you see him again," McKenna warned me, "cover your wallet with one hand and your ass with the other."

"Why? What's he selling?"

"A videotape claiming that some guy has discovered a cure for cancer, the elixir of immortality and the Philosopher's Stone—but needs investors to just dot a few *i*'s and cross a few *t*'s."

Attendees at the workshop included a woman who was a professional raver; a man who strolled the streets of Paris with a lobster on a leash;

a mother and her son, whom she brought as a gift for his 21st birthday; a woman who spent the entire weekend sucking on a little straw coming out of the top of a plastic water bottle in the shape of a large, pink, erect penis—she introduced herself as "a hooker from L.A.," adding that "I'm here to party with the elves." McKenna turned to the person sitting next to her and said, softly, "Top that."

Someone told him, "I heard that you're one of the greatest minds in the universe." McKenna responded, "More outlandish claims. We'll compare notes at the end." Someone else publicly confided to him, "If my life were a ride through the funhouse at Disneyland, you're like one of the characters who keeps popping up." McKenna confessed, "I'm an epistemological cartoon."

When the formalities are over, he begins his rap, a swirling kaleidoscope of speculation on the influence of another dimension and what was happening at the end of the 20th century to fracture our understanding of reality. This weekend would turn out to be much more than I bargained for. Mushrooms were only a starting point.

"Why," McKenna asked, "is there so much social tension over this psychedelic issue? Nobody who has informed themselves claims that great criminal fortunes are being made, or that kids are being turned into psilocybin runners in the ghetto. We know that all the stupid reasons given for suppressing psychedelics are in fact some kind of lie.

"And then the more naive on our side therefore assume that, well, shortly, some with reason will climb to its zenith, and all these things will be made legal—*not*. Because this phenomenon is a dagger pointed at the heart of every social system that's ever been in place, from the grain tower at Jericho to modern fascism in China.

"No social system is so confident of its first premise that it can tolerate this. But we don't live for the greater glory of social theories and institutions. We live because we find ourselves, as Heidegger said, *thrown* into being, and we have to sort that out on an individual basis."

And this is where McKenna's concept of novelty came in. Novelty was the absolute core of his quest. The ultimate battle is between the increase of novelty as opposed to habit or entropy.

"Look at the history of the universe," he said. "Novelty has been increasing since the Big Bang. We need to undergo radical deprogramming before the eschaton—the last thing. We are on the brink of moving into the domain of the imagination. Novelty is maximized and preserved. It changes our position in the cosmic drama, the cosmic accident. We're damn lucky to be here as spectators, we are told by science. Suddenly we matter. We still have freedom to act, to create.

"The bottom line, the final true message of psychedelics—the positive input that comes to you if you accept change—is the message that the culture outside of psychedelics is so keen to deny, with materialism, everything from the calendar to theories of democracy. But nothing lasts, not your friends, enemies, fortune, children, not even you. Nothing lasts.

"Well, if you live your life in denial of that, then it's essentially like being dragged kicking and screaming 60 years to the yawning grave. Strangely enough, the way you cheat the grim reaper is by living as fast as you can, because all time is the seriality of events, and the more events there are, the more time you have, so awareness becomes very important, and even, as the Buddhists say, awareness of awareness."

I had a question: "You mentioned 'living as fast as you can.' Now, I thought that doing things fast was one of the problems that brought us to this place, and that the antidote would be to slow down and savor the implications of what we do. Maybe you and I are saying the same thing?"

"Well," he replied, "I didn't really mean do more and more things, I said more and more will happen. I think the thing to do is to eliminate foolishness, having your time vampirized. I agree with you the goal is not to just jam in as much stuff as possible. Basically, one strong motivation for moving to Hawaii was just to escape the silliness, the triviality of it all, and I've discovered there was apparently no information loss. I can keep up with an O.J. Simpson discussion even though I only spent three minutes a week keeping track. The people who watched every day of the testimony, my God, they must be slow learners. And it's amazing how many fields you can participate in as a fully empowered player without investing much time.

"As pleasant as it is, I can't hold the whole thing in my mind in the States, as we citizens of the sovereign State of Hawaii refer to your country. I just feel like I've been parachuted behind enemy lines, and this is no time for philosophy, let's blow up the damn bridge and get out of here. But in Hawaii I can look at it all and see trends and tendencies and pontificate about it in my rainforest, and it all makes sense. Somebody said, 'Yeah, well, it all makes sense because you never talk to anybody else.' Probably some truth to that."

• • •

Saturday morning at Esalen. Fresh fruit and vegetables galore. Hot cereal and stewed prunes. People will be passing gas all over the place, and I remember with fondness my deaf uncle who once struggled to say, when somebody farted, "I can't hear it, but I can smell it."

At the first session that day, McKenna maintained that "There are not good beliefs, there are just bad beliefs, because they inhibit human freedom. A belief is a closed system. Psilocybin, like all psychedelics, has this quality of dissolving preexisting mental and behavior patterns. This ability to entertain possibilities is what starts us on the road to free will.

"Our legacy is the legacy of the children of the stoned monkeys. And the chaotic element that a psychedelic introduces into the mental structures of a population is an inevitable precondition for the overcoming of habit and the production of novelty. We are dysfunctional because we have been away from this symbiotic relationship to mushrooms for such a very long time.

"We have got to make a transition to some kind of higher consciousness. If yoga can do it, great. If transcendental meditation can do it, great. The Pope and the Dalai Lama, fine. But in my experience, the only thing that changes consciousness as fast as we're going to have to change it is psychedelics. We have to change it on the dime, because the processes that we have set in motion are going to drag us down.

"If we *don't* make this higher ascent within 50 years, all the easily extracted metal will be gone, petroleum supplies will be dwindled, epidemic diseases, fascism, the erosion of any knowledge by most people with a historical database. We're just turning ourselves into victims of our own processes. That's why I think this is the choke point. The next 20 years are make or break for the human enterprise. It's a forward escape into a world we can barely conceive of, but the only choice is grim death and extinction.

"We are all very toxified and poisoned by the society we live in, we're critics of it, but nevertheless we're products of it. We need to unify heart and head in the presence of super technology. The culture is being left behind by the technology. We have to reengineer ourselves.

"Fortunately, I have managed to transcend the idea that politics or some social reformation or some messiah is going to bail us out. The reason I'm an optimist is because I think that nature is about some very complex business here, and we are its instruments, and 10 thousand years of our discomfort is, from the point of view of the planet, a small price to pay for what is going to be achieved. I don't know about a God, but the laws of physics favor the production of novelty.

"I really believe our evolutionary past holds the key to our evolutionary future, and drugs and computers are just two ends of a spectrum. The only difference between them is that one is too large to swallow. And our best people are working on that.

"So I really see recovering ancient values through modern technology and a reconstruction of our lifestyles and our relationships to each other. This is how to make the ride to the singularity of the end of time a more pleasant and palatable experience. If you don't do this, the ride to the end of time will proceed at the same rate, but you may lose it.

"It may go from a white-knuckle ride to truly terrifying, because the change that lies ahead is going to require a great deal of flexibility and open-mindedness and a willingness to transform in order to take place without generating a megadose of anxiety.

"Anxiety is already rising. Most governments in the world, their entire function is simply to manage catastrophe at this point, because they have no plan, they have no vision, they're utterly clueless. Basically, they're waiting for flying saucers or the Second Coming to somehow cancel the nightmare that their own institutions and methods have made inevitable."

Jesus, I think, what if McKenna wasn't an optimist? And what if he were not so charismatic? Would he be just another guy with a long beard, wearing a toga and sandals, walking along the sidewalk and carrying a big signboard to remind us, *The End of the World is Coming! Are You Prepared?* Only, McKenna has a specific day for it.

"The end of the Mayan calendar," he says, "is the same day that I had calculated. Well, this is not a reason for believing my theory, for you, but for *me* it was a reason. Too weird a coincidence. The only thing that I have in common with the Mayan civilization is that we both used psilocybin, and it's almost as though when you purge the virus off your disc, there is at the bottom line and written in assembly code that cannot be expunged a discard date that says, 'Abandon this locality before December 21, 2012 A.D.'"

So, kids, be sure to mark that date on your calendar. Circle it in red.

McKenna had a distinct speech pattern—which he would pronounce *pat.tern*, as though his inner dictionary were separating his syllables, certainly a *shat.tering* experience.

"If there are aliens," he said, "they don't talk to people in trailer courts, *species* are addressed. Aliens don't talk to individuals, they talk to species. And they don't say things like, 'Be vegetarian,' they say things like, 'Now do language. Now physics.' Ultimately, everything is a mystery. And it's good, after such an exalted, plodding journey toward explanation, to remember that nowhere is it written that higher apes *should* be able to divine cosmic purpose.

"What wants to save itself is biology, and we're simply a kind of specialized cell that can work at high temperatures or can encode data, and so we've been deputized. I'm sure we're as expendable as any other species and as clueless. The problem is that so much novelty will be lost, and the universe doesn't like that. It wants to conserve novelty at all costs. That seems to be more important to it than conserving biology. It will sacrifice biology if necessary to save novelty. Novelty is the top of the value hierarchy, as I see it, and biology, culture, technology, physics— all are simply means to an end."

McKenna was most proud of his computerized timewave graph, indicating the rise and fall of novelty in history. He described what we were seeing on the screen:

" . . . We're now at six million years, and this is the story of the evolution of the higher primates, and these are solar energy cycles, glaciations, we're still moving in the realm here of large-scale cosmic input . . . this is a domain of high novelty, a very long period, longer than the time that separates us from Moses . . . this may be where that partnership paradise occurs, the early influence of psychoactive plants on consciousness . . . now we're under a million years. And remember, it wouldn't have any of these correlations if the end date were different . . . this is the last 62,000 years . . . 42,000 years . . . this is the mushroom paradise back here . . . the crucifixion is here . . . this is the fall of Rome here. . . .

"This is the birth of Muhammad here, this is the consolidation of Islam—570 to 630, Muhammad's birth and death—the world had never seen anything like Islam. These guys were desert tribes dealing water to each other for millennia at the edge of organized civilization. They were desert barbarians and suddenly one guy, Muhammad, not only founds a world religion but claims the allegiance of 700 million people, and he founds a political order, too. Buddha didn't pull that off, and neither did Christ. There's a book, *The 100*, that seeks to list the hundred most influential people in human history, and number one, Muhammad, built a political and religious and philosophical order that maintained its coherency."

However, novelty is not necessarily a good thing from the human point of view.

"What happened in 1355?" McKenna asked. "Within 18 months, one-third of the population of Earth died—bubonic plague—and no one knows how many died in Europe. It's an interesting signature. It certainly is novel to have one-third of the population drop dead." Because McKenna's predictions of the past were in accurate accordance with history, he was able to extrapolate into the future. "I predicted the fall of the Berlin Wall, Tienamen Square, Chernobyl—I predicted all of these things—I didn't say what would happen, but I said the day. 'This day will be the most novel day of this year.'

" . . . World War I, the Russian revolution, Dada, surrealism—it's the 20th century, for crying out loud—Hitler, bigtime novelty . . . World War II, culminates with the atomic bomb, the end of the war and the return to normalcy . . . 1950, invention of the hydrogen bomb.

"For those of you who are true fans of predictive accuracy, the day of the Human Be-In, January 13, 1967, is the day we go over the hump. Isn't it wonderful that it validates—well, but hell, it *was* the symmetry-breaking moment. And then, just after that, the landing on the moon and the cascade into novelty. Saddam invades Kuwait . . . Tienamen Square, three million, the largest crowd in human history . . . we're right about here. This is the pause before the storm. This is the most habituated moment that we will know for maybe the rest of time."

Boy, was I exhausted. Talk about your long, strange trips. Maybe it was all really just self-fulfilling prophecy, but you had to admire McKenna, if for nothing else, for just how far out on a limb he was willing to go.

"Hell," he said, "I *live* on a limb. I suppose if I were a different kind of personality, I would haunt the hallways of major universities and try to drag these guys into my theory. But for some reason, I think the time-wave itself empowers a certain kind of fatalism, and I just say if I'm right, I'm right, if I'm wrong, I've probably told enough people already.

"It is a remarkable thing for a non-mathematician to have created, and I know how little I knew when I started. If it's true, I really don't think we'll have to wait till 2012. If it's true [*and this became my mantra, in McKenna's voice*], the world is going to get *nut.tier* and *nut.tier* and *nut.tier*. Eventually it will get so nuts that those at the top, in charge of managing all these interlocking systems, will begin to ask, first themselves and then others, 'What is going *on*?'

"It's a done deal, folks. I feel like I am inside an enormous joke.

And that to some degree, each of you is too, to the degree that you understand what's going on here, what's *really* going on here. Then all you can do is act with style and a certain panache, and try to carry things forward, keep everybody happy, keep the levels of anxiety under control. It's a huge, huge joke of some sort, and the real belly laugh is beyond the yawning grave, and then you just look back and say, 'Why didn't I *see* it? It was in front of me all the time, and I lived my whole life in anxiety and doubt and frustration.'"

I had a question: "You say we'll look back from the grave and laugh at the futility with which we struggled through life. Are you implying that you believe individual consciousness can survive after physical death?"

"Not really, only that life will show its pattern and plan when we look back on it, and that will redeem some of the weirdness of having to live it essentially without a clue."

"You could become like the Unabomber, just send psilocybin in the mail to these professors, and insist that the *Washington Post* publish your thesis on the stoned monkeys."

"Good, well, you can be my advance man. Then they'll believe me."

"Oh, right. I have less credibility than you."

For all his pursuit of mysticism, Terence McKenna was essentially a scientist. He may have a cult following, but he was not a cult leader in the sense that he *encouraged* challenge rather than forbade it. "A scientist's job," he said, "is to prove that he's wrong. You don't get that at the ashram, or up in a monastery—[*mimicking what such a guru would not say*] 'Well, we crushed *that* hypothesis to smithereens.'"

Post-workshop, I had a question for McKenna.

"At Esalen, you talked about not knowing where the mind is. Do you think that the mind can function without the brain?"

"I have not made up my mind on this, but think of the mind as a hyperspacially deployed organ that is ordinarily invisible. As to whether or not it can exist independent of the brain, I am not sure. If the physical world is conceived as a 4-D manifold, it is logically impossible for a physical thing, a 4-D solid, to move or otherwise change. It must be our state of consciousness which changes as we become successively aware of adjacent cross-sections of the 4-D manifold. But this makes sense only if we, the observers, are not in space-time. This would imply that our minds exist on a level beyond anything that physics can tell us about."

"So that saying, 'May you live in interesting times,' is supposed to have been a Chinese curse, but if the ruling class had control of the language, it was a curse to *them*, but it was a blessing to the people who *made* it interesting times."

"I think it's saying the same thing as the Irish toast [*heavy brogue*]: 'May you be alive at the end of the world.'"

"Meanwhile, my Chinese fortune cookie predicts that you and I will cross paths again, and also that I will enjoy another Chinese repast soon."

"We must meet in a Chinese restaurant and save the oracle unnecessary embarrassment."

As for my psilocybin bust, I was lucky. With the aid of a terrific attorney, Doron Weinberg, I got off with a $100 fine and nothing on my permanent record. But I finally understood what that cop had meant when he snarled, "So you like mushrooms, huh?" What was his *actual* message? Back through eons of ancestors—all the way back to those *un*stoned apes—this cop was continuing a never-ending attempt to maintain the status quo. He had unintentionally revealed the true nature of the threat he perceived. What he had really said to me was, "So you like the evolution of human consciousness, huh?"

Well, yeah, now that you mention it, I do. I mean, when you put it like that—*So you like the evolution of human consciousness, huh?*—sure, I do. I like it a whole lot.

Terence McKenna died before we could meet again for a Chinese dinner. His was one of the most vibrant minds I've ever encountered. So it was with karmic irony that the cause of death was brain cancer. He had a tumor which he described as "the size of a quail egg" three inches behind his right eye. It had to be cut out immediately, under local anesthetic. He was conscious during the entire operation.

"Guys," he joked with the doctors, "let's keep the 'Oops' factor to a minimum here."

Later, his son asked the surgeon, "So, this tumor, it's thinking?"

The doctor thought for a while, and then he said, "Oh, yes, it's thinking about *some*thing."

Two weeks later, McKenna said that he kept "looking into my mind trying to see what difference" there was. "And," he mused, "I'm trying to figure out *what* it was thinking about that I'm *not* thinking about anymore."

remembering
john lilly

In 1967, while tripping on LSD at the Seaquarium in Miami, I had a delightful nonverbal encounter with one particular dolphin. I would run to my left, and the dolphin would swim in the same direction. Then I would run to my right, stop short, run to my left again, then back to my right, and the dolphin would swim in perfect synchronization. We resembled that scene in the Marx Brothers movie, *Duck Soup*, where Harpo mimicked Groucho's motions in a nonexistent mirror.

"By the way," I asked, "what are you always smirking about?"

The dolphin replied—and I'm willing to concede that this might have been my own acid projection—"If God is evolution, then how do you know He's finished?"

Obviously, it was a male chauvinist dolphin.

In 1970, I attended a weekend workshop conducted by John Lilly at Esalen Institute in Big Sur. It was about exploring mysticism with the scientific method. We weren't allowed to use words like "imagined" or "fantasized" or "projected." Whatever we experienced had to be accepted as reality.

As an exercise, for example, Dr. Lilly played a tape loop of one word being repeated continuously, but after a while you'd begin to hear other words. "When faced with repetition," he explained, "your human bio-computer automatically programs in novelty."

Lilly had worked with dolphins for so long that he had begun to look like one. And even sound like one, interspersing his own speech pattern with dolphin-like staccato clicks and squeaks. He always wore a jumpsuit, and his license plate said DOLFIN. He had done pioneering research on both psychedelics and interspecies communication, so naturally I told him of my acid-trip encounter with that dolphin in Florida, the one who said, "If God is evolution, then how do you know He's finished?"

"No," Lilly corrected me. "How do you know *you're* finished?"

It was a simple yet profound revelation. And so conscious evolution became the name of my game.

Lilly considered dolphins to be smarter and more benevolent than humans. His work inspired a movie, *The Day of the Dolphin* (1973), in which the Navy trains dolphins to be underwater weapon carriers. Lilly was dismayed. "They've turned dolphins into little grey niggers of the sea," he told me.

Lilly and his artist wife, Toni, later founded the Human Dolphin Foundation, and in 1980, with computer scientists, he designed a computer system, Janus, to formulate a human-dolphin computer-synthesized language.

In 1981, I introduced Lilly to freelance reporter Sandra Katzman, and she became his "invaluable friend." She kept a journal. Sample entry: "The rooms have mirrors. Above a bathroom sink a concave mirror stretches. Walls completely fronted with mirrors. Light bounces back and forth between mirrors. I ask, 'How much light is lost in each reflection?' 'One-eighth,' replies the scientist."

Back in 1954, Lilly was pondering what effects would occur in the brain if deprived of external stimulation, and he invented the isolation tank, where a person could lie suspended, perhaps for hours, in a dark coffin-like enclosure filled with warm salt-water. In the '60s, he added the ingestion of LSD to the mix. And a decade later, he began experimenting with ketamine—essentially an anesthetic—to enhance the out-of-body experience.

(Paddy Chayefsky wrote a novel, *Altered States*, based on Lilly's isolation-tank research, and also wrote the screenplay, but was so disappointed in director Ken Russell's film version, released in 1980, that he insisted on a pseudonym for his writer's credit.)

Lilly adored ketamine. His standard greeting to friends became, "Got any K?" Whenever he said that to David Jay Brown (coauthor of *Mavericks of the Mind: Interviews For the New Millennium*), the response would be, "I love you too, John."

Brown recalls, "John was one of the most brilliant people I've ever known; he was also one of the funniest. He had an extremely unusual perspective on the world, and with it, a sense of supreme confidence. He just really didn't seem to care what other people thought about him. Even though he appeared grumpy and cranky a lot of the time, everyone agreed how totally lovable he was. He just couldn't take himself seriously, and he always made people laugh."

Once, as a consequence of his experimentation with ketamine, Lilly was hospitalized. Toni called and asked me to speak with him, which I did for about an hour. He kept repeating a mysterious sentence, "Joe took father's shoe bench out—meet me by the lawn." I thought that he had gone totally crazy, but he later clarified his utterance, which was a test sentence by the telephone company to test transmissions. It was his way of communicating that he was okay.

Another time, while carrying out his torrid affair with ketamine, Lilly almost drowned in the hot tub at his Malibu home. This near-death experience confirmed for him that his life "was guarded by higher powers in the extraterrestrial reality, a hierarchy of entities operating through the control of coincidence on a global scale."

Lilly had propounded that concept—calling it the Earth Coincidence Control Office—which struck me as a witty metaphor until I realized that he actually meant it literally. I decided to act as if I believed in the existence of such a process, and as a result I began to lose my perspective. I had bought into John Lilly's cosmic conspiracy. I had gone over the edge, from a universe that didn't know I existed, to one that did. From false humility to false pride.

A couple of decades later, Lilly would dismiss his own concept. "Tooth problems," he explained. "I was trying to get in touch with my teeth."

A close friend of Lilly, known only as Brummbaer, told me: "For over 10 years, we were fellow ketamaniacs. The last time we shot up was a couple of years ago in Hawaii, and already then it took quite a toll on my body and even more on John's. Taking ketamine isn't just a flirt with death—it's a tantric fuck with death—all nine holes of your body participating—and it's not free!

"I observed John as somebody who was interested in sexual identity, and I once jokingly suggested how it would be if we all had a sex change in the middle of our life and so would experience both genders. When I heard he wanted breast implants, I was hoping for the protective sanity of his friends, but he wouldn't have been John Lilly—genius— if he couldn't find somebody to do him the favor. John also wore makeup in those days. The boobs were awful! Square and hard!

"Then one day they found John minus most of his blood on the bedroom floor—the wound from the implant hadn't healed—ants were marching around in a wound that John had tried to close with paperclips in the best sense of a pioneer who uses the materials at hand. When I told Tim [Leary] about this, he cracked up: 'My god, Brummbaer, look what a bunch of bores we are—trying desperately to pitch ideas to a software company while John is walking around with boobs.'

"I think the breast-implant story says what John always proclaimed: That you don't know it if you haven't experienced it yourself. And since he regarded his body as some kind of a laboratory/measuring device, to get boobs or any other implant wasn't such a big thing for him."

In the early '90s, Lilly visited Australia. According to his hosts, "All that was on his mind was scoring, no matter what it was. Also he was quite sick and feverish. His breast implants had gotten infected somehow, probably because his liver was none too clean. We rushed him to the local hospital, where they took the things out, and the next day he was fine and delivered a fantastic talk in the local surf club about dolphins."

About 10 years ago, Lilly moved to Maui, where he not only collaborated with the Kahua Institute on their project, Dolphin and Whale Adventures in Consciousness, but he also became a rap artist, for better or worse, with such songs as "I Know Nothing" and "The Journey."

On September 30, 2001, John Lilly's journey was over. He died of heart failure at the age of 86. His legacy includes 19 books, from *Center of the Cyclone* to *Tanks for the Memories*. A week before his death, he greeted Brummbaer with the ritualistic, "Got some K?"

At a memorial, Brummbaer described how Lilly had "refused to work for the government because, when he mapped the brain of mammals to measure brain activity, he lost access to his own experiments by not having the secrecy clearing of the Pentagon.

"Interestingly, the experiment he wasn't privy to was to remote-control a mule loaded with explosives into enemy territory, using John's electrodes and his brain maps. How odd this sounds today where we have a whole new idea about mules and how to deliver explosives. I think because of this event he became the maverick and never changed until the end."

celebrity
culture

country
joe mcdonald
wore khakis

Of course, this was not the first time I'd been broke.

Previously, after the original Woodstock Festival in 1969, my financial problem was so bad that Country Joe McDonald graciously hired me to spread false rumors about him. So, on my radio show, I mentioned that he had become a Scientologist. McDonald himself suggested a rumor that he had done a commercial for Coca-Cola.

"The people who know my work will know it's not true," he explained, "and it doesn't matter what the others think."

This was in keeping with what Ken Kesey once said about his energy and his image: "My energy is what I do, and my image is what people *think* I do."

I included this question in an interview with Kesey: "Would you care to speculate as to the motivation of performers like Paul Newman [who had actually done a Coke commercial] and Country Joe McDonald in contracting to lend their graven images to advertisements for Coca-Cola?"

"They need the money," responded Kesey.

But now, tied in with the promotion of Woodstock '94, there was an *actual* commercial for *Pepsi*-Cola, with McDonald being asked by fellow musician John Sebastian, "Remember when we did this 25 years ago?"

"No," replies Country Joe, who admittedly received $25,000 merely for saying that single word. It gives a whole new meaning to the slogan, "Just say no."

However, I was in no position to be self-righteous about this. In fact, I was so desperate I even offered myself to the Gap people for a "Paul Krassner Wore Khakis" ad. Would I be selling out, or would they be buying in?

After all, when Allen Ginsberg, the epitome of integrity, had posed for that "Wore Khakis" series in a full-page ad appearing in such diverse publications as *Interview* and the *New Yorker*. In tiny print you could barely read that "All fees for Mr. Ginsberg's image are donations to the Jack Kerouac School of Poetics, The Naropa Institute. . . ."

All fees for *my* image would have been donated to my landlord. but I received the following reply from Kelly Corroon, account manager for Gap Advertising:

"We appreciate your offer to do a khakis ad, but we usually only use vintage photographs in our khaki campaign. I am thrilled to know you wear Gap clothing, and that you love our khakis. Thanks again for your offer."

I had admitted to owning a pair, but I *never* said I loved 'em.

steve allen and
lucille ball

In April 1989, on the same evening that Lucille Ball was about to undergo serious surgery, I had dinner at a Hollywood restaurant with Steve Allen. CNN's entertainment reporter had made an appointment to meet Steve at the restaurant, and he interviewed him there—*twice*— once for if Lucille Ball survived the operation and once for if she didn't. Although I could understand the practicality of such foresight, I was somehow offended by it.

Sure enough, the next day there was Steve Allen on CNN, standing outside the restaurant and saying, "We all hope Lucy will pull through. There have been many success stories in the history of television, and yet the affection that millions of Americans hold for Lucille Ball is unique."

A week later, she died, and sure enough, there was Steve Allen on CNN again, standing outside that same restaurant and this time saying, "Lucy will be greatly missed. . . ." Then George Burns came on and said, "I had a lot of fun with Lucy." I couldn't tell whether he had taped that statement before or after Lucy was dead. There is, after all, no business like show business.

A week after Abbie Hoffman killed himself, the autopsy report was released, and his picture was on the same front page of the *Los Angeles Herald-Examiner* as a photo of Lucille Ball on the day she was scheduled to undergo serious surgery.

At a memorial in Los Angeles, Daniel Ellsberg unfurled a banner given to him by young people at an anti-nuclear protest—beautifully embroidered with the message: "Sweet dreams, Abbie. You helped start it. We'll help finish it."—and he presented it to Abbie's widow, Johanna

Lawrenson. A few months later, another memorial was held in New York. Ellsberg was there, and he would unfurl the same banner.

"How'd you get *that* back?" I asked.

"Johanna gave it to me so that I could present it to her again today."

And I finally understood. Restaging the unfurling of the banner dedicated to Abbie was just a variation on the CNN reporter interviewing celebrities twice about Lucille Ball. And didn't *I* mostly repeat at the New York memorial, almost word for word, what I had said at the Los Angeles memorial? I could no longer feel holier-than-thou about CNN's premature sentimentality. There *was* a business like show business after all, and it was the radical memorial business.

I told Steve Allen about that incident.

"American reality," he said, "has become part show biz through and through, whether you're talking about politics, religion, the military, or whatever. The Jewish scriptures report God frequently doing tricks and shticks to get people's attention."

On Halloween, 2000, Steve was at his son's home, carving a pumpkin with his grandchildren, and then he took a nap from which he never awoke. Steve had just come from an interview by NPR correspondent Jon Kalish, who was preparing a feature for "All Things Considered." It was to be a profile of me, because I had been planning to publish the final issue of *The Realist*.

Steve was the very first subscriber when I launched the magazine in 1958. He sent in several gift subscriptions, including one for controversial comedian Lenny Bruce, who in turn sent in gift subscriptions for several others, and that's how it grew, in Malthusian fashion, eventually to a circulation of 100,000.

Although one of Steve's *Tonight* show successors, Johnny Carson, made frequent references to his sidekick Ed McMahon's alcoholic proclivities, that banter was never censored. However, the head of NBC Broadcast Standards admitted to me: "If you were going to make jokes about Ed McMahon getting stoned on an illegal substance, it would not be approved."

In a society where arbitrary distinctions were drawn between legal and illegal drugs, children were being taught that it was wrong to put cyanide in Extra-Strength Tylenol but acceptable to spray paraquat on marijuana crops.

Cable TV now allows more freedom of expression than the networks, but not for me in the summer of 1980. Emmy Award-winning producer

Ann Elder had hired me as head writer for a special, satirizing the presidential election campaign. The show, titled *A Funny Thing Happened on the Way to the White House*, would take place in a modern newsroom, with Steve Allen as anchor. Supposedly, HBO wanted hard-hitting satire, but it turned out to be refried cotton candy.

This was the first time in American history that three major presidential candidates—Ronald Reagan, Jimmy Carter and John Anderson—had all publicly declared themselves to be born-again Christians. So the election was no longer a choice between the lesser of two evils; it had become a matter of choosing among the least of three sinners. But my concept of a "More Born Again Than Thou" competition was deemed "not appropriate" for HBO.

The original presentation included my idea for a sketch, "The Big Sister Abortion Clinic," wherein a poor teenaged girl who is pregnant and unmarried arranges for a fetal transplant to a wealthy woman who is not pregnant but is pro-choice and *can* afford an abortion. There was no objection from HBO, but Steve sent this memo:

"You could run into problems with the abortion sketch. More than any other important issue of our time, this one has become deadly grim business. I wrote the book that comedy is about tragedy, but because of the fact that killing—justified or not—is involved here, the issue is far more touchy than any other. If you decide to do such a sketch anyway, I would not want to be involved with it."

And so the sketch was aborted. It was frustrating, though I respected Steve for sticking to his principles. That's also how I felt about his more recent campaign to clean up television. On the day of his death, his full-page ad appeared in the *Los Angeles Times*, blasting the industry for "the filth, sex and violence you send into our homes."

I understood where Steve was coming from. He had said that he respected the sometimes-bawdy irreverence of Lenny Bruce and me because we performed for adults, but it was another thing for him to watch television with his grandchildren. The vulgarians had already gotten *past* the gate. Now they were invading his living room, and he had chosen to call for a boycott of sponsors rather than just using the off switch on his TV set.

Steve Allen's death was sudden. He had not been about to undergo serious surgery like Lucille Ball, so there were no double interviews of celebrities by CNN's entertainment reporter. On the way to his son's home, Steve's car was hit by another, and he suffered a concussion, which led to his death that Halloween evening. He would have enjoyed discussing the notion that, had NPR interviewer Kalish not asked him just *one* more question, Steve would be alive today.

a letter to
hunter thompson

Hey, Hunter—

Well, I thought you'd get a charge out of the fact that I'm pissed off at something you did almost three decades ago, which I just now discovered. In the new collection of your old letters—what's it called, *Fear and Loathing of Fear and Loathing?*—you sent a letter to Jann Wenner in 1974 about "Bend in the River," a grassroots conference in Oregon that Ken Kesey was organizing. Apparently, Kesey had recommended that Wenner appoint Tom Wolfe or me to cover the event for *Rolling Stone*.

"As much as I like both Krassner and Wolfe, personally," you wrote to Wenner, "I'd be strongly inclined to avoid whatever temptation there might be to assign either one of them to this story, if only because of the potential news-management problem. . . . I don't think assigning somebody to do a friendly, in-house whitewash will help Kesey, us, or anyone else."

That same day, you wrote to Kesey: "Let's face it—assigning Wolfe & especially Krassner to cover your debut in politics would have a pretty obvious touch of the Fix in it."

Listen, Hunter, you saboteur, who ever anointed *you*—of all people—as the Supreme Knight of Objectivity? I told our mutual friend, Lee Quarnstrom, about your letter to Jann and he responded, "It's *Rolling Stone* we're talking about here, not *The Economist*. Hunter was writing for *Rolling Stone*. It's not writing from the point of view of a disinterested scientific observer."

Tom Wolfe was doing pretty well then, but I was desperately broke, living on borrowed money. Although I was *there* at Bend in the River with my reporter's pad and tape recorder, I never got the assignment. Lee Quarnstrom did. In view of your courageous attempt to protect *Rolling Stone* from biased journalism, Kesey—ever the pragmatic prankster—had advised Quarnstrom to query Jann without mentioning his name.

So Quarnstrom went to the conference with Annie Liebowitz, who then came back to the Kesey farm, where Kesey requested that Annie not take any photos of a bunch of us suckling on a tank of nitrous oxide. I guess that's what you must've meant by news-management, huh? Ironically, Quarnstrom's editor at *Rolling Stone* got replaced, and Quarnstrom's article was never published. But he did say to thank you for the kill fee.

I guess I feel retroactively betrayed by you. When your first book, *Hells Angels*, was published in 1967, I assigned you to write about your promotional tour for *The Realist*, and because you were having financial problems, I paid you $200 in advance. Later, I extended your deadline and offered to send you some LSD if it would help.

"Good," you wrote back. "I've blown every deadline I've had for the past two months and it's good to find somebody with a schedule as fucked up as mine. The action here for the past two months has been unbelievable. All at once I got evicted, my wife went into a lingering two-month miscarriage and my lawyer came out from San Francisco and flipped out so badly that two sheriff's deputies took him one Saturday night 200 miles across mountains to the state loony bin. . . . As for acid, thanks but I'm suddenly OK."

Soon after, another letter arrived from you, asking, "Can I get any leeway on the July 1 delivery date? . . . In the meantime, you can send me some acid to help me level out. And I'll send you a dozen just-born marijuana weeds. You can plant them in Central Park."

As it turned out, you bungled your book tour by appearing on radio and television as either a blathering drunk or an insane mumbler. You walked off your first TV show when the interviewer said, "Tell me, Hunter, what do you think of the Hells Angels?" Who could blame you?

But at least you were honorable with me. In October, you wrote, "There's no avoiding the fact that I blew this one completely. I'm sending you $200 of the $1,900 I now show as book-profit on the hardcover edition. . . . With Johnson as president, I feel on the verge of a serious freakout but if I ever get over that hump I'll write a good article for you.

In the meantime, we're at least even on the money. This check is good. I've sworn off money articles a/o December, so maybe I'll level it out then. If not, I might run for the Senate or send off for a Carcano [the rifle ostensibly used to kill JFK]."

As a writer, I could understand; as an editor, I was frustrated. But I simply had to accept your nature. I mean, you once blew $6,500 worth of assignments in two weeks! Compared with completing articles, it was much easier for you to write three or four letters every night, including those that assured editors you were busy working on pieces you hadn't even started.

I know you consider yourself antisocial, but Kesey told me about your particularly peculiar reaction to a party being thrown in your honor: "When *Fear and Loathing [in Las Vegas]* came out, there was a big send-off party in a New York hotel penthouse, and Hunter wasn't there when it started at 9, he wasn't there at 10 and finally about 11 he showed up, and everybody's drinking white wine and eating brie, and he came in and looked around, his eyes wide, and just walked right through the place into a bedroom, closed the door and locked it. He was in there about half an hour. Suddenly the door opened up, and he came back out and left. Without a word to anybody. And everyone is speculating on what the hell he's been doing in there. And about half an hour later, Room Service showed up with 200 ham and cheese sandwiches and 200 Heinekens."

Lee Quarnstrom, who became an executive editor at *Hustler* and wanted to interview you, told me, "Hunter wanted $5,000 for the interview. He said, 'Get Larry Flynt to kick in some of his money.' I said, 'Well, we don't pay for Q&As.' So he called me back and he said, 'Okay, I'll do the interview for nothing, if *Hustler* will fly us both to Bora Bora and you can conduct the interview on a veranda as we sip mai-tais and watch the sun set into the Pacific.' I didn't hold it against him. I didn't think it was sleazy. I just thought it was opportunistic. Why not give it a shot?"

Phil Bronstein, executive editor at the *San Francisco Examiner*, had wanted you to cover the O.J. Simpson trial. He told me, "I thought Hunter would be the perfect person to write about the trial." You even met with him at a waterfront restaurant to discuss that possibility.

"Hunter's face was all banged up" Bronstein recalled. "He claimed he had gone night-diving and scraped his face on a rock. The waiter had some glandular problem, causing his eyes to bug out, but Hunter accused him of staring. Then he started telling me about these rumors he heard from friends in the L.A. coroner's office about nasty activities with dead bodies, including the infamous bodies involved in the Simpson case. Teeth marks on the butt and things like that. He said that he would cover the trial if we put him up at the Chateau Marmont in a suite with three satellite dishes, four fax machines and several assistants."

Inevitably, that assignment was withdrawn because you were such a flaky prima donna. And this wasn't the first time you'd made such a demand. Art Kunkin, publisher of the *L.A. Free Press*, told me, "Hunter wanted me to put him up at the Chateau Marmont, and I wouldn't do it, and he threatened to kill me. He was pissed at me for not having the kind of budget to do that."

Yet, like all the other editors, I too was willing to tolerate your irresponsibility in the hope of presenting your talent. In 1970, I assigned three countercultural figures who were running for sheriff—Stew Albert in Berkeley; George Kimball in Lawrence, Kansas; and you in Aspen, Colorado—to write about their experiences and observations during those election campaigns. Albert and Kimball came through, but when I heard nothing from you, I sent a follow-up note and you replied:

"Yeah, your letter got thru & found me in the middle of writing almost exactly the piece you asked for—but I've already agreed to give it to *Rolling Stone*. Wenner asked about a month ago. . . ."

Anyway, now that I've vented, I feel better, and I forgive you in retrospect for being such a gonzo prick.

Carry on,
paul

"**C**ircus freaks, celebrities," says Roseanne, "it's all the same thing."

As a kid violinist, I understood that connection; I was the object of an audience before I was a member of one. At the age of six, wearing a Little Lord Fauntleroy suit and playing my violin, I became the youngest concert artist ever to perform at Carnegie Hall. It didn't seem like such a big deal to me—I almost fell asleep in the middle of the Vivaldi Concerto in A Minor—but strangers kept complimenting me and rubbing my hair. I understood viscerally that they were doing it for their needs, not mine. One woman even asked me to sign her program.

"What for?" I asked.

"This makes it more personal," she explained, "and I can show my friends that I met you."

I wrote my name right above my photo, unaware that the word to describe my feeling was *absurd*. But, besides being a child prodigy, I was also a professional brat, and I said, "Well, if they're really your friends, why won't they believe you?" She laughed, and I discovered my true calling.

Twenty years later, instead of becoming a violin virtuoso, I launched a satirical magazine, *The Realist*. I was still intrigued by the implications of fame and would occasionally ask an interviewee how celebrityhood had changed his life.

"Sometimes it helps," replied professional curmudgeon Henry Morgan. "It gets you tables in full-up restaurants, and sometimes people give you stuff for nothing because you can afford to buy it and they just charge the people who can't afford to buy it. All you have to pay for it is a loss of privacy for the rest of your damned life, giving autographs to mindless little girls, listening to jokes forced up your leg by imbecile truckers, answering questions in small papers of dubious repute and minuscule circulation—and which use jerky words such as 'celebrityhood'—overpaying tradespeople because they know you're a big star and make a million dollars a year and don't need the money, being stared at in the street whether you're blowing your nose or not. On the other hand, I used to be shy when I went to a party. Now I'm not."

And Woody Allen said, "None of the *internals* get changed, and that's what really kills you. You get in trouble with a better class of women, that's all that happens. Years ago, I lived in a tiny one-room apartment and went out with fairly drab women. Now I come in contact with more exciting women, but the problems are still the same. I may get a suit custom-made, but I still can't relate to the tailor. I can afford a car, but I don't buy one because I have too many emotional problems driving. You know, all the things just recur on a higher economic scale."

Recently, a friend told me how she was once at an event where she was standing near the young, handsome Marlon Brando while she was eating a *samoza*, and she was so flabbergasted by his presence that she ate right through the napkin, with pieces of it hanging from her mouth. I also heard about a woman who saw Robert Redford in an ice cream parlor and ended up putting her ice cream cone in her purse, but in another city I heard the same story, except it was Paul Newman and frozen yogurt, so it's probably an urban myth.

Orson Bean admits, "I deliberately chose to walk that thin line between fame and oblivion because being a celebrity is part ego trip and part inconvenience. They say that savage tribes get upset if white hunters or anthropologists take their photograph; part of their soul will disappear. Conversely, autograph hounds think they're stealing part of the soul of a celebrity when they get his autograph, and they run away with it, thinking that some of that fame is gonna rub off on them."

Joan Baez used to sign autographs only for children. To others, she'd smile and say, "Let's shake hands instead. That way I'll get something out of it, too." And, at a peace demonstration during the Vietnam War, Muhammad Ali would only sign his autograph on draft cards.

Alley Mills told me about the conclusion of a research project. "It's

an actual phenomenon," she said. "When you've seen someone on cel-
luloid, and then you see them in person, your heart starts to pound and
you start getting all excited, even if you hate them. I remember seeing
Jamie Farr, that guy from *Mash*, in a restaurant, and I got all excited. I
don't like Jamie Farr. I didn't even like *Mash* that much. It's a physical
thing."

Stanley Young, who interviews celebrities for *People*, agrees. "There's
an inevitability behind it, because when somebody whose face is on the
screen for an extended period of time, or on the tube and they're in your
house, eventually you begin to emotionally identify with them. That's
why faces sell on magazines, because people have an emotional identification with them."

Joe Levy, an editor at *Rolling Stone*, says, "I don't think it's the end
of the world that celebrities are on the cover of all these magazines. I
do think it's the end of the world if they're on the cover of *every* magazine. If it gets to the point where you can't put a large-mouth bass on
the cover of *Field and Stream* unless you've got Jenna Elfman holding
that large-mouth bass, then you've gone too far."

Celebrities and the media have developed a totally symbiotic relationship. They need each other so desperately it's giving codependency
a bad name. Although *In Style* publishes a feature titled "Truth or
Tabloid," fundamentally the only difference between the *National
Enquirer* and *In Style* is in the slickness of their packaging and the elegance of their language. Whereas the *Star* calls Calista Flockhart "scrawny"
and "waif-thin," *In Style* refers to her "swanlike beauty" and "a frame
as slender as a tulip stem." In a *George* magazine interview (where she
is described as "wafer-thin"), Flockhart is asked about a story in an
Australian magazine that reveals her "secret lover." She laughs and replies,
"He was a reporter from *In Style* who was interviewing me. He was one
of their own."

Each fan projects upon a star their own individual perceptions. When
the Beatles came to America, there was a concert at Shea Stadium. You
could hardly hear them sing above the screaming of the crowd. One
young girl held up a poignant poster: "It's all right, John—I Wear Glasses
Too!"

The perverted extension of that sense of identification occurred when
Mark David Chapman asked John Lennon for an autograph, then a few
hours later killed him. Ken Kesey observed, "You have to remember,
whenever there's a spotlight, there's always a crosshair in the middle."

A couple of months later, John Hinckley tried to execute Ronald Reagan in the hope that Jodie Foster would be so impressed that she'd go bowling with him. And don't forget, Rebecca Schaeffer was killed by a deranged fan, while Selena was murdered by the president of her own fan club.

With the aid of technology, however, things happen so fast that even the rate of acceleration has been increasing, and irreverence has been accelerating along with everything else. Although it took more than a decade after the assassinations of John and Robert Kennedy for there to be a band called the Dead Kennedys, it took only a few months after the attempted assassination of Ronald Reagan for there to be a group called Jodie Foster's Army. Other bands have been named Sharon Tate's Baby, Jim Jones and the Suicides, and Lennonburger.

I asked Lew Harris, editor-in-chief of *E! Online*, how the Internet has changed the nature of fan clubs. His response: "Anybody who has anything they want to say about a celebrity has a voice now. The anarchy of the net is the most exciting thing, but celebrities don't like it very much, because we're in a period now where celebrity control is higher than it's ever been in the history of show business. The contract system in the studios is over, all these celebrities now have their personal publicists and most of the time their job is to keep their clients *out* of the press.

"The fascination with celebrityhood is unparalleled at any time in the history of the world, and now there's a medium for it. Along comes the Internet, you've got thousands of people out there, millions, who can say anything they want about a celebrity, they can put their pictures up, they can put somebody else's nude body—*TV Guide* got in trouble for running a picture of Oprah with Ann-Margret's body—this happens on the Web all the time, except they're nude. You've got Alyssa Milano nude, and her mother is now out trying to get all these nude pictures off the Web. Meanwhile, there are pictures of everybody else—Courtney Cox, Drew Barrymore, Brad Pitt—superimposed, done by PhotoShop. And the fans don't care. To them a fake picture of Brad Pitt nude is just as good as a real picture of Brad Pitt nude."

Just like it doesn't make any difference to those matrons who seek autographs from Elvis Presley lookalikes.

Larry Flynt has offered a million dollars to many celebrities to pose nude in *Hustler*—Cher, Farrah Fawcett, Olivia Newton-John—who have refused, but no matter. There is now a CD-ROM being sold on the

Internet with this pitch: "Are you tired of spending countless hours searching for pictures of nude celebrities? Well, the search is over! Celebrity Nudes CD-ROM with over 8,500 different images . . . contains some of the hottest actresses, *Playboy* centerfolds, singers, models and every other celebrity out there."

As Colin Quinn said on *Saturday Night Live*, "Charlize Theron is upset about appearing nude in *Playboy*, saying she intended the photos for her private use. I guess that makes two of us."

On KPFK, Amanda Parsons was talking about researching her new book, *High Exposure, Hollywood Lives: Found Photos From the Archives of the Los Angeles Times*:

"I discovered what may be, and I came to think of as, the most powerful cultural phenomenon of our century. These [celebrities] are people that are under our skins in ways that we can't possibly imagine until we let it happen, and it's a phenomenon felt all the way around the world. There's also something about it that's tawdry and unpleasant. What I learned from working on this subject of fame—I learned that I don't want it—as I sit here on radio. I think it's toughest for the person that *is* the celebrity, but for those of us who are out there, the fans, I think that we use these celebrity lives in ways that transform our own. I sometimes think of it as these are our gods and goddesses, these are our icons, and their stories become kind of parables for how to lead our lives."

Indeed, fan clubs on the Internet are known as altars. One site is actually named "Worship Janeane Garofalo." Another, more specialized, Web site declares, "No one in his right mind would call Janeane Garofalo fat. No one, that is, except the agents, casting directors and other assorted weight Nazis who've sworn to protect America from the sight of a woman without visible hip bones. Sure, Hollywood thinks we're ready to see a leading lady come out of the closet, but not out of a bakery." The site—surprise!—is sponsored by a weight-reduction plan: "Click here and we'll send you all the secrets of automatic fat control."

[After the terrorist attacks, Garofalo gained 19 pounds, which made her consider quitting acting.]

There is a sense of continuity in fan fetishism, from a sale of the Beatles' bedsheets cut up into thousands of one-inch squares—fully authenticated by hotel managers and suitable for framing—to the Fox network siphoning water from the swimming pool in *Melrose Place* and filling hundreds of tiny plastic vials that can be distributed to fans as souvenirs.

If the Beatles were, as John Lennon said, more popular than Jesus, then Madonna is more popular than his mother. Salman Rushdie sent her an autographed copy of his latest novel, *The Ground Beneath Her Feet*, coincidentally about a troubled rock star who is constantly reinventing herself. The bedeviled author was told that she shredded the book. Rushdie announced, "I suppose 'Shredded by Madonna' is a higher recommendation than 'Burned by fundamentalists.'"

Fame, as both Rushdie and Madonna know only too well, is a two-sided coin. Where there is love, there is always the potential of hatred. Last month, in *E! Online's* mean-spirited, reality-twisting, weekly series, "Diary of Madonna's Baby," the precocious child wrote:

"Well, Mommy's been in a good mood lately, 'cause she just started shooting that dumb ol' movie *The Next Best Thing*. You remember that, doncha, Diary? It's where Mommy plays a woman who uses a man to help her have a baby. No, it's not an autobiography, silly! It's a romantic comedy. . . . Mommy's so into this movie that as soon as she wakes up, she starts right off shouting and cursing at the nearest bodyguard. Then, by the time she reaches the set, she's all warmed up and ready to yell at the makeup girl, the hairdresser, the masseur, the pedicurist, the yoga teacher, the Tarot card reader and anyone else she hoodwinked the producers into hiring who has the misfortune of being within 20 feet of her luxury trailer."

The anonymous writer of this feature told me, "I see it personally as the antithesis of celebrity. It's the true meaning of iconoclasm—a shattering of the icon. It's satirical iconoclasm, an attempt to deflate—I think of it as celebrity deconstruction—and some of the support that I've heard from people who read it around the world is that they feel that more of that needs to be done, there's not enough vinegar out there being poured on these celebrities, there's only adulation and adoration. I think it's something in the human psyche."

At the various award ceremonies, so many celebrities thank God that you realize God is the Ultimate Celebrity. And a forgiving deity, at that. The MTV Awards telecasts have served as a redemption center for fallen celebrities. One year it was Pee Wee Herman asking the audience, "Heard any good jokes lately?" The next year it was Michael Jackson kissing his wife onstage as a public relations gesture to dispel the notion that they had gotten married as a public relations gesture.

A letter to Walter Scott in *Parade* magazine—"I fell in love with Latin hunk Ricky Martin at the Grammy Awards. Is he married?"—reeks with a vague delusion that the letter-writer has a chance with him. That same delusion was catered to by Tom Jones' manager, who kept it a secret that Jones was married, and it is still catered to by the publicist for Reese Witherspoon and Ryan Phillipe, who didn't want it known that they were girlfriend and boyfriend.

Here's a case history of a literary fan. Robert Weide first met Kurt Vonnegut in 1982. Over the past 10 years, Weide has been filming a documentary on the author's life. He wrote and produced *Mother Night*, based on Vonnegut's novel. "In high school and college," he told me, "I worshipped Vonnegut out of all reasonable proportion. I guess I still do, but it's hard to remain that fanatical over someone who's become one of your best friends. Despite the age difference, we've become something akin to brothers. This is a guy who, 20 years ago, I would have walked a mile, naked, in a blizzard, to shake his hand or get an autograph.

"Now we speak on the phone almost daily, and see each other whenever we're visiting the other's coast. I've spent weekends at his country home, we've had countless meals together, downed numerous glasses of scotch together. He even mentioned me in his book, *Timequake*. So I'm basically carrying on the friendship with him that every fan dreams of having with their idol. You know, 'If only he met me, I know we'd hit it off and become best friends.' I guess you could say I'm the world's most successful stalker. I've told Kurt that I'm glad he accepted me as a friend because it's much easier than having to camp out across the street with binoculars."

In *Notting Hill*, Julia Roberts, who got $20 million for her marquee value as well as her acting ability, tells Hugh Grant, "The fame thing isn't really real, you know."

Nevertheless . . . Ben Stiller has stopped counting the number of times people come up to him and say, "You've got something in your ear." A man who would never go to a peep show brings his binoculars to the theater, the better to see Nicole Kidman's bare buttocks. Michael Jordan becomes the top celebrity endorser, while Dennis Rodman is dumped as a TV pitchman. The removal of Pamela Lee's breast implants generates worldwide interest. A crazed fan in a restaurant asks Ron Howard, "Can I have your chicken bones?" And Monica Lewinsky—the *New York Post* calls her "the portly pepperpot" and the *Globe* refers to her as "the tubby temptress"—has come to represent the ultimate triumph of notoriety over talent. Yes, some day everybody's name will be in boldface type.

When my autobiography was published, I was a guest on *Late Night* with Conan O'Brien. Since I was scheduled to do a reading immediately after the show was taped that afternoon, NBC arranged for a limousine to take me downtown. That morning, there had been an article about me in the *New York Daily News*, and now a group of strangers was waiting along with the uniformed driver for me to exit the stage entrance.

A few people asked for my autograph. Then an attractive woman requested to have her photo taken with me. The presence of her friend's camera automatically gave us strangers permission to put our arms around each other. A man walking down the street observed this whole scene and realized that there was a celebrity in sight. So, when this photo-op was over, he approached the woman who was posing with me and asked for *her* autograph. As the limo drove away, I looked out the window. She was signing her name.

And, simultaneously, restoring my perspective.

the house that frank destroyed

Frank Sinatra would have been 86 on December 12, 2001, a date canonically designated as "Sinatra Day" in Nevada this year by Lt. Gov. Lorraine Hunt and Las Vegas Mayor Oscar Goodman. Also, 50 years after his debut at the Desert Inn resort, a new slot machine called "Sinatra Slots" has been introduced by International Game Technology. The dollar machine pays a progressive jackpot of up to $500,000 and features sound bites of Sinatra singing some of his hit songs, including "Fly Me to the Moon" and "My Kind of Town."

The marker on Sinatra's grave in the Palm Springs Cemetery District bears an epitaph, "The best is yet to come." At Wolfson Park on Frank Sinatra Drive in Rancho Mirage, you can push a button and you'll hear Sinatra's voice describing the area. At Livreri's Italian Restaurant in Palm Springs, Phil Moody and the Moody Singers perform "A Swinging Salute to Sinatra" in a cabaret room. And in Palm Desert, at Castelli's Andreino's, Joe Jaggi sings, in the words of one local critic, "more like Sinatra than the early Sinatra did."

When I was in my pre-adolescence, Frank Sinatra became my role model after he made a short film, *The House I Live In*, decrying prejudice. The lyrics of the title song summed it up: "All races, all religions, that's America to me"—I had a new hero—"The right to speak my mind out, that's America to me."

I would sing his love songs to myself: "Saturday night is the loneliest night of the week" and "It was just a ride on a train, that's all that it was, but, oh, what it seemed to be." I even went to a masquerade party as Sinatra—wearing an oversized bow tie, padded shoulders and pegged pants, and crooning into my broom-*cum*-microphone. I won first prize.

From then on I continued to comb my hair like his, with a blatant pompadour.

However, I became disillusioned with Sinatra in 1960. He fired Albert Maltz at the request of Joseph Kennedy, whose son was running for president. Maltz was the pilot case of the House UnAmerican Activities Committee in seeking contempt-of-Congress citations against Hollywood's "Unfriendly Ten" in 1947.

Maltz's novel *The Cross and the Arrow* was issued in a special edition of 140,000 copies by a wartime government agency for American servicemen abroad. His film *The Pride of the Marines* was premiered in 28 cities at Guadalcanal Day banquets under the auspices of the Marine Corps. His film *Destination Tokyo* was premiered aboard a U.S. submarine and adopted by the Navy as an official training film.

Yet this was the man considered too subversive to write the screenplay for Sinatra's movie production of William Bradford Huie's nonfiction book, *The Execution of Private Slovik.*

Maltz had said in a statement to the UnAmerican Activities Committee that he and others had been refused "the opportunity that any pickpocket receives in a magistrate's court—the right to cross-examine these witnesses, to refute their testimony, to reveal their motives, their history, and who, exactly, they are. . . .

"In common with many Americans, I supported the New Deal [which, according to Chairman J. Parnell Thomas, was 'working along hand in glove with the Communist Party']. In common with many Americans, I supported, against Mr. Thomas and [co-chairman] Mr. Rankin, the anti-lynching bill. I opposed them in my support of OPA [price] controls and emergency veteran housing and a fair employment practices law. . . .

"I will not be dictated to or intimidated by men to whom the Ku Klux Klan, as a matter of Committee record, is an acceptable American institution. . . ."

Sinatra was on Maltz's side in those days. He asked, "Once they get the movies throttled, how long will it be before the Committee goes to work on freedom of the air? How long will it be before we're told what we can and cannot say into a radio microphone? If you make a pitch on a nationwide network for a square deal for the underdog, will they call you a Commie? Will we have to think Mr. Rankin's way to get in the elevator at Radio City? Are they gonna scare us into silence? I wonder."

Sinatra needed to wonder no more. He himself silenced Albert Maltz—the man who wrote *The House I Live In.*

the war on
non-corporate
drugs

When Jack Herer (rhymes with *terror*) was a kid growing up in Buffalo, any time the Herer family visited his grandmother in Brooklyn, there were so many cockroaches permanently residing in her home that the whole family would always stay at the Edison Hotel instead. But now, in California, even though he lives in a funky little Van Nuys apartment that is a monument to clutter, there is not a single roach to be found, not even the smokable kind, since Herer uses a pipe.

He credits this bug-free environment to Borax, which he praises with such enthusiasm that you'd think he was talking about his *true* passion— the multifarious benefits of hemp. Indeed, whenever the phone rings, anyone in the household—Jack, his girlfriend Jeannie Hawkins, his son B.J., his daughters River and Chanci, or his assistant Thelma Malone— answers not by saying "Hello" but "Hemp."

Herer is wearing the same T-shirt that he wears every day, one of an identical dozen proclaiming "HEMP: Help Eliminate Marijuana Prohibition," and on the flip side, "Hemp for the Overall Majority for Earth's Paper, Fiber, Fuel." The T-shirt also prominently displays his jelly belly, which 20-year-old River leans against and sinks into, smiling.

"He's very lovable," she tells me. "Growing up with my father, I was a little bit rebellious. I'm just growing into being a part of the family now, accepting everything." River split time between her dad and mom, Vanetta, who raised her and her siblings in Portland, Oregon.

"Through the years," says 16-year-old B.J., "a lot of people have persecuted my dad. He could have given up 20 years ago. They said his information was wrong, but he stuck with it. That's very admirable."

Over tuna on rye and matzoh ball soup from a local deli, there is speculation among the extended family hanging out in the apartment as to who would be the best actor to play Herer in a movie. John Travolta? Jack Nicholson? Marlon Brando? The 58-year-old self-styled "hemperor" likes the idea of Brando, but contends that the actor "would have to take off some weight first."

•   •   •

Jack Herer first started smoking pot when he was 30 years old. That was the summer of 1969, and his life would never be the same. Everything was immeasurably enhanced—eating food, making love, listening to music—so it was absolutely understandable that Herer, who is a decidedly sharing kind of guy, started dealing marijuana in the spring of 1970.

Four years later, "Captain" Ed Adair, Herer's ally in the marketing of counterculture posters, tie-dyed clothes and general head gear, insisted that they take a joint oath: "We swear by our life, and our love for it, that we will work every day of our lives, all day, all night, to legalize pot—until we're dead, or it's legal, or we can quit when we've turned 84."

The more Herer learned about marijuana and about the suppressed history of hemp, the angrier he became that he had never heard of any of it during his entire formal and informal education. Herer became a stoned Talmudic scholar, and his mantra was "Paper-Fiber-Fuel."

In May 1980, he began a series of protests on the front lawn of the Los Angeles Federal Building in Westwood that would last for as many as 100 days at a time. The demonstrators would feed, clothe and provide portable bathrooms for petitioners attempting to get legalization initiatives on the local and state ballots.

On the flagpole they would hang a huge marijuana-leaf flag right underneath the American flag. The local and federal police were friendly and trusting. Often, instead of busting drunks, the cops would drop them off to sober up with the pot protesters.

One morning in January 1981, President-elect Ronald Reagan came to Westwood. It was five days before his inauguration, and he needed a haircut from his favorite barber. With his entourage of Secret Service agents, Reagan visited the Federal Building.

"You're doing a fine job," he told the manager, "and I want you to know that you can bring any of your problems to us. Incidentally, why are those Canadians on the lawn?"

Reagan had mistaken the five-pointed hemp leaf for the maple leaf that is featured on the Canadian flag.

"They're not Canadians," the building manager explained. "Those are the marijuana protesters, and they live down there 24 hours a day."

"Well," said Reagan, "I'll be on the job in a few days, and I'll see what I can do for you."

The above dialogue was reported by one of the secretaries in the manager's office who happened to support the marijuana initiative. Evenings after work she got high with the demonstrators and let them take showers at her home.

A week later, after only two days in office, amidst celebrating the return of the State Department hostages from Iran, Reagan reissued a World War II anti-sabotage act that had originally been passed in 1943 as a wartime measure to prohibit anyone, such as saboteurs, from being on federal property after regular business hours. Thus, Herer and five others were arrested for registering voters on federal property after dark.

Unlike his five cohorts, Herer refused to accept a year of unsupervised probation and pay the maximum fine of $5. That was the original amount specified, since the law was reenacted so hastily that federal authorities had neglected to adjust the fine for inflation.

In court, Federal Judge Malcolm Lucas (a Nixon appointee, later named Chief Justice of the California Supreme Court by his former law partner, then-Governor George Deukmejian) asked the supervising officer, "Now, what were these people doing there all night long?"

"Registering voters and listening to music."

"Oh? What kind of music?"

"Things like the Grateful Dead."

Whereupon the judge suddenly stood up and roared, "I threw my own son out of the house in 1975 for listening to them. As far as I'm concerned, the Grateful Dead would be better off Appreciably Deceased!" He then sentenced Herer to spend 14 days in jail.

In his defense, Herer told Judge Lucas, "I can't think of a higher honor that I could ever have in my life than going to jail for registering voters after dark on federal property at the busiest intersection in the country. If I'm not willing to do that, how can I call myself an American?"

Herer appealed his conviction all the way to the U.S. Supreme Court, but they wouldn't hear the case. In July 1983, he served his time in the Terminal Island Federal Prison.

"It was the best thing that ever happened to me," he now declares. "I had never been given the opportunity to write so clearly and without interruption."

In that dreary cell, Herer composed an outline for a comprehensive book about hemp, which he would call *The Emperor Wears No Clothes*, after the Hans Christian Andersen fable, and subtitled *The Secret History of Hemp and the Conspiracy Against Marijuana*.

Andersen's original emperor gave his gold to swindling tailors to be made into fabric for his imperial robes, but it was stolen. Herer sees a metaphor here for the U.S. government: "It struck me as the perfect analogy for creating laws against hemp/marijuana. The most useful plant would become the most criminal." And he extends the metaphor: "Only those with pure eyes could see that the clothes were not made of gold."

In his jail cell, Herer scribbled notes, based on original treatises he had written and published about hemp, titled *Everything You Should've Learned About Marijuana, But Weren't Taught in School*. That outline turned into the first edition of *The Emperor Wears No Clothes*, which was published in 1985.

Filled with stinging revelations about the U.S. government's six-decade war against marijuana and the suppression of America's original hemp history, the book rang as a clarion call for activists to reverse the policies that had resulted in millions of arrests over the years, and to relearn the story of why this plant, with so many beneficial uses, had been prohibited for so long. It was a manifesto that would turn on a generation to the truth.

Self-published, without major distributors, wholesalers, advertising or reviews, *The Emperor Wears No Clothes* became an underground best-seller: 400,000 copies were promptly sold in the U.S., mostly on college campuses during Herer's hemp tours in the late '80s and early '90s; another 250,000 copies of translated editions were sold in Germany (150,000), France, England, Italy, Japan and Australia. Additional translations would be published in Spain, Poland and Greece.

•   •   •

There are cynics who wonder whether Jack Herer is merely a toker in the guise of an activist, using hemp education as a smokescreen for marijuana legalization.

"I'm usually accused by people who are ignorant and don't believe that hemp is the number-one source of paper, fiber and fuel on earth," he responds.

So it was especially ironic when 70 representatives of hemp-related businesses met in Arizona in 1995 to launch the Hemp Industries

Association. Although most attendees cited Herer as their primary inspiration, they didn't want a public image that would link their livelihood
with dope-smokers.

"I'm sorry," he announced at the conference that sought his blessing, "but I just keep thinking about the 130,000 people currently incar-
cerated in the U.S. for cannabis. People just like us, who hung out
enjoying a joint just like we're doing right now. Wouldn't it be great to
teach the hemp information to everyone and put down this inquisition
once and for all?"

Three years later, with the controversy having simmered down, Herer
said, "Captain Ed Adair and I thought people would learn to make paper
and fiber and clothing and different elements of food, and they would
get into businesses and compete with each other and they'd find little
niches for themselves. Captain Ed and I were so proud that we had helped
start all these hemp businesses. But what's happened is that the majority of those people have decided, 'We're not here to legalize marijuana,
we just want to legalize clothing. We're only interested in one-percent-
THC plants.'

"So now, if we ever get any of these laws passed, we'll have to save
the world with a plant that's inadequate. Every time I run into one of
these guys that swears they're only doing it for hemp—and they used to
smoke bowls with me—they're only looking to save their little portion
of a business, and they're afraid that big businesses are going to get in
there and run them out. Well, tough shit."

• • •

His partner in hemp, Captain Ed, died in 1991, but Jack Herer goes
on and on, like the Energizer Bunny on ginseng.

In 1993, he attended the sixth annual Cannabis Cup in Amsterdam,
where he received a lifetime achievement award. On his return, Customs
officials at the airport in Los Angeles couldn't help but notice the
"Possible DEA Suspect" notation next to his name on the computer
screen. Which is why every time Herer reenters the U.S., he is stopped
and searched.

Four agents detained him for three hours, and even though their
narco-dog couldn't sniff out anything, with an artist's miniature paint-
brush they were able to scrape up less than one-half a gram of pot, not
enough to roll a thin joint, encrusted in lint at the bottom of his pants
and jacket pockets. They threatened to lift his passport unless he gave

them $10,000. They finally settled for $500. A sardonic Customs agent directed Jack's attention to a sign on the wall that warned, "Zero Tolerance." It said nothing about extortion.

The following year, at the seventh annual Cannabis Cup, Sensi Seeds produced a new strain of marijuana, four years in development, which they christened "Jack Herer."

"It's like Robert Burns tobacco," Herer muses, "or Baron de Rothschild wines, or even right up there with—eat your heart out, Ernest and Julio Gallo—long after I've died, people will be smoking Jack Herer."

Yes, we pluck no weed before its time. Out of 28 brands of sinsemilla competing for the Cup, 700 judges voted "Jack Herer" *Numero Uno* in virtually all categories, yet he couldn't even bring home a baggie of his own namesake marijuana. This time, though, when Herer's name came up on the computer at JFK Airport, the Customs supervisor asked, "Why do they want to search you so bad?"

"Probably because I'm the leader of the California hemp movement," he said, matter-of-factly. "So go ahead, turn my pockets inside out. I stayed up all night cleaning them. I'm all prepared."

For the first time in all his travels, he was let go by Customs without a search.

• • •

George Clayton Johnson, who wrote the screenplays for [the original] *Ocean's Eleven* and *Logan's Run* as well as the premiere episode of *Star Trek* and a number of classic *Twilight Zone* scripts, told me, "There are very few men in their own century who will probably be called great men. Martin Luther King was a great man. Some men have great power, but they're not truly great men. I think that Jack Herer, like Emile Zola or Thomas Paine, will prove to be a great man. Jack is a force of nature."

Herer totally believes that we can save the world by replacing all environmentally deleterious products with hemp. Of course, some people—like those who think the concept of global warming is a left-wing conspiracy—view him as a cannabis-crazed zealot.

Several years ago, at a conference held by the Drug Policy Foundation —a respectable drug-reform organization based in Washington, D.C.— former presidential candidate George McGovern and economist Milton Friedman received awards. Herer approached them, and upon learning that neither one knew anything about hemp, he proceeded to delineate its facts and virtues.

"The way they were looking at me," he recalls, "I realized that to them I was insane. But I think it's *literally* insane to *outlaw* hemp and keep our mouths shut about the stupidity."

But in 1994, to his surprise, Herer—once a thorn in the side of the Drug Policy Foundation—was presented with an award for activism at their annual conference. He delivered his acceptance speech wearing a green 100 percent hemp suit, a hemp shirt and tie, hemp hat and sneakers, even a hemp wallet and, underneath, that same HEMP T-shirt he wears every day.

Herer said that he was accepting his award for Captain Ed, too. He neglected, however, to thank Ronald Reagan.

checkmating with pawns

It was a hot day at the chess tournament in Phoenix, Arizona—103 degrees, to be exact—and 14-year-old Nathaniel Dight was elated over his custom-made chess set. Those carved wooden pieces had been weighted precisely for the smooth moves he liked to make. Each one had been lacquered and, for this extreme heat, carefully protected by matte acrylic spray. But before the game could begin, young Nathaniel was ordered to take a urine test.

"I know why you're doing this," he snarled. "It's because I've won three tournaments in a row, isn't it?"

"No, son, that's just a coincidence. This is a random drug test."

"I don't do any drugs. I mean like when I get a headache from playing chess too long, I won't even take an aspirin."

"Look, here's a cup. I need you to go fill it, right now. . . ."

All right, I confess, I made all that up, but consider the implications of something that I *haven't* made up.

America's drug czar, Barry McCaffrey, wrote in an article published in *Chess Life* magazine: "Research proves that mentoring youngsters and teaching them games like chess can build resilience in the face of illegal drug use and other destructive temptations. Drug testing is as appropriate for chess players as for shot-putters, or any other competitors who use their heads as well as their hands."

Accompanying the television image of a couple of eggs sizzling in a frying pan, the phrase "This is your brain on drugs" has always carried negative connotations, but apparently General McCaffrey has changed his mind about that. He now seems to believe that drugs can actually *improve* the way your brain functions.

There was an infamous chess player named Alexander Alekhine who held the world championship longer than anybody else. His games often had superb surprise endings, known in chess circles as "brilliancies." For instance, he would checkmate with a pawn move that no sane and sober mind could ever imagine. However, he was a notorious alcoholic, and McCaffrey is only referring to illegal drugs.

"Just when I thought I'd heard it all from McCaffrey," was the reaction of Allen St. Pierre, executive director of the NORML (National Organization for the Reform of Marijuana Laws) Foundation. "Drug testing for chess players? What's next from this overreaching drug czar? Drug testing for tiddlywinks players? How about bingo players?"

Moreover, McCaffrey's proposal smacks of subliminal racism. Social psychologist Walli Leff told me, "I think most of the movement to involve young people in chess is directed toward the African-American community, and the assumption is, if the kids are black they're going to be drug users. I think white middle-class suburban parents would have a fit if their kids had to take drug tests for their extracurricular activities. Or am I out of it and am I missing a new, white middle-class, suburban submissiveness?"

McCaffrey had been influenced by Chesschild, a group sponsored by the Office of National Drug Control Policy (ONDCP). Chesschild is a substance abuse prevention program conducted in libraries and schools, promoting a combination of drug-free lifestyles and chess.

"Policy recommendations like this one from ONDCP," said St. Pierre, "demonstrate a deep and disturbing pathology that goes well beyond opposing drug-law reform efforts."

Maybe the drug-law reformers should follow the example of gay-rights activists by having celebrities come out of the pot-smoking closet. Already, veteran stand-up comic George Carlin—in an interview by the *Daily Show's* Jon Stewart following Carlin's HBO special—admitted that he smokes a joint to help him "fine-tune" his material. "One hit is all I need now and it's punch-up time."

At the Shadow Convention that took place while the Democrats were in Los Angeles, Bill Maher revealed to the audience, "I'm not just a pot reformer, I'm a user"—something which ABC forbids him to say on *Politically Incorrect*—then quickly added, "Just making a light remark there, federal authorities."

Actor and hemp activist Woody Harrelson has stated, "I do smoke." Willie Nelson confirmed in his autobiography that he smoked pot in the White House. And on KRLA radio talk-show host Michael Jackson's program, Michelle Phillips, actress and former member of the Mamas and the Papas, said that she still enjoys smoking marijuana.

Just as Ellen DeGeneres appeared on the cover of *Time* magazine saying, "Yep, I'm gay," there might come a day when a presidential candidate will appear on the cover of *Newsweek* saying, "Yep, I'm stoned." Isn't that what young pot-smokers need—good role models—so they won't be ashamed of their private pleasure seeking?

Meanwhile, drug czar McCaffrey would continue his crusade, not only against illegal substances, but perhaps also against certain food supplements, such as a popular herbal mixture with a reputation for aiding memory and concentration. Who could ever have dreamed that chess players might get in trouble for using ginkgo biloba as a performance enhancer?

ask your doctor

Although I believe that medical checkups are the main cause of disease, I recently went for a medical checkup anyway. The doctor wondered why I was in such good shape.

"I never take any legal drugs," I explained.

"Well," he responded, "whatever works for you."

But prescription drugs—a $100-billion industry—have become such an integral part of the culture that Viagra and Prozac were actually included in a time capsule commemorating the 150th birthday of Yolo County, California. And users of Prilosec can get a free subscription to the *Prilosec Newsletter*.

Prilosec, a medicine for heartburn, is the world's best-selling drug. You can be sure, though, that their newsletter will never mention the fact that, though the cost of Prilosec in the United States is $3.30 a pill, it's $1.47 in Canada. And Prilosec is just one among many such rip-offs. No wonder there are now organized prescription-shopping excursions— or, as senior citizens refer to such trips, "drug runs"—across the border by chartered bus.

Pharmaceutical companies spend $1.3 billion a year on TV commercials for prescription drugs. By comparison, beer companies spend only $763.6 million. Marketing prescription drugs directly to consumers is permitted only in America. The game is to advise viewers to "Ask your doctor about such-and-such." This method of manipulation has proved to be extremely successful. According to *Prevention* magazine, in just one year 55 million patients asked their doctors about drugs they'd seen advertised, and doctors wrote prescriptions 84 percent of the time they were asked.

The ads for prescription drugs are so schmaltzy that even their side effects sound glamorous, yet they can be more dangerous than the diseases whose symptoms they purport to treat. The FDA at first sided with the manufacturer and minimized the hazards of Lotronex, a popular prescription for irritable bowel syndrome, but later decided to reevaluate its safety after five women who took Lotronex died as a result while 49 others developed ischemic colitis, a potentially life-threatening complication.

The diabetes pill Rezulin—which, like Lotronex, gained huge sales via fast-track approval by the FDA—was banned after 63 liver-failure deaths. In the last three years, the FDA has had to withdraw nine drugs from the market because of deaths and injuries. Anyone who takes Accutane, a powerful drug for acne, now finds attached to the bottle a special warning brochure outlining side effects—including a possible link to suicide. They must then sign a paper certifying that they understand the risks.

Prozac has no such requirement, but an investigation by the *Boston Globe* revealed that "One in 100 previously non-suicidal patients who took the drug in early clinical trials developed a severe form of anxiety causing them to attempt or commit suicide during the studies."

A study by Dr. David Healy, a brain chemistry expert at the University of Wales, indicates that 50,000 people have committed suicide on Prozac, people who would not have taken their lives if they hadn't been on the drug. And yet Eli Lilly halted development of a new and improved version of Prozac, its top-selling drug. The patent for the new formula, which cost Lilly $90 million, claimed to reduce "the usual adverse effects" of the original Prozac, including "nervousness, anxiety, insomnia, inner restlessness, suicidal thoughts, self-mutilation, manic behavior."

Why, it makes you want to take Prozac merely to get rid of the side effects brought about by taking Prozac. In October 2000, Arianna Huffington wrote, in a column the *Los Angeles Times* chose not to publish, but which she e-mailed to me:

"Almost from the time it was introduced in 1988, Lilly has been maniacally denying claims that Prozac produces violent or suicidal reactions. Could the recent startling reversal have anything to do with the fact that Prozac's extremely profitable patent—which brought Lilly $2.6 billion last year—was set to expire in 2004? What's more, just this August, a federal appeals court shortened Lilly's exclusive patent by three years, allowing generic versions of the mega-drug to hit the shelves next summer.

"The damning admissions in the enhanced Prozac's patent will be the center of a federal lawsuit scheduled to go on trial in Hawaii next summer. This will be the latest round in a legal battle initiated by the children of a man who, while on Prozac, fatally stabbed his wife and then himself. During the first trial, Lilly's lawyers and witnesses repeatedly claimed that violent or suicidal acts are not a side effect of Prozac.

"In fact, the president of Lilly's neuroscience product group, Dr. Garry Tollefson, testified under oath: 'There is absolutely no medically sound evidence of an association between Prozac and the induction of suicidal ideation or violence.' Clearly impressed with such expert testimony, the jury found the drug company not liable for the murder-suicide. The latest suit charges that 'a fraud was committed on the court' when Lilly failed to disclose the potentially explosive data contained in the patent [for the new and improved version of Prozac], which it had purchased three months before the first trial began."

Put *that* in your time capsule and smoke it.

I thought it would be appropriate to discuss this trend—ads telling people to ask their doctor about prescription drugs which have harmful side effects—with Scott Imler, president of the Los Angeles Cannabis Resource Cooperative.

"Gee," he mused, "can you imagine if *we* had ads like that advertising our services and products? And I agree with you, I think some of the side effects sound really scary, like don't touch a broken pill if you're pregnant. Don't get your Rogaine and your Viagra mixed up. Jeffrey [the staff horticulturist] came in one morning and his hair was standing up."

This was a week before the election, I'm writing this a month *after* the election and still, only Wavy Gravy's candidate for president—Nobody—has won. On Scott Imler's desk was a copy of *Time* with Al Gore and George W. Bush on the cover.

"The interesting thing about this prescription drug plan that they both have," Imler observed, "it just seems like welfare for the pharmaceutical companies, just guaranteed income right from your pocket to theirs. 'Prescription drug plan.' 'Ask your doctor today.' And what's interesting is a lot of people, with marijuana, *do* ask their doctor, and a lot of people that come to us are like, 'Do you know a doctor I *can* ask?'"

As for me, I plan to go for another medical checkup with a whole *list* of prescription drugs that TV commercials have advised me to ask my doctor about. My favorite is Pravachol, which promises to prevent your first and second heart attacks, so that when you get your first heart attack you'll think it's really your third.

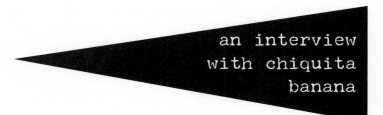

an interview
with chiquita
banana

When I was growing up, Chiquita Banana first triggered my sense of skepticism. In those days, she was just a poor street hooker with curvature of the spine, a yellow complexion and false eyelashes. She would do her sultry dance and beckon me, singing, "I'm Chiquita Banana, and I've come to say, bananas have to ripen in a certain way . . . So you should never put bananas—in the refrigerator. No-no, no-no!"

"That's bullshit," I told her. "You absolutely *can* put bananas in the refrigerator. But your corporate pimp just wants consumers to leave them out in the open to rot, so then people throw the rotten bananas away and buy a bunch of *fresh* bananas."

These days, Chiquita Banana is a very expensive call girl. Her posture has improved, she's had a full-body skin-peel and a boob job, and she lives in a lavishly furnished, post-modern, duplex condo. It seems her pimp has been awarded a settlement of $10 million in a lawsuit. The *Cincinnati Enquirer* had published a series detailing inhumane labor conditions and environmental crimes by Chiquita's pimp, and the paper was sued—not because it reported anything that was untrue, but only because it intercepted internal voice mail in obtaining its documentation.

I began our interview on that note.

Q. "Chiquita, let me ask, which do you think is worse—the invasion of your pimp's privacy or his running a business that involves third-world slavery, deforestation, poisonous residues, intimidation by thugs, bribery—"

A. "I'm sorry, Paul, but the attorneys won't allow any discussion about that subject. I mean, even though our suit was settled with the *Cincinnati Enquirer*, we're still under investigation by the government."

Q. "Okay. When Honduras was severely struck by Hurricane Mitch, international environmental activists reported that the death and devastation were made worse by deforestation and destruction of animal habitats to make way for banana plantations—"

A. "Excuse me, in the first place, Hurricane Mitch was certainly not *our* fault. And I'll have you know that we sent *aid* to Honduras."

Q. "No, Chiquita, what I'm saying is that it was the policies of your pimp that led to much of the destruction. And he didn't just send aid to Honduras. When Bill Clinton ran against Bob Dole back in 1996, your pimp sent huge bribes—oops, I mean mega-contributions—to *both* of them. And it worked. You got favors from the government. Clinton's people went to Geneva for World Trade Organization authority to impose tariffs on European products, and this was done on your pimp's behalf."

A. "Paul, you've changed. Why are you so hostile? You know something, I'll bet it was *you* who was behind that Internet hoax, warning everybody about bananas from Costa Rica being infected with flesh-eating bacteria. That false information went around the *world*. We were saddled with a rather challenging public-relations problem."

Q. "No, it wasn't me, I swear. And I'm not hostile, I'm just disappointed that you would lend your image to this trade dispute over bananas between the United States and Europe. The U.S. is fighting to end preferential treatment for Caribbean bananas in Europe. And Caribbean nations are watching this battle in total fear, because it would desolate their tiny economies, and banana farmers would have no choice but to cultivate marijuana instead—they're already making that switch—and then their marijuana fields become the target of American eradication projects."

A. "You know what? I'm gonna roll a joint, and we're gonna smoke it, I'm gonna put on some music, I'm gonna light some incense, and you, you're gonna mellow out, and *then* we'll continue talking. . . ."

[*A half-hour later*]

Q. "I'm so zonked out. That sure is powerful weed."

A. "Bananas aren't the only thing we grow, sweetie pie. In fact, marijuana is a much more lucrative crop, did you know that?"

Q. "I'm not surprised. But try to see this from the *poor* banana farmers' point of view. America provides weapons, machinery and manpower to destroy their little pot farms, and yet America is also trying to deprive them of the European market for bananas. Don't you think that this kind of unfair competition interferes in the internal affairs of other countries?"

A. "Honey, I'm so stoned I don't know *what* the fuck you're talking about. Why don't you just interfere with *my* internal affairs for a while?"

[*An hour later*]

Q. "Wow, you went around the world like you were false information."

A. "Well, I think you conducted a very *probing* interview."

Q. "Look, all I want you to do is at least *acknowledge* your symbolic contribution to your pimp's undue influence, which trickles down to farmers who need to be able to put bread on the table for their children to eat. It's that simple."

A. [*Singing*] "I'm Maria Marijuana and I've come to say, marijuana has to ripen in a certain way. . . . So you should never put marijuana— in the glove compartment. No-no, no-no!"

how sinsemilla came to america

Little did a certain photojournalist in Mexico know what he would be unleashing when he took a particular photo in the late 1950s. Nor did a horny 19-year-old—who was in the middle of masturbating while searching for bare-breasted African women in *National Geographic*—realize what fate would lead him to when he came upon that photo.

The full-color photo, which accompanied an article about beatniks who had left San Francisco and the Lower East Side, showed a trio of them—Zen guru Tom Newman, writer Lionel Olay and old Pancho Villa war hero Pancho Lepe—sitting around a lush green tropical paradise. They were in Yelapa.

The 19-year-old was David Wheeler. He was looking at this photo of the three grooviest-looking dudes he had ever seen. They were drinking mint tea in front of a papaya tree, and they were obviously stoned on grass. To Wheeler, that photo captured "the hippest community in the world," and in 1961 he traveled to Mexico in search of it.

In Guadalajara, he traded a '54 Ford station wagon for four horses with saddles. Then he and an Army buddy and their girlfriends took off for Yelapa. It was a treacherous, month-long journey, 380 miles across mountains. Only the two men made it all the way. The rains had beaten the color from their Levis and T-shirts into their skin. Wheeler's friend was tied over one of the now raw-boned horses because he was practically shitting himself inside out. They were saved by Indians who had never seen white men before, let alone blue ones.

Soon, even the men who were in that photo heard about these two gringos riding from Puerto Vallarta down the Mascota River through all that jungle to the coast. Wheeler's wet dream came true when Lionel Olay said, "Hey, kid, come and stay with us at Pancho Lobos."

One day Olay told him that his friend Juanito would bring something special down the hill—marijuana with no seeds. They called it *sin-ueso*—boneless grass. At a time when you could buy pressed bricks of Mexican pot in San Diego, 100 at a time for $8 a kilo, Juanito wanted $80 for a quarter-kilo. Olay came up with the money fast.

"The grass you're smoking in the states," he told Wheeler, "has about 3 percent active ingredients. This has 15 percent. They're all on the upper end. None of this laying around, drooling on yourself and give-me-more-doughnuts. You're going to want to do adventurous things."

It had a sweet smell, like no grass Wheeler had ever sniffed before. He took two hits, feeling like he was about to pass out, so he pressed his body against a post, hanging on to avoid falling down and breaking his head. Meanwhile, the others continued to smoke joints and enjoy their erudite conversation.

"Sit down," said Olay. "Watch it, that's the first time you smoked this stuff."

A year later, after smoking nothing but that stuff, he and Tom Newman went to live with the Nahuatl Indians, who lived under the glacier with the people who grew the best grass in the world. Then to Michoacan with *bigotones*—bandits with Zapata mustaches—and their Michoacan green, grown only by the Indians. But how did it get there in the first place?

An 80-year-old Indian told Wheeler a story he'd heard from his grandfather. In 1510, the explorer Hernando Cortez came there with a boatload of Moors, who laid around and drank coconut beer. But 10 of them hiked all the way to Paso de Cortez, between the two volcanoes of Vera Cruz and Tenochtitlan. Right there was where that superb grass had been grown. The Moors had brought their favorite grass, from Afghanistan, Turkey and Pakistan. They saw the most beautiful apples and figs grown by the Indians and asked if they could grow this marijuana for them. And that was the introduction of cannabis to the Western Hemisphere.

Newman got up at seven every morning, sitting in his underwear on a *serape*, meditating and smoking joints for four hours. He asked Wheeler what he wanted to do next.

"Well, I thought I'd become a holy man like you."

"No, that's not in the cards for you. I recognize your glands. I see the way you look at women. You're going to have to go through the whole householder thing, read Gurdjieff, *Siddartha*, marry, have kids, then come back."

"Bullshit. I'd rather have adventure."

"Okay, why don't you grow a ton of seedless and bring it back to the States? We spent seven months with these two tribes, learning how to recognize and kill the male plants. Why don't you bring a meaning-ful amount back to the States and fuck with the main chakra up there? Rattle some kundalini lines, which are dormant anyway."

It took two years to get it together. First, begging Indians to sell him handfuls of seeds. Then, going down the hill to search for grass traf-fickers with integrity. Planting a field and trying to explain why he would come back and destroy half the plants. Dealing with a semantic crisis: Killing the *machos* was a negative symbol to Mexicans. You don't kill the males—who's going to fight?

Finally, a ton. But Wheeler, who thought smuggling would be fun, now didn't have a clue on how to move the stuff. He sought out an expert known as Buckwheat, who fronted him $65,000. And they began to move the stuff—two kilos here, 200 kilos there—teaching people along the way. Their personal stash was four kilos of the stickiest, shini-est, psychedelic grass.

Buckwheat, who was in the music business, gave some to the Byrds at a concert and to David Crosby, who announced onstage, "I just smoked the most fantastic grass. It's called San Simeon, and it comes from right up the coast." San Simeon, of course, is the name of the famous William Randolph Hearst estate. Wheeler corrected Crosby. "That grass is *sin-semilla*, and try this here, it's Michoacan green." Crosby smoked a lit-tle, went onstage again and said, "I just smoked the best Michigan green."

And that was the start of it—at least according to David Wheeler. However, in *Deep Cover*, former DEA supervisor Michael Levine writes that Wheeler "was eager to impress me—too eager. He told stories, all of which involved him doing some outrageous, inventive or ingenious feat, usually illegal and usually in the company of some famous trafficker, corrupt politician or Hollywood star—stories, I noticed, that were dif-ficult, if not impossible, to verify. At times he spoke of things any pru-dent man—even an informer—would be silent about, such as his father's alleged CIA work. He even hinted at his own CIA connections. He seemed unafraid to claim knowledge of everything but was obviously expert at nothing.

"When he claimed responsibility for the introduction of sinsemilla to Mexico, I asked him a couple of questions about what wealth or property he had. Introducing sinsemilla to Mexico, in the drug world, was roughly equivalent to inventing the wheel. He should have earned hundreds of millions, if not billions of dollars. He spoke openly of taking part in drug deals that sounded as big as a hostile buyout of General Motors. When I learned that he was broke and that the government [Customs] was now fully supporting him and his two kids, I checked the faces of [fellow DEA agent] Hoopel and the Customs agents sitting around the room listening with rapt attention and saw not a glimmer of suspicion. He had them 100 percent conned. But then I had to admit that while his claims were wild, he hadn't really said anything that could be *proven* a lie."

Wheeler responds: "Everything Michael Levine writes is fiction, but it's all about him and his exploits. He's the most famous narc in the U.S. We did a two-year operation to sustain the governments who were bringing cocaine in. That's what I arranged, and it drove him up the wall. We used him for three weeks to play a Puerto Rican pimp in Panama. If you read Levine's book, you're reading my enemy's book."

Incidentally, speaking of outrageous feats, Wheeler claims to have been celibate for the last seven years. Does that include masturbation?

"Less and less," he says.

ritalin wars

Over 30 years ago, Yippie leader Jerry Rubin told me that he had written his book *Do It!* on Ritalin. I thought he was talking about some newfangled electric typewriter, the Ritalin. I didn't realize it was a prescription drug with speed-like qualities. On the other end of the political spectrum, conservative columnist William F. Buckley has admittedly been taking Ritalin every day for more than three decades.

Peter McWilliams once asked Buckley about it, and he replied that his doctor had said, "My blood pressure is so low that I should either take a quarter pound of chocolate in mid-afternoon, or a Ritalin. . . . But after 30 years, nobody has detected any change in me, haahahahhhhhaaaaaaa, oooooooooooooooooooooooooooooooo oooooo! Now I'm feeling quite fine, as you can see."

But that same drug seemed to have the opposite effect on young children. For over a decade, they've been given Ritalin because they have Attention Deficit Disorder (ADD). That's an imaginary disease which was invented to cover up the causes of boredom by suppressing healthy curiosity. Practically everyone I know—and most likely you, too—would be force-fed Ritalin from a Pez dispenser if we were currently attending school.

In the late 1990s, use of Ritalin by children nearly tripled. Six million schoolchildren have been diagnosed with ADD and ADHD (Attention Deficit Hyperactivity Disorder). At least two million are given Ritalin. Members of Congress have called for action to reverse the increase in Ritalin use to combat ADHD, which is characterized by a short attention span, impulsive behavior and difficulty sitting still.

When divorced parents disagree about giving their children Ritalin,

judges rule in favor of the parent who medicates a child—thereby com-
pounding authoritarian educators with authoritarian courts—despite hor-
rendous side effects and despite the fact that the long-term effects of
such drug use have never been studied.

In Albany, N.Y., a family court forced a couple to put their seven-
year-old son back on Ritalin even though, when he started second grade,
not only was the drug not helping, but the boy was eating only one meal
a day and sleeping just five hours a night. His parents had told school
officials they wanted to take him off Ritalin for two weeks and, as a result,
they were charged with child abuse—specifically, "medical neglect"—
and placed on a statewide list of child abusers.

This is not a unique situation. "Just say no" has become "Medicate
or else!" Dr. Lawrence Diller, author of *Running on Ritalin: A Physician
Reflects on Children, Society, and Performance in a Pill*, is alarmed about
this "new and troubling twist in the psychiatric drugs saga . . . public
schools have begun to issue ultimatums to parents of hard-to-handle
kids, saying they will not allow students to attend conventional classes
unless they are medicated. Parents unwilling to give their kids drugs are
being reported by their schools to local offices of Child Protective Services,
the implication being that by withholding drugs, the parents are guilty
of neglect."

Moreover, an estimated 90 percent of ADD and ADHD cases were
unjustified diagnoses in the first place, according to syndicated radio host
Dr. Dean Edell. "They're better behaved," he observed, "but that's not
solving the problem, which could be a personality clash between a teacher
and a student." He added that those who take Ritalin are "more likely
to use this class of drugs." In fact, a study at UC-Berkeley tracked 500
children for 25 years and found that the use of Ritalin in treating ADHD
doubles the risk that a child will later smoke tobacco, snort cocaine or
take prescribed stimulants.

USA Today editorialized: "Absent evidence that the lives of children
are at stake when they're not on Ritalin, no arm of the state should be
ramming the drug treatment down parents' and childrens' throats." And
the *Las Vegas Review-Journal*: "The underlying problem here is the notion
that children belong first to the state, that biological parents are allowed
to retain custody only at the discretion of school and 'child welfare' officials, who after all have professional diplomas, and thus know best. No
free country can long operate under such a presumption, with its inevitably
corrosive effect on the family."

Class-action lawsuits have been filed in New Jersey and California, claiming that the manufacturers of Ritalin conspired with the American Psychiatric Association (APA) to inflate the drug's potential market— conspired, in the words of the complaint, to "create" a disease—then later hyped the drug's ability to counteract that disease in order to boost sales and profits. The makers of Ritalin are accused of working with the APA to include the diagnosis of the two diseases in the standard medical text used by doctors.

BBC News reports that "Treatment rates for hyperactivity in some American schools are as high as 30% to 40% of a class, and children as young as one have been known to have been given the drug." Yet, psychiatrist Peter Breggin, author of *Talking Back to Ritalin: What Doctors Aren't Telling You About Stimulants for Children*, writes that "Ritalin does not correct biochemical imbalances—it causes them." He says there is evidence that Ritalin can cause permanent damage to a child's brain.

In *The Indigo Children*, Lee Carroll and Jan Tober agree that "some children may have calmed down and may have conformed, but was it because their 'evolved consciousness' was numbed out?" The authors present several alternatives to Ritalin, from herbal and nutritional supplements to biofeedback and neurotherapy. Also check out Mary Ann Block's *No More Ritalin: Treating ADHD Without Drugs*.

Finally, there's a tremendous irony to all this Ritalin use among schoolchildren. It is now on the DEA's Top 10 list of the most often stolen prescription drugs. Young hustlers in cities across the country manage to score large supplies of the drug and are selling those pills to other students. That's against the law, of course. But will there soon be a national epidemic of faked hyperactivity by kids who just want to get legally high?

plan humboldt

All right, class, today we're going to focus on the Great Drug War at the turn of this century, specifically the notorious Plan Humboldt, a counter-narcotics and crop-substitution program funded by the government of Colombia.

It seems that, because the Colombian people enjoy smoking the highly potent marijuana grown in Humboldt County, the Colombian government funded $1.3 billion to help the United States stop the flow, including herbicide spraying at the source.

But the herbicides were sprayed so indiscriminately that not only were the targeted marijuana fields destroyed, but food crops across northern California were also wiped out. Furthermore, the natural environment was being stripped bare, and a film of poison permeated the water, the animals and human beings. It became common for children in the state to develop skin rashes, along with other symptoms of pesticide poisoning such as headaches, dizziness, diarrhea and nausea.

Finally, Amnesty International persuaded former president Jimmy Carter to conduct an independent inquiry. His investigators learned that those Americans who were flying helicopters for CAMP—the Campaign Against Marijuana Production, which for many years had been waging war on Humboldt's growers—were actually under the supervision of combat-trained, so-called "advisers" from Colombia.

At a press conference, investigators charged that Colombian-supplied technology could not distinguish between legal and illegal cultivation. This was particularly ironic, since Colombia had funded the substitution of legal crops to be grown by Humboldt farmers, in the

hope of disengaging them from dependence on income from marijuana—
and now these substitute crops were being destroyed with equal-oppor-
tunity recklessness.

However, the U.S. government would only release statistics about
marijuana crops—boasting, for example, that 65,000 acres of marijuana-
growing land had been ruined during one particular six-week eradication campaign by Colombian-trained troops and police.

But this destruction was no longer going to be allowed without anyone fighting back. A group known as Anarchists Without Borders (AWB)
would soon begin waging guerrilla warfare, gathering enthusiastic sup-
porters in such cities as Mendocino, Ukiah and Eureka—all seriously
affected by the spraying—as the Anarchists wended their way southward
from Seattle.

On the East Coast, it was a member of Friends of the AWB who
managed to shmush a tofu cream pie in the face of Tom Brokaw. In an
interview with Attorney General John Ashcroft, the NBC news anchor
had left unchallenged Ashcroft's false assertion:

"Our eradication program relies on state-of-the-art Colombian satellite intelligence and other electronically gathered data, along with human
intelligence obtained from aerial surveillance of areas with marijuana cultivation. There is absolutely no possibility that any aircraft flown by the
Drug Enforcement Agency can spray over legal crops or populated zones."

That he was spouting a lie could easily have been attested to by the
thousands of farmers who had been growing legal crops in California,
Washington and Oregon, only to lose their livelihoods as a result of the
widespread aerial fumigation.

Meanwhile, the president of Colombia, Andres Pastrana, expressed
his own concern that Colombian personnel had become involved in the
Humboldt County battle, rescuing the crew of a crop duster which had
been brought down by the AWB with small-arms fire.

The pilot—a DEA operative flying a Colombian-supplied aircraft—
was hit in the barrage, but he managed to land. Two helicopter gun-
ships circled above, firing on the AWB while the crew of a third helicopter
rescued the crew. The pilot of that ship, a Colombian, was wounded,
almost fatally.

"If Colombian military advisers start dying while carrying out Plan
Humboldt," President Pastrana announced, "the Colombian people simply will not allow that to continue."

Still, he refused to answer any questions that reporters asked about the AWB claims that Colombia's principal interest in Humboldt was not the marijuana farms, but the oil, which was running out in Colombia, yet was so abundant in northwest America. Not until Colombian oil companies started drilling—despite the protestations of native Americans in the region—did Pastrana admit to his government's ulterior motives.

Right-wing death squads from Michigan and Montana escalated the situation. Serving as vigilante armies, these mercenaries slaughtered innocent American civilians. They were paramilitary outfits financed by organized crime, pot-plantation owners and linked to the American military being trained for jungle warfare by Colombian forces.

Moreover, investigative journalists discovered that in Colombia, defense contractors were the primary lobbyists for Plan Humboldt, which included 30 helicopters that had been delivered to the States.

But George W. Bush took it all in stride. He insisted that the 300 Colombian troops deployed in Humboldt County were there to train the U.S. counter-narcotics battalions, not to fight the AWB guerrillas. As for Colombian fatalities in California, they were disguised as accidental. Their bodies were flown back to Colombia, where helicopter crashes and car wrecks were staged to account for the deaths.

Even as the American president accepted Colombian funding—and, in the process, ignored the takeover of American oil fields by Colombian multinational corporations—he criticized the Colombian government for not being successful in cutting down the insatiable demand for Humboldt's extra-strength marijuana.

false alarm

It was one of those rare occasions when my wife Nancy and I could take off for a weekend vacation in the desert. I made sure to bring our favorite designer drug, Ecstasy, along with marijuana, snacks, vitamins and bottled water. In our room at the spa, we smoked a joint to ease us into the Ecstasy, then swallowed our capsules. We hung out, soaking in the hot-springs pool with a beautiful view of the mountains as we got higher and higher.

Because taking Ecstasy is such a sensual and loving experience, there is an agonizing irony about its distribution. Just as the Mafia began distributing LSD in the '60s, so has organized crime—the pinnacle of mayhem and murder—been distributing Ecstasy. Thus, Salvatore "Sammy the Bull" Gravano, former hit man and government snitch responsible for the imprisonment of mob boss John Gotti, got a dose of his own medicine when he was arrested and convicted.

Although the DEA declared Ecstasy (MDMA) illegal in 1985, its popularity has been increasing steadily—one out of 12 high-school seniors has tried Ecstasy—and it is the drug of choice at rave parties. But, just as there was hysterical media panic in the '60s about brain damage caused by LSD, there is now the same kind of propaganda being spread about Ecstasy.

Recently, *60 Minutes* presented a 12-minute documentary on Ecstasy, featuring material intended to scare the living shit out of viewers, including footage of a young man who had gone into a coma and died as a result of taking five hits of Ecstasy.

Not included was footage of Ecstasy pioneers Sasha and Anne

Shulgin—despite an extensive interview with them—or any mention of the therapeutic and medicinal uses of MDMA. Also omitted was the footage of the Dutch government's national drug prosecutor saying that pill-testing "saves lives," and the interview with Trinka Poratta, former Los Angeles police officer and National Police Consultant on Dance Drugs, who expressed her support for harm reduction and on-site pill-testing, specifically by DanceSafe.

Emanuel Sferios of DanceSafe was interviewed for two hours, two minutes of which appeared on the program, with him talking about harm reduction. He was depicted testing pills at a rave, and the DanceSafe Web site was shown.

"In short," he says, "they chose to portray us as the lone representative of harm reduction, with no support from police or policy makers. This is unfortunate and grossly inaccurate but not entirely unexpected. Prime-time television likes controversy. We are and were aware of that. Our choice to work with *60 Minutes* was based on a recognition that, at this point in time, national press coverage on raves and Ecstasy that mentions harm reduction is better than no mention at all.

"Now don't get me wrong. It was a ridiculous, overly alarmist and totally sensationalistic hit piece on Ecstasy, but this is what made DanceSafe and harm reduction look so reasonable. The undercover Orlando police officer, Mike Stevens, came across as over-zealous and ideological, whereas we came across as pragmatic and reasonable. You could hear the emotion in his voice as he spoke—'Ecstasy is no different from crack or heroin'—whereas I sounded calm and collected.

"Middle America is getting fed up with the drug war. They are looking for an alternative. We should consider this *60 Minutes* segment a huge victory for harm reduction. If we hadn't interviewed with them, they would have run the same show, just without us at the end, and harm reduction would not even have been mentioned."

And, of course, TV viewers have since been flooding their Web site.

Meanwhile, someone sent Peter McWilliams a new product that contains concentrated coffee and is promoted as giving the consumer a "lift." He responded: "Are you letting people know that caffeine is an addictive drug to which the body builds up an immunity within two weeks, and after that you're pretty much taking it to ease the pangs of addiction and to get back to 'normal' again? A little warning label such as that, and you'll have a great product marketed with integrity."

McWilliams continued: "Caffeine is marketed to children in Coca-Cola and a dozen other sodas. It is a harsh drug akin to cocaine. It should be used sparingly by adults—once or twice a week at most. Children should *never* use it. What it does to their developing nervous systems is nothing short of horrific! That tens of millions of kids swill sodas every day is the most serious drug problem in this country. That's why I call caffeine the most dangerous drug in America."

Well, Nancy and I hardly ever drink coffee or soda. But that time we took Ecstasy in the desert—or *thought* we did—we finally realized that we had ingested vitamin C by mistake. We had been getting high from a combination of THC and the power of suggestion.

who killed peter mcwilliams?

E*njoy*. That was his favorite word. He always signed his e-mails *Enjoy*, even if it was bad news. And Peter McWilliams, a Los Angeles author and publisher, was living with bad news every day. In 1996, he was diagnosed with AIDS and cancer, yet he was bursting with enthusiasm.

His other favorite word was *consent*. His license plate said CONSENT and his self-published, best-selling book was titled *Ain't Nobody's Business If You Do: The Absurdity of Consensual Crime in a Free Society*.

McWilliams survived the cancer and got the AIDS under control with pills that nauseated him. Ironically, if he threw up his lunch, that regurgitation would also include the nausea-producing pills he needed in order to stay alive. But if he smoked marijuana, it would not only increase his appetite, it would also counteract the nausea.

That same year, California Proposition 215 was passed, legalizing marijuana for medical use when recommended by a physician. It had been recommended to McWilliams by four physicians. Cannabis clubs were opened up where AIDS patients could purchase marijuana. McWilliams devised a plan to supply marijuana to these buyers' cooperatives that were providing a legal service for their sick and dying customers, at reasonable prices in a pleasant setting.

He hired Todd McCormick—a cancer patient since the age of nine—to research and write a book, *How to Grow Medical Marijuana*. McCormick proceeded to grow 4,000 plants in a house known as the Cannabis Castle. But the DEA insisted that federal law superceded state law, and he was arrested in 1997. Federal prosecutors obtained an order forbidding a medical-marijuana defense, and in order to avoid a manda-

tory 10-year minimum sentence—leaving him with no defense at all—
he pleaded guilty and is currently serving a five-year sentence.

In 1998, Peter McWilliams was arrested as the kingpin of this conspiracy to cultivate and distribute medical marijuana. In *Ain't Nobody's
Business If You Do*, he had chronicled the cruelty of putting people in
prison who had not harmed anyone. Now, not only had McWilliams not
harmed anyone, he was trying to *help* others.

But, like McCormick, he was not allowed a medical-marijuana defense
and ultimately pleaded guilty for the same reason as McCormick. Without
a medical-marijuana defense, he had no defense at all. He would be considered the godfather of an insidious cartel.

Furthermore, a federal judge prohibited him from smoking his
medicine while he awaited sentencing, which was scheduled for August
15, 2000—the second day of the Democratic convention in Los
Angeles, so it was unlikely that there would be any media coverage
of his incarceration.

Anthropologists of the future will look back upon these times and
wonder how legislators could have been so barbaric. Although eight
states and Washington, D.C., have passed initiatives to legalize medical
marijuana, Indiana congressman Mark Souder (known as "Mad Mark")
claims that any effort to make medical marijuana legal "is just a phony
excuse to be a pothead."

"I agree that medical marijuana will eventually lead to the legalization of marijuana use for all adults," McWilliams told me, "but not for
the reasons the drug warriors paint. There is no 'massive, well-funded conspiracy' to legalize marijuana that General Drug Czar McCaffrey and his
drug warriors maintain. Certainly the few million spent each year by all
the marijuana legalization groups combined becomes an ineffective drop
in the ocean when compared to the $50-billion annual Drug War budget.

"Medical marijuana will lead to recreational marijuana legalization
through the natural process of experience and education. Once people
personally discover how benign marijuana is, the next logical question
becomes, 'If alcohol and tobacco are legal, why not marijuana?' There
is simply no reasonable, factual response to that question. As Jack Herer
pointed out, once enough people ask, 'Why isn't the emperor wearing
any clothes?'—the game is over. All it takes is enough people asking the
question.

"Enter medical marijuana. Once in general use, tens of millions of
Americans will be asking that question. How many people? Well, let's

consider pain relief alone. In 1997, the National Academy of Neuroscience, based on studies from four major universities, determined that 97 million Americans each year could benefit from the use of medical marijuana to treat pain. Once those 97 million—half the adult population of America—realize that the horror stories they have heard about marijuana are simply not true, there will be a chorus of *Why isn't the emperor wearing any clothes?* It will shake the narco-prison-industrial complex to its very foundations.

"Something that a lot of people don't realize is that when you smoke marijuana regularly—several times a day—it loses its euphoric effect. The medical benefits continue—relief of nausea, pain (physical or emotional), spasticity, excessive eye pressure (glaucoma) and so on—but the euphoric effects go away. While I was using marijuana to treat my nausea, I can't tell you how much I missed getting high. Although I'd smoke it several times a day, the average high school student was getting high more times a month than I was. That's because after the first month, I never got high, and I really enjoy marijuana's high. Simply put, recreational marijuana you use to get high; medical marijuana you use to get by."

Marijuana is the country's fourth largest cash crop, after corn, soybeans and hay. There are 80 million Americans who have smoked marijuana. Eleven million still smoke it every month, and half of them smoke it every day. And they inhale. And they enjoy it. But marijuana arrests have accelerated during the last decade. In federal prisons, average drug offenders spend more time behind bars (82.2 months) than rapists (73.3 months). In California, more inmates are doing life terms for possession of marijuana than for murder, rape and robbery combined.

In the larger prison outside those walls, more and more companies are requiring employees to submit to random drug tests, and their privacy goes down the drain while their urine is sent to the lab. *The New York Times* and *Rolling Stone* are among the publications which have such a policy. When a *Times* employee takes a drug test, the faucets are removed from the sinks in the bathroom so that the testee will not be able to dilute his or her urine with tap water.

Peter McWilliams was subject to random drug tests for two years while his sentencing date was postponed over and over. His AIDS medications caused nausea, but he couldn't smoke marijuana to keep it down. And he vomited, and vomited, and vomited again. Every day.

"The stomach acid that comes up along with everything else with the regularity of Old Faithful," he told me with a touch of mordant humor, "has eroded my teeth into spiky little remnants of their former selves—my mouth resembles a photograph from *The Amazing Ozark Mountain Book of Dental Oddities.*

"Over time, I tried various techniques to keep the AIDS medications down a little longer before vomiting. In addition to large doses of Marinol, which is essential, I added herbs, lying in hot water, curled up in a fetal position in bed, and two electric massagers—a smaller one to stimulate the acupuncture points for anti-nausea and a larger one for my stomach.

"Gradually, over many months of trial and mostly error, I was able to increase the length of time I could hold down my medications from 30 minutes to one hour and 15 minutes. That 45-minute increase is apparently enough for the medications to get into my system. The procedure of keeping them down is agonizing, exhausting and debilitating, and I must do it three times a day. It is entirely unnecessary if I could use medical marijuana."

Peter was hoping to be sentenced to home detention with an ankle bracelet for electronic monitoring, while simultaneously trying to prepare himself for five years' incarceration in a federal prison. On June 14, 2000, two months before he was due to be sentenced, he was found dead in his bathtub. He had died from asphyxiation. He had choked to death on his own vomit. He had been murdered—but by whom? And for what reason?

I accuse President Bill Clinton for coming out against medical marijuana, as if to say, "I feel your pain, I just don't want to help you relieve it."

I accuse Drug Czar Barry McCaffrey, who proclaimed, after medical-marijuana initiatives were passed in Arizona and California, "There is not a shred of scientific evidence that shows that smoked marijuana is useful or needed."

I accuse California Governor Gray Davis for opposing recommendations by his own Attorney General's Task Force on Medical Marijuana.

I accuse Assistant U.S. Attorneys Jackie Chooljian and Mary Fulginiti, the prosecutors who sought to prevent the use of a medical-marijuana defense.

I accuse Federal Judge George King who denied Peter McWilliams—slumping in his wheelchair in the courtroom—his legal right to smoke medical marijuana.

These individuals participated in an unspoken conspiracy, all for the same reason. And what was it that they had in common? They all wanted to keep their jobs. They all wanted to advance in their careers. They all wanted prestige. They all wanted to live in a nice house. They all wanted to send their kids to college. They all wanted to be responsible to their families. And the price was simply their own humanity.

McWilliams's death, at the age of 50, occurred on the same day that the governor of Hawaii signed into law a medical-marijuana bill passed by the state legislature, making Hawaii the first state in the United States to authorize the medical use of marijuana through the legislature rather than by a vote of the people. That had been attempted twice in California, and although the legislature passed the bill in each case, then-Governor Pete Wilson vetoed it both times, and so the people decided to eliminate the middleman and passed a referendum.

A few politicians have had the compassion and courage to speak out against the insanity of the war on drugs. I mean the war on *some* drugs. I mean the war on some *people* who use some drugs. Sometimes. Among such heroes: New Mexico Governor Gary Johnson (a Republican), who stated "We're trying to get tougher with things that *we* got away with. And there's a hypocrisy to that, in my opinion." And California State Senator John Vasconcellos (a Democrat), who introduced legislation to implement recommendations whereby persons legally possessing ID cards would be immune from arrest under state law for possession, transportation, delivery or cultivation of medical marijuana. In July 2000, the bill was passed.

That same month, the DEA—forced by recent scientific evidence—began legally binding procedures that could conceivably result in the end of marijuana prohibition. Meanwhile, like a pair of dinosaurs trying to survive, both major presidential candidates were drowning in chickenshit. Al Gore and George W. Bush both took public anti-medical marijuana positions. Another presidential candidate, democratic socialist David McReynolds, came out publicly as a pot smoker (and lauded the relationship between marijuana and communication in *Pot Stories for the Soul*).

At the Green Party convention, Ralph Nader's opponents—Jello Biafra (lead singer of The Dead Kennedys and political activist) and Steve Gaskin (founder of The Farm commune and author of *Cannabis Spirituality*)—each preceded Nader with a 10-minute speech. Biafra called the war on drugs "ethnic cleansing, American style." Gaskin, sad and angry over Peter McWilliams's death, spoke with great passion, declaring that it was "as if Barry McCaffrey came out with a pistol like that South Vietnamese general and executed him."

Nader watched this on the TV monitor, and during his own 10-minute speech—clearly influenced by Gaskin's tribute to McWilliams—he proclaimed, "We've got to stop this drug war that does these horrible things to our people." Later, in his lengthy acceptance speech, he said:

"At home, our criminal justice system, being increasingly driven by the corporate prison industry that wants ever more customers, grossly discriminates against minorities and is greatly distorted by the extremely expensive and failed war on drugs. These prisons often become finishing schools for criminal recidivists. At the same time, the criminal justice system excludes criminally behaving corporations and their well-defended executives."

At the National Libertarian Party convention—where presidential candidate Harry Browne came out firmly for decriminalization of marijuana—Peter McWilliams became the posthumous winner of their Champion of Liberty Award. Peter will be missed. He was the victim of a political assassination, but his inspiring legacy continues to live on.

● ● ●

I e-mailed the above to a few friends, and received the following responses.

Robert Anton Wilson: "Nobody except Tim Leary ever faced oncoming death with as much bravery and *hilaritas* as Peter. He will be missed by multitudes. I do not think you exaggerate in using the word 'murder.' Depriving the ill of the medicine they need ranks as 'depraved indifference' or Murder Two in most states."

John Vasconcellos: "I am deeply saddened, deeply angered. Poor Peter! Poor each and all of us in this crazed society we inhabit! What shall we do next?"

And Ken Kesey, with his uncanny ability to cross-fertilize compassion and irreverence: "Well, I would rather choke on my own vomit than on somebody else's."

My immediate instinct was to forward Kesey's little message to Peter, whose particular sense of humor would have enabled him to really appreciate such a sardonic observation. And, of course, I would have signed the e-mail *Enjoy.*

the penis
monologues

the missing
episode of
seinfeld

[*Jerry is onstage at the comedy club.*]

Jerry: Did God look down at Adam and Eve one day and say, "Oops, I forgot something. Let there be erections." So Adam got the first hard-on in history. But God forgot to say *when*. And that's why men don't always get an erection when they *want* one. Women don't know it, but sometimes men have to actually *pray* for an erection. "Please, God, I'll be sensitive to her needs, I promise, oh God, please, just make it hard. . . ."

• • •

[*George is having dinner with his parents. There is no conversation, but George's father is smiling, then chortles out loud.*]

George: What! What! What's so funny? Is it because I'm becoming more like *you* every day?

George's father: Should I tell 'im? I'm gonna tell 'im.

George's mother: No, don't tell 'im. It's private between you and me. It's none of his beeswax.

George: C'mon, stop teasing me, I want to know, whatever it is, I want to know, so c'mon, tell me.

George's father: Okay, I'm gonna tell 'im. I've been taking Viagra. George, it really works. Your mother and I have been making whoopie like it was going out of style.

George's mother: Yeah, but it's not *me* he gets excited over. It's only because of the Viagra.

George's father: What *difference* does it make? George, listen to this, they cost $10 each. But a friend of mine goes to Mexico and he gets me a bottle of 50 for $42.

George: Gee, that's less than a buck a fuck, isn't it?

George's mother: George! You must never say the F-word in this kitchen! See, I told you, we never should've told 'im.

• • •

[*In Jerry's apartment, Kramer bursts through the door.*]

Kramer: Jerry! Jerry! I'm gonna be rich! I bought a bunch of shares in Pfizer when it was real low and now they put Viagra on the market and all the doctors are getting writer's cramp from writing prescriptions and the stock is going up and up like *it* took Viagra! Jerry, I'm gonna be able to retire!

Jerry: Retire from *what*? Kramer, you don't do anything *now*.

Kramer: Yes, I do. I scheme. I spend a lot of time scheming, Jerry. But now I'll be able to *finance* my schemes. I'm gonna be able to call my own bluff, every day! It that's not retirement, I don't know what is.

Jerry: Anyway, I might get this stand-up comedy award tonight, and I'm trying to think of what to say that will sound completely spontaneous. So, what's your *current* scheme?

Kramer: Okay, I got this idea because of the insurance companies. Blue Cross will pay for six Viagra pills a month. Well, that's very arbitrary, isn't it? I mean I get six hard-ons in one *day*.

Jerry: That's the national average, you know, six hard-ons a day.

Kramer: Jerry, believe me, Kramer doesn't *have* "average" hard-ons. But here's my merchandising idea. It's for one-night stands—a combination package of Viagra and RU486, the morning-after pill. It's a natural for the unisex market.

• • •

[*At the restaurant, Elaine and George are sitting at the table.*]

Elaine: But, George, that's stealing.

George: Yup. And from my own parents.

Elaine: You have no scruples. How do you know your father isn't counting the number of times he "makes whoopie" with your mother? He'll know that you took some of his Viagra pills when he thinks he has seven more times to go and the bottle is empty.

George: You think he keeps a tally sheet? He'll never suspect.

Elaine: You're in denial again—but you have to give me a couple. I would just *love* to put a Viagra into Jerry's and Kramer's coffee.

George: Oh, really? I thought you had *scruples*, Elaine. Dosing somebody is unethical, especially friends.

Elaine: Oh, didn't I tell you? I had *my* scruples removed with laser surgery.

George: But what about the side effects of Viagra?

Elaine: Stop worrying, George. Hurry, let me just have two. Jerry and Kramer will be here any minute.

• • •

[*At the stand-up comedy award ceremonies, Jerry, Elaine, George and Kramer are sitting at the table. Suddenly the table rises slightly.*]

Jerry: Kramer, stop that, what are you *doing*?

George: Maybe he's holding a one-man seance.

Kramer: I can't get it *down*! Jerry, I can't get it *down*!

Elaine: Gosh, Kramer, you must have been thinking about sex, huh?

Kramer: No, I was thinking about my business plan. That's the only thing that really arouses me. When I'm with a babe, I just think about my latest scheme and I get aroused. But I always let the babe take the credit.

• • •

[*Courtney Cox is emceeing the event. Now she's announcing the winner.*]

Courtney: And the best stand-up comic award goes to . . . Jerry Seinfeld!

[*Jerry walks up to the stage. Courtney and Jerry embrace warmly. She gives him the statuette. As the audience applause subsides, the blood flow increases to the spongy tissue in Jerry's penis. He tries unsuccessfully to hide his erection with the statuette.*]

Jerry: Thank you very much. Well, as you can *see*, I'm very excited about receiving this reward. I feel all tingly. And I have a headache. I'm a little dizzy too. An erection is like a cop. When you *want* one, it's never there. But when the *last* thing in the world you want is a hard-on—a *public* hard-on—then *boing*! I'm busted, right here onstage, with a spotlight, in front of 500 strangers. I may have to vomit. I'll try to avoid the first few rows. And everything looks blue. Especially my balls. Is there a groupie in the house? Well, I'm not actually a group. Is there a *singly* in the house? Who would like to get laid tonight? I'll point the way. So I've become a human dousing rod. Now I think I'm gonna faint. But even while I'm lying unconscious here on the stage [*Jerry is fainting*], my penis will still be a stand-up. . .

As an adolescent, I often masturbated in the bathroom with the aid of female fantasies, so it was quite logical that a great many of my dreams would include a coed bathroom as a locale. During the punk era, there were nightclubs that featured unisex bathrooms. And then, of course, that all-purpose bathroom in *Ally McBeal* empowered my original dreams to make their way into mainstream awareness.

But now, social engineers in Sweden have gone even further. According to an article by Jasper Gerard in *National Post Online*, young Swedish women are demanding that men use the lavatory in a strictly sedentary posture—that is, sitting down—not only for hygienic reasons, but also "because a man standing up to urinate is deemed to be triumphing in his masculinity and, by extension, degrading women. To micturate from the standing position is now viewed—among the more progressive Swedes—as the height of vulgarity and possibly suggestive of violence. Among the young, leftish intelligentsia there is also a view that to stand is a nasty macho gesture."

Indeed, a feminist group at Stockholm University has been campaigning to scrap the urinals on the grounds that their basic construction, which allows only males to use, is intrinsically sexist. And, in fact, a Swedish *primary* school has already ditched its urinals to acculturate young male Swedes to this standing—I mean sitting—order.

"It has long been one of the more imaginative examples of feminist paranoia," Gerard states, "that men engage in unacceptable, anti-women practices while standing at the urinal. According to this conspiracy theory, men repair to the lavatory to plot in exclusive circumstances. As all men know, the reverse is true. One stands in shuffling silence staring with mock interest at the wall in front. Under no circumstances does one divert a glance by a single degree. Far from being a venue to display one's masculinity, one feels embarrassed even to be there. Conversational gambits are as welcome as when a priest asks if anyone present objects to the marriage.

"No, the answer is more subtle, according to [a certain] non-squatting Englishman. It is not so much a function of female suspicion as of women's desire for absolute equality. Voting, fighting, learning and indeed yearning were all pastimes once denied women. So to achieve absolute equality, the Swedish sisters have stripped men of their remaining dignity and plunked them on the potty. Young Swedish men comply, he says, 'out of a sense of justice.' In other words, they don't feel it is right that they should be the sole advantage of a fire-and-forget physique."

Does that sound like science fiction? Ironically, in the science-fiction film, *Gattica*, Ethan Hawke's character changes his identity, which even includes changing from a left-hander to a right-hander, but his cover is blown when a bathroom monitor notices that he still urinates by holding his penis with his left hand. The crux of that movie depends on him standing at a urinal.

However, I discovered a basic flaw in this line of reasoning. I mean here's how I urinate, and I assume it's generally true of right-handed men who wear briefs. I unzip with my right hand. Pull open my fly with my left hand. Grab my underwear with my right hand, pulling it over my genitals and holding onto it while I urinate by holding my penis with my *left* hand.

But consider if there were no longer urinals. Then what would happen to the manufacturers of urinal accouterments, such as those pastel marzipan-like deodorizers and the rubber bull's-eye pads with urine-draining holes and messages like "The Star Wars Missile Missed Its Target! Will You?"

Lost to the culture forever would be that unspoken ritual we men practice at urinals, leaving about six feet of space between the first person waiting on line to take a leak—say, after a movie—and the guy who's actually pissing, a ritual that women have experienced only while waiting on line to use an ATM.

And how would the new order affect random drug testing? What would happen with those men who have been pissing drug-free urine through a plastic tube? Or through a plastic penis in case the drug tester stands real close to you? Even then, you've got to be careful. In San Antonio, a Mexican-American was caught using a fake penis while being urine tested for drugs by his parole officers. The telltale signs were evident by the bleached pink appearance of the penis and the fact that his urine came out in a sprinkler-like fashion. The final giveaway came when he fumbled his organ and it fell to the floor.

Meanwhile, the U.S. Navy is planning to replace urinals on the surface fleet with unisex toilets. Paul Richter reported in the *Los Angeles Times* that it's considered "a way to make warships sweeter smelling and more comfortable for today's increasingly diverse crews." This commode is called the "Stainless Sanitary Space System."

Within several years, 3,000 "heads" (Navy jargon for bathrooms) are to be converted—at a projected cost of $187,000 each—to a new, stainless steel, modular design with no difficult-to-clean crevices or seams. They will be cheaper to maintain and more suitable for female crew members. Women constitute about 13 percent of the Navy.

"The goal," announced a Navy memo, "is to make all sanitary spaces gender-neutral to facilitate changes in crew composition."

But Rep. Roscoe Bartlett (R-Md.)—a member of the House Armed Services personnel subcommittee—intends to launch an investigation because he fears the conversion could hurt military readiness by "advanc[ing] social engineering experiments on the military and [giving them] higher priority than the core function."

Navy officials insist that, from an engineering perspective, urinals are an onboard disaster. Because of a design that uses a low water flow, urinals on ships generate more odor than standard toilets, and have a greater "over-spray" problem that corrodes flooring and walls, their piping tends to become blocked by mineral buildups, and it's difficult and expensive to replace the plumbing when these problems occur.

Conversely, while our Navy will be spending $561 million on unisex commodes, a less expensive South African invention will break down a barrier between genders by enabling women to urinate standing up.

The "Eezeewee" is described in a Reuters dispatch as "a reusable device with a shaped plastic cup and a length of pipe." It has taken six years to develop and is already patented in 106 countries.

Stephen Odendaal, managing director of Mouldmed, the company that invented the device, said that it "will be invaluable for women who are traveling, hiking, camping, fishing, sailing, skiing, or bed-ridden. Having a wee has never been so easy. It even has a handy, discreet carrying pouch so it can be taken everywhere."

Wait till the Swedes find out about *that*.

countercultural
icons

the persecution of lenny bruce

Lenny was in mock shock. "Do you realize" he asked rhetorically, "that they're busting kids for smoking *flowers*?" But Lenny was an optimist. It was in 1960 that he said, "Now let me tell you something about pot. Pot will be legal in 10 years. Why? Because in this audience probably every other one of you knows a law student who smokes pot, who will become a senator, who will legalize it to protect himself."

A sense of optimism was the essence of Lenny Bruce's humor, especially at its most controversial. And so, when it was discovered that Nazi leaders from Germany had resettled in Argentina with false passports, he displayed from the stage a newspaper with a huge headline: "Six Million Jews Found Alive in Argentina!" Now, that was the ultimate extension of optimism.

Lenny poked fun at the ridiculously high fees of show business by comparing them with the absurdly low salaries of teachers. He explored the implications of pornography, masturbation and orgasms before they were trendy subjects and became the basis of an $8-billion industry.

He ventured into fields that were mined with taboos, breaking from a long tradition of mainstream stand-up comics who remained loyal to safe material. They spewed forth a bland plethora of stereotypical jokes about mothers-in-law, Chinese waiters, women drivers, Marilyn Monroe, airplane food, Elvis Presley, and the ever-popular complaints about "my wife," whether it had to do with her cooking, her shopping, her nagging or her frigidity.

I first met Lenny in 1959 when he came to New York for a midnight show at Town Hall. He was a charter subscriber to my magazine,

The Realist, and he invited me to his hotel, where he was staying with Eric Miller, a black musician who worked with Lenny in certain bits, such as "How to Relax Colored People at a Party." Lenny would portray a "first-plateau liberal" trying to make conversation with Miller, playing the part of an entertainer at an all-white party.

Lenny's satire was his way of responding to a culture wallowing in its own hypocrisy. If it was considered sick to have a photo of him on the cover of his first album, picnicking in a cemetery, he knew it was really sicker to enforce racial segregation of the bodies that were allowed to be buried in that cemetery.

At this point in his career, Lenny was still using the euphemism *frig* on stage. Although the mainstream media were already translating his irreverence into "sick comic," he had not yet been branded "filthy." I handed him the new issue of *The Realist* featuring my interview with Albert Ellis, which included a segment on the semantics of profanity.

"My premise," said Ellis, "is that sexual intercourse, copulation, fucking or whatever you wish to call it, is normally, under almost all circumstances, a damned good thing. Therefore, we should rarely use it in a negative, condemnatory manner. Instead of denouncing someone by calling him 'a fucking bastard,' we should say, of course, that he is 'an unfucking villain' (since *bastard*, too, is not necessarily a negative state and should not only be used pejoratively)."

Lenny was amazed that I could get away with publishing it without resorting to asterisks or dashes as other magazines did.

"Are you telling me that this is legal to sell on the newsstands?"

"Absolutely," I said. "The Supreme Court's definition of obscenity is that it has to be material which appeals to your prurient interest. . . ."

Lenny magically produced an unabridged dictionary from the suitcase on his bed, and he proceeded to look up the word *prurient*, which has its roots in the Latin *prurie*, "to itch."

"To itch," he mused. "What does that *mean?* That they can bust a novelty store owner for selling itching powder along with the dribble glass and the whoopee cushion?"

"It's just their way of saying that something gets you horny."

He closed the dictionary, clenching his jaw and nodding his head in affirmation of a new discovery: "So it's against the law to get you horny. . . ."

•   •   •

In September 1961, Lenny was busted, ostensibly for drugs (for which he had a prescription), but actually because he was making too much money and local officials wanted a piece of the action. He was appearing at the Red Hill Inn in Pennsauken, New Jersey, near Philadelphia. Cops broke into his hotel room to make the arrest, and that night an attorney and bail bondsman came backstage and told him that $10,000 was all it would take for the judge to dismiss the charges. Lenny refused. A lawyer friend (David Blasband, now a top First Amendment attorney) happened to witness this attempted extortion. The others assumed he was a beatnik just hanging around the dressing room. That was on Friday. On Monday, Lenny went to court and pleaded not guilty. "Incidentally," he added, "I can only come up with $50." The case was dismissed.

Five days later, at the Jazz Workshop in San Francisco, Lenny was arrested for portraying a Broadway agent who used the word *cocksucker* to describe a drag queen. This was the first in a series of arrests, ostensibly for obscenity, but actually for choosing religious and political icons as targets in his stream-of-consciousness performances.

Lenny was writing an autobiography, *How to Talk Dirty and Influence People*, which *Playboy* magazine planned to serialize, then publish as a book, and they hired me as his editor. We hooked up in Atlantic City, where Lenny drove me around in a rented car. We passed a sign warning, "Criminals Must Register," and Lenny started thinking out loud:

"Criminals must register. Does that mean in the middle of the hold-up you have to go to the County Courthouse and register? Or does it mean that you *once* committed a criminal act? Somebody goes to jail and after 15 years' incarceration, you make sure you get them back in as soon as you can by shaming anyone who would forgive them, accept them, give them employment, by shaming them on television—'The unions knowingly hired ex-convicts.'"

And so Lenny decided to dedicate his book, "To all the followers of Christ and his teachings—in particular, to a true Christian, Jimmy Hoffa—because he hired ex-convicts as, I assume, Christ would have."

Lenny was taking Delaudid for lethargy and had sent a telegram to a New York City contact—referring to "DE LAWD IN DE SKY . . ."—as a code to send a doctor's prescription. Now, in Atlantic City, he got sick while waiting for that prescription to be filled. Later, while we were relaxing on the beach, I hesitatingly brought up the subject.

"Don't you think it's ironic that your whole style should be so free-form, and yet you can also be a slave to dope?"

"What does that mean, a slave to dope?"

"Well, if you need a fix, you've got to stop whatever you're doing, go somewhere and wrap a lamp cord around your arm . . . "

"Then other people are slaves to *food*. 'Oh, I'm so famished, stop the car, I must have lunch immediately or I'll pass out.'"

"You said yourself you're probably going to die before you reach 40."

"Yeah, but, I can't explain, it's like kissing God."

"Well, I ain't gonna argue with *that*."

Later, though, he began to get paranoid about my role. "You're gonna go to literary cocktail parties and say, 'Yeah, that's right, I found Lenny slobbering in an alley, he would've been nothin' without me.'"

Of course, I denied any such intention, but he demanded that I take a lie-detector test, and *I* was paranoid enough to take him literally. I told him that I couldn't work with him if he didn't trust me. We got into an argument, and I left for New York. I sent a letter of resignation to *Playboy* and a copy to Lenny. A few weeks later I got a telegram from him that sounded as if we had been on the verge of divorce—"WHY CAN'T IT BE THE WAY IT USED TO BE?"—and I agreed to try again.

● ● ●

In December 1962, I flew to Chicago to resume working with Lenny on his book. He was performing at the Gate of Horn. When I walked into the club, he was asking the whole *audience* to take a lie-detector test. He recognized my laugh.

Lenny had been reading a study of anti-Semitism by Jean-Paul Sartre, and he was intrigued by an item in *The Realist*, a statement by Adolf Eichmann that he would have been "not only a scoundrel, but a despicable pig" if he hadn't carried out Hitler's orders. Lenny wrote a piece for *The Realist*, "Letter From a Soldier's Wife"—namely, Mrs. Eichmann—pleading for compassion to spare her husband's life.

Now, onstage, he performed the most audacious piece I've ever seen by a comedian. Lenny was empathizing with an orchestrator of genocide. Reading Thomas Merton's poem about the Holocaust, Lenny requested that all the lights be turned off except one dim blue spot. He then began speaking with a German accent:

"My name is Adolf Eichmann. And the Jews came every day to what they thought would be fun in the showers. People say I should have been hung. *Nein*. Do you recognize the whore in the middle of you—that you would have done the same if you were there yourselves? My defense: I was a soldier. I saw the end of a conscientious day's effort. I watched through the portholes. I saw every Jew burned and turned into soap.

"Do you people think yourself better because you burned your enemies at long distance with missiles without ever seeing what you had done to them? Hiroshima *auf Wiedersehen.* [*German accent ends.*] If we would have lost the war, they would have strung [President Harry] Truman up by the balls, Jim. Are you kidding with that? Not what kid told kid told kid. They would just schlep out all those Japanese mutants. 'Here they did; there they are.' And Truman said they'd do it again. That's what they should have the same day as 'Remember Pearl Harbor.' Play them in unison. . . ."

Lenny was busted for obscenity that night. One of the items in the Chicago police report complained, "Then talking about the war he stated, 'If we would have lost the war, they would have strung Truman up by the balls.'"

The cops broke open Lenny's candy bars, looking for drugs.

"I guess what happens," Lenny explained, "if you get arrested in Town A and then in Town B —with a lot of publicity—then when you get to Town C they *have* to arrest you or what kind of shithouse town are *they* running?"

Chicago was Town C. Lenny had been released on bail and was working again, but the head of the vice squad warned the manager, "If this man ever uses a four-letter word in this club again, I'm going to pinch you and everyone in here. If he ever speaks against religion, I'm going to pinch you and everyone in here. Do you understand? You've had good people here, but he mocks the pope—and I'm speaking as a Catholic—I'm here to tell you your license is in danger. We're going to have someone here watching every show."

And indeed the Gate of Horn's liquor license was suspended. There were no previous allegations against the club, and the current charge involved neither violence nor drunken behavior. The only charge pressed by the city prosecutor was Lenny Bruce's allegedly obscene performance, and his trial had not yet been held.

Chicago had the largest membership in the Roman Catholic Church of any archdiocese in the country. Lenny's jury consisted entirely of Catholics. The judge was Catholic. The prosecutor and his assistant were Catholic. On Ash Wednesday, the judge removed the spot of ash from his forehead and told the bailiff to instruct the others to do likewise.

The sight of a judge, two prosecutors and 12 jurors, everyone with a spot of ash on their foreheads, would have had all the surrealistic flavor of a Bruce fantasy.

The jury found Lenny guilty. The judge gave him the maximum penalty—a year in jail and a $1,000 fine—"for telling dirty jokes," in the words of one network news anchor. A week later, the case against the Gate of Horn was dismissed, but it had become obvious that Lenny was now considered too hot to be booked in Chicago again, a fear that would spread to other cities.

"There seems to be a pattern," Lenny said, "that I'm a mad dog and they have to get me no matter what—the end justifies the means."

In less than two years, he was arrested 15 times. In fact, it became a news item in *Variety* when Lenny *didn't* get arrested one night. While the Chicago verdict was on appeal, he was working at the Off-Broadway in San Francisco. The club's newspaper ads made this offer: "No cover charge for patrolmen in uniform." Since Lenny had always talked onstage about his environment, and since police cars and courtrooms had *become* his environment, the content of his performances began to revolve more and more around the inequities of the legal system.

"In the halls of justice," he declared, "the only justice is in the halls."

• • •

It was fascinating to watch Lenny work. "I found this today," he would say, introducing his audience to a bizarre concept. Then, in each succeeding performance, he would sculpt and resculpt his findings into a mini-movie, playing all the parts, experimenting from show to show like a verbal jazz musician, with a throwaway line evolving from night to night into a set routine. All Lenny really wanted to do was talk onstage with the same freedom that he exercised in his living room.

Sometimes it was sharing an insight: "Alcohol has a medicinal justification. You can drink rock-and-rye for a cold, pernod for getting it up when you can't get it up, blackberry brandy for cramps. . . . But marijuana? The only reason could be—to serve the devil—pleasure! Pleasure, which is a dirty word in a Christian culture. Pleasure is Satan's word."

Other times it could be just plain silliness: "Eleanor Roosevelt had the prettiest tits I had ever seen or dreamed that I had seen. [*In her voice*] I've got the nicest tits that have ever been in this White House, but because of protocol we're not allowed to wear bathing suits. . . ."

That harmless bit of incongruity would show up in Lenny's act from time to time. One night he was arrested at the Cafe Au Go Go in Greenwich Village for giving an indecent performance, and at the top of the police complaint was "Eleanor Roosevelt and her display of tits." Lenny ended up firing all his lawyers and defending himself at his New York obscenity trial. He was found guilty—in a sophisticated city like New York. Lenny was heartbroken.

At his sentencing, he again acted as his own attorney. His most relevant argument concerned the obscenity statute he'd been accused of violating. As part of his legal homework, he had obtained the legislative history of that statute from Albany, and he discovered that back in 1931 there was an amendment proposed which *excluded from arrest* in an indecent performance: stagehands, spectators, musicians and—here was the fulcrum of his defense—*actors*. The law had been misapplied to Lenny. Despite opposition by the New York Society for the Suppression of Vice, the amendment had been signed into law by then-Governor Roosevelt.

Lenny had complained that District Attorney Richard Kuh tried to do his act in court. A friend of mine who dated Kuh swears that he took her back to his apartment and played Lenny Bruce albums for her. Maybe someday he would play for her the soundtrack from the movie *Lenny*, with Dustin Hoffman doing Lenny's act onstage, where he complains about the district attorney doing his act in court. But now, before sentencing, Kuh recommended that no mercy be granted because Lenny had shown a "lack of remorse."

"I'm not here for remorse but for justice," Lenny responded. "The issue is not obscenity, but that I spit in the face of authority."

The face of authority spat back at him that afternoon by sentencing him to four months in the workhouse.

"Ignoring the mandate of Franklin D. Roosevelt," Lenny observed, "is a great deal more offensive than saying Eleanor has lovely nay-nays."

• • •

On October 2, 1965, Lenny visited the San Francisco FBI headquarters. Two days later, they sent a memo to the FBI Director in Washington, describing Lenny as "the nightclub and stage performer widely known for his obscenity." The memo stated:

"Bruce, who advised that he is scheduled to begin confinement, 10/13/65, in New York State as a result of a conviction for a lewd show, alleged that there is a conspiracy between the courts of the states of New York and California to violate his rights. Allegedly this violation of his rights takes place by these lower courts failing to abide by decisions of the U.S. Supreme Court with regard to obscenity. . . ."

On October 13 (Lenny's 40th birthday), instead of surrendering to the authorities in New York, he filed suit at the U.S. District Court in San Francisco to keep him out of prison, and got himself officially declared a pauper. Since his first arrest for obscenity, his earnings had plummeted from $108,000 to $11,000, and he was $15,000 in debt.

On May 31, 1966, he wrote to me, "I'm still working on the bust of the government of New York State." And he sent his doodle of Jesus Christ nailed to the cross, with a speech balloon asking, "Where the hell is the ACLU?"

On August 3, while his New York obscenity conviction was still on appeal, he received a foreclosure notice on his home. Lenny died that day from an overdose of morphine, on the cusp between suicide and accident. In his kitchen, a kettle of water was still boiling. In his office, the electric typewriter was still humming. Lenny had stopped typing in mid-word: *Conspiracy to interfere with the 4th Amendment const.*

At the funeral, his roommate and sound engineer, John Judnich, dropped Lenny's microphone into his grave before the dirt was piled on. Eighteen months later, the New York Court of Appeals upheld a lower court's reversal of his guilty verdict.

Fortunately for his legacy, there is a documentary, *Lenny Bruce: Swear to Tell the Truth*, which was a dozen years in the making. It was nominated for an Academy Award in 1999. But, as producer Robert Weide told me, prophetically, "If there's a documentary about the Holocaust, it will win." And then he added, "The odds against *my* film winning are six million to one."

Lenny really would've appreciated that.

"Sure we were young. We were arrogant. We were ridiculous. There were excesses. We were brash. We were foolish. We had factional fights. But we were right."

—*Abbie Hoffman*

The charismatic organizer of political radicals and stoned hippies alike, Abbie Hoffman, once told me that a group of filmmakers wanted to follow him around in order to produce a documentary, but he declined. I asked why. He grinned and said, "I want to make my *own* myth." But with the release of a posthumous biopic, *Steal This Movie*, one version of Abbie's myth was instead produced by Robert Greenwald.

I was disappointed with the script and the casting. Abbie had wanted Mel Gibson to play him in a movie. Robert Downey, Jr. was offered the role—I think Abbie would've liked that—but, as the story goes, Downey insisted that, in a drug-bust scene, the cocaine had to be real. It's not a true story, though; he simply turned down the part.

The role went to Vincent D'Onofrio, who is much taller than Abbie, whose imitation Boston accent sounded more like a speech defect, and who failed to capture Abbie's peculiar brand of charisma. The real Abbie oozed with passion and wit. His Medusa-like hair seemed to be crawling with snakes that hissed "Don't tread on me!" His smile displayed a set of bright white teeth despite the fact that he hardly ever brushed them.

D'Onofrio asked, "Can you imagine the MTV generation sending thousands of kids from across the country to gather in one place to talk about our country? No way. It's sad because teenagers today would never get what Abbie did with his life. No, our kids are home watching cable, and who the fuck even wants to leave the house? It would be inconvenient for them. Maybe if a pop star like Britney Spears asked the kids to gather, they might do it, but the truth is we don't have anyone with the kind of charisma of an Abbie Hoffman. . . ."

• • •

Abbie was a warrior who tempered his fearlessness with a gift for humor that was sharp and spontaneous. On a particularly tense night on the Lower East Side, we were standing on a street corner when a patrol car with four police cruised by. Abbie called out, "Hey, fellas, you goin' out on a double date?" These were the same cops from the 9th Precinct that he loved to defeat at the pool table.

Abbie and I had known of each other's reputation before we actually met. He was a subscriber to *The Realist,* and I had read his letter to the *Village Voice* criticizing Jefferson Airplane for doing a radio commercial for Levi's. He asked, "Don't they know that the Levi's workers are on strike in North Carolina?"

We first met in Central Park at a meeting before the Armed Forces Day parade in 1967. The Vietnam War was escalating, while the division between pro- and antiwar citizens at home was expanding, and a large group of protesters were discussing whether to leave the safety of the park for unknown dangers lurking on Fifth Avenue. Suddenly, Abbie assumed his leadership role.

"What is this?" he growled. "We're huddled together like in a fuckin' *ghetto,* afraid to watch a fuckin' *parade.*"

That did it. Demonstrators left the area, followed by a division of police. The Armed Forces Day parade began. When the Marines marched by, we chanted, "Get a girl, not a gun." The Navy marched by, and we sang "Yellow Submarine." Green Berets marched by, and we shouted, "Thou shalt not kill!" The Red Cross marched by, and we applauded. A missile rolled by, and we called out, "Shame!" Military cadets rode by on horseback, and we advised, "Drop out now!" The Department of Sanitation swept past, and we cheered.

After the parade, Abbie and I went to have soup and we talked about, not politics, but religion.

"When I was at Brandeis," he said, "I asked this professor, 'How come in one part of the Bible, Jesus says to God, 'Why hast thou forsaken me?'—but in another part of the Bible, Jesus says to God, 'Forgive them, for they know not what they do?' And the professor says, 'You gotta remember, the Bible was written by a lot of different guys.'"

Beneath the irreverence of Abbie's radicalism, there lay a solid spiritual foundation. Once, we had planned to see *The Professionals* with Burt Lancaster and Lee Marvin—"That's my favorite movie," Abbie said—but it was playing too far away, so instead we saw the Dino DiLaurentiis version of *The Bible*, and later we discussed the implications of Abraham being prepared to slay his son because God told him to do it. I dismissed this as "blind obedience." Abbie praised it as "revolutionary trust."

• • •

Abbie knew that if you didn't have a huge advertising budget, you could use creativity to break into the media, by borrowing a trick from the CIA: You don't have to manipulate the media if you can manipulate the events *covered* by the media. For example, Jim Fouratt, an organizer of the Central Park Be-In, had an idea for a piece of street theater—in this case, Wall Street—which Abbie put into action.

He led a group of hippies to the Stock Exchange, armed with $200 in singles that they showered onto the floor from the visitors' gallery. Stockbrokers weren't used to seeing real money there, and they instantly switched from screaming "Pork Bellies!" to diving for dollars. The hippies' symbolic gesture, together with its political rationale, graced the print and electronic media.

Abbie's TV screen had the word *Bullshit*! taped on the lower right-hand corner. We would study the media to learn how we could manipulate 'em. When CBS News wanted to film a hippie acid trip at the Hoffmans' apartment, we agreed to do it. As a joke, I suggested to CBS that they ought to pay for the LSD, because I was curious to see whether they would charge the expense to Entertainment or Travel.

Blaming my suggestion, they changed their corporate mind, expressing fear that the trip would now be "staged." We took the acid anyway— Abbie, Anita, my friend Phyllis and me—and we watched CBS. Every commercial seemed to be trying to sell us the high that we were already on. At one point, Abbie and Anita left the living room, and when they walked back in, they were both totally naked.

I thought they might have a little orgy in mind, but Phyllis whispered to me, "I think we ought to leave now."

Just then a phone call came about some trouble at the 9th Precinct.

Abbie and Anita quickly got dressed, and we all walked down to the police station.

"You know," I said to Abbie on the way, "you're the first one who's really made me laugh since Lenny Bruce died."

"Really? He was my *god*."

I told Abbie how Lenny had once printed the word FUCK on his forehead with strips of paper towel in a courthouse lavatory to discourage photographers from taking his picture.

Some black kids had been busted for smoking marijuana in Tompkins Square Park. Abbie wanted to indicate that there could be solidarity between hippies and blacks, so he insisted on getting arrested too. The cops refused to oblige his request, but Abbie just stood there in the lobby of the stationhouse. Captain Joseph Fink beckoned to me.

"Paul, do you think you can persuade Abbie to leave?"

"Abbie's his own man," I replied.

Abbie was standing in front of a display case filled with trophies. Suddenly he kicked backwards with his boot—he always wore boots—breaking the glass as if there were an emergency. Since Abbie was most meditative when he was engaged in action, this was a transcendental moment.

"*Now* you're under arrest," yelled Captain Fink.

And Abbie enjoyed the rest of that acid trip behind bars.

LSD had become illegal in October 1966, and a couple of underground papers reacted accordingly. The psychedelic *San Francisco Oracle* became politicized, and the radical *Berkeley Barb* began to treat the drug subculture as fellow outlaws. Now, a year later, there would be an event in the nation's capital that would publicly cross-fertilize political protesters with hippie mystics.

Our plan was simple—to defy the law of gravity. It was decided to hold an exorcism of the Pentagon—the pentagon being a baroque symbol of evil and oppression—including a special ceremony to levitate the Pentagon 22 feet—the height of a ladder, thoughtfully enough. After applying for a permit, Abbie informed the media that the government would allow us to raise the Pentagon no more than *three* feet off the ground, and of course the media accurately reported that quote, informing the public of the planned demonstration in the process.

• • •

In December 1967, Abbie, Anita and I decided to take our first vacation together. We flew to the Florida Keys, where we rented a small house-on-stilts on one of the islands.

Tripping on acid, we watched Lyndon Johnson being interviewed. The TV set was black and white, but on LSD it appeared that LBJ was purple and orange. His gigantic head was sculpted into Mount Rushmore. "I am not going to be so pudding-headed as to stop our half of the war," he was saying. The heads of the other presidents—George Washington, Thomas Jefferson, Abraham Lincoln and Theodore Roosevelt—were all snickering to themselves and covering their mouths with their hands so that they wouldn't laugh out loud.

We talked about the styles of protest that would be taking place at the Democratic National Convention in Chicago the next summer. I called Dick Gregory in Chicago, since it was his city we were planning to invade. He told me that he had decided to run for president, and he wanted to know if I thought Bob Dylan would make a good vice-president.

"Oh, sure," I said, "but to tell you the truth, I don't think Dylan would ever get involved in electoral politics."

(Gregory would end up with lawyer/assassination-researcher Mark Lane as his running mate.)

Next I called Jerry Rubin in New York to arrange for a meeting when we returned. And so it came to pass that on the afternoon of December 31, 1967, several activist friends gathered at Abbie and Anita's apartment, smoking Colombian marijuana and planning the Chicago action. Our fantasy was to counter the convention of death with a festival of life. But we needed a name in order to utilize the media as an organizing tool. And that was the birth of the Yippies.

Yippie (the Youth International Party) was simply a label that I invented for a phenomenon which already existed—an organic coalition of political activists and stoned dropouts. You could see them intermingling at peace rallies, at civil rights demonstrations and, yes, at smoke-ins, passing around joints. As Yippies, we had no separation between our culture and our politics.

Originally, however, there was an adversarial relationship. The politicos thought the hippies were irresponsible but came to realize that smoking pot in the park was an act of civil disobedience protesting an unjust law. And the hippies thought the politicos were playing into the hands of the government but came to understand the linear connection between putting kids in prison for smoking pot in America and burning them to death with napalm in Vietnam. It was the logical extension of dehumanization.

● ● ●

In February 1968, a group of New York Yippies attended a college newspaper editors conference in Washington D.C. Senator Robert Kennedy happened to get off the same train that we were on. He had announced that he would not run against Lyndon Johnson for the Democratic nomination. In return, LBJ was overheard at a barbecue referring to Kennedy as "that little shit." Now Kennedy was talking to an aide in the train station. Abbie, Jerry and I stood there, looking like the psychedelic Three Stooges.

"Look how tan he is," Jerry said. "What an opportunity. We've gotta *do* something."

Abbie, on the other hand, didn't hesitate a second to devise any strategy. He just followed his impulse. "Bobby," he roared from six yards away—"you got no guts!" The senator flinched ever so slightly.

This particular encounter crystallized the difference in personality between these two main Yippie leaders. Jerry was the left brain, intellectualizing about a situation, and Abbie was the right brain, acting purely on instinct.

Abbie and Jerry were allies, but they also had a competitive relationship. For instance, when Abbie came up with the "Kill your parents" slogan, Jerry eagerly latched on to it. A photo of Jerry made the cover of the *National Enquirer* with this headline: "Yippie Leader Tells Children to Kill Their Parents!" Abbie became slightly jealous of that publicity, even though we all borrowed ideas from each other.

There was also a fierce rivalry between Abbie and Emmett Grogan of the San Francisco Diggers. Before the Yippies were christened, Abbie had been using the Diggers' name to describe himself and other community organizers on the Lower East Side. Emmett demanded that he stop. Emmett had lent Abbie a pile of Digger leaflets in a spirit of cooperation, yet he resented Abbie for supposedly imitating the Diggers, even opening a Free Store.

"You're a fuckin' *copycat*," Emmett snarled.

And when Abbie burned a dollar bill at a rally in 1968, Emmett complained, "The Diggers were burning money a fuckin' *year* ago!"

I had told the Diggers of a conference at a campground in Denton, Michigan, sponsored by Students for a Democratic Society. They arrived in the middle of Tom Hayden's speech and were so disruptive that SDS accused them of being CIA. Emmett climbed onto a table and delivered a loud, mean-spirited, more-radical-than-thou rap. Then he jumped off the table and threw it toward the audience, which was just a prop in his theater of cruelty.

I didn't expect to see this kind of hostility. Originally I was charmed by the gentleness of Digger pranks. Peter Berg had conned two reporters, both wearing hippie garb, one from *Time* and one from the *Saturday Evening Post*, into interviewing each other as manager of the Free Store. But, on the other hand, the Diggers had also slaughtered a horse to protest an execution at San Quentin Prison.

Back in New York, Abbie reenacted Emmett's gesture, overthrowing a table during his own speech, an act which only made Emmett cling more adamantly to his proprietary attitude. When he learned in a bar that Abbie had compiled a booklet, *Fuck the System* (later to evolve into *Steal This Book*), which Emmett assumed was based on the Digger leaflets, he exploded with self-righteous rage.

At 3 a.m., he took a cab to Abbie and Anita's apartment. Emmett knew that Abbie was in Boston and, blurring the line between seduction and rape, he took sexual advantage of Anita in order to get even with Abbie. To compound the revenge, he would later boast in his autobiography, *Ringelevio*, which was written in third person:

"Emmett got himself a can of something from the refrigerator and watched the movie [on TV] and talked with Anita for a while, before he took what he had to take, to show Abbott Hoffman how something 'free' could be stolen and how it felt to have it taken."

When Anita told Abbie what had happened, he got into an old-fashioned fistfight with Emmett, like a couple of street urchins caught in a time warp. And nobody won. I asked Anita if she would prefer for me not to write about this.

"Naturally, no one likes to be identified as a victim," she said, "so I'm not fond of discussing this, but I certainly see no reason to protect Grogan."

• • •

A headline in the *Chicago Sun-Times* summed it up: "Yipes! The Yippies Are Coming!" Our myth was becoming a reality. Yippie chapters were forming on campuses, and Yippies across the country were finding out what to call themselves.

In March 1968, Robert Kennedy announced that he was going to run for president after all. Obviously, Abbie's epithet in the train station had gotten to him. In June, on the night that Kennedy won the Democratic nomination in the California primary, he was assassinated by Sirhan Sirhan.

A few Yippie leaders went to Chicago a couple of months before the convention. Abbie remained there to oversee local organization of the counter-convention, while Jerry and I flew back to New York. Said Jerry: "I feel like Fidel Castro when he left Che Guevara in the jungles of Bolivia."

A few weeks before the convention, Abbie phoned me in New York. He wanted me to fly to Chicago—"You're gonna be our Clarence Darrow in court," he said—because the Yippies were going to sue for a permit. But when I arrived, it turned out that the judge was Mayor Daley's brother-in-law, and he had already turned down a similar lawsuit by Tom Hayden's organization, Mobilization Against the War, so we withdrew ours.

That evening, we met with local Yippies at *The Seed*, Chicago's underground paper. Editor Abe Peck, not wanting to be responsible for attracting young people to a bloodbath, had written: "Don't come to Chicago if you expect a five-day Festival of Life, Music and Love." The New York Yippies were adamant about not calling off the counter-convention, and Hayden was called in to act as mediator. He came wearing his bedroom slippers and blamed the argument on "drug paranoia."

On the Saturday before convention week, officers were placed at every pumping and filtration plant to prevent the Yippies from putting LSD into the water supply, even though it was known that five tons of acid would be necessary for such an action to be effective.

In the evening, we were reminded that sleeping in the park would not be allowed, even though the Boy Scout troops had been permitted to do so. We were given an 11 o'clock curfew. Allen Ginsberg served as the pied piper of peace and safely led our troops out with the power of chanting. "Ommmmmmm . . . Ommmmmm . . . Ommmmmmm . . . " It was the first time I ever saw Abbie cry.

During the convention, Anita, Abbie and I were staying at the apartment of a friend, whose landlord had freaked out. He was now sitting on the front steps of the house, holding a .32 caliber revolver, waiting to shoot Abbie or me. I had taken a quick flight to speak at the University of Kansas, then returned to the temporary office of the *Ramparts Wall Poster* in Chicago.

Writer Art Goldberg was driving me back to the apartment from there. Because we both had long hair, a cop stopped us and searched the trunk. He asked for Art's driver's license and, when he saw the name Goldberg, he said, "We'll get you all in the oven yet." It was during this delay that other police arrested the landlord with the gun. Abbie was out in the park getting laid at the time. So, inadvertently, my life had been saved by an anti-Semitic cop, and Abbie's life had been saved by his own rampant horniness.

Later, Abbie was arrested while we were eating breakfast, ostensibly for having the word FUCK written in lipstick on his forehead, but really just to get him off the streets. He might have gotten away with it if only he hadn't tipped his hat to the police who were assigned to follow him.

Demonstrators planned to march to the Amphitheater, but since sadistic violence by the police had been building up from the beginning, some protesters decided to remain in the park for sanctuary. There were restrictions on where we could march, but Dick Gregory announced that he was inviting *everybody* to come to his house, which just happened to be on the other side of the Amphitheater.

But police violence prevented that march. Because of media omnipresence, our chant became, "The whole world is watching! The whole world is watching!" The Yippie Olympics were called off. No marathon high jump—people getting as high as possible on hash oil, then jumping up and down for as long as they could—and no joint-rolling contest, either. Abbie stood in the park and declared the Yippies dead: "Yippie was just a slogan to bring together the New Left and the psychedelic dropouts. The Yippies never really existed."

But the myth lingered on. There was a soft drink named "Yippie!" A TV quiz show had a question: "What was the name of the pig who was the Yippie candidate for president?" A question in the Trivial Pursuit game asked, "What were members of the Youth International Party called?" Another question: "Who first suggested putting LSD into the Chicago water supply?"

An episode of *Garry Shandling* revolved around the publication of an old photo of Garry's mother sitting naked on Abbie Hoffman's shoulders. And an episode of *Barney Miller* showed a police inspector looking at an arrestee's record and muttering, "A Yippie, huh?" He then read from the rap sheet: "Making bombs, inciting to riot . . . "

That's disinfotainment.

• • •

A couple of months after the Chicago convention, antiwar organizers became a target of the House Committee on UnAmerican Activities, and Abbie got arrested for wearing an American flag shirt. When he appeared on the Merv Griffin show wearing another American flag shirt, network officials blacked out his image. But not his energy.

The next summer, the Woodstock Festival of Music and Love felt like the vision we originally had for Chicago. Abbie and I took acid in the woods and laughed ourselves silly, but he got serious later when the Who were performing.

He went up onstage with the intention of informing the audience that John Sinclair was serving 10 years in prison for possession of two joints—that this was the politics behind the festival—but before he could get his message across, Peter Townshend turned his guitar into a tennis racket and smashed Abbie in the head.

It was nothing personal, though. A week before, when the Who played the Fillmore East, a plainclothes cop had rushed onstage and tried to grab the microphone—intending to warn the audience that there was a fire next door and the theater had to be cleared—but Townshend thought he was a wacko from the audience and kicked him in the balls.

Another kick in the balls came in the form of indictments for conspiracy to cross state lines for the purpose of inciting a riot at the Chicago convention. Jerry Rubin called it "the Academy Award of protest." At a fund-raising party on Abbie and Anita's rooftop, poet/musician Ed Sanders, radio free-form pioneer Bob Fass and I linked arms and became a chorus line doing the two-step and singing in *nyah-nyah* fashion, "We weren't indicted, we weren't indicted. . . ."

However, we would all be witnesses at the Great Conspiracy Trial. Street theater came to the courtroom. One day, Abbie and Jerry were dressed in judges' robes. The real judge ordered the pair to take them off, only to reveal that underneath Abbie's judge's robe, he was wearing a Chicago police officer's shirt.

Call me a sentimental fool, but when it came my turn to testify in January 1970, I decided to take a tab of LSD before I took the witness stand. Abbie was furious. "You were *creamed*," he shouted. He thought I had been totally irresponsible and stopped speaking to me.

Ten months later, I noticed a little ad in the movie section of the paper—*The Professionals* was playing at a theater on Avenue D—so I clipped the ad and mailed it to Abbie. That gesture broke the ice, and we had a reconciliation.

• • •

Abbie had been given an advance of $25,000 for the film rights to his autobiography, *Soon To Be a Major Motion Picture*, and he endorsed the check to bail out a Black Panther who then fled the country. Now, not only was Abbie out $25,000, but the IRS began hounding him for taxes on that amount. He was in desperate financial straits, started dealing cocaine, and was eventually set up for a bust. He was facing a sentence of 15-years-to-life.

"I got caught behind enemy lines without proper identification," Abbie whispered to me at a farewell party in 1974, just before he went into hiding for six years.

Abbie grew a beard and became Barry Freed. He felt like "a hunted animal," but with the aid of plastic surgery, he managed to become a leading activist in ecological causes. He had assumed another identity, but his courage and dedication remained intact.

•   •   •

In San Francisco, shortly before Christmas 1979, my phone rang. A voice said, "You want to buy me coffee?" He didn't have to say his name. It was Abbie, still on the lam from that drug bust.

"I'll meet you at City Lights Bookstore in half an hour," I said.

Johanna was with him. He called her Angel. They had become each other's anchor in a sea of paranoia.

"Our relationship is completely nonsexist," he explained. "She's my bodyguard, and I do the cooking."

They spent more time together than any couple I knew. But, Abbie confided, there was one problem: "She wants to have a kid."

"Oh, yeah? You gonna have one?"

"Don't you remember? I had a vasectomy."

"Oh, I forgot about that." In fact, a film titled *Vas!* had been made of his operation. "Well," I said, "if you need a sperm donor . . . after all, what are friends for?"

We wandered around North Beach. Abbie was not exactly keeping a low profile. He stood next to a Salvation Army Santa Claus on Broadway, borrowed his bell and rang it vigorously, urging unsuspecting passersby to drop some cash into Santa's cauldron. We moved on. He did a Harpo Marx parody of a tourist responding to the barker in front of a strip joint. Then he proceeded to take the place of the barker.

"Come on *in*," he shouted. "Whatever you want, we got! You want ladies with stretch marks? We got 'em here!"

Abbie was frustrated about a film, *The Big Fix*, in which a character obviously based on him sells out and works for an advertising agency. As Barry Freed, Abbie was an organizer in the anti-nuclear-power movement. One day, in separate stories in the same issue of his local newspaper in upstate New York, there were photos of both Abbie and Barry. While Abbie was being written about as a fugitive, Barry was being honored as an environmentalist.

Abbie confessed to me that he had come to prefer his new identity.

• • •

After he emerged from underground in 1980, it wasn't too long before Abbie found himself onstage at the University of New Mexico, debating G. Gordon Liddy, the mustachioed, tight-assed, Watergate conspirator. The moment had come for Abbie to ask Liddy a question he had been pondering for months. Abbie braced himself.

"Liddy," he yelled, "I got just one question for you. Do you eat pussy?" The audience cheered. This was really off the wall.

"Come on Liddy, answer me! *Do you eat pussy?*"

Liddy couldn't respond over the roar of the crowd.

Abbie bleated over and over, "*Do you eat pussy? Do you eat pussy?*"— like some kind of sexual street fighter chanting his mantra—"*Do you eat pussy? Do you eat pussy? Do you eat pussy?*"

The audience went wild. Abbie was triumphant.

Finally, Liddy was able to reply, "You have just demonstrated more than I ever could possibly hope to, the enormous gap which separates me from you. . . ."

• • •

Jerry Rubin had become involved in the world of finance and networking. He once wrote that a necktie was a hangman's noose, but now he was wearing one. "Money is the long hair of the '80s," he proclaimed. He even sent out a press release requesting that the media no longer refer to him as a former Yippie leader. I envisioned the headline: "Former Yippie Leader Asks Not to Be Called Former Yippie Leader."

In 1984, Abbie and Jerry were together again, on tour with a debate titled "The Yippies vs. the Yuppies."

Abbie was in top form. He suggested that Jerry "merge with Jane Fonda, so they can have 'networkouts.' What could be better? Strong, muscular bodies with shallow, underdeveloped minds." Abbie had come prepared with props and proceeded to make a "Yuppie pie" for Jerry. Into a Cuisinart he poured the ingredients—spirulina, brie, wine "from Chile, made by stepping on the eyeballs of political prisoners," some

tofu—"soft, rubbery, sort of like intestines of a Cabbage Patch doll"—
natural vitamins, stock certificates—"stocks and bondage: Yuppie sex"—
credit cards, business cards, the keys to a Porsche, a gold watch—"How
does a Yuppie spell relief? R-o-l-e-x"—and then he processed it all down
to a fine, unappetizing mess.

As moderator, I summed up: "This debate perpetuates the myth that
there is a separation between Yippie and Yuppie. We each have a combination of both spirits. The Yippie in us knows that there must be some
kind of social revolution to counter the injustices that horrify us every
day. The Yuppie in us knows that, too—but we want to watch it on our
VCRs, maybe have some friends over for Sunday brunch. After all, what
good is a social revolution if you can't watch it at your convenience? If
Abbie Hoffman were to throw money in the Stock Exchange today, this
time Jerry Rubin would invest it."

And Britney Spears would ask G. Gordon Liddy, "Do you eat pussy?"

• • •

The last time I saw Abbie was in Chicago in August 1988. We were
there for the 20th anniversary of the '68 convention.

"There's no way that change will come about without people taking risks," he told the audience as well as himself—"risks with their
careers, their marriage plans, their status in the community, and their
lives. . . ."

Recently, the University of Connecticut exhibited nearly 100 pieces
of Abbie Hoffman memorabilia, ranging from unwashed socks to unclas-
sified FBI documents. Abbie would have appreciated such a display, but
he killed himself in April 1989. For a week I had to put my grief on hold
in order to deal with the constant stream of media people wanting a
comment from me on his death. Associated Press was the first to call.

"He was a fighter for justice," I said.

Abbie had taught me how to speak in sound bites.

jerry garcia
and his
magic shield

When Jerry Garcia was four years old, his brother accidentally chopped off the top half of the middle finger of Jerry's right hand while they were fooling around with an ax. But that wouldn't prevent Jerry from surrendering to his destiny. By seventh grade, he was playing a nine-and-a-half-fingered saxophone, as well as the piano, and also taking guitar lessons. At the time, his friend Laird Grant predicted, "You're gonna become a fuckin' rich, famous, rock-and-roll star some day." Grant neglected to foretell that he himself would eventually become the Grateful Dead's first roadie.

Garcia's musical genius was underscored by his personal character. Ken Babbs of the Merry Pranksters remembers an example of such harmony:

"One time in the '60s, Jerry and I took a ride through San Francisco and he said, 'There's someone we have to go see,' and he gave me directions to this little dive apartment down some bleak street, and we went into an ugly dark room full of a messy life and its accouterments, and Jerry yelled out, 'Dave, Dave, wake up!' And a bleary-eyed, down-and-out guy staggered up off a mangled couch and rubbed his eyes. 'Jerry,' he said, 'what's the haps?' 'The haps are,' Jerry said, 'that we are going to start a new group, and we want you in it.' 'Ah, I can't play anymore.'

"'Sure you can,' and Jerry commenced to convince him of his worth and the worth of the new band and how he, Jerry, would play slide guitar and he, David, would play rhythm and sing, and by the time we left it had all been set up. Out in the car, Jerry told me that he had really been worried about David and was hoping this would bring him up out of his downer funk. It worked. David Nelson joined up with Jerry in New Riders of the Purple Sage, and David has been playing and touring ever since."

• • •

Even though Bill Clinton and Al Gore have worn Jerry Garcia DMT-inspired designer neckties, Jerry never wore a tie himself. But he did have a drawer filled with black T-shirts, along with a copy of the *Urantia Book*. He once told me of a legend that anyone who read that 2,097-page bible from cover to cover—which he had done—would receive a mysterious visit from three elderly women. Although they never arrived at *his* door, he accepted that disappointment with grace.

One of my most memorable encounters with Garcia occurred in 1967, at a concert in Pittsburgh featuring the Grateful Dead, the Velvet Underground, the Fugs and, for comic relief, me. There were two shows, both completely sold out, and this was the first time anybody had realized how many hippies actually lived in Pittsburgh. Backstage, between shows, a man sidled up to me.

"Call me Bear," he said.

"Okay, you're Bear."

"Don't you recognize me?"

"You look familiar, but—"

"I'm Owsley."

Of course—Owsley acid! He presented me with a tab of Monterey Purple LSD. Not wishing to carry around an illegal drug in my pocket, I decided to swallow it instead. Soon I found myself in the lobby, talking with Garcia. As people from the audience wandered past us, he whimsically stuck out his hand, palm up.

"Got any spare change?" he asked.

Somebody gave him a dime, and Jerry said, "Thanks."

"I guess he didn't recognize you," I said.

"See, we all *do* look alike."

In the course of our conversation, I used the word *evil*.

"There are no evil people," Jerry said, just as the acid was settling into my psyche, and I imprinted on what he was saying. "There are only victims."

"But what does that mean? If a rapist is a victim, you're supposed to have compassion when you kick him in the balls?"

I did the second show while the Dead were setting up behind me. Then they began to play, softly, and as they built up their riff, I faded out and left the stage. I was definitely tripping.

Some local folks brought me to a restaurant which, they told me, catered to a Mafia clientele. With my long, brown, curly hair underneath my Mexican cowboy hat, I didn't quite fit in. The manager came over and asked me to kindly remove my hat. I hardly ate any of my spaghetti after I noticed how it was wiggling on my plate.

I glanced around at the various Mafiosi figures sitting at their tables, wondering if they had ever killed anybody. Then I remembered what Garcia had said about evil. So, then, these guys might be executioners, but they were also victims.

The spaghetti was still wiggling on my plate, but then I realized that it wasn't really spaghetti, it was actually worms in tomato sauce. The other people at my table were all pretending not to notice.

• • •

Although Garcia had a brilliant mind, he also had a certain streak of sweet naivete, especially while tripping. His ex-wife and friend for almost three decades, Mountain Girl, told me this revealing anecdote:

"In 1972, when the Grateful Dead were young and sassy, and highly motivated to stand out and be weird, we were trekking across Europe in two big rent-a-buses. A very long haul from Germany down through Switzerland, over das Alps mountains and ober dem valleys, oop und doon, oop und doon, so everyone dropped acid (natcherly) for the ride to Paris. A 12-hour trip stretched into the infinite, wheeled along by two nice rent-a-drivers, Kurt and Mick. Long, long day. Cows grazing the high mountains, shimmering vistas—and, inside the buses, giggling and goofing.

"At the very tip top of the highest pass in Switzerland in view of the mountains and skiers paradise, the pressure relief valve on the butane tank blew out in a long horrible howling hiss, somewhere just behind our seat. The bus driver slammed on the brakes, sliding to a halt, as we panicked and leaped for the exits. But before the doors could open, Jerry rose from our seat, waving a box of matches and shouting, 'Gas leak? I know what to do to find a gas leak! Strike a match! I'll find it!' And he began lighting matches and tossing them into the rear of the bus. And that is a true story."

• • •

There was an elegant alliance that developed between the Grateful Dead and the Merry Pranksters. Ken Kesey had this recollection of a particular media appearance:

"Once I was on the Tom Snyder show with I think it was Garcia and Bob Weir. We'd been talking in the studio waiting room wondering whether we should split because Snyder was being very hardball with whomever he was interviewing on the monitor. It was during Tom Snyder's hardball period.

"'You ready, gentlemen?' the waiting room blondie asks, her voice dripping smirk.

"'Ah, what the hell, let's do the gig,' Garcia says, and we file in.

"I can't remember the questions but I'll never forget our responding style: Bobby would begin to answer, then Garcia would interrupt him. Then I would interrupt the interruption. And when Tom got a chance to speak again we would finish the question for him and begin gibbering answers and interruptions and elaborations. He never got a chance to go into his hardball windup. After his stammered thank-you's, we shook hands with him, then with each other, as we left the stage, still gibbering. We watched him on the monitor in the waiting room as he introduced his next guest. He was still stammering.

"'He never had a prayer,' Garcia giggled. 'We Huey-, Dewey- and Louie-ed him.'"

• • •

In 1978, I accompanied Kesey, his family and a bunch of Pranksters to Egypt, where the Dead would be performing. We saw an incongruous quartet of semi-trailers invade the rhythm of Cairo's streets. These huge trucks were bearing sound equipment on loan to the Dead by the Who.

Kesey's Day-Glo sneakers were peeking out from under his *galabia*— a long skirt-like piece of clothing worn by Egyptian men. We chose our own fabric. Kesey described rock impresario Bill Graham's fabric as "the wallpaper on the upper rooms in the old Fillmore." Bob Weir looked up at the Great Pyramid and cried out, "What is it!"

Actually, it was *the* place for locals to go on a cheap date. The Pyramids were surrounded by moats of discarded bottlecaps. The Dead were scheduled to play on three successive nights at an open-air theater in front of the Pyramids, with the Sphinx looking on.

Now a bootleg tape of Dean Martin and Jerry Lewis doing filthy *shtick* was being used for a preliminary sound check. Later, an American

Army general would complain to stage manager Steve Parish that the decadent spectacle of a rock-and-roll band performing here was a sacrilege to 5,000 years of history.

"Listen," Parish said, "I lost two brothers in Vietnam, and I don't want to hear this crap."

The general retreated in the face of those imaginary brothers.

An air of unspeakable excitement permeated the first night. Never had the Dead been so inspired. Backstage, Garcia was giving final instructions to the band: "Remember, play in tune."

The music began with Egyptian oudist Hamza el-Din, backed up by a group tapping out ancient rhythms on their 14-inch-diameter tars, pizza-like drums, soon joined by Mickey Hart, resembling a butterfly with drumsticks, then Garcia ambled on with a gentle guitar riff, then Bill Kreutzmann, then Phil Lesh, Donna, Keith and, as the Dead meshed with the Egyptian percussion ensemble, basking in total respect of each other, Weir segued into Buddy Holly's "Not Fade Away."

"Did you see that?" Kesey said. "The Sphinx's *jaw* just dropped!"

There was something especially magical about the third concert on Saturday. I had a strong feeling that I was involved in a *lesson*. It was as though the Secret of the Dead would finally be revealed to me, if only I paid proper attention.

There was a full eclipse of the moon, and Egyptian kids were running through the streets shaking tin cans filled with rocks in order to bring it back. "It's okay," I assured them. "The Grateful Dead will bring back the moon." And, sure enough, a rousing rendition of "Ramble On Rose" would accomplish that feat.

There was a slight problem with an amplifier, but a sound engineer told Garcia, "It's getting there."

"Getting there ain't good enough," he replied. "It's gotta fuckin' *be* there."

The moon returned just as the marijuana cookie that Bill Graham gave me started kicking in along with the LSD that a Prankster had smuggled into the country in Visine bottles. I belonged to a vast army of secret dancers who only danced when they were alone, but on this night the music was so powerful that when the Dead played "Fire on the Mountain," I danced my ass off on that stage as if I had no choice.

"You know," Bill Graham confessed, "this is the first time I ever danced in public."

"Me too," I said.

That was the lesson. That was the secret.

The next day, a dozen of us had a farewell party on a *felucca*—an ancient, roundish boat, a kind of covered wagon that floats along the river. We were all completely zonked out of our minds in the middle of the Nile. The Egyptians kept us dizzy on hashish, and we in turn got them tripping on acid. A true cultural exchange.

Jerry was carrying his attaché case, just in case he suddenly got any new song ideas. I asked him about the paradox of that refrain, "Please don't murder me," in such a joyful song.

"Well," he said, "when things are at that level, there's kind of a beauty to the simplicity of it. I wrote that song when the Zodiac Killer was out murdering in San Francisco. Every night I was coming home from the studio, and I'd stop at an intersection and look around, and if a car pulled up, it was like, 'This is it, I'm gonna die now.' It became a game. Every night I was conscious of that thing, and the refrain got to be so real to me. 'Please don't murder me, *please* don't murder me. . . .'"

That tidbit of information ought to be mentioned in a course on the Grateful Dead which is given every other semester at the University of Santa Cruz, alternating with a course on the Beatles.

● ● ●

Twenty years ago, Jerry Garcia read Dennis McNally's biography of Jack Kerouac, *The Death of an Angel*. He asked McNally, "Why don't you do *us?*" Meaning a biography of the band, not just Jerry, who had originally been inspired by Neal Cassady to identify with a *group*.

Two decades later, McNally completed the second draft of *A Long, Strange Trip*. Since Garcia had acted as the matchmaker for McNally and his wife-to-be, Susanna, and inasmuch as her father was dead, she asked Jerry to give her away at the wedding. To her surprise, he agreed to do it.

"He generally did not go out of his chosen path that much," says McNally. "He loved people, one on one, or in small groups, but he wouldn't want to go to a party because it was full of strangers. Although he was authentically gregarious, he was actually quite shy. To the end, he got stage fright before a performance."

Jerry had once told me that the pre-concert tension he experienced was always necessary to perform well, yet if it got any stronger, he would have to go see a psychiatrist. Now he was standing in a back room of the restaurant where the wedding would take place. The maid of honor observed how fidgety he was.

"You look nervous," she said. "What are you nervous about? You get up in front of 50,000 people!"

"Yeah," he responded, "but then I have my magic shield in front of me, and I *don't* have it today."

The wedding music began—"Attics of My Life" from *American Beauty*—calling for a stately, slow walk, but Jerry and Susanna practically sprinted down the aisle. For Garcia, this marriage ceremony proved to be a scary misadventure—a public performance without the protection of his guitar.

• • •

In 1983, between concerts in Canada, I interviewed Garcia in his hotel room. Here's an excerpt from our dialogue:

Q. "Do you think, since the roots of the Grateful Dead are psychedelic, that affects the structure of a song in particular, or the structure of a concert, in terms of the build-up?"

A. "It doesn't so much affect the structure of a song particularly."

Q. "Except when you have a free rein in the middle of it?"

A. "That's right, some of our songs are big affairs, and some of them are also meant to be opened up. They're kind of like loose-leaf files, you can open 'em up and stick things in them; some are arranged so you can contain an experience, sort of direct it, and our second half definitely has a shape which, if not directly, is at least partially inspired by the psychedelic experience, as a wave form—there's sort of a rise in that—the second half for us is the thing of taking chances and going all to pieces, and then coming back and reassembling."

Q. "And that's the leap of faith of psychedelics—which is, somehow I'll get back to that core—I may make a few convolutions in the process."

A. "That's right, you might lose a few pieces, but you don't despair about seeing yourself go completely to pieces. You don't despair about it, you let it go. We've been doing some interesting things the last couple of years in our most free-form stuff that's not really attached to any particular song. It's just free-form music, it's not rhythmic, it's not really attached to any musical norms, it's the completely weird shit.

"We've been picking themes for that, and thinking of it as being like a painting, or a movie. Reagan in China was one of our themes. One time we had the Khadafy Death Squad as our theme. Sometimes the theme is terribly detailed, and sometimes it's just a broad subject.

We do this when we think about it, when we remember to, it's not a hard-and-fast rule, but that part of the music at times has some tremendous other level of organization that pulls it together, makes it really interesting.

"It's like whether you worry about the world *out there* when you're having some kind of personal experience, a psychedelic experience or whatever, anything that's happening in your life—and the world out there, how it affects you, how it sort of colors things that are happening in your trip. The music is like psychedelics in a way, and there are times even when I come off stage, and I swear I've been dosed but I know I haven't. And it's happened to all of us in the band.

"There is some biochemical reality in there that has to do with maybe the loudness of the music, or maybe like the East Indians believe, that intervals in music contain emotional realities. Their music is organized where each interval has an emotional truth that goes along with it, and so when they're playing, they're playing your heart, or they're playing a kind of nervous-system music. That's the way they believe, and it feels that way when you hear it too, so there may be those kinds of realities in there that are kicking off some kind of biochemistry, subtle brain proteins, and changes of that sort."

Q. "What theme would you paint right now?"

A. "Well, let's see, we should be on enormous divans with silk cushions all over, surrounded by nubile maidens feeding us peeled grapes, with huge bubbly hookahs."

• • •

Garcia started smoking pot in his early teens. He loved to get stoned with his friends and go to a drive-in movie. In those days you could get a matchbox of marijuana—15 skinny joints' worth—for as little as $5. It was not surprising, years later, that one could find a kilo of Acapulco Gold in the kitchen of the Dead house in San Francisco.

"Jerry taught me how to roll joints," recalls Steve Parish. "He was a great joint roller. He liked seeded weed best. He thought weed went downhill when everybody did sinsemilla."

Garcia used to tease Dead songwriter Robert Hunter by threatening to leave a big pile of joints in the middle of the dining-room table for Hunter's parents to find.

When Hunter later became a participant in the Veterans Administration program of experimentation with psychedelic drugs, Jerry pumped him for information about LSD. And, in 1965, with David Nelson and Sara Rupenthal—who became his first wife—Jerry took his first acid trip . . . but certainly not his last.

"We had enough acid to blow the world apart," he would tell Robert Greenfield, author of *Dark Star*. "We were just musicians in this house and we were guinea-pigging more or less continuously. Tripping frequently if not constantly. That got good and weird."

It was while tripping on acid that Garcia listened to the Beatles and to Bob Dylan's first electric album—destroying, in the process, Garcia's prejudice against amplified music. And so, with his band, the Warlocks—forerunner to the Grateful Dead—Jerry gleefully turned his talent from bluegrass banjo picking to rocking with an electric guitar.

When the Dead appeared on *Saturday Night Live*, they almost dosed the NBC coffee machine with acid. In the mid-'70s, Jerry got dosed himself, with something else. He had been given what he was told was Persian opium, but what he was actually smoking was 95 percent-pure-heroin based, and he became addicted, secretly snorting smack, though his friends knew.

Laird Grant asked, "What happened with pot?"

"That's not good enough, man" Jerry said. "It fucks with my throat. I can't sing on it."

On his way to a treatment program in Oakland, he stopped to free-base on cocaine, just one last time, in his BMW in a no-parking zone in Golden Gate Park, and he was arrested for possession of heroin and coke. Jerry had become sick and debilitated, but David Nelson—in a karmic turnaround—encouraged him to play banjo and guitar and sing the old songs again, just for the fun of it, and that proved to have a healing effect.

• • •

"Even though your music is, on one level, entertainment," I once said to Garcia, "I think it's also a service."

"Actually," he said, "I've always thought that we were like a public works, really, a utility as much as anything else. That's the way it feels, and for a lot of people it's *therapeutic* to have a real good time once in a while. I know it is for me, definitely, and that's what we do as far as I'm concerned, really. And being able to direct that in some way or another is awfully nice.

"I remember one time a long time ago—Ken Kesey and Wavy Gravy

were involved with it too, I guess not coincidentally—we played some-
place funny, like Cincinnati, at a university there, and they had Kesey
speaking there, and the Hog Farm [traveling commune] was there also,
and this was in '69, maybe '68.

"We went there and played, and the people got off on it, just enor-
mously, and we left town, but the Hog Farmers stayed behind, and the
day after the concert they got on the local FM radio station—back in
those days they had loose, free-form radio—and they said, 'There's this
vacant lot'—there was this lot in the black section of town that had old
tires and bedsprings and junk and garbage and all kinds of shit—and
they said, 'Let's clean up this lot.' And they got people to stop there,
sort of steaming on the energy of the concert from the night before,
kind of continuing that feeling.

"At the end of the day, when those ladies came home from their
jobs over on the white side of town, there was a *park* there. It's like taking the energy of that high—Wavy Gravy and the Hog Farmers have
such grace in doing things like that—and to me, that's always been a
great service model. You know—how can you turn this into something,
how can you take it another step, without it turning into some kind of
willful mind manipulation?

"And that was one of the times that happened, really spontaneously.
It was just great, and we got such lovely feedback from it. But for me,
it's always been this model of—if you get the right elements going there,
and people who are clear about that good energy, there's definitely stuff
that you can make happen that turns out good, and everybody feels good
about it."

• • •

There was, then, a special bond between Wavy Gravy and Jerry
Garcia, transcending the fact that they both had Ben & Jerry ice-cream
flavors named after them—an ironic christening since Garcia had experienced a diabetic coma and wasn't supposed to touch *any* ice-cream flavor, let alone Cherry Garcia.

In 1995, Wavy was attending the last of the Shoreline shows, a series
of Dead concerts at the Shoreline Amphitheater in Mountainview,
California.

"I was successfully altered," Wavy reminisces, "and in my amoeba
Day-Glo many-pieced attire, totally swaddled in op-art, and carrying a
pole with a large orange extension cord, and black light, I was wandering

backstage when Jerry, also altered, came zooming through a backstage door, late for the gig, and he saw the suit floating in space. He screamed and fell to the sward as Bob Barsotti [producer at Bill Graham Presents] screamed in my ear, 'Don't give my headliner a heart attack!' Thank God I didn't or I would've been ripped to shreds by hordes of hippies."

Shortly after that incident, Garcia did die, of heart failure, at Serenity Knolls, a rehabilitation center he had checked into less than a week after he left the Betty Ford Clinic.

Jerry Garcia remains an icon representing the sense of community that inextricably accompanied the music of the Dead. There had been an amazing continuity spanning a few decades of their events, from benefits such as one for the Black Panthers where everybody got frisked, to concerts where the entire audience seemed younger than the number of years the band had been together.

A Dead concert always served, not only as a musical oasis, but also as a healing ceremony, an extended family reunion, the celebration of a shared value system, a spiritual happening, a gathering of the tribes, a convention of Martians. That's the essence of Garcia's legacy, and it will survive, even though the Zodiac Killer finally tracked him down and snuck into his room at Serenity Knolls and murdered him in his sleep, and then Jerry was mysteriously transported to another plane of existence by three elderly women from the *Urantia Book* publishing company.

On a radio call-in show, a teenage girl, who had mourned the loss of Kurt Cobain the previous year, reassured listeners now mourning the loss of Jerry Garcia, "The pain never goes away, but it does fade." Another caller predicted, "There will now be actual chunks of Jerry Garcia in Ben & Jerry's Cherry Garcia ice cream." Jerry would surely have laughed at that one.

At his funeral, three women—not including Mountain Girl, though the description may well have fit her most accurately—each claimed that she had been told by Jerry that she was "the love of his life."

His body was laid out in an open casket. His glasses were down on his nose, just as he had worn them in life. But his left hand had been placed so that it was covering his right hand, the one with the missing middle finger. When Jerry's daughter Annabelle noticed that, she changed the position so that his hand with the missing finger would now be on top. This was, somehow, a most appropriate daughterly thing to do.

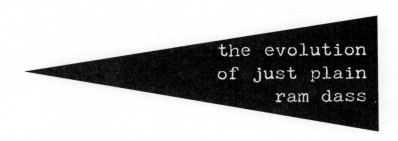

the evolution
of just plain
ram dass

Prologue:

In 1964, I assigned Robert Anton Wilson to interview Timothy Leary for *The Realist* at his LSD research center in Millbrook, New York. That was also the first time Wilson met Ram Dass, who at the time was still Richard Alpert, the psychologist who was fired with Leary for their acid experimentation with students at Harvard University.

When Wilson was about to leave the Millbrook mansion, he went looking for his overcoat. Somebody told him that he had put it on the bed on the third floor, so Wilson started up the three flights of stairs, and halfway up he met Alpert coming down, carrying his overcoat.

"How'd *you* know I was looking for my overcoat?" Wilson asked.

A mischievous, mystical expression passed across Alpert's face as he replied, "We have powers."

• • •

After Wilson's article was published, Leary invited me to visit the Millbrook estate. While we were discussing game theory in the living room, a minor fire broke out in another building, a bowling alley that was now used as a meditation house. Leary rushed outside and filled a bucket with water.

"Get pails and do what I'm doing!" he shouted. "Somebody call the fire department!"

They arrived promptly, but the flames were already out. Alpert sent a letter to the *Millbrook Roundtable* commending the volunteer firefighters. I observed that he was playing a nice "community relations game."

Mainstream media were then warning that LSD could cause brain damage, but I became so intrigued by the playful and subtle patterns of awareness Leary and Alpert manifested that I couldn't help but wonder: If their brains have been so damaged, how come their perceptions are so sharp?

I began to research the LSD phenomenon, and in April 1965, I returned to Millbrook for my first acid experience. Leary was supposed to be my guide, but he had gone off to India. Alpert was supposed to take his place, but he was too involved with getting ready to open at the Village Vanguard as a sort of psychedelic comedian-philosopher. So my guide was Michael Hollingshead, the British rascal who had first turned Leary on.

While tripping, I visited with Alpert for a while. He was soaking his body in a bathtub, preparing his psyche for the Village Vanguard gig.

"It's only an audience," I reassured him. "What can they do to you? If they don't laugh, it doesn't make any difference. What do you have to lose?"

"My ego?"

It was an absurd moment. Alpert had taken 300 acid trips, but there I was, a first-timer, standing in the open doorway, reversing roles and comforting *him* in his anxiety about entering show business.

As our friendship developed, we enjoyed what he called "up-leveling" each other with honesty. On one occasion, we went to a party, and I was acting unduly manic, but he commented on my behavior, choosing an eggbeater as his metaphor. I appreciated his reflection and, without being defensive, I calmed down.

Conversely, onstage at the Village Theater (later the Fillmore East), Alpert was sitting in the lotus position on a cushion. He talked about his mother dying and how there seemed to be a conspiracy on the part of relatives and hospital personnel to deny her the realization of that possibility. He also told about some fellow in a mental institution who thought he was Jesus Christ. Later, I teased him about having discussed his mother openly but concealing the fact that the man who thought he was Jesus was his *brother*—death obviously carrying more respectability than craziness. At his next performance, Alpert identified the man as his brother.

●   ●   ●

After my LSD-laced testimony at the Chicago Conspiracy Trial in 1970 was completed, in order to get centered I asked myself, "All right, now why did you take acid before you testified?"

"Because," I answered myself, "I'm the reincarnation of Gurdjieff."

This was slightly confusing, inasmuch as I didn't believe in reincarnation—I thought it was the ultimate ego trip—and besides, I had never even *read* anything by Gurdjieff. Then I flashed back to a conversation with Alpert during my first visit to Millbrook. I had been curious about Leary.

"Do you think Tim ever gets so involved that he forgets he's playing a game?" I asked.

"Well, you know, he's an old Irish Catholic booze hound, and he tends to get caught up in his own game sometimes, but Tim is a very skillful game player, and he knows what he's doing."

"Well, who would you say—among all the seekers you've ever known of—who would you say was always aware of playing a game, even the game of playing a game?"

Alpert thought for a minute and then said, "Gurdjieff."

So that's why I had ingested the LSD, because the Chicago trial was just another game. But not, of course, to the defendants. They felt that I had been totally irresponsible. When I told Alpert about this, he called it "psychedelic macho."

He wanted to go to India, and I was able to purchase a large enough supply of Owsley White Lightning LSD from him to finance his trip. The day before he left to meditate for six months, we sat in a restaurant discussing the concept of choiceless awareness while trying to decide what to order on the menu.

In India, Alpert gave his guru, Maharaj-Ji, three of those same LSD tablets—each one containing 300 micrograms—and apparently nothing happened. Alpert sent me a postcard saying, "Come fuck the Universe with me!" It sure sounded tempting, but after all, I had a magazine to run, so I stayed tripping in America, where I kept my entire stash of acid in a bank-vault deposit box.

Meanwhile, Richard Alpert was transformed into Baba Ram Dass. His father called him Rum Dum. His brother called him Rammed Ass. He grew a beard, wore a white guru gown with beads, and in 1971 his book *Be Here Now* was published. It sold two million copies, and he became a world-renowned spiritual icon.

At first, when people began to kiss his feet, he was embarrassed, but then he learned not to take it personally.

• • •

Muruga Booker is an internationally celebrated master percussionist. He toured with Ram Dass and Swami Muktananda, a prominent spiritual leader, in 1971 when Ram Dass was going through changes because he had been asked by Muktananda to speak at a college event.

"I remember Ram Dass backstage," says Booker. "He was crying, 'I'm no one to be out here, *he's* the guru, and I have a guru in India— *they're* the gurus—I'm not even worthy to speak here.' But he came out, and before he spoke, he told everybody, 'I want you to know, I'm not worthy to speak here.'"

It sounds like Ram Dass had suddenly found himself in the middle of *Wayne's World*.

Booker continued: "When he was saying how he's not worthy, we were thinking that a person of knowledge is just someone who knows everything, and what we learned from him was humility. And truth. Truth isn't necessarily saying, 'I know that I'm one with God.' Truth could also be saying, 'I know that I don't know.' Or, 'I know that I'm not worthy.' And admitting that brings you to the worthiness of truth. And it is truth. We were looking for truth to be some high ditty, and he showed us that truth is saying, 'Here's where I am now, and I'm working on this.'"

On another occasion, Booker was in a tent while everybody else was chanting. Muktananda wanted him to play the drums but, Booker told me, "I was then starting to experience that *I'm* not worthy of being there, and I didn't want to go in. And then I went to sleep and into a trance, and my breathing stopped. An energy field came around me, and I went into a breathless state.

"Ram Dass came in to get me and he says, 'Why aren't you in there?' I said, 'I'm not worthy, I'm not breathing, I went into this state.' He actually helped bring me out. I'm in this state where I can't even breathe and these things are happening to me, and he says, 'This is what's *supposed* to be happening. The ones chanting in there are *trying* this state, the nonbreathing state.' And so he really helped me on the path in that respect."

• • •

I had moved from New York to Watsonville in central California. My home was on a cliff overlooking a deserted beach. The roar of the ocean had replaced the rumbling of the subway. I was living in paradise, but I was also heavily into conspiracy research. I had published Mae Brussell's article on the plot behind the Watergate break-in several months before Woodward and Bernstein in the *Washington Post*, and now I was investigating the Charles Manson case on my own, and it was scary. My religion had always been Coincidence, but now that had been replaced by Conspiracy.

One sunny afternoon in 1973, after Baba Ram Dass had returned to the States, he visited me in Watsonville. His beard was gone, and instead of his guru gown and beads, he was wearing a tan cashmere sweater and slacks. A few years previously, he had been staying with Aldous Huxley's widow, Laura. "I was going to give a lecture," he told me, "and I got all up into my dobi and kurtan, and she said, 'Why do you have to do all that stuff?' I said, 'Well, Laura, you don't understand, because you're not in the spiritual domain, and I've just got to wear it.' But she started me reflecting, and I realized that I was just using it— clinging onto it to protect myself from life.

"And I *used* the uniform as hard as I could, because it forced people into reacting to me a certain way which elicited certain responses for me and not others. These people didn't come on to me in certain kinds of worldly or sexual or other ways because I couldn't handle them. Now I'm ready to handle them. And now I just want to be somebody—another person. The other thing is that my faith in what I'm doing is much stronger than it was a few years ago, so that I don't need all the gimmicks."

"Do you think that your name might be a gimmick?"

"If I didn't really feel that Ram Dass was really much more euphonious than Richard Alpert, I really could easily go back to Richard Alpert now. I mean, I've dropped the Baba in my head. I'm just Ram Dass now. I'm not Baba Ram Dass anymore."

So here we were, two old friends—he was on a spiritual path, I was on a conspiracy path—and now our paths had crossed again. We decided to record our conversation. Before we began, he wandered around the living room to absorb the ambiance. I asked him about the manipulation of the spiritual movement by the government.

He answered, "I see that the spiritual program *could* be used by the government in a way to undercut revolutionary activity—or to undercut disruptive things—because it tends to cool kids out and keep the scene quiet. All right, I could understand that. In its true sense, when it really works, it is an *exquisite* form of heresy in the sense that it really undercuts *every* system—government or anybody that has another system that they think is better—it undercuts that one too.

"And what interests me now—I really am very much aware of what I would call Martian Takeover. I don't think it's Martians—I'm using that as an analogy—but I mean the takeover of more conscious beings into every part of life. And I think they are not manipulable by the usual kinds of propaganda, and that they're a very different breed of being. And that a lot of the young people who have—primarily through drugs, I think, but now more and more through meditation and stuff like that—are just living inside in a different space than what the government is living in, and what most people who are pro- or anti- with great attachment are living in.

"And these kids are going into every walk of life, but they're not consumers in the usual traditional sense. Their lives get very simple, and their clothing styles—they're over a lot of the kind of hip, super clothing—I mean, they're not spending money that fast, nor are they concerned about earning it, nor are they concerned about the standard of living so much, nor insurance.

"Tim Leary had a curve 10 years ago, if you recall, about how fast the ideas would take over, and like what percent of the kids had to drop out before the whole thing collapsed. And I think that it's much more subtle than that, but I feel there is an incredible underground force going on, connected with the spiritual scene, but I don't think it's manipulable by man's mind that way."

"But," I said, "you know the old phrase, 'The devil never sleeps'— at the same time that your Martian Takeover is occurring, there is also going on a counter-consciousness, really."

"No doubt about it. It's just that I think the consciousness is much stronger."

On another subject, I said, "In 1963, I predicted as a joke that Tiny Tim would get married on the Johnny Carson show, and in 1969 it happened. You and I talked about that, and you called it 'astral humor,' but I never knew exactly what you meant by that phrase."

"Well," he said, "it's like each plane of reality is in a sense a manifestation of a plane prior to it, and you can almost see it like layers, although to think of it in space is a fallacy because it's all the same space, but you could think of it that way. And so there are beings on upper planes who *are* instruments also of the law.

"I *talk* about miracles a lot, but I don't live in the world of miracles, because they're not miracles to *me*. I'm just dealing with the *humor* of the miracle concept from within the plane where it seems like a miracle, which is merely because of our very narrow concept of how the universe works."

Referring to my involvement in conspiracy research, he continued, "I'm just involved in a much greater conspiracy. You can't *grasp* the size of the conspiracy I understand—but there's no *conspirator*—it's the wrong word. That's why I say it's just natural law. It is all perfect."

"Would you agree with the concept—what William Blake said, that humans were created 'for joy and woe'—the implication of which is that there will always be suffering?"

"I think that suffering is part of man's condition, and that's what the incarnation is about, that's what the human plane is."

"If you and I were to exchange philosophies—if I believed in reincarnation and you didn't—how do you think our behavior would change?"

Ram Dass hesitated for a brief moment. Then he smiled and said, "Well, if you believed in reincarnation, you would never ask a question like that."

His low chuckle of surprise and amusement blossomed into an uproarious belly laugh of delight and triumph as he savored the implications of his own Zen answer. I would find myself playing that segment of the tape with his laughter over and over again, like a favorite piece of music.

• • •

Larry Flynt had been converted to born-again Christianity by Ruth Carter Stapleton, the evangelist sister of then-President Jimmy Carter. This religious epiphany took place aboard Flynt's Lear Commander Jet, which, when it belonged to Elvis Presley, had been painted red, white and blue. Flynt purchased the plane for $1.1 million and had it painted pink. In the afterglow of his conversion, he announced, to my total astonishment, that he was appointing me to be the publisher of *Hustler*. It was an offer too bizarre to refuse.

During that weird stint in 1978, I had the pleasure of introducing Ram Dass to Larry Flynt. Ram Dass, Flynt, his wife Althea and I went to a health-food restaurant, where we discovered that we all shared something in common. We were all practicing celibacy: Flynt at the suggestion of comedian/activist/nutritionist Dick Gregory (who had also put Flynt on a food-fast); Althea by extension; Ram Dass for spiritual purposes; and me just for the sheer perversity of it.

Over lunch, Flynt told me that he was actually *bored* with pornography, but felt so strongly about his right to publish it that he had gone to Atlanta to defy a ban and sell *Hustler* personally. He got arrested for that, but before being tried in Atlanta, he had to stand trial for obscenity in Lawrenceville, Georgia. The next week, Flynt called me from there.

"Now I know why you introduced me to Ram Dass," he said. "By the way, is his name one word or two?" I told him it was two words and he continued: "Ram Dass really helped me to get rid of my hang-up about labeling myself as a 'celibate.' I can just say that I'm not having sex."

"And you don't have to worry about the label 'fasting' either. You can just say that you're not eating food."

"Oh, listen, Paul—you know those ads for guns we have in *Hustler*— well, you know, I'm against violence, but I'm also against censorship, so just move 'em to the back of the magazine, okay?"

A few days later, while walking on the sidewalk in Lawrenceville, during a lunch break in the obscenity trial, an American-flag pin on his lapel, Flynt was shot twice in the abdomen. The .44-caliber magnum bullets came from across the street, one lodging near his spine. His local attorney was also wounded. According to the doctors, if Flynt hadn't taken an enema (another Dick Gregory influence) on the morning he was shot, he would not have lived, because the contents of his intestines would've caused a fatal infection.

After this attempted assassination, Althea took over *Hustler* and fired me. My job had lasted only six months. Larry Flynt would later attribute his born-again conversion to "a chemical imbalance" in his brain.

•   •   •

In the film *Save the Tiger*, Jack Lemmon plays a middle-aged man who has a brief affair with an assertive teenaged hippie. At one point they match role models—one pair of names after another—from their respective cultural and countercultural backgrounds. Lemmon would name famous baseball one-hit wonder Cookie Lavagetto and the hippie girl would counter with Baba Ram Dass.

But in real life, when I told my daughter Holly that Ram Dass was coming to visit us in San Francisco, she had never heard of him. The game was different now. Ram Dass was *my* Cookie Lavagetto. But Holly had adapted easily to my assortment of friends, listening intently whether it was Abbie Hoffman reminiscing about the Yippies or Margo St. James talking about organizing prostitutes or Mae Brussell revealing a new conspiracy or Ram Dass discussing masturbation as a form of spiritual meditation.

"For a guru," Holly said, "he's a pretty regular guy."

To Ram Dass, the initials of LSD have always stood for Love, Service and Devotion. He launched the Prison Ashram Project, a program of meditation for prisoners. He cofounded Seva, an organization involved in curing preventable blindness in underdeveloped countries and replanting rainforests after they have been razed for profit. He has worked with environmental groups, socially conscious businesses and dying individuals. But who could have predicted that he would be temporarily peddling a rejuvenating skin cream at a Saks Fifth Avenue cosmetics counter?

• • •

Stanley Krippner has spent a few decades investigating the field of human consciousness. In 1966, he went to Manaus, Brazil, for a conference on transpersonal psychology. The theme was "Technologies of the Sacred." Many of the participants, including Ram Dass, wanted to try Ayahuasca.

There are three major Ayahuasca churches in Brazil, all operating with government approval, and one of them, the Santo Diame Church, gave the group permission to hold a session there, but not as an official part of the conference. Krippner wanted to go because his roommate, Marcus—an adventurous friend on a spiritual path—had never taken Ayahuasca and would be very interested. Krippner signed up for both of them.

That day, they fasted as was recommended and showed up at the gates of their hotel, where the bus was waiting to take them into the rainforest to this church. But the organizers had miscounted, there weren't enough seats on the bus for everybody, and some people would have to be left behind. Krippner confided to his friend Kumu that he would stay behind, but he felt responsible for Marcus, not wanting him to have such an unusual and intensive experience without Krippner being there to support him.

"So I was sort of locked into coming," he told me. "I could go and not drink the Ayahuasca, but that's not the point. There's plenty of Ayahuasca, there's just not plenty of seats. So after Kumu made that announcement, Ram Dass, who was preparing to get on the bus, says, 'Well, I will give up my seat to somebody else.' And Kumu says, 'Oh, no, Ram Dass, we want you there more than anybody else. It would be such an honor to have you at the event.' Ram Dass says, 'Well, I would like to go, but I have to follow the principles of my teaching, and I am taught to be of service and to give up my place to others when the occasion demands it.'

"Now he did not say this in front of the whole group—he was not making a show out of this—he was saying it only to the two of us. Ram Dass says, 'I've been fasting all day, I'm going to go down to the restaurant now and have something to eat.' So Kumu was almost in tears, he was so disappointed, and I said, 'Well, what you have just seen is the mark of a truly spiritual person who will give up this opportunity for somebody that he doesn't even know, and for somebody who, for all we know, might not get anything out of the experience, so this is truly an unselfish act.'"

People started to get on the bus, when unexpectedly a van showed up out of nowhere. One of the organizers had figured they'd better have another vehicle in case there wasn't enough room on the bus. So now there was enough room for everybody. Kumu went running down to the restaurant to get Ram Dass, but he was already eating a delicious Brazilian meal.

"Ram Dass," said Kumu, "there's room for you in the van, you can go."

"No," he replied, "it's too late, I've been eating—I've been really pigging out, I'm so hungry—and it just wouldn't work for me to go, having eaten such a big dinner."

"And," says Krippner, "of course he was right. I think he had come to peace with that decision. And also, of course, it's part of his discipline—these are not events that you enter into frivolously—and so, seeing that the discipline was to fast, once he broke his fast he couldn't really turn around and make another decision. So I said to Kumu, 'Well, this is the second spiritual act that you've seen. Having eaten something and broken his fast, it simply would not be the same. It wouldn't have the integrity that he would have wanted the experience to have.'"

•   •   •

There was a sign over Ram Dass's computer—"Old Dogs *Can* Learn New Tricks"—while he was working on his recently published *Still Here: Embracing Aging, Changing and Dying*. He wasn't sure how to end it, though. Ironically, as he was finishing the manuscript, he had a stroke and was not expected to survive, but he did, and now he knew how to conclude the book. His speech and right arm were affected—but he's left-handed, so he can still inscribe copies of *Still Here*—and he lives in a wheelchair, which he calls his "swan boat."

My friend Gerri Willinger also lives in a wheelchair. I asked her what she wanted for her birthday, and she said, "A ticket to see Ram Dass." He was scheduled to speak at a Learning Center event. I also bought tickets for my wife Nancy and me.

When we arrived at the hotel ballroom, there were a thousand people giving an intense, raucous, standing ovation to welcome Ram Dass, who was sitting in his wheelchair on the stage. His hairline had receded, but his hair was long in back, totally white, as was his mustache. He looked like a retired Tarzan.

His speech was slow but clear. He referred to his mind as "the dressing room that dresses my concepts with words." There were long pauses between phrases. He told the audience that "silence is texture" and advised them to "serve the silence, and I'll worry about the words." It was evident that his sense of humor was still intact as he paid tribute to "Rent-a-Mouth."

Ram Dass talked about soul and faith and spirituality, and this New Age audience ate it up, thrilled just to be in his presence. One devotee told how she had once hugged him and he "felt like Liquid Light." He discussed the motives of helpers. Some, for example, wanted to gain social power from serving him.

Gerri Willinger was sitting in her wheelchair up front, and she managed to ask the first question. Actually, it was intended more as a wake-up call than a question. She pointed out the contrast between Ram Dass's revered position with loving caretakers and her own situation—being treated as less than human at a cocktail party, for example, while constantly getting screwed by the system in her quest for official help. She said that those who helped him would not look at her or talk with her, and that he's lucky he was a holy man before he became disabled.

Ram Dass acknowledged that "there are assholes at cocktail parties." And when he told how a group of doctors once treated *him* like "a psychotic," Gerri knew that he understood, and that was all that mattered. There were a thousand people there, but Gerri had *connected* with him.

During the break, as his wheelchair passed her wheelchair, unable to give her a hug, Ram Dass reached out to shake her hand with his good hand, And that was Gerri's birthday gift, a touch of Liquid Light.

•   •   •

Occurring simultaneously with the Republican and Democratic conventions in Philadelphia and Los Angeles were the Shadow Conventions. Ram Dass and I both participated at the Shadow Convention in L.A. on the day that was dedicated to the war on drugs. Ram Dass was introduced by Laura Huxley.

"Aldous said, 'Our business is to wake up,'" she told the audience of 700 crowding into Patriotic Hall. "I think," she added, "you are the wakers-up." Ram Dass, wearing a floppy straw hat, wheeled himself forward on the stage, silent for a long while. Then he began speaking, quite slowly:

"I've spoken . . . all around the world . . . about consciousness and spirit . . . but it is only in California . . . that I can say to the audience . . . prior to my speech . . . I smoked a joint." [*Cheers and applause*] "This war has made us . . . less than truthful with one another . . . because we can't tell anybody . . . what you feel with marijuana . . . so medical marijuana has put me . . . ahead of the game. . . . It gives me control . . . of the spastic elements . . . I have from the stroke . . . and some of the pain. . . . It gives me perspective . . . so I can look at the stroke . . . with a certain love . . . with a certain witnessing of it."

As he continued, the speed of his speech—buoyed by the audience's enthusiasm—definitely started to catch up with his thoughts.

"My history, you probably know. I started out as a psychology professor. And then I took psychedelic mushrooms [*applause*] given to me by Tim Leary. And with mushrooms, I plumbed the depths of my being. I inhabited my soul. I got very deep into my being. It seems very strange that a culture would prohibit a plant that would keep one spiritual, that would keep one conscious. These psychedelic drugs that I took led to changes in the '60s. The culture is frightened of change. And the drugs were only part of the change.

"When I take a drug, for a moment I surrender the cultural progress my mind supports, and I get to an intuitive place where I can see clearly. Politicians don't want the populace to see clearly. With these drugs, I see creativity. What's the problem? Doesn't this culture want creativity? A joint takes me through realms of consciousness, perspectives about life. This gathering is a perspective of life.

"In the hospital, when the doctors invited me to discuss my case, I said, 'You don't seem to understand. Because, you see, I don't really exist. My consciousness is here and there and everywhere.' And they looked at me funny. To be able to handle this stroke, with all the negative energy around me—'Oh, too bad, you had a stroke'—a joint did it every time. Every time I would get depressed, there would be the medicine, for my body and for my head.

"We are lock-step in a culture that won't let go. The culture has to be free, and your consciousness has to be free. And what we are doing here is freeing consciousness. We've had the Information Age, and now we need to go on to the Age of Consciousness. And we are the leaders. This group."

• • •

One of my favorite encounters with Ram Dass occurred in a roller-skating rink—the site of a birthday party for our mutual friend, Dean Quarnstrom. All the guests were provided with roller skates, and as we skated around the rink in a counterclockwise direction, accompanied by a tape of organ music, Ram Dass skated alongside me.

He called out, "How do you stop?"

I called back, "Aim for the wall!"

It worked. The wall stopped us.

I saw Ram Dass most recently at a benefit for NORML in Marin County, where I performed after greetings to the audience by simpatico luminaries such as California State Senator John Vasconcellos and San Francisco District Attorney Terence Hallinan.

Although Ram Dass had requested not to speak publicly, he was approached by many folks at the event. This scene reminded me of a character I once based on him—Baba Blabla, in a fable, *Tales of Tongue Fu*—who confessed: "I grew *accustomed* to being silent. Matter of fact, I *preferred* it. And I discovered that adults would share the most *bizarre* confidences with me, who always understood but never judged."

A year after I wrote that little book, in 1975, Ram Dass led a five-day meditation retreat. Wavy Gravy came late, not knowing it was a *silent* retreat, and started yapping to a group until finally someone informed him of the silence rule.

At the closing ceremony, Ram Dass presented each of the 200 participants with a postcard-sized photo of his guru. Taped on the back was a thread from the guru's woolen shawl. Wavy covered his face, pretending that he was weeping in ecstasy, then moved his hand to reveal that he was wearing a red plastic clown nose. Ram Dass cracked up.

• • •

Epilogue:

For three decades, since their first meeting, Robert Anton Wilson and Ram Dass never crossed paths with each other again. Wilson read a couple of his books, and he kept running into people who met him regularly, but somehow he and Ram Dass never saw each other again until the memorial for Timothy Leary in Los Angeles, where they were both scheduled to speak.

They were sitting in the audience waiting their turn, and Wilson was thinking, "Gee, I wish I could get a cup of coffee. I wonder where the hell you get coffee around here." And then he noticed that Ram Dass had disappeared. A few minutes later he returned, with three cups of coffee—which were difficult to carry—one for himself, one for Wilson and one for Nina Graboy, who was Leary's secretary in the '60s.

"How'd *you* know I wanted coffee?" Wilson asked.

A mischievous, mystical expression passed across Ram Dass's face as he replied, "We have powers."

It was an inside joke with a 30-year delay of the punch line.

On the mantel over the fireplace stood my Donald Duck with eight arms. But on this particular day, there was something vaguely different about him. Then I realized what it was. He now had *ten* arms. The additional arms were actually two pairs of shoelaces. Ken Kesey had been around. He had purchased a pair of shoelaces for himself, but they only came in packages of three. Such a prank was Kesey's way of showing affection.

On October 25, 2001, surgeons cut out 40 percent of his liver, but the remaining scarred-up hunk-o'-meat wasn't in such good shape either, extremely cirrhotic, plus diabetes and hepatitis C. On the morning of November 10, if you clicked on a headline, "Kesey Recovers From Cancer Surgery," on msn.com, you would have learned that he had died. Oh, if only this had been just another prank. But no, the culture had lost a novelist and folk hero, and I had lost a fine friend.

On the same night in 1987 that I had undergone surgery without the aid of health insurance, a benefit to pay my medical expenses was held in Berkeley. Kesey told the audience, "I spoke with Krassner today, and the operation was successful, but he says he's not taking any painkillers because he never does any legal drugs." Then he led the crowd in a chant: "Get well, Paul! Get well, Paul!" And it worked. And now, how I wished I could have done the same for him.

Kesey had been an early subscriber to *The Realist*, and when we met for the first time at an antiwar rally on the UC-Berkeley campus in 1965, he walked up to me and continued a conversation that we had never begun: "Faye [his wife] said that . . ."

There was a rumor that the Merry Pranksters were going to invite the Hells Angels to a big bash at his house in La Honda, and a group of bikers began hanging around. It was a strange alliance. I mean, Day-Glo swastikas? So, when the Vietnam Day Committee invited Kesey to participate at this demonstration, Pranksters and Angels painted a bus together and made toy ack-ack guns to shoot at enemy aircraft.

Kesey was the final speaker. Accompanying himself on a harmonica, he told the audience that we should love our neighbors, that wars have been fought for 10,000 years, and that the protest march we were about to embark on wouldn't *change* anything. "Just look at the war," he advised, "turn your backs and say, 'Fuck it!'" Kesey found himself in the unusual position of bringing people *down*. The crowd was chafing at his bit, and the march began.

Although I disagreed with Kesey, I admired his willingness to be so politically incorrect, especially in front of this audience. At a benefit the next night, I played a harmonica and parodied his position. Suddenly, Kesey jumped up onstage and, with a characteristic twinkle in his eye, shouted, "I protest!" And we proceeded to have a spontaneous dialogue right there. It was the beginning of *Keez and Kraz*, our own private buddy movie.

In January 1966, young people all over the Bay Area were ingesting LSD in preparation for the Acid Test at the Fillmore Auditorium, organized by Kesey and the Pranksters. The ballroom was seething with celebration, thousands of bodies stoned out of their minds, undulating to rock bands amidst balloons and streamers and beads, with a thunder machine and strobe lights flashing, so that even the security guards were contact high. Kesey asked me to take the microphone and contribute a running commentary on the scene.

"All I know," I began, "is that if I were a cop and I came in here, I wouldn't know where to begin. . . ."

•   •   •

In February 1971, publisher Stewart Brand invited Kesey and me to coedit *The Last Supplement to the Whole Earth Catalog*. Kesey was seated in a Palo Alto backyard at a table with an electric typewriter. His parrot, Rumiako, was perched on a tree limb right above him, and whenever Rumiako squawked, Kesey would type a sentence as though the parrot were dictating to him. Kesey looked up. "Hey, Krassner, I've just been sitting here, thinking about the anal sphincter."

By the magic of coincidence, I reached into my pocket, withdrew a piece of printed wisdom that had traveled 3,000 miles with me when I moved from New York to San Francisco. It was titled "The Anal Sphincter: A Most Important Human Muscle." I handed it to Kesey and said, "My card." It was a most auspicious new beginning.

Each morning, Kesey and our managing editor, Hassler (his Prankster name), would come to the Psychodrama Commune where I was staying. We'd all have crunchy granola and ginseng tea. Then, sharing a joint in an open-topped convertible, we'd drive along winding roads sandwiched by forest, ending up at a huge garage filled with production equipment. Kesey and I would discuss ideas, pacing back and forth like a pair of caged foxes. Gourmet meals were cooked on a potbellied stove. Sometimes a local rock band came by and rehearsed with amplification that drowned out the noise of our typewriters.

Kesey had been reading a book of African Koruba stories. The moral of one parable was, "He who shits in the road will meet flies on his return." With that as a theme, we assigned R. Crumb to draw his version of the Last Supper for our cover of *The Last Supplement*.

One morning at breakfast, I couldn't help but notice that Kesey had taken a box from the pantry and was pouring some white powder from it into his crotch. "I've used cornstarch on my balls for years," he explained. It sounded like an organic commercial in the making. Our public service ad would appear with step-by-step photos on the inside back cover of the *Supplement*—which, after all, was about tools, information, ideas and visions—with Kesey giving this pitch:

"Y'know how it is when you're swarthy anyway and maybe nervous like on a long freeway drive or say you're in court where you can't unzip to air things out, and your clammy old nuts stick to your legs? Well, a little handful of plain old cornstarch in the morning will keep things dry and sliding the whole hot day long. Works better than talcum and you don't smell like a nursery. Also good for underarms, feet, pulling on neoprene wet suits and soothing babies' bottoms. And it's biodegradable."

One afternoon, two black women from Jehovah's Witnesses stopped by the garage, and within 10 minutes Kesey convinced them that in Revelations, where there's talk of locusts, it was really a reference to helicopters.

Kesey threw the *I Ching* every day as a religious ritual. When his daughter Shannon was invited out on her first car date, he insisted that she throw the *I Ching* in order to decide whether or not to accept. Once he forgot to bring his family *I Ching* to the garage, and he seemed edgy, like a woman who had neglected to take her birth-control pill, so I suggested that he pick three numbers, then I turned to that page in the unabridged dictionary, circled my index finger in the air and it came down pointing at the word *bounce*. So that was our reading, and we bounced back to work.

After two months we finished the *Supplement* and had a party. Somebody brought a tank of nitrous oxide. Kesey suggested that in cave-dwelling times, *all* the air they breathed was like this. "There are stick figures hovering above," he said, "and they're laughing at us."

"And," I added, "the trick is to beat them to the punch."

• • •

He called himself One-Legged Terry. His right leg had been gobbled up by a machine at a kibbutz in Israel. Terry was an unusual man. He took LSD on a post-war visit to the Nazi concentration camp at Dachau. He fought with the Israeli Army, but he became sympathetic to the Arab cause.

In New York, he presented me with a chunk of hashish, the size of a thick wallet, which he had smuggled into the United States inside the cloth that was wrapped around what was left of his thigh. Nobody at Customs would say, "I beg your pardon, sir, but I'm afraid we'll have to search your stump."

In the hospital after his accident, the songs of Bob Dylan helped him to recuperate. Prophetically, in 1970 he ended up teaching Hebrew to Dylan.

One day, Terry called and said, "Bob Dylan wants to meet you." I walked over to Dylan's studio, trying not to plan what I would say, thinking nevertheless that I might start off by referring to a mutual folksinger friend—"You know Happy Traum, don't you?"—but I tried to block even that out of my mind.

When Dylan and I shook hands, though, *he* said, "You know Happy Traum, don't you?"

I had just been with my little daughter Holly, and I told him how she insisted on calling her fingers "toes," and her toes "fingers." Dylan in turn told me how his young son wanted to be called "daddy" and insisted on calling Dylan "son." In the middle of our conversation, Dylan suddenly stopped.

"This isn't an interview, is it?" he asked.

"No, it isn't."

"Because," he said, "Bob Dylan—that's somebody who's waiting for me out in the car."

One-Legged Terry moderated a debate about the Middle East on ABC radio. The panelists included Jewish Defense League founder Meir Kahane (who later turned out to be an FBI informant), Arab-American spokesperson Mohammed Medhi, Abbie Hoffman and me. One of the few things I had a chance to say was, "It's important to realize that we're talking about value judgments. Not only may Jews not be the chosen people, but people may not be the chosen species." At the end of a rabid two-hour discussion, everybody summed up his position. I summed up mine in three words: "Nyah, nyah, nyah."

Dylan was sitting in the back of the studio, and later he said to me, "Hey, you didn't say very much."

Of course, Dylan didn't say very much himself. When I had asked why he was getting Hebrew lessons from Terry, he said, simply, "I can't speak it." Now I pointed an imaginary microphone at him and asked, "How did you feel about the six million Jews who were killed in Nazi Germany?"

"I resented it."

I told him that I was moving to San Francisco.

"Well," he said, "if you see Joan Baez, would you tell her that I'd like to do a benefit with her again some time?"

When I moved, I took that chunk of hash with me, and it fueled the production of *The Last Supplement* by Kesey and me and our staff. Later, when I interviewed Kesey at my new home, he used a portion of the chunk to brew a saucepan of hash tea, which we sipped as we sat facing one another at the dining-room table, each armed with an electric typewriter. This was Kesey's idea.

At one point, writer Ron Rosenbaum rang the doorbell. He wanted to borrow a sugar cube of acid. I explained that I was in the middle of an interview and invited him in, but after watching Kesey and me typing and silently passing pages back and forth across the table for a while, he decided to leave.

Here's an excerpt from the interview:

Q. "You've said, regarding the media, that if you follow the wires, they all lead to the Bank of America. Would you expand on that?"

A. "When you've had a lot of microphones poked at you with questions like, 'Mr. Kesey, would you let your daughter take acid with a black man,' 'Mr. Kesey, do you advocate the underwear of the Lennon Sisters [singers on *The Lawrence Welk Show*],' 'Mr. Kesey, how do you react to the findings of the FAD indicating that patchouli oil causes cortisone damage,' you get so you can follow the wires back to their two possible sources. Perhaps one wire out of a thousand leads to one of the sources, to the heart of the man holding the microphone, while the other 999 go through a bramble of ambition, ego, manipulation and desire, sparking and hissing and finally joining into one great coaxial cable that leads out of this snarl and plugs straight into the Bank of America."

Q. "How did Cassady respond the time you told him you feared you were losing your sense of humor?

A. "With great concern and sympathy, as though I had told him that I had cancer of the lymphthf."

Q. "How did you regain it?"

A. "The lymphthf? It came back on its own, after I dropped a five-gallon jar of mayonnaise on my foot."

Q. "No, I mean how did you regain your sense of humor?"

A. "Oh, that. I never did, I guess. Rehabilitation, as my counselor up at the Sheriff's Honor Camp used to tell me, is a two-way street."

Q. "Would you say that Christ was hindered or helped by his celibacy?"

A. "You gotta remember that Jesus was fathered by a celibate so he comes by it naturally. I *do*, however, think it contradicts some of the longevity claims made by the advocates of this particular crotch yoga discipline."

Q. "Would you agree that sexual jealousy is essentially puritan?"

A. "No, I think all denominations are probably afflicted by it."

Q. "What do you think of mechanical aids to sexual stimulation, such as vibrators?"

A. "I've always, if you'll pardon the expression, made out quite well with the traditional equipment, thank you."

Q. "Would you go so far as to say that orgies derive out of boredom?"

A. "All the orgies in my meager experience derived not from boredom—in fact, far from boredom—but from effort, ingenuity and a good deal of horniness."

Q. "Unlike Tim Leary and his magic embrace, you don't seem to be physically demonstrative. Do you attach any significance to that?"

A. "My dad, a Texan, raised me on good ole *Amurcan* handshakes; I reckon folks just does what comes natural to them. Sometimes I hug people, but it's usually when I'm interested in the configuration of their pectoral region."

Q. "Did you have to overcome any homosexual defenses when you were a wrestler?"

A. "Just one, and he was terrific."

Q. "Do you have as much faith in sports as you once did?"

A. "No. I played and loved sports, but I'm not going to steer my sons into them the way my father did me. I don't like the heavy fascist hit I get off the pro heroes, and I don't like the Little League consciousness that forces a kid to knuckle under a father's fading, and ill-proportioned, values. I'm afraid the old 'builds a boy's character and self-confidence' argument is just an earlier version of the Marine recruiter shuck."

Q. "There was a film critic who said that the Marx Brothers often used Sufi parables to launch into their excursions into madness."

A. "Far out! But I can believe it. There was a pervading smell of sanity in the fuss the brothers raised that seemed to come from some place other than the local yeshiva. Sufo Marx? Who'da thought it?"

Q. "Do you see the legalization of grass as any sort of panacea?"

A. "The legalization of grass would do absolutely nothing for our standard of living, or our military supremacy, or even our problem of high school dropouts. It could do nothing for this country except mellow it, and that's not a panacea, that's downright subversive."

Q. "It's no accident that the initials of your protagonist in *Cuckoo's Nest* are RPM—Revolutions Per Minute—and you don't take that word lightly, but where is your vision of revolution in relation to both Ho Chi Minh and [author of *The Greening of America*] Charles Reich?

A. "Chuck and Ho? Naturally, I can't hope to under the circumstances with reference to each of their personal visions, huh?"

Q. "I'm talking about the spectrum from Chuckie's bell-bottoms to Ho's antiaircraft."

A. "Ah, I see. Well, I think that either sticking a leg in a pair of bell-bottoms or loading a canister into an antiaircraft weapon may or may not be a revolutionary act. This is only known at the center of the man doing the act. And *there* is where the revolution must lie, at the *seat of the act's impetus*, so that finally every action, every thought and prayer, springs from this committed center."

Q. "Didn't you once believe that writing is an old-fashioned and artificial occupation?"

A. "I was counting on the millennium. Now I guess I'm tired of waiting."

Q. "In *Sometimes a Great Notion*, you had this idealistic logger in the role of a strikebreaker, and yet now, back in real life, you're glad that the union has shut down the local [Oregon] paper and pulp mill. What's made the difference—ecology?"

A. "Women's lib."

Q. "Are you just being a smart-ass or do you mean that?"

A. "Women's lib has made us aware of our debauching of Mother Earth. The man who can peel off the Kentucky topsoil, gouge the land empty to get his money nuts off, then split for other conquests, leaving the ravished land behind to raise his bastards on welfare and fortitude, is different from Hugh Hefner only in that he drives his cock on diesel fuel. Women's lib was the real issue in *Notion*. I didn't know this when I wrote it, but think about it: It's about men matching egos and wills on the battleground of Vivian's unconsulted hide. When she leaves at the end of the book, she chooses to leave the only people she loves for a bleak and uncertain but at least *equal* future.

"The earth is bucking in protest of the way she's been diddled with; is it strange that the most eloquent rendition of this protest should come from the bruised mouth of womankind?"

Q. "And yet, since you're against abortion, doesn't that put you in the position of saying that a girl or a woman must bear an unwanted child as punishment for ignorance or carelessness?"

A. "In as I feel abortions to be probably the worst worm in the revolutionary philosophy, a worm bound in time to suck the righteousness and the life from the work we are engaged in, I want to take this slowly and carefully. . . ." [Kesey proceeded to go into a lengthy dissertation here.] "I swear to you, Paul," he concluded, "that abortions are a terrible karmic bummer, and to support them—except in cases where it is a bona fide toss-up between the child and the mother's life—is to harbor a worm of discrepancy."

Q. "Well, that's all really eloquent and misty-pooh, but suppose Faye were raped and became pregnant in the process?"

A. "Nothing is changed. You don't plow under the corn because the seed was planted with a neighbor's shovel."

Q. "I assume that would be her decision, though?"

A. "Almost certainly. But I don't really feel right about speaking for her. Why don't you phone and ask?"

So I called Faye in Oregon and reviewed the dialogue. She asked, "Now, what's the question—if I were raped, would I get an abortion?"

"That about sums it up."

"No, I wouldn't."

A couple of years later, Kesey changed his position on abortion and became pro-choice.

"A woman's reproductive rights are inextricable from her freedom in general," he said. "She should have control of her body as well as her mind."

After the interview, we went to a benefit rally for the United Farm Workers. Joan Baez was performing there, and I was happy to give her Dylan's message. I felt like a special courier. Mission accomplished.

Kesey and I hung around La Honda for a while. He had once discovered a tunnel inside a cliff overlooking the beach. We were smoking hash in the tunnel, which had been burrowed during World War II so that military spotters with binoculars could look toward the ocean's horizon for oncoming enemy ships. All we spotted was a meek little mouse in the tunnel. We blew smoke at that mouse until it could no longer tolerate our behavior. The mouse stood on its hind paws and roared at us: "*Squeeeeeeek!*"

This display of mouse assertiveness startled us, and we almost fell off the cliff. The headline would have read, "Dope-Crazed Pranksters in Suicide Pact." And it all would've been One-Legged Terry's fault.

● ● ●

In 1974, I was sharing an apartment with Stewart Brand. On the wall of my room I taped a photo of my daughter Holly and two posters: President Nixon, whom I disdained; and a Native American, Geronimo, whom I admired.

One evening I sensed that there was something vaguely different in my room. Then I realized what it was—my Richard Nixon poster. His eyes, which had always looked toward the right, were now looking toward the left. It had that eerie effect of the Jesus-face plaque in a novelty-shop window, where his eyes would follow you as you passed. Except that Nixon's eyes were frozen in this position.

I examined the poster more closely and was able to discern that the original eyeballs had been whited out from the right side, and new eyeballs had been drawn in the left-hand corners. Then I checked to see whether the eyes in Holly's photo had also been changed, but she was still looking directly at me. So was my Indian guide. Only Nixon's eyes had been altered. It seemed out of character for Stewart to have done this, but I asked him anyway.

"No, it wasn't me," he said. "But Kesey was around for a while."

"Of course! I should've realized it was Kesey when I saw that tell-tale trail of cornstarch."

•   •   •

In 1977, I was spending the Christmas holidays with the Kesey family in Oregon. Larry Flynt had just become a born-again Christian and, in the afterglow of his conversion by President Carter's evangelist sister, he hired me to run *Hustler*—the first men's magazine to "show pink" in their photos of naked women. For *me* to function as redeeming social value was an offer too absurd to refuse.

Kesey's daughter Shannon was giving him a haircut, stretching out each individual coil and then clipping off the end of it, while Kesey—himself a practicing Christian—gave me his farewell blessing: "Christ's plan has a place for pink. All you have to do is lace it with love. . . ."

I hired my former wife, Jeanne—who had been my managing editor at *The Realist*—as researcher and cartoon editor. On the phone with Kesey, I asked, "Does hiring one's ex-wife count as nepotism?"

"Well," he replied, "nepotism is better than nopetism at all."

I repeated this to Flynt. He laughed and said, "Look, the next time you perform somewhere, maybe you could use that line and mention that I said it."

"Oh, sure—in fact, why don't I call Kesey right now and tell *him* that you said it?"

My job at *Hustler* lasted six months. Flynt was shot, his wife Althea took over, and she fired me. I went back to my office and locked the door, feeling an overwhelming sense of relief. I phoned family and friends to tell them the news before they learned about it from the media.

When I called Kesey, he said "Why don't you come to Egypt with us? The Grateful Dead are gonna play the Pyramids." What perfect timing! I put my radio on and started dancing around the office, singing, "Oh, thank you for firing me, Althea, thank you, thank you, thank you."

•   •   •

I received the following letter from a Hollywood actor:

"When I was working up on some mountain, I heard a rumor about Kesey migrating to the great beyond. I asked everybody: 'Somebody said

Ken Kesey is dead?' Not one out of 20, 25 knew who Ken Kesey was! Much less read his books. 'Jesus Christ,' I thought, 'am I alone in this world?'

"Very much later, sitting by the fire and beer cooler, the makeup girl showed up with a joint; smoked in silence—not a word. Stoned to the teeth, I threw a log on the coals and picked two cold ones. She said, 'What was the bartender's name in *Sometimes a Great Notion*?' I knew but asked. She said 'Teddy.'"

Kesey once told me that when he was working on *One Flew Over the Cuckoo's Nest*, "I wasn't trying to write a novel, I was trying to go all the way."

He would occasionally share his literary talent by reading from his work, but in 1989 he completed a unique collaborative writing project with a group of students at the University of Oregon. He left them with some scrupulously chosen words to fire up the intensity of their literary integrity.

"What's the job of the writer in contemporary America?" he began. "I'm not sure, but here's an example. You're going to be walking along on the street one of these days and suddenly there's going to be a light over there. You're going to look across the street, and on the corner over there, God is going to be standing right there, and you're going to know it's God because he's going to have huge curly hair that sticks up through his halo like Jesus, and he's got little slitty eyes like Buddha, and he's got a lot of swords in his belt like Muhammad.

"And he's saying, 'Come to me. Come across the street to me. Oh, come to me. I will have muses say in your ear you will be the greatest writer ever. You will be better than Shakespeare. Come to me. They will have melon breasts and little blackberry nipples. Come to me. All you have to do is sing my praises.'

"Your job is to say, 'Fuck you, God! Fuck you! Fuck you! Fuck you!' Because nobody else is going to say it. Our politicians aren't going to say it. Nobody but the writer is going to say it. There's time in history when it's time to praise God, but now is not the time. Now is the time for us to say 'Fuck you! I don't care who your daddy was. Fuck you!' And get back to our job of writing."

● ● ●

If you were to ask Kesey what he thought was his greatest work, his answer would not have been the title of a book. He would've said, "The bus."

Twenty-five years after Tom Wolfe wrote *The Electric Kool-Aid Acid Test*—mythologizing the cross-country trip of the former school bus, revamped and misspelled "Furthur"—Ken Kesey and his Merry Band of Pranksters were once again driving the bus, this time from the farm in Oregon to the Smithsonian Institution in Washington, D.C. There would be various stops along the way. Tim Leary asked me to call him when the bus arrived in Los Angeles before heading east. Kesey said that in Philadelphia, a troop of Girl Scouts with a hip scoutleader was scheduled to board the bus.

"We're calling it Cookies and Kool-Aid."

This was not the first time such a trip was planned. In 1974, a group of second-generation Pranksters were repainting the designs and symbols and inner-vision comic-strip characters on "Furthur," because there had been an inquiry from the Smithsonian. Kesey figured that if the outside of the dilapidated bus could be brightened anew, why, then, the inside would automatically work again and the bus could be driven all the way to Washington.

In 1984, the bus was still there on the farm. In fact, *People* magazine was planning to publish a special section on the '60s, and a photo of the bus would be on the cover, with Kesey and me sitting on each of the headlights and Wavy Gravy perched on the hood. Posing for the cover of *People*, I couldn't resist subtly holding on to my crotch with one hand. However, they made Michael Jackson the main story, and put *his* carefully chosen picture on the cover, with his gloved hand blatantly grabbing *his* crotch. On the inside, a full-page photo of us atop the bus identified me as "father of the underground press." I immediately demanded a paternity test.

In November 1990, I was assigned by the *San Francisco Examiner* to cover the pilgrimage on wheels. I felt torn between reporting the truth—that this was *not* the original bus—or snitching on a friend. What a terrible conflict of interest. Was my responsibility to reveal what I knew or to be loyal to Prankster tradition?

The original bus, a 1939 International Harvester, was still resting in peace at the farm—a shell of its former shell, metal rusting and paint fading—a psychedelic relic of countercultural history. But the bus I boarded now was a 1947 Harvester. The Grateful Dead had donated $5,000 for a sound system, which was blaring out Ray Charles's "Hit the Road, Jack" as we left.

This version of "Furthur" had been deemed the Most Historical Float at the Oregon 4th of July parade. It was painted by 15 individuals starting in April. The result was a magnificent visual feast. A Sun God with refraction discs so the eyes followed you. A totem pole and a tiger. Adam and Buddha. Pogo and the Silver Surfer. A lizard—following Dorothy and her companions down the yellow brick road—named the Lizard of Oz. A banner on the side of the bus warning, "Never Trust a Prankster."

There was a painting on the back door of an eye-in-the-Pyramid, and a helium tank on the back platform, so that Kesey could blow up balloons and give them to kids at stops along the way. One mother offered him a quarter. "I'm an important author," he explained—"you can't give me a *quarter*." So now she wasn't sure whether the balloon was free or she should give him a dollar.

Pedestrians flashed the V sign and the *Star Trek* signal. Drivers waved and honked their horns. A police car was behind us, and a cop used his megaphone to call out, "Good luck on your journey." Our hood ornament was a beautiful sculpture of a court jester holding a butterfly net, named Newt the Nutcatcher, with a profile resembling Neal Cassady, legendary driver of the original bus.

On the inside, a picture of Cassady watched over the current driver, Kesey's nephew, Kit, who refused to wear a taxicab cap. Kesey's son, Zane, was also on the crew, so the trip had a strong sense of family tradition. Altogether there were 12 males and one female—a 23-year-old Deadhead who got on the bus in Berkeley instead of going to a Halloween party. She was still dressed as Pippy Longstocking.

Lee Quarnstrom had quit his job as a reporter to join the original Pranksters, and now he was covering this event for the *San Jose Mercury-News*. Since we were now in San Jose, the bus circled around the parking lot of the *Mercury-News*. Kesey quickly found a CD of '60s songs and played "Mr. Lee" by the Bobbettes over the sound system. Lee was sitting on the top deck of the bus as the entire editorial staff of the paper stood outside the building, cheering for him while the lyrics rang out: "One, two, three, look at Mr. Lee. . . ."

Ed McClanahan had been a classmate of Kesey's in the Stanford writing class where it all started. He gave up a chance to go on the original trip, regretted it for 26 years, and was now covering this trip for *Esquire*.

"If the bus goes past the *Esquire* building," he asked Kesey, "are you gonna play the theme from *Mr. Ed*?"

Later, I overheard Quarnstrom whisper to fellow Prankster Zonker, "Shhh, Paul doesn't know." There was some sort of hoax in the air, but

I decided to maintain conscious innocence and just allow it to unfold.

Quarnstrom and Kesey had something awful in common. They had each lost a son. Eric Quarnstrom had been shot in a meaningless street encounter. Jed Kesey was killed in an accident when the van carrying his wrestling team skidded off a cliff.

Jed and I had a special relationship. I flew to Oregon for the memorial. It was heartbreaking. Faye was outwardly stalwart, but Ken shook with emotion. "You were his favorite," he sobbed as we embraced—for the first time.

Kesey had always been against seat belts—"They sanction bad driving"—but after this he would campaign for legislation to *require* vehicles to have seat belts, the kind that could've saved Jed's life. For now, though, Kesey's grief was unrelenting.

"I feel like every cell in my body is exploding," he said.

Near the start of the reunion bus trip, Quarnstrom and Kesey had talked privately about their mutual tragedy in Wavy Gravy's kitchen.

"I think about Eric every day," said Quarnstrom.

"I think about Jed every day," said Kesey. "And it's appropriate that we should."

Meanwhile, a color photo of the bus appeared in *Time* magazine, and an employee at the Smithsonian recognized it as not being the original "Furthur." Their spokesperson issued a statement: "The current bus is not even close to the original. Even if it were, the Smithsonian is not interested in a replica." Kesey was aghast.

"I don't think of this bus as a replica," he said. "The Smithsonian—they want to clone the other one from the carburetor, which is about all that's left of it—the way they wanted to do in that Woody Allen movie, *Sleeper*, when they only had the nose for that. And they wanted to put on new metal, new chassis, new motor, and hire some artists to paint and, you know, they're going to restore it, and I thought, 'In what form? Are they gonna go back to when it was bright red and we all drove it into Berkeley on Vietnam Day with swastikas and Stars of David and American flags all over, with guns stickin' out of the top? Or when we went to New York with Pop Art stuff on it?'

"It's had dozens of different permutations. If they really want to restore it, they'll take it back to yellow. But the thing about the Smithsonian is that I've never spoken to them. They've been dealing with some rich people up in Portland—they wanted me to give them the bus—they're going to fix it up and donate it to the Smithsonian. My metaphor for this is that they've also been negotiating for Tom Selleck's dick, but they haven't mentioned it to Tom."

We reporters had a discussion about journalistic ethics, specifically how we planned to handle any possible use of drugs on the bus. What with stomach paunches, gray hair and bifocals, the drug of choice this time around could well be *ant*acid. Kesey would permit neither cigarettes nor diet soda on the bus. In response to a decade of "Just say no" propaganda, he advised, "Just say thanks."

He had been disinvited from a *Nightline* panel on drugs because he was pro-marijuana. He made a distinction between pot, mushrooms, LSD, psilocybin—"the organic, kinder, gentler, hippie drugs"—and cocaine, crack, ice, "drugs that make you greedy and produce criminals." He called drugs "my church," confessing that he had taken psychoactives "with lots more reverence and respect than I ever walked into church with."

The bus headed for Stockton, where Kesey was scheduled to speak at the University of the Pacific, and the machinations of the prank would begin. I was the only one who didn't know what the plan was. While Kesey was inside speaking, Zane was drawing a chalk outline on the street around the perimeter of the bus. Inside, Kesey was finishing up his question-and-answer segment, aided by a microphone wedged into a foam rubber football, which each questioner in the audience would throw to the next questioner.

"Okay," Kesey said, "that's enough. Now we will sing our national anthem." He led the audience in singing the Grateful Dead song, "What a Long Strange Trip It's Been." Outside, the crew made sure my bag was off the bus. Inside, Kesey left the stage.

He said to Zonker, "Why don't you run out there and tell us the bus is missing?"

"Because I didn't know it *was*," Zonker replied.

Quarnstrom rushed in and reported "Kesey, they done left us!"

"Kesey shouted, "The bus is gone! The bus is gone!"

Where the bus had been, there was now only that chalk outline and a message in white tape spelling out: NOTHING LASTS! The bus was on its way back to Oregon. Kesey and a couple of others would stay at a hotel in Stockton and take the train back. They had planned from the very start that the bus would not be driven to the Smithsonian.

"I always knew we wouldn't carry this prank too far," Kesey said, adding, in mock shock, "*That's* not the real Elvis!"

254 ◄ ◄ ◄Murder at the Conspiracy Convention

I called Tim Leary to inform him that the bus was *not* coming to Los Angeles after all. Leary had been in Europe, returning with an East German flag that he wanted to donate to the Smithsonian, but he didn't say whether it was the original flag or just a replica.

Zonker offered to drive me to San Jose, where I could catch a plane back home the next morning. Before I went to get my bag from Kesey's room, I told Zonker, "I hope I don't come out of the hotel only to find a chalk outline of the car."

Kesey asked me to call *San Francisco Chronicle* columnist Herb Caen and tell him that the bus had disappeared. All of a sudden, I was experiencing the Stockton Hostage Syndrome. A hoax had been played and, although I was a victim of that hoax myself, I was now expected to help perpetuate it.

"Tell him there's been a mutiny," Kesey instructed me, "and that you're an irate Prankster who's been left behind."

"What, and ruin my credibility?"

•   •   •

In 1997, Kesey and the Pranksters were on their way to the opening of a special exhibit—"I Want to Take You Higher: The Psychedelic Era"—at the Rock and Roll Hall of Fame in Cleveland.

The *Bowling Green Daily News* published a photo of "a man who didn't want to be identified" licking the side of the bus. He apparently believed that LSD had been mixed in with the painted designs.

"We got bumped from the induction ceremonies," Kesey told me. "We were supposed to be honored on the 6th of May, but Michael Jackson's people contacted the museum. They didn't think it would be fitting if Michael Jackson was on the same list as the bus, so they moved us to the 10th."

"You mean they think psychedelic exploration is worse than child molestation?"

"Yes," said Kesey. "We are lower than pedophiles."

"Words to live by."

"I remember this old saying my dad had: 'I'm so low the snail shit on the bottom of the ocean looks like shooting stars in the sky.'"

•   •   •

Revealing images of Kesey keep popping up in my memory.

*When my daughter Holly was living with me in San Francisco, we managed to play a haphazard version of the domestic game. We had taken to piling up the paper bags from shopping on the kitchen table—neither of us would bother to flatten them out and put them away—but one time Kesey came over and just crumpled all the bags up into one big bag, which he tossed out the back window into our garden.

*At his house in La Honda, former site of vigorous Prankster parties, the loudspeakers that had been placed in the hill across the road remained intact. One day, a car stopped on the road—which was separated from the house by a little bridge—and a couple in the car were engaged in a loud, hostile argument that brought us outside. When Kesey realized what was going in, he quietly strode back to the house and put a romantic Frank Sinatra song on the stereo, which came blasting out of the hill. The couple in the car stopped arguing and drove off.

*When my wife Nancy and I drove to Mexico with Kesey in his old cream-colored, open-topped Buick convertible, he was wearing a Panama hat and a white suit, which suffered not the slightest stain while he changed a tire that went flat on the way.

The last time I saw Kesey was at Whee! (The World Hemp Expo and Extrava*ganja*) near Eugene, Oregon. The Pranksters made a campily majestic entrance on "Furthur." Kesey was seated on top of the bus—"like a sweating and red-faced pasha," in Nancy's words, "nestled in a customized luggage rack, shaded by ribbons and banners." At their booth, the Kesey family served as their own logo.

The Pranksters presented a satirical performance with an anti-gun theme on the main stage—inspired by the recent high-school shooting in Springfield, just a few miles from Kesey's home—suggesting not only that teachers be armed, but also that all students be armed.

"Let us have no law that will infringe on the right to have guns," Kesey expounded, "but let us ban all ammunition!"

(In an article in the *Los Angeles Times* on January 5, 2002, 15-year-old twins Niko and Theo Milonopoulos, cofounders of Kidz Voice-LA, wrote: "Many Los Angeles kids have been saved from gun violence by a decade-old city ordinance that prohibits gun dealers from selling ammunition over the holidays. The holiday ammunition ban, which halts the sale of thousands of bullets from Christmas Day through New Year's Day, is a welcome reprieve in a city where more than 50 kids are shot to death each year. . . .

("A year-round citywide ban on the sale of ammunition would save the city millions of dollars in health care, emergency services and criminal-related court and prison costs, which come into effect each time someone is shot. According to the American Medical Assn., taxpayers pay an average of $17,000 per gun injury. Cities such as Chicago and Washington, D.C., not only ban the sale of all ammunition and guns but also prohibit an individual from possessing these tools of destruction within their city limits.

("With a ban on the sale of ammunition in effect year-round, law-abiding individuals would be able to purchase guns in Los Angeles and keep ammunition in their homes. The real difference would be that ammunition would be less accessible. On Sept. 7, Councilmen Nick Pacheco and Eric Garcetti introduced a motion to ban the sale of all gun ammunition citywide throughout the year. The initiative was sent to the Public Safety Committee. The proposal stalled as City Hall focused on protecting Angelenos from terrorist attacks.")

The last thing Kesey wrote for publication was more than a week after the terrorist attacks for a special issue of *Rolling Stone* on 9/11.

"Bush has just finished his big talk to Congress," he wrote, "and the men in suits are telling us what the men in uniforms are going to do to the men in turbans if they don't turn over the men in hiding. The talk was planned to prepare us for war. . . .

"The Real War has already been waged, and it's not between the U.S. and the Taliban, or between the Moslems and the Israelis or any of the familiar forces, but between the ancient gutwrenching bonebreaking fleshslashing way things have always been and the timorous and fragile way things might begin to be. Could begin to be. Must begin to be, if our lives and our children's lives are ever, someday, in the upheaving future, to know honest peace. . . ."

Kesey barely made his deadline, and this final paragraph was cut for lack of space:

"I can remember Pearl Harbor. I was only six but that morning is forever smashed into my memory like a bomb into a metal deck. Hate for the Japanese nation still smolders occasionally from the hole. This 9/11 nastiness is different. There is no nation to blame. There are no diving Zeros, no island-grabbing armies, no sea filled with battleships and carriers. Just a couple dozen batty guys with box knives and absolute purpose. Dead now. Vaporized. Of course we want their leaders, but I'll be damned if I can see how we're gonna get those leaders by deploying our aircraft carriers and launching our mighty air power so we can begin bombing the crippled orphans in the rocky leafless already bombed-out rubble of Afghanistan."

• • •

After his son Jed died in 1984, Kesey told me that the sadness he felt made him realize how his own death would make so many people sad. This was not an egotistic statement, just an objective observation.

"With Jed's death," he later elaborated, "what I finally came to grips with was that love and grief have to be united. You can't separate them. As soon as you really love somebody, at some point you're going to grieve. And that's why people move away from each other, so they don't have to be there to experience the loss."

And now Kesey was buried alongside Jed on the farm at a private funeral. His casket, painted in multi-colored psychedelic swirls, had been transported there from a public memorial by "Furthur," resting on the same back platform where he once blew up balloons and gave them to kids along the way.

There are those who'd like to imagine Kesey on That Great Bus in the Sky, with Cassady at the wheel and Garcia on the guitar and Leary on acid, but everybody remembers him in their own way. When his little granddaughter learned of Kesey's death, she asked, "But now who will teach us how to hypnotize the chickens?"

defying
conventions

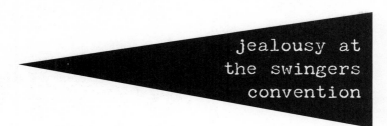

jealousy at the swingers convention

The 24th annual Lifestyles Couples Convention has filled three hotels in Palm Springs, California. The Convention Center is connected to one of them, the Wyndham, which surrounds a large outdoor pool and patio populated by couples busy socializing in 116-degree dry heat. Women and men alike are wearing thongs. From afar they appear like so many eyeless smiley faces among the bathing suits. The law that Sonny Bono signed when he was mayor, banning thongs in public, does not apply to this event, or, for that matter, to Cher.

The convention is for couples only. Except for me. I've been hired to perform stand-up comedy at their Friday luncheon, and I'm here alone. On the small, propellered plane from Los Angeles to Palm Springs, the right side consists of two-seat rows, occupied entirely by couples on their way to the convention—horny with the expectation of getting laid by the spouse of a stranger, perhaps sitting in front of or behind them—and the left side of the plane consists of one-seat rows, occupied entirely by me. I'm afraid that the plane might tip over upon trying to land.

At the Convention Center, even the plastic-encased lapel nametags are coupled off: "Ken and Barbie" on his, "Barbie and Ken" on hers. Not all the couples are paired off in real life, though. One person can simply bring along another—known in swinger circles as a "ticket" for gender balance—in order to get into the convention. So everybody has entered two by two, and I feel like a unicorn stowaway on Noah's Ark, surreptitiously balancing on the cusp between love and lust.

There are 3,000 participants at this convention, mostly upper-middle-class, in their 30s, 40s and 50s. They consider people in the outside world to be "straight," even though one would ordinarily consider *them* straight. I mean there are suburban soccer moms here, openly celebrating their secret lifestyle at an oasis of supportiveness. There's a man in a suit with a flesh-colored penis necktie, another wearing a T-shirt declaring, "I'm Not Going Bald, I'm Getting More Head," and another dressed only in a leather jockstrap, who recognizes me and introduces himself.

"I'd give you my card," he says, "but I have no place to keep them."

Inside the 100,000-square-foot Convention Center, the Exhibit Hall has been turned into an "Adult Marketplace," buzzing with commercial activity. I overhear one shopper's complaint: "But we've *already* spent $400." There's a multitude of merchandise on display—pornographic videos, naughty lingerie, fetish paraphernalia, edible lotions—plus booths galore. At the Golden Nipples booth, women are cheerfully having exact duplicates of their nipples created in sterling silver or 14-karat gold, which can be used as pendants, key fobs, money clips or—yes, of course— nipple covers. At the Penimax booth, an Asian vendor is selling disposable cock rings, which, he promises, will maintain your erection even after you ejaculate.

There are several booths dedicated to booking vacations especially designed for swingers, at nude beaches, clothing-optional resorts and ocean cruises. I follow around an elderly woman who is busy picking up brochures at every such booth. It seems incongruous, but I try not to indulge in stereotypes. Finally I engage her in a conversation, and she explains that her boss told her to get as much material as she could, because he owns some property surrounded by government land, and he wants to start a new business.

At the Erotic Massage Wear table, a woman uses my arm to demonstrate a device that turns her fingertip into a vibrator, not intended for nose picking. Then she puts Jergen's Lotion on my right hand, dons a pair of Love Mitts—made of vinyl with little nubs all over—and proceeds to massage my hand, while on the VCR there's a tape of a woman wearing Love Mitts and massaging a man's lubricated penis. This is a bizarre mixed-media sensation. Although I don't get a hard-on, the lobes of my brain seem to fuse, and for the next few hours my left hand persists in feeling neglected.

Checking out the functional furniture, I eavesdrop on a (fully clothed) couple testing out the "rocking torso feature" on a Love Table, but I actually climb *into* the Love Swing, assuming a position ordinarily assumed by a woman while the man stands up, crotch to crotch. My body is suspended half upside-down in mid-air with legs spread and feet up in stirrups. I'm feeling mighty vulnerable. As I hang there, the inventor hands me my tape recorder, then proceeds to show me how "the woman can place the man's penis on her G-spot by moving her legs from a position of being out front like this to being in the fetal position" and how "the man, instead of just going in and out like that, he can make his penis a joystick, so every step he takes is a movement inside of her, more like a dance step." He guarantees, "You'll never use a bed again."

Next I inspect the Bungee Sexperience—a harness designed by a company that makes bungee cords—it bounces in the air, so the "rider" can enjoy weightless sex in a variety of positions. I ask the woman demonstrating this how many hours a day she bounces up and down. "At an event like this," she responds, without missing a bounce, "I'd say eight to 12 hours." She tells me that her circulation is excellent, and that her 18-year-old son refers to the contraption as a "bungee humper." In addition to bouncing, it can also create "the illusion of bondage, yet the person can actually be comfortable while restrained."

The Auto Erotic Chair, however, provides *real* bondage. It's equipped with leather restraints and panic snaps for arms and legs, and comes complete with a power box, pneumatically operated anal and vaginal plugs. "Our power source unit is designed to stimulate nerve fibers throughout the genital areas by delivering controllable electro-pulse energy through conductive electrodes on our sex toys. Our precision-engineered technology gives you safe and pleasurable electric play." So, for example, in the Electro-Flex Penile Ring/Anal Plug Configuration, "A single conductor butt plug is used in conjunction with a single conductive cock ring to complete the circuit. With a single conductive cock ring, one side of a double conductive butt plug can be used to stimulate either the prostate or the sphincter."

If you'd prefer something, well, less electric, there's always the Crystal Wand, a 10-inch-long, S-shaped coed tool, hand-carved from pure crystal-clear acrylic, that doubles simultaneously as a G-spot stimulator and prostate massager. I'm reminded of a swing party I heard about, one that took place at the Whispers Club in Michigan. Couples removed from the refrigerator 12-inch summer sausages and cucumbers that the hostess had planned to use for food that evening. When she walked into the "party room," she couldn't help but notice that although the food was being consumed, it was not exactly in the fashion she had originally envisioned. Instead, the sausages and cucumbers were being utilized as organic sex toys.

As I continue to wander around the Adult Marketplace, I realize that the name of the game is penetration. All paths lead to penetration. But I'm not referring to penetration of the sexual kind, although that's an implicit goal—pick an orifice, any orifice, and there's always a corresponding appendage or gadget that can fulfill its desire for penetration—no, I'm talking about penetration of the *market*. There's lots of money to be made here. The persistent question is, how can I penetrate this market? Maybe I could come up with a combination FM radio and vibrating dildo.

•   •   •

I'm beginning to feel like I'm experiencing an alien encounter, only *I'm* the alien here. Nevertheless, I'm aware that swingers and comedians do have something in common. We both like to have a good opening line. As a performer, I always try to slant my opening line toward a particular audience.

My opening line at the World Hemp Expo was, "Last night, for the first time in my life, I used a hemp condom." My opening line at a Skeptics Conference, attended by the Amazing Randi and the Amazing Kreskin, was: "This is the first conference I've been to where there were two people with the same first name of Amazing—but the Amazing Randi was born with that name, it's on his birth certificate, whereas the Amazing Kreskin changed his name for showbiz, his real name is the Obnoxious Kreskin." And my opening line at a luncheon during the Los Angeles County Bar Association conference was, "I'd like to begin with a moment of silence, so that you can think about your client's problem, and then you can make this a billable hour."

Now I find myself in a lavish hotel suite, trying to crystallize an opening line while contemplating the bald spot on the back of my head, infinitely cloned in the mirrors of the hotel bathroom, actually the only place I ever get to *see* that bald spot as others do. This will be a serious opening line, since I have been told that, in the introduction to my performance, I will be presented with the Lifestyles Freedom Award. I decide that my opening line will then be, "I just want to say that freedom of expression existed long before the First Amendment." Though it's not my motivation, I realize that this opening line will undoubtedly please

Robert McGinley, the bearded cofounder and president of the Lifestyles Organization.

"We hate government intervention in our lives," he has assured me. "We hate censorship. We're against laws that require helmets for cyclists. It's good that a law was just passed allowing women to breast-feed in public, but we shouldn't need permission from the government to do it." He admits to being "libertarian, but not Libertarian Party." He draws his philosophy from Jack London—"The proper function of man is to live, not to exist"—and, more specifically, his credo is, "Adult sexuality is normal." Dr. McGinley (he holds a Ph.D. in counseling psychology) tells me a riddle: "What do you call an Italian swinger?" I give up. The answer: "A swop."

At the luncheon, it turns out that I am *not* presented with the Freedom Award after all, and I have to come up immediately with a replacement opening line: "I'm delighted to be at the Lifestyles Convention—this is the first convention I've ever been to that was named after a condom."

Indeed, condom consciousness (if not condom use) is present at the convention. In one workshop, "The ABCs of Swinging," condom etiquette is described as bringing "the right safety equipment, just as you would for scuba diving or parachuting." Another presentation on "Safer Sex" covers new drug therapies for AIDS, information on other sexually transmitted diseases that are increasing among heterosexuals, and "things you should be doing to protect yourself."

Originally, herpes had caused a certain panic in swinger circles. Some swing clubs closed, though private parties increased. But, paradoxically enough, with the advent of AIDS, *new* clubs opened, as if the disease were anti-climactic. Currently, there's a surge of growth in this subculture—thanks to the Internet—with estimates ranging from 20,000 to three million participants. And, according to Dr. McGinley, "There's been very little increase in condom use. It's the woman's choice."

Nonetheless, at the Adult Marketplace, a woman in a black lace negligee roams around giving out free samples of condoms. There are also Creme Cookie Condoms for sale. They appear to be vanilla and chocolate Oreo-style cookies, individually wrapped in cellophane. I ask the vendor whether these are condoms that look like cookies, or cookies that look like condoms. She tells me that they are edible cookies, but each one has a condom inside.

"They're only a dollar each," she says, adding, as I edge away from her booth, "it's a great joke."

• • •

The Art Gallery at the Convention Center, featuring the Lifestyles Convention's 7th annual Sensual & Erotic Art Exhibition, almost didn't happen. The state's Department of Alcoholic Beverage Control had tried to prevent it from opening. When their authority was challenged, an ABC representative became an alchemist, transforming logic into absurdity. Legally, he said, you can't even have sex in a hotel room which has a minibar. Sure, pal, just try to enforce *that* one.

Two days before the convention, the ACLU obtained a restraining order against ABC's interference with the art exhibit. But ABC didn't just give up and assume the fetal position in a love swing. Rather, the agency threatened to revoke the Wyndham Hotel's liquor license if they allowed a special two-hour session, the convention's traditional Evening of Caressive Intimacy, to take place in the Wyndham Ballroom on Friday as scheduled. This popular, closed-door, clothing-optional massage clinic, limited to the first 200 couples who sign up, would include the "human car wash," involving, as one veteran swinger portrays it, "a lot of naked bodies and some serious rubbing."

But the ABC regulations on Attire and Conduct—behavior "deemed contrary to public welfare and morals, and therefore no on-sale license shall be held at any premises where such conduct or acts are permitted"—includes this clause as a no-no: "To encourage or permit any person on the licensed premises to touch, caress or fondle the breasts, buttocks, anus or genitals of any other person." The Wyndham chickens out, the massage clinic is cancelled, the money is refunded, Lifestyles will sue the hotel for breach of contract, and the convention will be held in Las Vegas in 1998.

A lawyer, standing on the border of cynicism, suggests, "Just buy a town in Mexico and all the officials."

In 1996, the convention was held at the Town & Country Hotel in San Diego (for the fourth time), but two ABC officers claimed that they witnessed oral copulation in the convention hall, and the hotel's liquor license was suspended for five days, hence Lifestyle's move to Palm Springs this year. Lately, ABC has been spreading its particular brand of paranoia in Los Angeles, where the agency has raided gay, black and Latino bars in Los Angeles and in Hermosa Beach, where it has imposed restrictions on restaurants, requiring patio patrons to order food with their drinks, and forbidding customers to dance. Proprietors now play less upbeat music so that nobody will be tempted to dance. Those who can't resist are asked to stop.

Incidentally, I find out that, instead of giving the Freedom Award to me, convention officials have decided to present ABC with an Anti-Freedom Award, but that notion gets lost somewhere in award limbo, along with my unspoken opening line.

On Friday night, the massage clinic that doesn't take place is followed by the Wild West Casino and Dance. One man comes attired in a sheriff's outfit with a rubber penis drooping almost to the floor. A security guard tells him that he'll have to check it. Fake knives, guns and bullets are acceptable, but not a fake sex organ. Another cowboy, with a *real* (unloaded) gun, is stopped by a security guard, but he resists, asserting in his best John Wayne manner, "This is an 1887 pistol, and I'm not about to check it."

Several folks leave the dance at midnight to attend an unofficial 3rd annual spanking party. It ends at 3 a.m. with a bout of fist fucking. Dear Abby was right. One thing *does* lead to another.

● ● ●

I've been sampling many workshops at the Convention Center, and I notice that whenever I sit down on a chair next to a chair with someone else's stuff on it, and the owner of the stuff is sitting on the other side of that chair, they always tap the top of their stuff in a subconscious gesture of territoriality. I also observe that a man with one leg (he walks with crutches) and his wife seem to arrive at every single workshop that I attend. Hmmmmm. I'm beginning to get suspicious. Obviously, I've seen too many spy movies.

A cartoon in the 1991 convention program showed two rooms where lectures were being given. The room featuring "Do It Yourself Porn: Make Your Own XXX Movies" was overflowing into the corridor, and the room featuring "Socio-Political Ramifications of Current Trends in the Erosion of Civil Liberties" was empty, except for the baffled lecturer. It was a nice touch of self-deprecating humor, an exaggeration not too far from reality. At this '97 convention, porn actress Nina Hartley's "So You Want to Throw a Party: Recipes for a Successful Orgy" attracts 10 times more audience than attorney Bob Burke's "Sexual Politics: A Behind the Scenes Look."

Unfortunately, one workshop, "The Undertone of Sexuality in the *Star Trek* Series," has been cancelled—"due," someone added to the notice, "to Federation Regulations and Star Fleet Emergency Order 1007-932." Deborah Warner, in describing her presentation, had written: "Paramount and its parent company, Viacom, have a vested interest in presenting the *Trek* franchise as a family-oriented show. To this end, they overtly depict the characters as asexual. Yet there exists erotic subtext. . . . This has spawned a very large community of fans who create volumes of explicit erotica that is enjoying great popularity in print and an explosion of interest on the Internet."

Now, outside the room where her workshop would have been, there is disappointment—"Oh, and she was gonna bring a Klingon"—and nostalgia—"Remember the time Quark and Deanna were french-kissing?"

That theme continues at "American Tantra: How to Worship Each Other in Bed." This workshop—whose motto, "Orgasm long and prosper," paraphrases *Star Trek*'s blessing, "Live long and prosper"—is conducted by Paul Ramana Das and Marilena Silbey. "Interspecies intercourse," he muses. "This can't be the only planet where love is made." A writer for *Adult Video News* has reviewed their *Intimate Secrets of Sex & Spirit* and confessed, "I've rarely laughed so hard in my life. No shit, this vid earns a prenomination for 'most outrageous sex scene.' Paul actually uses Marilena's pussy as an echo chamber!"

Now, in his regular voice, he is telling our workshop of the need to "approach the body, not for sexual release, but for every single inch of this body, the groundwork, the geography of pleasure. Can anybody name one spot on your body that is not capable of receiving pleasure?" Nobody can. Later, the entire audience, seated around the perimeter of this extra-large room, is instructed to come stand in the center area and face their partners. I start to slide out, but not inconspicuously enough. Ramana Das, who knows me from a previous incarnation calls out, "There goes Paul Krassner. Are you afraid to participate?"

"I'm here as a journalist."

"Ah, he can't participate because he's a journalist. See how everybody has excuses."

Suddenly I'm saddled with a dose of New Age guilt, as though I have aborted my inner child. Meanwhile, there's a lovely blonde who doesn't have a partner, and I'm tempted to participate, but some guy who's also without a partner links up with her. Unexpectedly, my guilt changes to jealousy. Just a slight pang of jealousy, mind you, but a terrible taboo in this particular world.

Jealousy is an outmoded emotion to be shunned like dandruff. There's even a workshop that advises "How to Handle Jealousy" and another titled "Swing Without Guilt or Jealousy." And so now I not only feel guilty about not participating, I also feel guilty about feeling jealous. I've committed a swinger crime. Any second, I expect to hear security guards shouting "Jealousy alert!" Loud sirens go off. "Jealousy alert!"

Now where will I go? I have been reading about tantra in *Real Magic* by Isaac Bonewits: "Energy control is a very important part of the exercises; it is essential, for example, that during *Kama-kali* the male be able to refrain from ejaculating under the most harrowing circumstances." I decide to drop in on a workshop, "How to Prevent Premature Ejaculation," but everybody has already been there, and they all left early. Sorry. I blurted that out before I could stop myself.

• • •

There are swing clubs all around the country, from "Shenanigans" in Indiana to "Liberated Christians" in Arizona ("for Christians seeking liberation from false sexual repression based on mistranslation of scripture who wish to explore responsible non-monogamy and polyfidelity"). Many clubs designate themselves as an Equal Opportunity Lifestyle Organization, where membership is open to all races, and they belong to NASCA (North American Swing Club Association).

The Spring 1997 issue of *NASCA Inside Report* editorializes:

"There are political attacks on freedom that citizens should be aware of. It is far too easy to lose, through complacency and ignorance, the freedom that we Americans cherish. These attacks include the proposed censorship of the Internet, now under review by the U.S. Supreme Court, the recently court-upheld attempts by states to keep 'harmful' literature from the eyes of children by controlling street news racks, the reintroduction in Pennsylvania of legislation to outlaw swing clubs and a similar measure in California. Regarding the latter two, do we smell a conspiracy here?"

In Pennsylvania, Richard Kasunic, a Democratic state senator, failed in his 1996 attempt to outlaw "sex clubs." This year, he has reintroduced legislation to outlaw "swinger clubs." He states, "My bill will outlaw these immoral establishments in every community in Pennsylvania and provide significant penalties for those who choose to continue this offensive practice." The penalty for operating a swing club, even in one's own home: up to two years in jail and $5,000 in fines. For a second conviction: up to seven years and $15,000. For patronizing a swing club: $300 plus court costs.

In California, Tim Leslie, a Republican state senator, has introduced a bill which would provide that "every building or place which, as a primary activity, accommodates or encourages persons to engage in, or to observe other persons engaging in, sexual conduct including, but not limited to, anal intercourse, oral copulation, or vaginal intercourse, is a nuisance and shall be enjoined, abated and prevented, and for which damages may be recovered, whether it is a public or private nuisance."

Swinger periodicals range from *New Friends* to *Fuck Thy Neighbor*. Patti Thomas, author of *Recreational Sex: An Insider's Guide to the Swinging Lifestyle*, is editor at *Connection*, which publishes 13 titles, including *Cocoa 'n Creme*, catering to interracial swingers (not to be confused with *Black 'n Blue*, catering to sadomasochist swingers). *Connection* is suing the federal government over a bill that Ronald Reagan sent to Congress in 1987, the Child Protection and Obscenity Act, an outgrowth of the Meese Commission on Pornography.

The specific statute being challenged—known as the record keeping and labeling law, or the ID law—was supposed to be aimed at child pornography, but has been applied to adults-only swing publications. It requires anyone placing an explicit-photo ad to provide a photo ID, nicknames, maiden names, stage names, professional names, aliases. These records must be available for inspection by the attorney general's office.

Connection had attempted to comply with the law by cutting out every explicit photo ad from its magazines and sending them with a letter to those advertisers, explaining the new law and its requirements, asking that they submit the proper ID or send a "soft" photo that didn't require ID. Out of 500, only 26 advertisers responded with IDs. Patti Thomas spoke about this in her keynote speech at the Conclave '97 Convention in Chicago:

"It definitely makes it difficult to produce the magazine our readers and subscribers have come to expect, when you don't have enough so-called 'legal' ads to fill all those pages. And considering that *swinging itself is not illegal*, why should we have to 'register our sexual choices' with the government just to place a personal ad in a magazine? . . . I've never really thought of myself as an activist, or as one who was 'politically involved,' but over the last few years I think I've finally come to realizing that it's going to be *necessary* to be involved, even if it does mean 'exposing' my lifestyle to those who would repress it. I am *fucking sick and tired of do-gooders* trying to tell me how I should live my life!"

In 1995, *Connection* filed a suit challenging the constitutionality of the law and seeking a permanent injunction. In 1997, the motion was denied. Attorneys filed an appeal and a motion for a temporary injunction relieving *Connection* from complying with the act during that appeal. The motion was granted.

"The justice system in this country just makes no sense to me whatsoever," Patti Thomas tells me. "As far as I know, once we do present our case to the Court of Appeals, if our decision isn't favorable, we will make every attempt to go to the Supreme Court. Our attorneys are the best First Amendment attorneys anywhere. Our lawsuit has been very costly, as you can imagine, but our company believes very strongly in fighting for our constitutional rights. Our suit was filed not only for the benefit of our company, but because we felt that this outrageous law was totally infringing on the civil rights and freedoms of people involved in alternative lifestyles. Obviously, the average person involved in swinging would have no way of combating this law on their own."

I ask her whether attempts at repression have resulted in politicizing the swinger community.

"I'm afraid we haven't been very successful," she replies. "We try to inform our readers about political issues threatening our lifestyle and attempt to get them involved. Unfortunately, many in the lifestyle either don't believe that the government will actually take away their rights or are too afraid to make a stand. Swingers who have been 'exposed' as active participants in the lifestyle have lost jobs, family, community standing, friends, etc., as a result.

"People I've personally known who have lost their jobs when their swinging activities were discovered just wouldn't fight back because of the fear of further exposure through the publicity that could have been generated. As a matter of fact, my ex-husband was fired from a management position (back in 1980) when someone discovered his photo in one of our magazines and brought it to the attention of his superiors. Luckily, he was able to find a position with one of *Connection*'s affiliate companies. So, we pretty much remain an 'underground minority.'"

Her point is underscored by a 29-year-old woman at the convention. "None of us like publicity," she says. "None of us want to be out in the open. The business world is very conservative." She is wearing an American flag bikini, although she has never heard of Abbie Hoffman. She was born the same year that he got arrested for wearing an American flag shirt. Nor did she have any way of knowing that when he wore another American flag shirt on the Merv Griffin show, his half of the TV screen was blocked out all across America. She was, in short, unaware of the roots of her own, limited freedom.

• • •

It's Saturday night, and the Carnival Masquerade Ball is being held in the huge Convention Center Ballroom. On the wall behind the stage are gigantic masks. Above the tables are gold and purple balloons, fashioned after either somebody's school colors or a Chinese restaurant's hot mustard and soy sauce plate. The taped music is loud, and the dancing is raunchy, enhanced by gaudy yellow, blue and red lights. Pheromones are flying, and the costumes are kinky.

"Costumes," the program states, "may be anything of fertile imagination (genital area must be covered) for an exotic night of adult social fun." Hey, look who's here: Superman. The phantom of the opera. The devil. Mickey Mouse and Minnie Mouse (in a see-through top). An executioner. An Arabian potentate. A gold-plated pharaoh. A chicken lady covered with big yellow feathers. A guy in a dog collar being led around on a leash. And the one-legged man, who is wearing a roller skate as his costume.

At one point, an announcement is made that the next dance number will be filmed, so anybody who doesn't wish to be recognized should get off the dance floor. About 80 percent of the dancers leave. Similarly, taking part in the costume-judging means that permission to be photographed is automatically granted, which results in many contestants not making themselves available to be chosen as possible finalists.

The Best Male Costume goes to a 75-year-old man dressed as a biker stud. The Best Female Costume goes to his 75-year-old wife, dressed as a biker slut. The Best Couple's Costume goes to a woman with *papier mâché* breasts the size of beach balls and her mate with matching enormous testicles, but covered by pillowcases and a sign that warns "Censored by the hotel and ABC."

A marriage ceremony is performed onstage. The blissful pair have written their own vows; nothing is mentioned about forsaking all others. The newlyweds, their party and a few other couples are invited to a gathering in the suite of a three-time Emmy Award-winning TV producer and his wife. It turns out to be a tantra-filled wedding night. All the women massage the groom, and all the men massage the bride. One woman, a computer animator who wants to become a sexual surrogate, predicts that, as the millennium comes to an end, tantric men will be popping up everywhere.

A retired chairman and CEO of a title and escrow company, who attended another tantra party, tells me, "The difference between the tantra party and the party next door is the fact that at the beginning of the tantra party there was a lot of ceremony and shared tantra ritual, but once we had experienced that, it was every person for themselves. It was like the party next door." These were closed parties by invitation only. But you didn't need an invitation for open parties. All you had to do was find them.

The Wyndham Hotel is permeated by a sense of uninhibitedness. In the elevator, a beautiful black woman is looking in the full-length mirror and admiring her new Clit Clip—nonpiercing, adjustable, genital jewelry—"not designed to be painful," I learned at the Adult Marketplace, "just very sensual and aesthetically attractive. The Clit Clip is a long, narrow, *U*-shaped piece of metal, designed to fit around the clitoris hood, with some light-catching Austrian crystals, in your choice of clear, red, blue and purple, dangling from the ends." The woman in the elevator turns toward me and says "Isn't it nice?" Her husband smiles proudly.

"It's charming," I reply, "but what are you gonna do if the metal detector goes off at the airport?"

I leave them giggling in the elevator as I get off on a floor where I've heard there would be lots of action. I follow one group, but only the couple in front really know where they're going. They are on the way to their own room, and when they get there, they go in, close the door, and we are all left out in the corridor, looking like a perplexed ant farm. Everybody turns around. I am now at the front of the line, so I let them all pass by me as they head in the opposite direction, strolling briskly, except for the one-legged man with the roller skate and crutches, who is gliding gracefully along the carpet. Passersby are asked, in vain, "Where's the party?" We finally find a room with a porn photo on the door, which is slightly open.

Inside, there are perhaps 50 people in semidarkness. Exhibitionists and voyeurs together again. Here a blowjob, there a copulation, everywhere an undulating juiciness. There is an unspoken homophobia—no man is relating sexually to another man—but there is lots of lesbian libido. In order to keep a low profile, I have ripped several pages out of my notebook and folded them in half, so that I can take notes unobtrusively.

However, a woman with a feather duster asks me to hold her panties. She is about to join a threesome on the corner of the king-sized bed near the bureau I'm leaning against. I marvel at the choreography of this foursome. But they're playing, and I'm working. Their moans become my background music.

I wasn't *always* a wallflower at the orgy. I flash back 30 years . . . I'm at a Sexual Freedom League couples-only party at a large theatrical studio in San Francisco. There are 150 people dancing in the nude. Behind the closed curtains on the stage there are 15 small mattresses in constant use.

I remember making love on one of those mattresses with a sweet flower child only 15 minutes after we'd met. It was an exhilarating experience. We were on the front lines of the Sexual Revolution. We had to hold back from screaming out political slogans at our moment of climax. The seeds of contemporary swinging were planted at that party, but who could have known it would blossom into an industry?

• • •

If it's true that, as Bill Maher once stated so poetically, "The real problem with marriage is that it's just very difficult to bump your uglies with the same person every night your whole life," then for some people, swinging is the answer. To them, cheating is not an issue, unfaithfulness is obsolescent, and adultery is merely a concept that deprived former Air Force Lieutenant Kelly Flinn of the opportunity to drop a nuclear bomb.

The Lifestyles Convention provides a nurturing environment for these couples the same way a convention of crossword-puzzle enthusiasts or barbed-wire collectors would provide for those folks. Yet, in the case of swingers, one is left with a puzzle. Is impersonal intimacy an oxymoron? I ask that question of Stella Resnick, author of *The Pleasure Zone*. Her reply:

"We can't put a value judgment on this. These are all consenting adults. It doesn't really matter that it's rather impersonal because they are in long-term relationships, so they're getting their intimacy needs met, but not necessarily their needs for excitement in sex, and this is certainly a way to do it. Often they are sexually identified in the sense that they're sexual people, they have strong sexual desires, they're not necessarily into politics or other causes, but this is a good cause—being in the body, being healthy—and it's a way of relaxing and enjoying their bodies. Whatever turns you on, as long as you're not doing any damage to anybody else and you're taking care of yourself, fine, enjoy."

When Tom Arnold was a guest on *Late Show* with David Letterman, he was being pressed by Letterman about his friendship with Kathie Lee and Frank Gifford. This was shortly after the *Globe* had entrapped and videotaped Gifford's extramarital tryst with a flight attendant in a hotel room. Letterman insisted, "I don't revel in the miseries of others," but Arnold reminded him of his monologues with jokes about Gifford. Letterman defended himself: "It's part of the job." Arnold stammered, searching for just the right words. He finally found them: "Frank Gifford took a bullet for a lot of us." And the audience applauded the accuracy of his assessment.

Certainly, noncelebrities don't have to worry about supermarket tabloids revealing infidelities to *their* spouses. Such exposure could never occur with swinging couples, not only because, as a rule they are honest with each other, but also because they party *with* each other, so there are no surprises. They are sharing a secret lifestyle, one with an ethic that transcends ordinary romance. Sneaky affairs are for straight people, but swingers can have their wedding cake and eat their fantasies, too. Which explains why there have been no hookers hanging around *this* convention.

murder at
the conspiracy
convention

"The history of civilization is the history of warfare between secret societies."

—*Ishmael Reed*

I n the men's room at the airport, a man standing at the urinal a couple of urinals away from my urinal was urinating without aiming his penis. Both hands were busy flossing his teeth. A monument to multitasking. I'll admit that I occasionally brush my teeth while I'm urinating—at least that leaves me with one hand free to steer—but this guy could possibly be the only human being on earth who pisses and flosses simultaneously.

He must have practiced at home before he decided to go public. And of course he was proud of his manual dexterity. Maybe he even has a license plate that says PFLOSS, though other drivers would assume it's his name, not his avocation. In any case, that image immediately replaced my previous visual mantra: seeing one of the kids on a school bus holding up to the window a sign that read "HELP US!"—and laughing with his classmates.

Now, on Memorial Day weekend, I was catching a flight to San Jose. I was headed for Conspiracy Con 2001, a convention featuring the prophets of the sinister. Of course, the word "Con" might well be an unintentionally accurate description of the presenters, as compared to conspiracy researchers who would *not* be there, such as Peter Dale Scott, Jon Rappoport, Martin Lee, John Judge.

My friend Roy Zimmerman, who writes and sings satirical folk songs in the tradition of Tom Lehrer, has a spoken piece of patter which goes:

"I just got back from the conspiracy convention. Have you been? It's fun. Seven hundred conspiracy theorists all in one hotel, with the little name tags, 'Hello, my name is—none of your fucking business!' Great seminars—'Triangulation and You,' 'Paranoia for Profit,' 'Victoria's Real Secret Was J. Edgar Hoover.' In the lobby, I saw five people get off the elevator—what, you think that's a coincidence? There was entertainment, of course—a group of horny anti-government folk singers called the Randy Weavers."

Zimmerman was surprised to learn that there would actually be an event such as the one that he thought he was making up. Although the real conspiracy convention didn't have the 700 attendees he had imagined, there were over 500, including 40 percent from out of state and 10 percent from other countries, including Canada, England, Australia, Denmark, Austria and Ireland. Also taking place at the Santa Clara Convention Center that same weekend as Conspiracy Con was the Charismatic Catholic Convention. Dueling religions, together again.

The Mae Brussell Connection

When President Kennedy was assassinated on November 22, 1963, Mae Brussell was a suburban homemaker with five children. Her seven-year-old daughter Bonnie was worried about Lee Harvey Oswald. She saw him on TV. He had a black eye and he was saying, "I didn't do it. I haven't killed anybody. I don't know what this is all about."

Bonnie decided to send him her teddy bear. It was all wrapped up and ready to mail when she saw Oswald murdered by Jack Ruby two days later on Sunday morning TV. Mae had to wonder, "What kind of world are we bringing our children into? My concern over who killed John Kennedy was basically selfish, to find out if there had been a *coup*. Was the United States going fascist?"

Mae began a weekly radio program, originating on her local FM rock station and syndicated to half a dozen other stations. She purchased the *Warren Commission Report* for $86, studying and cross-referencing the entire 26 volumes, without the aid of a computer. It took her eight years and 27,000 typewritten pages. She was stunned by the difference between the evidence and the conclusion that there had been only a single assassin.

"And then," she told me, "I began paying attention to the deaths of judges, attorneys, labor leaders, actors, professors, civil-rights leaders, reporters, authors, Black Panthers, Indians, Chicanos, students and hippies—studying what I considered to be untimely, suspicious deaths—and why the masses were being drugged, dosed for control. Rock musicians had an ability to draw together youth at a time when protest meetings were being broken apart and the hippie, antiwar youth became too visible with their own unique art form at Woodstock. Those persons seeking racial harmony and social protest were defined as enemies of the state."

Mae began to study the history of Nazis brought to this country after World War II under Project Paperclip and infiltrated into hospitals, universities and the aerospace industry, further developing their techniques in propaganda, mind control and behavior modification. She would knit sweaters for her children while breathlessly describing the architecture of an invisible government. The walls of her home were lined with 40 file cabinets containing 1,600 subject categories.

Every day she would digest 10 newspapers from around the country, supplementing that diet with items sent to her by a network of researchers and young conspiracy students known as Brussell Sprouts, plus magazines, underground papers, unpublished manuscripts, court affidavits, documents from the National Archives, FBI and CIA material obtained through the Freedom of Information Act, and hundreds of books on espionage and assassination. On Sundays, she would sort out the previous week's clippings into various categories as though she were conducting a symphony of horror.

What started out as a hobby for Mae had turned into a lifetime pilgrimage. Each piece of her jigsaw-puzzle investigation inevitably led to another piece. Although the ultimate mystery of existence would remain forever inconceivable, conspiracy research became her Zen grid for perceiving reality, drawing her deeper and deeper into a separate reality that Carlos Castaneda himself never dreamed of. Castaneda was, of course, one of the three tramps arrested at the Grassy Knoll.

When I first met Mae in 1971, my religion had always been Coincidence, but that instantly changed to Conspiracy. My head was swirling in the afterglow of a fresh conversion as I pondered the theological question—the Conspiracy koan—that she posed: "How many coincidences does it take to make a plot?"

On June 17, 1972, the attempted burglary of Democratic headquarters at the Watergate Hotel in Washington suddenly brought Mae's eight-and-a-half years of dedicated research to an astounding climax. She recognized names, *modus operandi*, patterns of cover-up. She could trace linear connections leading from the assassination of President Kennedy to the Watergate break-in and all the killings in between.

Three weeks later—while Richard Nixon was pressing to postpone any investigation until after the election, and the mainstream press was still referring to the incident as a "caper" and a "third-rate burglary"— Mae completed her first article, which I published in *The Realist*, documenting the conspiracy and delineating the players, from the burglars all the way up to FBI Director L. Patrick Gray, Attorney General John Mitchell and President Nixon himself.

"The significance of the Watergate affair," she wrote, "is that every element essential for a political *coup d'etat* in the United States was assembled at the time of the arrest. The team of men represented at the hotel went all the way from the White House with its Emergency Contingency Unit, walkie-talkies and private radio frequency, to the paid street provocateurs and troops who would create the emergencies. Was the target of their associations the cancellation of elections in 1972?"

Mae and I really believed that we could prevent Nixon from being reelected. How incredibly naive.

The Cathy O'Brien Connection

The leadoff speaker at Conspiracy Con was Cathy O'Brien, who claimed to be a victim of the CIA's MK-Ultra child-sex-slave program, Project Monarch. She was introduced by her husband, Mark Phillips, as "the love of my life." Phillips claims that, having worked for the CIA, where he learned hypnosis, and for a Department of Defense subcontractor with exposure to mind-control research, he was able to rescue O'Brien, deprogram her and collaborate on their book, *Trance Formation of America*.

"There is not one person in this audience," he exhorts, "that could not be legally experimented on, killed or financially destroyed."

He has the bearing, the cadence and the pompadour of a dramatically pious televangelist. He oozes with practiced integrity. In contrast, Cathy O'Brien has the demeanor of a guileless, bleached-blond checkout cashier in a small-town supermarket who sends money every week to her favorite televangelist. She speaks with a certain tremor in her voice.

"Mind control," she warns, "is the most important issue facing humanity today."

She reveals her relationship with Gerald Ford, who was "very much interested in mind control, so the local Michigan Mafia child pornography ring was actually sanctioned, and they could target children like myself who were so horribly abused that they would be used in child pornography. When my father was caught sending this pornography through the mail, Gerald Ford approached and told him that he could receive immunity from prosecution if he would sell me into the project. My father eagerly agreed. He was so happy that the government actually condoned child abuse that he went on to have five more children to raise for the project, so there were seven of us in all. He was never prosecuted and remains free for reasons of national security."

At the age of 13, she met the man "who would become my owner" —Senator Robert Byrd. In *Trance Formation*, she describes their first meeting:

"I undressed and climbed into his bed as ordered. I was momentarily relieved to find that his penis was abnormally tiny—so small it didn't even hurt! And I could breathe with it in my mouth! Then he began to indulge himself in his brutal perversions, talking on and on about how I was 'made just for him' due to the vast amounts of pain I could withstand. The spankings and police handcuffs I had previously endured were child's play compared to Senator Byrd's near-death tortures. The hundreds of scars on my body still show today. . . .

"I was one of the only kids in my school who listened to country music. But then, Senator Byrd fancied himself a country music fiddler, and it was 'my duty to love what he did.' I was ordered to listen to country music or no music at all. Music was my psychological avenue for escape, a dissociative tool. . . . CIA operator Merle Haggard, who often used well-documented cryptic language in his songs pertaining to government mind-control slave operations . . . released songs including 'Freedom Train' and 'Over the Rainbow.'

"My father told me repeatedly that Merle Haggard was my 'favorite' singer, and his songs reinforced my programming. Of course, Senator Byrd remained my 'favorite' fiddler as ordered. He played train songs like 'Orange Blossom Special' while making train sounds on his fiddle. Sometimes I was his captive audience, bound and gagged, while he played his fiddle. Other times he instructed me to spin round and round like a music box dancer in order to add 'new dimensions to our sex.' These new dimensions included more and more physical pain through 'kinky' torture."

It was Senator Byrd who directed her father to send her to Catholic school, and it was Gerald Ford who became "my first president." That night, she recalls, "I wore my Catholic uniform as instructed and went into a dissociative trance as my father drove me to the local National Guard Armory, where I was prostituted to Ford. He took me into an empty room, pushed me down on the wooden floor as he unzipped his pants and said, 'Pray on this.' Then he brutally, sexually assaulted me. Afterward, my memory was compartmentalized through use of high voltage. I was then carried out to the car where I lay in the back seat, muscles contracted, stunned, in pain, and unable to move."

And then there was Dick Cheney, President Ford's chief of staff. After Cathy was hunted down and caught in Cheney's game of "human hunting," she stood naked in his hunting-lodge office as he paced around her and gave her this choice: "I could stuff you and mount you like a jackalope and call you a two-legged deer. Or I could stuff you with this (he unzipped his pants to reveal his oversized penis) right down your throat and then mount you. Which do you prefer?"

Apparently, Cheney's oversized penis balanced out Senator Byrd's tiny penis in a tawdry version of Emerson's Law of Compensation.

With unintentional prophetic irony, Cathy describes her 1983 meeting with Ronald Reagan, George Bush and Dick Cheney: "Reagan gestured toward Bush and said, 'This is my vice president. People don't usually know what the role of the vice president is because he's always behind the scenes making sure everything that the president wants done happens the way it's supposed to.' He looked at me and said matter-of-factly, 'I catch the public's attention while the vice president carries out orders.' Bush's close friend, Dick Cheney, said, 'And *gives* them.'

"George Bush, Jr. stood by his father and covered his backside whenever Bush would become incapacitated from drugs or required criminal backup. It appeared that Jr. was there to serve both purposes while his father and Cheney enjoyed their work-vacation. Jr. had never shown any interest in me sexually. Like his father, he had only shown sexual interest in [my daughter] Kelly, who had been away with him most of the day."

Cathy told the Conspiracy Con audience that, at the age of 19, "I worked on a White House/Pentagon level during the Reagan/Bush years and carried out many criminal covert operations for the CIA. The war on drugs was no more than the CIA eliminating competition worldwide, turning our streets into a bloodbath. I was exposed to many drugs, perversion, sex activity, filmed through a little lens in the ceiling because these criminals do not trust each other, so they blackmail each other. I used cocaine, sometimes heroin, Bush's drug of choice.

"Of all the drugs I was exposed to, there was one that was strictly forbidden, and that was marijuana, because the effects on the brain actually opened those neuron pathways so that any compartmentalization of memory, of any kind of trauma, or so-called secret, actually begins to erode. That's why they don't want to have even medical marijuana. I'm not standing here to be pro-marijuana at all, I am here to tell you I am extremely *anti*-marijuana, but I know why this anti-marijuana campaign is out there, with their efforts to control all of us by making sure that this particular drug is controlled so that no one in any kind of position would have free thought."

When she finished her presentation, Mark Phillips returned to the stage. "We ask you respectfully," he said, "to please allow us to provide you with"—that is, to sell—"our book and share it with someone you love. It's a horrible book . . . probably the most incredible validated story that is going to soon be a major theme in maybe more than one motion picture and a TV documentary series. After all these years, Cathy and I believe that this is our last year."

And therein lies the paradox of this convention. All the speakers totally distrust the controlled mainstream media, yet they all sense imminent triumph, believing that they and their messages will soon be vindicated by those very same controlled mainstream media.

You want statistics? Here's what the polls show. That 68 percent of Americans believe President Kennedy was killed as part of a conspiracy. That 51 percent believe federal officials assassinated JFK. That 40 percent of Americans think the FBI set the fires at Waco. That more than four in ten Americans think the FBI deliberately withheld evidence in the Oklahoma City bombing case. That 80 percent of Americans think the government is concealing knowledge of extraterrestrial life. That 75 percent of Americans believe the war on drugs is a failure. That 47 percent of people using public toilets flush with their feet.

The Michael Aquino Connection

In a book about the National Security Agency, *Body of Secrets*, James Bamford reveals that, in 1962, U.S. military leaders proposed a plan to commit violent terrorist acts and kill innocent Americans, blaming Cuba in order to create a pretext for invading the island and deposing Fidel Castro.

One document prepared and signed by all five Joint Chiefs of Staff, states: "We could develop a Communist Cuban terror campaign in the Miami area, in other Florida cities and even in Washington. We could blow up a U.S. ship in Guantanamo Bay and blame Cuba. Casualty lists in U.S. newspapers would cause a helpful wave of indignation."

In an interview, Bamford said, "What the Joint Chiefs indicated in their plan was they would have people shot on American streets, bombs blown up, refugee boats sunk on the high seas—and all this would be blamed on the Cuban government."

I have no problem believing such insidious intentions, and yet I can't accept Cathy O'Brien's story. I think it's an elaborate hoax, intertwining celebrity porn with historical context to foster credibility. Example: "Noriega had been an intricate part of arming the Nicaraguan *contras* for Reagan, as well as an international hub in the cocaine operations that funded the black budgets for ultrasecret projects such as Project Monarch. . . .

"Aquino put a vaginal prod in my hand and ordered me to masturbate myself with it, pushing the button to electrically jolt myself internally upon command. Noriega's eyes were enormous. He paled to a sickly grey, his mouth fell open and he ran out the door while Aquino assured him that he had 'nowhere to run, nowhere to hide from Reagan's powers.'"

So who *is* this Aquino guy? According to Cathy, "In the early 1980s, my base programming was instilled at Fort Campbell, Kentucky, by U.S. Army Lt. Colonel Michael Aquino. He holds a top-secret clearance in the Defense Intelligence Agency's Psychological Warfare Division (PSYOP). He is a professed neo-Nazi, the founder of the Himmler-inspired satanic Temple of Set and has been charged with child ritual and sexual abuse at the Presidio Day Care in San Francisco. But like my father, Aquino remains 'above the law' while he continues to traumatize and program CIA-destined young minds in a quest to reportedly create the 'superior race' of Project Monarch mind-controlled slaves."

I contacted Aquino, who retired in 1994, and he responded:

"Not only was I never stationed at Fort Campbell at anytime throughout my entire Army career, but I've never even visited that particular post, on- or off-duty. I have never had any contact at anytime, anyplace, anywhere with Cathy O'Brien. I have never programmed sex slaves for the government or anyone else. I have never participated in any form of child abuse whatever."

What does he think her motivation is?

"I can only assume that O'Brien is either a crank or simply an unethical individual who seeks money, notoriety and/or publicity by inventing sensationalistic lies. Her book is strewn with sex accusations not just about myself, but concerning a parade of high government officials, celebrities and country music stars. I haven't sued O'Brien for libel for the simple reason that her book is clearly in the lunatic fringe, and to take legal notice of it would only give it a dignity it doesn't deserve. I presume that the other public figures libeled by it haven't sued her either for the same reason.

"I certainly am not going to defend/excuse any of the MK-Ultra projects. These were all before my time—I was commissioned a 2nd Lt. in 1968—and I read about such things in *Search for the Manchurian Candidate* and *Acid Dreams*, shaking my head, much the same as you probably did. I *can* affirm that my work in Army PSYOP was strictly legitimate and in keeping with the Field Manual #33-1 guidelines taught at the Special Warfare Center, Fort Bragg.

"In a nutshell: techniques for trying to convince an enemy not to fight but to cooperate with you. I originally became interested in it because (a) I believed that the USA was generally on the side of goodness, and (b) winning wars by persuasion rather than bullets and bombs seemed a great idea to me. This may sound like a naive idealist, but that's the way I looked out at the world in 1968."

I asked Aquino, "Do you think that Cathy O'Brien and Mark Phillips utilized you in the book [published in 1995] because the Presidio case would give their accusations a patina of verisimilitude?"

"Well, I think that's obvious," he replied. "After the highly publicized and sensationalized attack on my wife and myself at the Presidio, all sorts of nutcases tossed my name around in whatever their fantasy of the moment. The combination (high-ranking Army officer, intelligence officer, Special Forces officer, PSYOP officer, #2 official of the Church of Satan 1970-75+, etc.) was just too juicy.

"As for the Presidio affair, following the publication of the 'recovered memories of Satanic Ritual Abuse' book *Michelle Remembers* in 1980, the United States and other Anglo-American countries went through a decade of 'Satanic Ritual Abuse' scares and witch-hunts. After the 1984 McMartin Preschool became internationally publicized in one such scare, day-care facilities generally became targets of 'Satanic Ritual Abuse' witch-hunts.

"The epidemic extended to U.S. military services as well, including 15 U.S. Army day-care centers and elementary schools by 1987. In late 1986 it was the turn of the Presidio. The San Francisco Police investigated, verified that my wife and I had been 3,000 miles away in Washington, D.C.—where I was on duty every single day [the alleged victim] was at the day-care center September 1st to October 31st, 1986—and closed the case with no charges accordingly.

"In October 1988, however, I appeared as a panelist on a *Geraldo Rivera Halloween Special.* Rivera was trying to aggravate and escalate the 'Satanic Ritual Abuse' witch-hunt mania, and I was speaking out against it. The broadcast came to the attention of Senator Jesse Helms who became enraged that a Lt. Colonel in the Army should dare to hold a 'Satanic' religion. As Freedom of Information filings later revealed, Helms then secretly contacted his close personal friend, Secretary of the Army John Marsh, and insisted that Marsh devise some way to destroy my career.

"I am a Priest of Set. Set is an ancient Egyptian god about 5,000+ years older than any Judeo-Christian mythology. 'Satan' is a figure of Judeo-Christian mythology. I do not believe in 'Satan.' I *do* think that Judeo-Christian mythology manufactured its 'devils' from many older, competing Mediterranean religions, including that of Egypt. Its 'Satan' was accordingly given features from the Greek Pan, the Mesopotamian Baal, the Phoenician Astarte, the Egyptian Set) and probably Amon, Baneb-Tett, et al.) and *then*, not surprisingly, pronounced 'The Personification of Evil.' This happens a lot between different religions, incidentally. The Set of whom I am a Priest is not in the least Evil, does not advocate Evil and does not appreciate Evil. He doesn't care about Judeo-Christian mythology one way or the other. . . .

"What was actually taking place: a blatant attempt by Senator Helms, Secretary of the Army Marsh and the Criminal Investigation Division of the Army to discredit an Army officer with a 'politically incorrect' religion. It didn't work."

The Mark Phillips Connection

Although I believe that *Trance Formation of America* is an elaborate hoax and Michael Aquino thinks it's in the lunatic fringe, conspiracy researcher Robert Sterling perceives a more devious motivation. In

Apocalypse Culture II, edited by Adam Parfey, Sterling writes:

"Effective disinformation is never an absolute lie. The purpose of disinformation is to confuse truth and validity, and to do so, boldfaced lies are rarely convincing. Effective disinformation mixes truth and deception to obfuscate the two. The closer the disinformation approaches truth, the more damning it becomes. Then all the disinformation, even the legitimate parts, discredits targeted research and ideas.

"At the time of the release of *Trance Formation*, there was a growing awareness in the conspiracy subculture of intelligence agency involvement in satanic ritual abuse. Literature on the subject was reaching a critical mass where it could not be ignored. Would intelligence agencies devote resources to counteract such information? Not only is it possible, it almost certainly has occurred.

"The CIA, even with an officially acknowledged history of abusing people through mind-control experiments (the most famous being MK-Ultra), certainly has a vested interest in denying such operations exist, especially when the operations are as insidious as sexually abusing children. And supposing that [the] tales are part of a CIA disinformation campaign, it would make sense that some names on the list would actually include guilty participants. After all, what better place to hide the truth than out in the open, knowing full well it won't be believed."

Sterling posted a review of O'Brien's book by Jaye Beldo on his Web site, *The Konformist*:

"If you are bored out of your mind with the usual Pamela Anderson Lee 'power-fuck porn,' I suggest grabbing a copy of *Trance Formation of America* and heading to the nearest bathroom with a jar of Vaseline. Why not infuse new life into your worn-out sexual fantasies by envisioning some of the scenes spelled out in Cathy O'Brien's supposed exposé of the pedophile shenanigans of our Government officials? I mean, how could you not get excited over picturing Hillary Clinton going down on the author's deformed vagina like a starved wolf while Bill walks in on them and casually ignores them? . . .

"I cannot help but get the impression that Cathy is, at times, really no different from some of the questionable UFO abductees making extravagant claims of being transported to other solar systems and back again. I have little doubt that some of the horrible things she mentions actually happen on a day-to-day basis. Completely denying them would be folly."

Mark Phillips was not too thrilled with this review, and he wrote to Beldo:

"I feel compelled to inform you of the inevitable consequences of your unsolicited written vulgar assaults upon Cathy O'Brien, Kelly, myself and the overall integrity of our book. I have placed you on the shortlist of potentially dangerous sexual predators, which is automatically reviewed by interested local law enforcement personal [*sic*] (that we are in regular professional communications with) whenever a sexual crime is committed in the area you reside. Until you are apprehended for being a physical threat to yourself and/or innocent others, you will remain at large but nevertheless well identified.

"Stay away from contact with children and out of any county/state/federal prison system, as within moments from the time you may eventually be arrested for some alledged [*sic*] charge of illegal/immoral activities, I will be notified and will do all in my power of influence to see that you are legally seperated [*sic*] from society until you have had the time necessary to do what you proposed for others less appreciative of your sick 'review'—to get a hold of yourself or allow an inmate to take matters into their own hands and change your thoughts towards acceptance of brutal criminal activity."

Konformist editor Sterling wrote to Phillips:

"I harbored no personal animosity to either you or Ms. O'Brien, but I had serious questions about the accuracy of what was in your book. Even more disturbing, I had a very bad feeling that, wittingly or not, the claims in *Trance Formation* could easily be used to manipulate people into a hysterical witch-hunt state, and could be used to smear those who are innocent of charges made by you and Cathy, Brice and others. I felt if people were not careful, they could be whipped into a fascist state of mindlessly agreeing to any charge made by alleged CIA sex slaves to a conspiracy underground version of McCarthyism."

The "Brice" he refers to is Brice Taylor, author of the first competitor of *Trance Formation*, published in 1999—*Thanks for the Memories: The Memoirs of Bob Hope's and Henry Kissinger's Mind-Controlled Slave*— in which she asserts that Walt Disney raped her on Mr. Toad's Wild Ride; that she had sex with all three Kennedy brothers plus JFK, Jr. when he was 12; and that she has cavorted with public figures ranging from Prince Charles to Alan Greenspan, from Elvis Presley to Neil Diamond, from Johnny Carson to Ed McMahon. Hi-yo!

Sterling observes that, "After suffering horrible torture and abuse at the hands of countless famous politicians and celebrities, both O'Brien and Taylor declare of being spoken to by Jesus Christ, whose glorious powers healed them of all trauma and left them immune to further manipulation. At the time of her 'memory recovery,' Brice was corralled and influenced by Christian fundamentalists, who convinced her that her previous life was the prelude for an afterlife in Hell. It should be obvious that the New World Order sex slave genre is nothing more than thinly veiled porn disguised as parapolitics."

Sterling told me that Cathy and Mark's book has "sold over 20,000 copies. Their following is heavily right wing Christians and patriot groups, and if you hang out with either sector you'll eventually hear some pro-*Trance-Formation-of-America* sentiments. Not surprising—part of the book's thesis is that mind control is part of the New World Order plot."

Also published in 1999 was *Paperclip Dolls* by Annie McKenna, and in 2001, *A Nation Betrayed: The Chilling True Story of Secret Cold War Experiments Performed on Our Children and Other Innocent People* by Carol Rutz, who writes: "No one could understand why I still sucked my thumb or actually fell asleep during naptime in kindergarten. One moment I was watching *Howdy Doody, Kookla, Fran and Ollie* or *Mighty Mouse* saving the day. The next I was being molested or poked and prodded by some government official."

In Cleveland, NewsChannel 5's Brad Harvey interviewed Cheryl Hersha, a registered nurse who told of an abusive military father who forced her and her sister into a CIA child-spy program, namely MK-Ultra, infamous for the use of mind control, sex, torture and murder. The CIA admits to the existence of MK-Ultra, but denies that the program included children.

Hersha claims, "The military training began when I was about eight, and that consisted of teaching us weapons, knives, revolvers and shooting." She says that she would seduce and drug top foreign diplomats and then take them to a secret location. "Sometimes he would be passed out and they would take pictures and that would be enough to blackmail them into compliance."

A private investigator and a local author teamed up for a book based on Hersha's story, but they both admit that the evidence is thin.

The predecessor of this whole nonliterary genre was *The Control of Candy Jones*, published in 1976. Jones was a highly successful model supposedly transformed into a CIA Manchurian Candidate. The book was ghostwritten by her husband, carnival hypnotist and late-night radio talk show host "Long John" Nebel. His friend, stage magician and psychic debunker James "The Amazing" Randi, told me that Nebel made up the entire book because he needed money. When I mentioned this to Walter Bowart, author of *Operation Mind Control,* he insisted that Randi himself was an intelligence agent. Amazing, indeed.

The Extraterrestrial Connection

In 1972, while celebrating the publication of Mae Brussell's conspiracy research in *The Realist* by ingesting three tabs of Owsley's White Lightning acid (a total of 900 micrograms), I happened to meet a cabalistic guru who insisted that he had communicated with beings from outer space. "It's time," he warned me, "for God to regain *control* of these bodies that have been entrusted to us." In my state of vulnerability, this was a slightly disturbing encounter, and I phoned a couple of friends.

I called Ken Kesey, and he said, "It has to do with a struggle for the will." I called Mae Brussell, and she said, "These people have their own reality. The occult is their safety valve for not having to deal with the problems on Earth."

But now, a few decades later, the notion of a symbiotic relationship between extraterrestrial visits and human needs is being heralded by some conspiracy researchers. Dr. Steven Greer, director of the Center for the Study of Extraterrestrial Intelligence, writes in a New Age magazine, *The Light Connection*:

"For most people, the question of whether or not we're alone in the universe is a mere philosophical musing—something of academic interest but of no practical importance. Even evidence that we are currently being visited by nonhuman advanced life forms seems to many to be an irrelevancy in a world of global warming, crushing poverty and the threat of war. In the face of real challenges to the long-term future, the question of UFOs, extraterrestrials and secret government projects is a mere sideshow, right?

"Wrong—catastrophically wrong. Advanced spacecraft of extraterrestrial origin have been downed, retrieved and studied since at least the 1940s and possibly as early as the 1930s. Significant technological breakthroughs in energy generation and propulsion have resulted from the study of these objects and from related human innovations dating as far back as the time of Nikola Tesla, and these technologies utilize a new physics not requiring the burning of fossil fuels or ionizing radiation to generate vast amounts of energy.

"Utopia? No, because human society will always be imperfect—but

perhaps not as dysfunctional as it is today. These technologies are real—
I have seen them. Antigravity is a reality and so is free energy generation. We are talking about the greatest social, economic and technological
revolution in human history—bar none. The disclosure of these new
technologies will give us a new, sustainable civilization. World poverty
will be eliminated within our lifetimes. [No wonder] that the so-called
Star Wars (or National Missile Defense System) effort has really been a
cover for black-project deployment of weapon systems to track, target
and destroy Extraterrestrial Vehicles as they approach Earth or enter
Earth's atmosphere. . . ."

Fortunately—or unfortunately—there is now a Web site that tells
you how to make a Thought Screen Helmet, which blocks telepathic
communication between aliens and humans. Aliens cannot immobilize
people wearing thought screens, nor can they control their minds or
communicate with them. Aliens have not taken any abductees while they
were wearing thought screen helmets using Velostat shielding. Also,
London's Goodfellows insurance company sells the Alien All Risks policy—$400 a year for $1.7-million coverage—for being abducted or
impregnated by an alien. It has been sold to 40,000 people.

Since Conspiracy Con is "A Brian Hall Production from the people who brought you the Bay Area UFO Expo," presenter William
Lyne seemed like a heretic. Lyne, who had top secret clearance in Air
Force Intelligence, recalled the time that Arthur C. Clarke came to the
base to talk about unidentified aerial phenomena. Lyne said, "Dr.
Clarke, I very much enjoyed your speech. It was very interesting.
However, you and I both know you're a goddam liar, and flying saucers
are man-made machines powered by electricity. You can't fool me. I've
seen them close up."

Lyne said that he "knew Roswell [site of the infamous UFO crash]
was a hoax when it was created." He met a nurse who had been "present when they were doing the 'autopsy' of the alien, which was actually a rhesus monkey. She had to eat them in Bataan [during World War
II]. She survived the death march. It's a staple diet of Malaysians. Rhesus
monkeys and green peppers." Sounds like a book by Dr. Seuss.

Along those same lines, Michael Shermer, head of the Skeptics Society,
received a letter from Ken Phillips, Jr.:

"In 1995 I was a contractor for the U.S. Air Force at Wright-Patterson
Air Force Base. As a joke I asked a Colonel if I could see the alien bodies. While I don't discount the possibility of life beyond Earth, as an

amateur astronomer I have never seen a scrap of evidence for it. He laughed and told me that at one time they had some monkeys—used, I believe, in some biometrics experiments—that were kept in a freezer. They were stretched out, and devoid of most of their hair.

"Imagine a rhesus monkey, stretched out, hairless, and frozen. Long of limb, slight of build, head a little too big, large eyes. Then have a playful lab technician plant just a hint that the 'thing' in question is not of this world. If I had been in a position to hoodwink a gullible person, skeptic that I am, it would have been hard to resist. Even today, dozens, and perhaps hundreds, of laboratories still use aliens—er, small primates—in medical research. And years later, men might be willing to testify before Congress, misidentifying a natural, and very Earthly, phenomenon."

Shermer recounts his own recent appearance on *Politically Incorrect* with author Whitley Streiber:

"He told me that he has written 23 books, only 16 of which are fiction. In my opinion, all 23 are fiction, but what I found interesting both off the record in the Green Room and on the record on the air, is that he equivocated considerably about whether he really thought it was aliens who 'probed' him in the middle of the night while he was sleeping. I thought this was rather odd since in *Communion*, and in his other alien books, there seems little doubt that he *does* think it was aliens from another planet, and not neuronal aliens from his brain.

"Also enlightening was Streiber's response to my calling attention to the fact that before his 'alien abduction,' he had already written a fair amount of science-fiction, fantasy and horror stories. What he said was that initially he too could not distinguish between a possible alien-abduction experience and just his imagination and fantasy. Obviously he resolved that dilemma, at least long enough to add 'A True Story' after his book title *Communion*."

Furthermore, Alex Constantine, one of Mae's "Brussell Sprouts," in his book, *Psychic Dictatorship in the U.S.A.*, writes:

"The 'Alien' invasion is a very active cover story for the development of mind control technology. Supposedly, as those weird syndicated UFO television programs keep reminding us, alien scientists have voyaged millions of light years to place CIA implants in the bodies of human subjects. This incredible cover story is widely believed—yet most 'skeptics' scoff at the notion that human scientists might want to do the same thing. The aliens have been pounded into the heads of the American consumer by a slue of books penned by military intelligence officers."

In *Military Mind Control and Alien Abduction*, Dr. Helmut Lammer and Marion Lammer present evidence that "covert human military are involved in the alien abduction mystery. During the last years, more and more people who experienced alien abductions claimed that they were also harassed by covert military agencies. Some experienced traumatic flashbacks and recall kidnappings by unknown military personnel. These alleged alien abductees claim that they were also kidnapped, examined, interrogated, sometimes implanted with tiny foreign objects, by human military personnel, men in white lab coats or men in business suits."

Dr. Michael Persinger has conducted studies that indicate statistical correlations between high electromagnetism and various "fringe phenomena," including UFO contacts, poltergeists and extra-sensory perception. And, in *DMT, the Spirit Molecule*, Rick Strassman states that overabundant DMT production in the pineal gland explains psychosis, near-death and mystical experience, and alien encounters.

"Things," as Arsenio Hall says, "that make you go 'Hmmmmm . . . '"

The Mind Control Connection

It is an irony of quasi-cosmic proportion that Nikola Tesla's discoveries are used for the purpose of mind control while their potential humane applications remain suppressed. Tesla expert Ken Adachi writes:

"Unlimited electricity could be made available anywhere and at any time, by merely pushing a rod into the ground and turning on the electrical appliance. Homes, farms, offices, factories, villages, libraries, museums, streetlights, etc., could have all their lighting needs met by merely hanging ordinary lightbulbs or fluorescent tubes anywhere desired—without the need for wiring—and produce brilliant white light 24 hours a day. Motor energy for any imagined use such as industrial applications, transportation, tractors, trucks, trains, boats, automobiles, airships or planes could be powered freely, anywhere on the planet, from a Single Magnifying Transmitter.

"This new form of energy even had the ability to elevate human consciousness to levels of vastly improved comprehension and mental clarity. Undreamed of therapeutic applications to improve human health and to eliminate disease conditions could have been achieved fully 100 years ago had Tesla been allowed to complete his commercial development of Radiant Energy. But powerful barons of industry, chiefly J.P. Morgan, colluded to deny him the financial backing he needed and, in doing so, effectively denied mankind one of Nature's most abundant and inexhaustible gifts of free energy.

"Morgan had already orchestrated circumstances in Tesla's life in order to force Tesla to be dependent on him for financial backing. During an earlier period, when Tesla himself had millions from his Polyphase AC generator royalty payments and other earnings, Morgan wanted to woo Tesla with a deal that effectively gave Morgan majority control over his patent rights and projects, but Tesla turned him down, telling Morgan that he had enough money of his own to fund his projects. While returning to his hotel from that very meeting with Morgan, however, Tesla was told that his laboratory had been burned to the ground. From that time forward, other financial backers were not to be found. Morgan was powerful enough to blacklist Tesla among the Eastern Establishment elites that previously had hobnobbed and feted with Tesla as if he was one of their own."

Although people who hear voices in their heads are usually dismissed as just pain nuts, in 1991 Harry Martin and David Caul reported in the *Napa Sentinel*:

"The Department of Health, Education and Welfare and the U.S. Army have admitted mind-control experiments. Many deaths have occurred. In tracing the steps of government mind-control experiments, the trail leads to legal and illegal usages, usage for covert intelligence operations, and experiments on innocent people who were unaware that they were being used. Walter Reed Army Institute of Research [under the code name 'Project Pandora'] refined the technique so that the microwaves could transmit understandable spoken words.

"In fact, one of its researchers, Dr. Joseph Sharp, was himself the subject of an experiment in which pulsed microwave audiograms, or the microwave analog of the sound vibration of spoken words, were delivered to his brain in such a way that he was able to understand the words that were spoken. Military and undercover uses of such a device might include driving a subject crazy with inner voices in order to discredit him, or conveying undetectable instructions to a programmed assassin."

In an article in the *Village Voice*, James Ridgeway and Ariston-Lizabeth Anderson discuss a technology "that will make the H-bomb obsolete, replacing it with 'nonlethal' electromagnetic zaps from the ionosphere designed to take out an enemy's entire communication system, change weather patterns by turning sunny skies into torrential downpours, and drive you literally crazy by shooting sounds into your head.

"Part of the High-Frequency Active Aural Research Program (HAARP), this latest theoretical weapon shoots a zapping electromagnetic beam into the ionosphere, where it becomes superheated before being steered back to earth. The Pentagon claims this research will improve our communication system, but the technology could also be aimed at adversaries, domestic or foreign."

In a report from the Air Force's scientific advisory board on weapons for the 21st century, independent investigator Nick Begich stated:

"One can envision the development of electromagnetic energy sources, the output of which can be pulsed, shaped and allow one to prevent voluntary muscular movements, control emotions with both short-term and long-term memory, produce an experience set, and delete an experience set. What's more, the technology may be able to create high-fidelity speech in humans, raising the possibility of covert suggestion and psychological direction. It may be possible to 'talk' to selected adversaries in a fashion that would be most disturbing to them."

So now we return to the conspiracy convention. William Lyne, a researcher on Tesla and free energy devices for 50 years is speaking:

"I know a man who's in mind control—and they've used it on him and his father—they use a virtual reality type of technology that's projected to that person, transmitted to them so that they see images that aren't there, but what they want to do is terrify them and make them *think* they're seeing these things, except they're intelligent people and they know that they're not real images, they just want to know how they're *receiving* those images. If they want you to see something, they can transmit it to you.

"They can do it for a whole area. And the place where this person lives, they're all shutting down at 10 o'clock at night. Everybody in that whole part of town are actually going to bed at the same time. It's like they've got the whole area under control. And it's within eyeshot of Los Alamos Labs. The dirty part of the labs where they do this kind of stuff. I say dirty because there's coerced black projects being done out of there."

There's a mini-ballroom at the convention center where conspiracy books, audio and videotapes are being sold. A man wearing a space suit is hawking an Alien Abduction Survival Kit. Another vendor is selling aura cameras. And, for some incongruous reason, a woman is coning— that is, getting the wax out of a prone client's ears with the aid of a burning candle and a tin pie-plate. At a booth offering "Free Electricity for

Life," the proprietor is saying, "They killed one of my associates."

As for Lyne's own safety in the face of promulgating the concept of free energy, he says, "I'm encouraged lately because there's safety in numbers. Too many people have access to this stuff and are promoting it. Now there have been some real tragedies in the past. People had some of this technology and they disappeared or were squashed. I don't have any fear of the government. I lost my fear a long time ago. They tried to murder me several times, and I said to myself, 'Well, I might be dead tomorrow and nobody'd know why, so I'm gonna go out there and tell what I know and I'm not afraid,' and I think everyone should take the same approach."

The Cattle Mutilation Connection

William Lyne added another secret ingredient to the recipe.

"Cattle mutilations," he said, "is a testing process, but it also combines basically a mind-control element. Kinky sex cults started showing up at mutilation sites. They would try to create the impression that it was some sort of occult group, Osiris (Outer Space International Research) having their golden-cup ceremony, drinking bull blood. But they couldn't have, they weren't the type. It's a CIA project to throw the light off what the research was all about. They even use 'flying saucers'—zap those animals with a type of beam which knocks them out, bring them into the ship, do mutilations, removing ionized tissue.

"What they're doing is exposing cattle to particle beam weapons and developing a type of weaponry to murder somebody and there won't be any evidence. Remove the blood and genitalia and ears and eyes and tongue—all the tissue that's used to study ionizing effects on organic beings, and they run it through the counters to see if there is any evidence, and they develop this technology so that they can kill anyone. No one's safe. They can zap you from a flying saucer and everyone says you died of AIDS, contra virus or terminal pneumonia."

An editor at *Bizarre News* came up with a theory that the recent slaughter of European cattle to prevent the spread of Hoof-and-Mouth Disease was actually a cover-up for alien cattle mutilations.

Interviewed by the *News*, Linda Moulton Howe, author of *An Alien Harvest*, said that extraterrestrial aliens are responsible for the enigmatic animal killings in America "and the federal government knows it. I've talked to dozens of eyewitnesses who have seen silver discs landing in their fields. Ranchers have told me about non-human creatures carrying away their cattle."

But a reader sent this e-mail: "Everyone knows that cattle mutilations are perpetrated by U.S. Government's special ops teams using silent helicopters and advanced laser operating technology to remove the sex organs of mature bovines to test them for the effects of trace radioactivity left over from days of nuclear testing."

When Associated Press reported that, in central Texas, bulls' abdomens have been sliced open, their genitals, internal organs and tongues removed, a local sheriff was quoted: "If we could find any indication humans are involved, we would do more."

Radio commentator Jim Hightower reacted: "Say what? *If* humans are involved? Indeed, the sheriff claims that authorities have found no tire tracks, shoe prints, cigarette butts or other telltale evidence that people were on the scene. But, if not humans—what? The sheriff has ruled that the cattle died of 'natural causes.' Sure—their bellies just split open."

In August 2001, Kate Silver reported in the *Las Vegas Weekly* that, when a small farming town in Montana had a spate of cattle mutilations, the National Institute for Discovery Science was called in for help. Dr. Colm Kelleher, deputy administrator for NIDS, said, "One of the first things we did was investigate cult activity but were never able to nail it down. Traditional cults tend to use smaller animals like chickens and goats. Tackling a 2,000-pound bull is not the kind of thing cults are known for. Whoever's doing it is very organized and probably very well equipped. Some of the cuts have been very skillful; someone has a reasonable background in surgery."

He added that there is a correlation between animal mutilations and UFO sightings. For example, from 1974 to 1977, in the area surrounding Montana's Malstrom Air Force Base, there were 62 animal mutilations, and investigations of 192 UFO and unknown helicopter sightings. "We're not trying to add anything mysterious to this," he said. "The bottom line is we're not going to draw a cause and effect between UFOs and animal mutilation."

Nor would Alan Gudaitis, director of the Mutual UFO Network. "First, we'd have to prove aliens existed," he said. "And then, would they do something like this?"

Don Emory, manager of Area 51 Research Center—known for its research on military, UFO and aerospace matters—says, "Supposedly, that people start making the connection that this was alien mostly derives from farmers seeing strange lights in the field the night before. There's also the connection that maybe this wasn't alien, it was actually some kind of military testing. The UFO people think that it's UFOs. Conspiracy people think it's the government."

At Conspiracy Con, though, it was not an either/or proposition. For believers in both UFOs *and* conspiracies, when it comes to Unidentified Flying Objects, the word "Unidentified" does not necessarily mean that the Flying Objects are from *outer* space.

The Toxic Religion Connection

When Jordan Maxwell was confirmed in the Catholic Church, the bishop invited the children to ask him questions. Young Jordan stood up and said, "My father works with torches, like a welder. Could I take a torch and turn it up and burn an angel? If an angel got burned, would it hurt him?"

"No," replied the bishop.

"Why not?" asked Jordan.

"Well, an angel is a spirit. You can't burn a spirit—because you had to have wood or paper to burn—fire is a natural phenomenon. You can't burn a spirit."

"Then why am I worried about going to Hell, where my spirit will burn forever, if you can't burn a spirit?"

That encounter foreshadowed Jordan Maxwell's career, exploring the hidden foundations of religions and secret societies, which he's been doing since 1959. At the convention, his presentation, "Toxic Religion and the Occult Establishment," burst with anti-clericalism and was greeted by scattered laughter and applause.

"Catholic priests do not salute a flag in this country," he declared. "They owe no allegiance to this country. Priests wear black robes, judges wear black robes, Darth Vader wears black robes, vampires wear black robes, all the blood-sucking murderers wear black robes. If you're intellectually honest and are not afraid to speak out in public, you're going to know that Judaism and Christianity are the biggest bunch of hogwash the world has ever known, period.

"I'm not anti-Semitic, I'm not anti-Jewish, I'm anti-bullshit. I'm intellectually honest and I'm tired of bullshit. I'm tired of being told how holy Israel is because I will guarantee you there's nothing holy in Israel. The only thing holy coming out of Israel are the stories—they're full of holes. There's nothing holy in Israel, there's nothing holy in Salt Lake City, there is for sure nothing holy in Rome, there's nothing holy anywhere on earth.

"People are running around downstairs [at the Charismatic Catholic Convention] talking about the Antichrist, and they have no idea in the world what the word Christ means. It comes from a Greek word, *christo*, which gives us Crisco, cooking oil. And Christ means oil, okay? Jesus the Crisco. And when oil congeals it becomes lord. Look up the word in the *Oxford Dictionary of the English Language*, and it will tell you lord is correctly spelled lard—congealed christo. In the Hebrew dictionary, the word oil is *shemen* or semen. This is why, if you're going to be a priest, you've got to go to a *seminary* with altar boys."

Religion is not Maxwell's only target: "I think the dirtiest, the filthiest, the most licentious people on the face of the earth are the British royalty. They represent in the human race all that is evil and all that is filthy and degenerate. And that's why Princess Diana is dead."

That there was a conspiracy behind Diana's death seems to be a given among this crowd: the royal bloodline protected by the paparazzi. Conspiracy researchers often start with a premise—who benefits?—and work their way backward, molding their perception of reality like Silly Putty in order to *culminate* with the justification of that premise.

"All the trash you are experiencing right now in this system," Maxwell continues, "is caused by the Jesuits, the Catholic Church and especially British royalty—*there* is a conspiracy that you can count on. The people that we Americans fought on the field of battle to get our freedom— who were the redcoats, who were the enemy of the founding of this country if it wasn't the British royalty?"

Maxwell reminds us, "About ten years ago, a young black man broke into the Queen Mum's bedroom, and one of her servants happened to be walking by and the bedroom door was open a bit, and she saw this young black boy in the queen's bedroom. She quietly went to security, which came up and arrested him for breaking into the queen's bedroom, but the queen said he didn't threaten her and he wasn't armed and it was just a childish silly prank, and so she let it slide if he promised not to do that anymore. James Bond couldn't break into the queen's bedroom! If there was a young black man in the queen's bedroom in Buckingham Palace, the queen ordered him in like pizza. The Queen Mum with her black boyfriend. Tell me about racism."

The next day, Maxwell would have to defend himself against some complaints.

"Yesterday I jumped in your face about religion," he explained to the audience, "and I didn't mean to offend. I want to clarify. I have the highest respect for spirituality. I would like to think of myself as a spiritual man, but I also understand that true spirituality, from all the way back into ancient history, has always been between the individual and the God that created them.

"Religion is a product of man's mind. There are things going on out there in the universe—you have no *idea* what's going on. If there is a divine presence in the universe that encompasses life throughout all creation, we haven't yet the faintest idea what that one is, but I have the highest respect for it. But I don't appreciate large institutions who are federally protected.

"I will tell you a secret that it has taken me forty-two years to uncover. All religion in the western world is based on astrology. The people who run this world from behind the scenes—Illuminati, secret societies—one of the most powerful evil secret societies on the face of the earth that this country faces, one of the most devious and despotic and insidious conspiratorial apparatus operating in this country right now are the Jesuits.

"I think that we should send every Jesuit back to Rome and kick them out of this country. They're on the payroll of an organization that is dedicated to the overthrow of man's freedom. Out of the Catholic Church has come the Mafia, the Crusades, the most violent bloodshed across Europe, which was dominated by the Pope, and Europe has dominated the world. As an American, I'm not under the domination of *any-body's* power, including my mother."

That's some secret, huh? It took him 42 years to discover that neither the Pope nor his mother can control his behavior.

"The same people who gave you the Mafia gave you the Church. The Church *is* the Mafia. An FBI man called me: 'We've been watching you, we follow you wherever you go, we know what you're doing. But you are not a threat. We admire what you're trying to do. But your government does not consider you to be a threat—yet—but if you get enough people listening to you—and they're not just listening but they're actually *hearing* you—then you will be considered a threat and now we'll have to take another look at what you're going to do.

" 'But the reason I'm calling—this is an unofficial call—is to warn you when you talk about corruption and government, most people in government couldn't care less, they don't care, they're corrupt and they know it and you know it, so what are you gonna do about it? But when you talk about the church and religious institutions in this country, what you're doing is you are messing with organized crime at its highest level. The highest levels of organized crime in this country are the religious institutions. We're talking about a lot of money. We're talking about the control of men's minds, about the dream of absolute total domination. This makes the Mafia look like child's play.'"

Although Maxwell has hosted his own radio talk shows, guested on over 600 radio programs, written and produced many TV shows and documentaries, including three two-hour specials for CBS as well as the four-part *Ancient Mystery* series, the FBI agent didn't mention exactly when the government would finally consider his influence to be a threat. And yet, that seems to be his aspiration: "I want the president of the United States and the CIA to wake up every night in the middle of the night in a cold sweat wondering where the hell I am. I want them to know who I am."

Meanwhile, it would interest Maxwell to know: the bad news, that one in five American teenagers doesn't know the answer to the question, "From what country did America declare its independence?"; and the good news, that a billboard on Interstate 5 in Oregon says that "The Pope Is the Antichrist."

The Duck Breast Connection

Everybody makes mistakes. In my hotel room that first night, I should've ordered the Colossal Pacific Prawns simmered in Thai curry sauce with sticky rice and toasted coconut. Instead I ordered the Marinated Muscovy Duck Breast pan-seared medium rare with wild rice, porcini mushroom pancake, black currant/demi glaze and rhubarb chutney. The worst thing is I knew it was a mistake *before* I called Room Service, and I deliberately made the wrong choice.

The words "medium rare" had tipped me off immediately. It was bound to be tough fowl. So I chewed and chewed and chewed, but the best I could do was chew the duck-breast juice out of each bite, then leave the residue on my plate like an inedible mosaic. The pancake, the glaze and the chutney were all delicious, though.

Then I watched a movie, *Unbreakable*, which was threaded through with a comic-book metaphor, and I realized how much Conspiracy Con felt like a comic book. Organizer Brian Hall, who resembles Clark Kent in appearance and manner, mentioned that his boyhood hero was Batman. Now he had coordinated his very own summit of plainclothes superheroes, a modern version of the Justice League of America, where

Superman, Captain Marvel, Wonder Woman and their colleagues combined forces to achieve justice.

I pondered my favorite conspiracy theory, diligently created by Steve Lightfoot, who discovered "new evidence" in the killing of John Lennon on December 8, 1980. In 1982, disappointed that there had not been a public trial of Mark David Chapman, Lightfoot went to the library and reread the newsweeklies' reports.

"While flipping through the pages of *Time*," he explained, "I simultaneously discovered, one, that the December 15 issue came out a week earlier, the day of Lennon's death, and did not have the murder report, and two, with almost every turn of the page, the headline messages, from back to front, signaled like a double-meaning cryptographic code about, of all things, John Lennon's murder.

"It was when I turned to page 16 and noticed the headline 'Who's In? Who's Out?' above just-elected Ronald Reagan that I first thought I had stumbled onto a government code hidden in the headlines of *Time* magazine, a code having to do with John Lennon's assassination. I understood that the headline dealt with the selection of the Cabinet that was taking place then. However, I also noticed that Reagan was 'In,' and John Lennon was 'Out,' as he had just been shot to death the same day this magazine came out.

"The fact that Richard Nixon's book *The Real War* was prominently displayed at his side [on the desk] in the very foreground of the picture, accompanied by a vase of white flowers, reminded me of the fact that Nixon was Lennon's biggest enemy in life, as Nixon had tried to illegally deport John in the '70s when he was an outspoken peace activist and singing songs about 'Tricky Dicky' during the Vietnam war."

Lightfoot was falling deeper and deeper into a conspiratorial abyss. He checked out *The Real War* and found that many of Nixon's passages applied to his growing obsession, especially this one: "Perhaps a nation that equates celebrity with wisdom, that looks to rock stars and movie actresses as its oracles, deserves to lose."

He discovered "even more instances of double-meaning bold-print behavior" in *Newsweek*, while *U.S. News & World Report* "was the most discreet." In their November 24, 1980, issue, he found Mark David Chapman's name among Letters to the Editor. Well, not exactly *his* name but, in the middle column the phrase "Mark my words" in a letter from Roger Chapman, and in the third column, a letter from David King.

And then, busy examining microfilm of magazines published in

September 1980, he spotted what he perceived as the face of the same man—allegedly Mark David Chapman—getting Lennon's autograph in a photo he had previously seen. But the man in this photo wasn't Chapman. It was Stephen King. His latest novel, *Firestarter*, was reviewed in that issue of *Time*. It was while reading the book review that Lightfoot "got my first notion that Mark David Chapman was probably an alias that Stephen King used, as his writings betrayed shocking parallels to the Lennon murder. I have researched several of Stephen King's novels and I have found ample clues in every book except *Carrie*."

Steve Lightfoot was an alchemist, transforming synchronicity into premeditation. He had developed rationalization into a fine art, his synapses eagerly linking esoteric associations. He'd had, after all, a born-again experience. Now he felt a strong sense of identity and a definite purpose in life. "I need demonstrators," he pleaded, seeking media attention. His preposterous mission provides insight into the reasoning process of conspiracy researchers who are taken relatively more seriously, such as Sherman Skolnick:

"We were the first and probably among the very few to point out that Monica Lewinsky was reportedly positioned from an early age to be a Mata Hari type, to use sex to infiltrate the Clinton White House. From all the known facts, we were convinced and remain convinced, she was reportedly a creature of renegade units of Israeli Intelligence, the Mossad. Apparently the acting deputy chief for North America for the Mossad was Rahm Emanuel, on and off for some six years Clinton's senior advisor.

"If you understand 'spook' work, black-bag operatives and such, you can comprehend our assertion that Rahm was both a Clinton loyalist and a contributor to his scandals by way of manipulating him, all at the same time. Monica's father was originally from Central America. He was ostensibly a 'sleeper agent' for the Mossad. That is, an intelligence asset pressed into service when and as needed.

"Many have forgotten that Monica was later sent by Clinton to hold a key position in the Pentagon, as assistant to the Press Chief. She traveled on occasion with one or more of the top Pentagon officials. She admits one such official got her pregnant and she required an abortion. Her purpose, as we understood it, was to infiltrate close to the top U.S. military, including the Chiefs of Staff.

"Her task? To try to sniff out reportedly the names and details of the small circle of flag officers, admirals and generals, plotting as authorized by the Military Code, to arrest their Commander-in-Chief Clinton for treason. If Clinton were to have them arrested for mutiny, if they survived and were not assassinated, they intended to defend themselves with documented charges, for example, of Clinton's treason with the head of the Red Chinese Secret Police."

And what about Chandra Levy? The American Patriot Friends Network speculates: "Whether or not she actually had knowledge of two massive government cover-ups, the possibility or perception that she did would make her dangerous to powerful people and would be reason enough for her elimination.

"Chandra was peripherally involved in the Oklahoma City bombing story as she worked with journalists and TV personalities arranging coverage of Timothy McVeigh's execution. Dr. Louis 'Jolly' West was one of the premiere scientists involved in CIA mind-control experiments. He allegedly visited McVeigh up to 17 times in prison and may have been instrumental in persuading McVeigh to remain silent about coconspirators in the bombing. This becomes plausible when coupled with McVeigh's claim that he was implanted with a (biotelemetric) microchip during the Gulf War.

"Another government cover-up waiting to unravel, which could be triggered at the Bureau of Prisons, covers a litany of names familiar to researchers of CIA involvement in drug and arms smuggling. Carlos Lehder, a co-founder of the Medellin drug cartel in Colombia, was tried in the U.S. and sentenced to life plus 135 years. In return for his 'key' testimony against former Panamanian dictator (and CIA asset) Manuel Noriega, Lehder's sentence was reduced to 55 years. During Chandra's tenure at the Bureau of Prisons, a major story on the Internet (with convincing documentation) involves claims that Lehder is out of prison and traveling freely around the world. A separate rumor (not confirmed) is that Lehder is in Russia helping the CIA to set up drug distribution networks.

"Could Chandra have come across any Bureau of Prison records that confirm any part of either of these two blockbuster issues? Just a visitor's log confirming West's visits to McVeigh or documentation of Lehder's release from prison could have proved fatal to Chandra."

The weirdest plot that has come to my attention is a federal program of brainwashing and molesting children with electroshock and dolphins. This practice is "verified" by Brice Taylor—who claims that she and her 13-year-old daughter had a threesome with Sylvester Stallone,

and that he filmed them in "Dolphin Porn," videos of dolphins pene-
trating women in the ocean—and by Cathy O'Brien, who declares that
"Jesuit/NASA-based whale and dolphin programming suggests that
water is a mirror to other dimensions and is the means by which aliens
have mixed with our population."

I found myself playing with my food, molding the masticated remains
of my marinated Muscovy duck breast into the shape of a small horse's
head that eventually morphed into a large crucifix. Then I decided to
place the tray with that plate in front of the door to Jordan Maxwell's
hotel room. I just couldn't resist. If he's reading this, I apologize, but
what can you expect from a professional brat?

The Charismatic Catholic Connection

The Charismatic Catholic Convention has a busy schedule. "We are asking the Holy Spirit to bring forth the Gifts of the Spirit in all the sessions and gatherings of the convention," states their guidelines, "and
we have asked people to come and serve in that ministry of love.
However, the Lord has given us time constraints for each session so
we are asking the Holy Spirit to lead His people to observe the time
and order established."

There is a lot of live music, all praising the Lord so much that it
seems like their deity must be very insecure, with a tremendous ego problem. The official theme song of the convention, "You are the Light of
the World," begins: "He has called us, out of the darkness/ Into His
marvelous light/ We are His chosen, a royal priesthood/ That we might
declare His praise . . . "

A man at the podium is praying:

"Heavenly Father, Mother, King and Queen of this glorious universe, praise God, for all of your people, for this fellowship. Thank you
for the inspiration that you give us to learn the lessons we need to learn
to be more like You and more like Your Son, more like the people who
You designed us to be, that is, the God kind, not the man kind.

"Father, I ask for protection, for myself, I ask you to empower the
people here to be protected as well, and I ask for you to give them a full
powerful anointing so that they can live their lives fully in the no-fear
zone, in the total-love zone, to harmonize and to be totally uplifted in
Your Holy Spirit, to the Heavenly Kingdom where nothing but love and
blessings flow from the river of life that is eternal into their hearts.

"May it be expressed fully, glorifully, so that we pray to bring this whole planet back to You. I would praise You, Father, and I ask You also for divine protection as well as for making not only our path easy in its trip to Africa, but also one that's very, very productive for the cessation of genocide. We praise you, God, in Yeshiva's God. Say amen. Thank you."

Hey, wait a minute! Have I goofed? Am I attending the wrong convention? But, no, this is not a priest preaching to his flock of Charismatic Catholics. Rather, it is Len Horowitz, and he is addressing *his* congregation of conspiratorialists.

He had received a phone call from a naturopath who said, "I had a dream last night—I never have dreams—but there may be an assassination attempt on your life, and you need to ask for prayer as much as you can." Dr. Horowitz tells the audience, "Prophecies like that come about so that you can enter into the realm of the Kingdom of Heaven, that you can pray and have God come on and change everything, change that negative outcome."

Horowitz is the author of *Emerging Viruses: AIDS and Ebola*, which exposes the creation of AIDS by bio-warfare labs, and then its deployment into gay and black populations with vaccinations. His presentation is titled "Toxic Warfare Against Humanity: Globalism, Terrorism and 'Non-Lethal' Methods of Genocide."

He explains that "Non-lethal warfare is where you don't kill populations like with a bomb or a gunshot, but you make them sick. You make them dependent on pharmaceuticals which are actually a military-pharmaceutical complex run by the same players—the global elite—and then ultimately these populations become enslaved to the pharmaceuticals and economically debilitated along with their nation states."

Interviewed for streaming radio by Geoff Mecalf, he warns: "Today we are going to get vaccinated full of contaminated vaccines that deliver monkey cancer viruses and a hideous array of other things for the [purpose of] 'public health' for 'infection prevention.' What the vast majority of incriminating evidence in *Emerging Viruses* relays is the fact that the Army's sixth top biological-weapons developer, Litton Bionetics—they had the contract to supply the monkeys for the vaccine manufacturers—essentially also had the contract to develop numerous AIDS-like and Ebola-like viruses during a largely funded and mostly secret 'special virus cancer program.'"

There is a strange familiarity to his message. Two days before the convention, *The Boondocks* comic strip depicted its young black protagonist, Huey, sitting at a computer saying to his grandfather, "This site is huge. I didn't know there was so much in the world that can kill you. Medical accidents, pesticides, rare diseases, diet . . . Wait . . . hold on. What's this? Did we get immunized as babies?" His grandfather says, "Yeah," and the kid responds, "*Great*! Says here they use vaccines to test experimental government super-diseases. *Thanks, Granddad*!"

According to Horowitz, "At the hub of the wheel is the Rockefeller family. Everything from the spraying of malathion—produced by Chevron, a Rockefeller company—to the creation of West Nile virus outbreaks, or alleged outbreaks, along the Eastern seaboard. You're looking at the international bankers. In essence there are about 13 families that have virtually all the financial control that run the world economies.

"And these people also are committing genocide. That's defined as the mass killing of people for economic, political and/or ideological reasons. You've got global genocide. The people who run the economies have a desire to reduce half of the world population simply because smaller populations are easier to control. And they have all the money they need. It's not about making money anymore in this New World Order thing. God wants a New World Order too. He just doesn't want to have it run by corporate fascists.

"I prayed for the Achilles Heel to break the Illuminati code. God gave it to me: The six miraculous musical notes that are in a code in the Bible represent six notes of an ancient musical scale. Frequencies are there, everything about those specific frequencies represent a divine sacred song, Geometry, how this world is going to go back to God real soon with the bringing together of the 144,000, that's nine, that's completion. Humble servants of God are currently being assembled to where in the end times they sing God's praises in such a way as to instantaneously and miraculously deliver this planet back to God, and the frequency of that love signal will be so strong that those with closed hearts and evil will be in such dissonance that they'll virtually *implode*.

"Bust the Illuminati. Bust the cryptography code. The darkest time in our history is just beginning. Revelation tells you in God's word that you and I should count the number of the Beast 666. The revelations we've just been given is that wisdom. It takes it out of the realm of foolish conspiracy theory into hard, provable, scientific, statistically significant fact, and God bless you with it at this time. With that blessing, I want to thank you so much for allowing me to be here tonight [the time was now 12:30 in the afternoon]. Thank you. God bless you. Thank you [said nine times]. Say hallelujah! Praise God! Thank you all."

Horowitz was scheduled to fly to Africa and spread the word. "Okay, God," he prayed, "if it's not Your will for me to go—because apparently I'm hearing from all these people that I shouldn't go, I shouldn't go, fear, fear, fear, fear—please let me know what You want me to do, and if You have me go, if You choose to have me die if I go, then so be it, but I would prefer to live and carry your work forward, so please direct me." And God directed him to go.

After he left the stage, the P.A. system blared forth the sound of Jackson Browne singing, "There are lives in the balance. . . ."

The Chem-trails Connection

The first time I ever heard of chem-trails was in the *San Francisco Bay Guardian*. Merle Haggard—yes, the same country singer described by Cathy O'Brien as a "CIA operative"—asked an interviewer:

"Have you seen the chem-trails, the chemical trails from airplanes flying way up high? I wonder what it is they're spraying. It's my biggest question at the moment. They do a tic-tac-toe pattern—clouds do not come in streaks—wherever the prevailing winds are going to carry it over the city. I think it's the United Nations. I've been onto it for a couple of years. There's an epidemic around the United States of upper respiratory infections, particularly old people and people in ill health. It scares me. I want to know what's going on."

But when the *Desert Sun* made reference to the "thick saturated layer of a milky white substance left by jets crisscrossing our [Coachella] valley," a reader from Palm Springs wrote that it was actually "condensed water vapor. That is exactly the same stuff clouds and fog are made of. Sorry to disappoint you."

At the Conspiracy Con, William Thomas, author of *Chem-Trails: Mystery Lines in the Sky*, stated, "I've taken a lot of flak for this story. It cost me just about everything I hold dear. I've taken a beating even coming down here. Journalists with a reputation and a paycheck to protect do not attend and speak at conspiracy conferences. They do not speak the truth. It's very difficult to pursue a story like this, with the media controlled by five major corporations, part of the military-industrial-entertainment complex. You want to short-circuit the mind-control trip? You want to be a lot healthier in your spirit and body? Turn off the news!"

Nevertheless, he vowed that 2001 would be "the breakthrough year" in bringing the issue before the public through the mass media. He had just been "interviewed by mainstream television in Canada for the very first time on the chem-trails subject, and I guarantee we will be on American mainstream media before very long. People call you and others pointing to this phenomenon 'wing nuts.' Then I guess the pilots, the police officers, the former military personnel who first reported this and continue to say that this is not normal—they're wing nuts too. The real wing nuts are the people *doing* this.

"Unlike normal contrails, which are usually short in length and short-lived, these thick white plumes linger for hours, laid down by two or more aircraft in crisscross X patterns, tic-tac-toe grids, perfectly parallel rows. Chem-trails turn clear blue skies into a milky overcast in spite of forecasts calling for sunny weather. The FAA [Federal Aviation Administration] insists that these are normal flight operations, but I have an FAA source, 'Deep Sky,' who disagrees.

"On days and locations of heavy reported sprays, our hospitals are jammed, emergency rooms overflowing with sudden acute upper respiratory ailments. The Centers for Disease Control says there's an epidemic of fatalities, from sudden onset pneumonia, influenza-like illness and heart attacks. It's way beyond coincidence. People think this is done deliberately for some reason to sicken and kill us. It's not a deliberate biological attack—we run into the Law of Unintended Consequences—and yet the results are the same. Illness and death. If you know that program is frightening and sickening and killing people, and you continue to do it, at that point you cross the line, you become a murderer.

"The earth and its inhabitants are being subjected to unprecedented experimentation without our knowledge or permission. Some say the chem-trails are intended to kill us all. Others insist the disorientation and lethargy resulting from chem-trail exposure are intended to make citizens compliant to the New World Order and enslave us all. The most plausible explanation for massive aerial spraying is a planet-wide, high-tech campaign against catastrophic climate change. If true, such a desperate Band-Aid solution disregards fundamental causes of global warming in order to protect powerful financial interests by permitting pollution and profits.

"This story has cost me a lot, cost me the love of my life, my career. To the people doing this, you can break my heart and you can break my back, but you will never, ever, break my spirit." [Prolonged applause, shouts of *Bravo!*] "I'm not afraid of death."

The Reptilian Connection

If there is a star of this show, it's David Icke (rhymes with like). Author of *And the Truth Shall Set You Free*, he's a dynamic performer, somewhat pot-bellied, with longish yellow hair. His presentation is about the secret manipulation of the human race, going back thousands of years, revealing how the same interbreeding bloodlines continue to control positions of power today, and he ardently shares suppressed information on humanity's ancient extraterrestrial origins. Thus he offers an alternative explanation of our existence that transcends creationism and evolution alike.

All that, and he puts his underwear on backwards too. With his whimsical British accent, he confides to the audience: "A little while ago, I'm thinking I'll empty me bladder before I speak, so I'm fiddling and I can't make contact, and then I realize I put me underpants on the wrong way around. I didn't know whether I was coming or going."

Icke has spoken in 25 countries in the last five years—"little dusty filthy holes in little side streets, and what this information needs is setting an event to match the stature of the information. So we're not on the fringes anymore, hiding away, we're in the mainstream. This is real. A few can only control the mass of people when the mass of people are manipulated to police each other.

"You set the norms in society by controlling what passes for the media, education, science, and you set the norms of what is right and wrong, possible and impossible, good and bad, sane and insane, dangerous and not dangerous, and you create a mental and emotional sheeppen of norms. The vast majority of people are not questioning. And then you've got the few who are looking at these norms and seeing that they are fundamentally limited and limiting.

"The conspiracy in the end is a mind game. It's about controlling the way we think and feel, and disconnecting us from those levels that would filter and see through the veils that are thrown before us. And one of the greatest ways of keeping people in ignorance is stopping the free flow of information. So you frighten people into keeping their mouths shut.

"There is no need for hunger in the world, for poverty. The reason we have it in this world of abundance is a simple equation: abundance equals choice equals freedom. Scarcity equals dependency equals control. And so what we have all over the world is manufactured scarcity creating manufactured dependency creating control by the few. Transnational corporations have gone into those countries, taken over vast swards of food-growing lands. In Ghana, 53 percent of children were malnourished while 58 percent of food-growing land was growing cocoa for the western chocolate industry.

"The control of today's world is merely today's point in an unbroken stream of manipulation over thousands of years in which the same bloodlines working through their secret society network have put themselves in the positions of power. Have used that power to further and further centralize power to the point we've reached today where all that has been hidden all these years is actually coming to obvious public attention.

"Whenever you reach a point where something is about to become physical reality, the centralized global structure of power, there's always a window of time when what has remained hidden comes into the public arena because it's about to manifest. And that's the point of time we're in. We're seeing the fusion of mega-global corporations in media ownership, business ownership.

"This is a house of cards, dependent for its continuance on maintaining its secrecy, and that veil is lifting. Producing a solution to this is completely in our hands, because we are the solution and we are the problem. The secrecy part of it is lifting. Now it's down to us. We are the generation that has the opportunity if we don't run away, secede to fear, and we do what is necessary."

If Icke was delivering a vague pep talk, the next day he would enter specific domains of strangeness.

"I know I'm okay today, because I've got my underpants on the right way around," he began. "A few years ago, I met a scientist who joined the CIA as a youngster, serving his country. He is a genius in the area of magnetics. When he started to work for the CIA in these secret projects, he realized that they didn't want his knowledge to serve humanity, they wanted to create technology that would help to control the mass of the population, and he rebelled against it and said, 'I'm not doing this anymore.'

"He started to tell me a story and, as he did, he was opening his shirt. One day he left home and he started missing time. Doesn't remember anything about it. But he does remember waking up on a medical-type bench, and as he got his faculties back he realized there was something stuck to his chest. As he opened his shirt, I could see like a see-through shampoo sachet on his chest with an orange-gold liquid inside it.

"And he said that what they'd done was manipulate his body to need this drug to survive, and if he doesn't get it, then he starts to die what is apparently a very long and painful death. And this patch (which is what they call them on the inside) with the drug has to be replaced every 72 hours, and if he doesn't serve an agenda that sickens him, then it's not replaced.

"He told me about a microchip now so small it can be inserted in a vaccination program through a hypodermic needle. Even those who thought the microchip was coming along as a tagging device have not realized that it's not just about keeping a tag on where people are. It's not actually the signals going from the chip to the computer we should be concerned about, but the signals coming the other way *to* the chip, because the technology exists, outside the public arena and increasingly in it, which can manipulate human emotion and thought processes externally once one of these guys is inside. If people say no to one thing, say no to the microchip."

[In December 2001, Reuters reported that a chip the size of a grain of rice which can be injected into your body and give detailed information to anyone with the right scanning equipment is soon to be available from Applied Digital Solutions; the company has projected a potential market worth $70 billion.]

Occasionally, Icke throws in a tidbit of comic relief, such as two Martians in a bar: "Have you heard the latest about the Earthlings?" "No, what have they done now?" "They borrow money that doesn't exist and pay interest on it."

Other times, he'll throw in a generally unconsidered theory: "JonBenet Ramsey has all the feel of her being a multi-personality, dissociative identity disorder, trauma-based mind-control situation, and involved in Satanic ritual abuse. I think there's a massive cover-up there, because if you're going to stop the dominoes falling, you have to stop the first domino falling, and that's what that cover-up to me was all about."

But he is most challenging when he discusses interbreeding: "Why are these ruling families today obsessed with interbreeding? Why when you follow them back genealogically to the ancient world have they always been obsessed with interbreeding? I found an amazing common theme in the ancient world anywhere on the planet: the theme of gods interbreeding with humanity, creating hybrid bloodlines which ended up in positions of power.

"I talked five hours with a Zulu shaman about extraterrestrial connections to the Illuminati. African history is the same theme, of gods from another world, which have great connections to earth history, interbreeding with humanity, creating bloodlines which have ruled the world all these thousands of years. The royal black bloodline of Africa from the age of tribal days claimed descendants from the same gods that these other crowds do.

"One of the great themes that comes up in this interbreeding and these ancient accounts is of a serpent race, a race of a reptilian genetic history, which interbred with humans, creating hybrid DNA. I'm not just talking about this tiny frequency range we call the world. There are other frequencies as well, in terms of where manipulators of the manipulators actually come from. This force which manipulates through these bloodlines overwhelmingly operates right on the periphery of our physical senses, right on the edge. It can appear that someone's gone from one form to another. This is 'shape shifting' between human and reptilian form.

"From 1998 onward, I kept meeting people telling the same story, that they have seen people overwhelmingly in positions of power (but not always) move from a human form to a reptilian-type form. There is the Mayan legend of the iguana. Lizard-like aliens had descended upon the Mayans. Their pyramids—their advanced astronomical technology including the sacrifice of virgins—were supposedly inspired by lizard aliens. When the aliens interbred with the Mayans, they produced a form of life they could inhabit. They fluctuated between a human and iguana appearance in chameleon-like abilities, a perfect vehicle for transforming into world leaders.

"Those who have seen a reptilian-type ethereal figure enveloping and following around humans and locking into them in those lower two chakra points, vortex points, for me, is possession. The more I've understood this, the more I've realized just how many people, particularly these bloodlines, are actually controlled by these other-dimensional forces, and while we appear to be seeing a president or a banking leader in a physical form, the actual point of control is beyond that and overshadowing it, and on some occasions people see that overshadowing entity."

One wonders whether such a defense—"The reptile made me do it"—will someday be used in a court of law.

"To understand humanity you have really got to understand humanist reptilian past, reptilian inherited genetics. One of the most ancient parts of the human brain is known by science as the R complex, for reptilian brain. We get these traits—cold-blooded behavior, ritualistic behavior, desire for top-down power over structures. Now, dismiss the reptilian thing—let's just think they don't exist—I have just described the basic mentality of the Illuminati that allows wars to be created, millions of casualties without any emotional attachment to consequences. Why do people who have more money than they could spend in a thousand lifetimes go on accumulating it? Why do corporations that have *enormous* power and control over vast areas go on accumulating and seeking more and more power and control?"

So, then, is this whole reptilian agenda really just a metaphor for the varieties of human cruelty? Or does Icke mean it all literally?

"Some of the descriptions, like of the British royal family—people who claim to have been at the rituals—are of a literal shift. They seem to go from one physical state to another, very much in this dimension, which from our perspective of this-world physics is like, *what?* And then others are describing what appears to be a vibrational thing, where people are looking into another dimension slightly outside of our physical frequency range, the normal one, and suddenly they're seeing another level of the person which appears reptilian. And exactly where the truth is in all that or whether it's a shade of grey and both are true, there's a lot more information that is needed.

"Going back in African history, this reptilian group actually go back a phenomenal amount of time in relation to this planet, and they claim that it's actually rightfully theirs, and at some point in the ancient past there were some great wars that went on, and in fact they were kicked off, and they're trying to regain control of what they think is rightfully theirs, like being kicked out of a country.

"Other researchers, concentrating on the reptilian thing for a long time, say that in some way they basically go around to different places, just raping the resources, and then move on. Then there's the one about the fact that in some way a lot of these beings were almost imprisoned, in a vibrational prison, like they can't get out of it by going up because they can't vibrationally get there in their present state of being. And their only way out of that level is to come into a lower level of vibration, into this dense physical world, and operate through that. But I understand Cathy saying it's only a mind-control thing."

From the gospel according to Cathy O'Brien:

"When Bill and Bob Bennett together sexually assaulted my daughter Kelly and me at the Bohemian Grove in 1986, I had already known Bill Bennett as a mind-control programmer for some time. He apparently found perverse pleasure in whipping me. With my wrists bruised and my body stinging with pain, Bennett lit up a cigarette and cryptically asked, 'Was that your first cum-union with an alien?'

"[On another occasion] deep underground in NASA's Goddard Space Flight Center mind-control lab near D.C., Bill Bennett began preparing me for the program. NASA uses various CIA designer drugs to chemically alter the brain and create exactly the mindset required at the time. I could barely crawl up onto the cold, metal lab table as the drug took effect. In the darkness surrounding me, I could hear Bill Bennett talking. 'My brother Bob and I work as one unit. We are alien to this dimension—two beings from another plane.'

"The high-tech light display swirling around me convinced me I was transforming dimensions with them. A laser of light hit the black wall in front of me, which seemed to explode into a panoramic view of a White House cocktail party—as though I had transformed dimensions and stood amongst them. Not recognizing anyone, I frantically asked, 'Who are these people?'

"'They're not people, and this isn't a space ship,' Bennett said. As he spoke, the holographic scene changed ever so slightly until the people appeared to be lizard-like aliens. 'Welcome to the second level of the underground. This level is a mere reflection of the first, an alien dimension. We are from a transdimensional plane that spans and encompasses all dimensions. I have taken you through my dimension as a means of establishing stronger holds on your mind than the earth's plane permits. Being alien, I simply make my thoughts your thoughts by projecting them into your mind. My thoughts are your thoughts.' If this were so, why did he have to *audibly* tell me?"

Aha! A touch of skepticism from Cathy. And yet part of me still hopes that was all true, if only because of Bill Bennett's maxim about the Gary Condit affair: "Hypocrisy is better than no values at all."

The Paul Krassner Connection

Even Mae Brussell had such a heavy investment in conspiracy that it affected the objectivity of her perception. She was convinced that behind the death of John Belushi there was a conspiracy involving Robert De Niro and Robin Williams, who had both snorted cocaine with Belushi the night he died. I argued with Mae about this. After her death in 1988, I learned that the Los Angeles Police Department had been preparing a drug-sting operation in which they planned to ensnare De Niro, Williams and Belushi. So there *was* a conspiracy, just not the one that Mae had in mind.

Now I was having a flashback to 1972 when I experienced a paranoid freak-out from information overload. During that psychotic episode, I was positive that all the so-called Nielsen TV-rating families really consisted entirely of experts in behavior modification drawn from the 642 Nazis imported to the U.S. after World War II under Project Paperclip. And I broke up with a girlfriend because I somehow convinced myself that the FBI had sent her to spy on me. She asked if we could at least have a dialogue, but that only made me more suspicious.

I met a new girlfriend and seriously asked if there was a microphone in her cat's flea collar. I totally believed in the possibility at that moment, but she thought I was just being my usual funny self. Twenty years later, I would read in an article by Harrison Salisbury in *Penthouse*: "The CIA wired a cat to eavesdrop on conversations. Micro sensing devices were installed in its body, and its tail was wired as an aerial. But it was hit by a car before it got into action." One person's paranoia is another person's vision of the future.

I've also been the recipient of *other* people's paranoia. In July 1981, *New Solidarity*, official organ of Lyndon LaRouche's reactionary U.S. Labor Party, published a dossier on me:

"In the early 1950s, Paul Krassner was recruited to the stable of pornographers and 'social satirists' created and directed by British Intelligence's chief brainwashing facility, the Tavistock Institute, to deride and destroy laws and institutions of morality and human decency. Among Krassner's circle of Tavistock iconoclasts, peddling smut in the name of humor and 'creative expression,' were Lenny Bruce, the drug addict comedian who died of a heroin overdose in the early 1960s; 'literary' pornographer William Burroughs; Norman Mailer, whose plea of insanity saved him from conviction on charges of attempted manslaughter against his wife; and homosexual versifier Allen Ginzburg [*sic*]. Krassner's recruitment to Tavistock's psychological shock-troupe [*sic*] was facilitated by his intense childhood and adolescent masturbatory fixation. . . ."

On the other hand, was I now losing my religion? Had I forsaken the unholy trinity—the Federal Reserve Bank, the Council on Foreign Relations and the Trilateral Commission? How could I distinguish truth from lies any more if truth was cross-fertilized with greed, the need for attention, false memory, speculation, fantasy, self-delusion and intentional propaganda?

316 ◄ ◄ ◄

I contemplated the implications of something that Michael Aquino had told me: "Part of what we learned in PSYOP was that it's not just the propaganda you create that is a factor, but the pre-existing propaganda 'filters' in target audiences' brains as well. The key has to be designed to fit the lock, so to speak. And underlying all this is the challenge to the PSYOPerator to extricate *himself* from his own filters; otherwise he will see the situation only through his personal distortions and thus be inept at influencing it objectively and comprehensively."

Consequently, propaganda can become a two-way street. For example, Cory Hammond, former president of the American Society of Clinical Hypnosis, has had many clients who, under hypnosis, "remember" hideous incidents of satanic rituals, infant sacrifice, sadomasochism and coprophilia (get that shit-eating grin off your face). Dr. Hammond believes that three groups working together—neo-Nazis, the CIA and NASA—have been programming American children for over 50 years to make them part of "a Satanic order that will rule the world."

Likewise, the war on drugs is filtered through a *mass* of distortions. In the words of *The Economist*—a venerable British newsweekly that has been a longtime passionate advocate for the legalization of drugs—the growing, selling, consuming and outlawing of illegal drugs around the world is a complex mix of economics, politics and world culture.

There are silly conspiracies. Some folks believe that the moon landing was faked (those were close-up photos of oatmeal). Others believe that the Woodstock Festival never occurred (it was contrived by the media). Still others believe that Elvis Presley's death was fabricated (he's alive in Las Vegas, working as an Elvis impersonator). And surely there must be others who are convinced that militant vegetarian activists are responsible for Mad Cow disease.

Sometimes silly conspiracists get results. In 1995, Indiana transportation officials were forced to alter the maintenance codes marked on the back of highway signs because some state residents were convinced that the markings were coded messages designed to assist invading UN troops.

And there are serious conspiracies. Gasoline refiners conspire to limit supply and fix prices. The relationship between doctors and pharmaceutical companies is blatantly conspiratorial. Douglas Valentine wrote in *The Phoenix Program* (about the CIA's notorious terrorist campaign against Vietnamese villagers) that in 1968 the Army's 111th Military Intelligence Group kept Martin Luther King under 24-hour-a-day surveillance. Its agents were in Memphis on April 4 and "reportedly watched and took photos while King's assassin moved into position, took aim, fired, and walked away."

World War II was bracketed by presidential conspiracies of silence: Franklin D. Roosevelt knew that Japan was going to attack Pearl Harbor, and Harry Truman knew that Japan was about to make peace overtures but he nevertheless ordered that atomic bombs be dropped on Hiroshima and Nagasaki. Domestically, the Aryan Republican Army financed and helped to stage the Oklahoma City bombing, and the Bureau of Alcohol, Tobacco and Firearms knew about it three weeks before it happened.

Pokemon has become a target of religious leaders throughout the Arab world who charge that the game promotes theories of evolution, encourages gambling and, at its core, is part of a Jewish conspiracy aimed at turning children away from Islam. To David Icke, Jews are the pawns in an elaborate Rothschild-Illuminati breeding experiment, and are "impregnated with a reptilian genetic code."

I had felt a familiar wave of paranoia come over me at the conspiracy convention. Was I having a relapse of my 1972 freak-out? Did the anti-virus software honcho hackers finally find out that I knew they were behind the computer-virus outbreaks like some kind of electronic protection racket? Had there been a microchip in my forced flu vaccination? Was I myself a Manchurian candidate?

But . . . *Tavistock* . . . *Tavistock* . . . I just couldn't seem to remember anything about ever having been brainwashed at the Tavistock Institute. They must've programmed it right out of my consciousness.

The Mad Scientist Connection

Downstairs at the convention center, the Charismatic Catholics are singing joyfully: "I will call upon the Lord/ Who is worthy to be praised/ So shall I be saved from my enemies . . . "

Upstairs at Conspiracy Con, there is a final panel with questions from the audience. A reporter for *Stuff* magazine waits his turn on line, then steps up to the microphone and asks, "What is the secret to how you've managed to maintain such healthy heads of hair?" The answers: "Well, mine's glued." "I stopped pulling it a few years ago." "It was the fluoride." "Mine is the same color when I purchased it." "Genetics."

Another question, in the form of a statement from an audience member: "With all the power and control that the Illuminati appears to have, I'm struck by the fact that they still have not gained any knowledge of life over death, physical life existing, everlasting life."

Jordan Maxwell responds:

"How do you know they haven't? I'm sure that they have a lot more knowledge about such things than we do. I have been of the opinion that they very well—these people who are running the world behind the scenes—might be operating with a knowledge of reincarnation which is profoundly more finite than our understanding. A lot of us have a belief system in reincarnation, but I wouldn't be a bit surprised if these people have an actual system that they *know* works, and they've set up things so that when they die they come back and reincarnate and keep up the good work. It wouldn't surprise me a bit if reincarnation is something that they have mastered, maybe have a higher knowledge of."

David Icke agrees:

"I can absolutely support that. A number of people that I've met over the years who have had access to knowledge of some of these blood-line families have told me again and again that they set up a situation whereby they basically use the body like a disposable unit. They operate in these bloodline bodies for a certain period of time, and then when the body starts to come to the end of its useful life, they basically just whip out of it and whip into another one, because basically the focus of their consciousness is not in this dimension. They are *in* it, but they're not *of* it. The focus of their consciousness and their knowledge is in other dimensions."

A correspondent for *UFO* magazine first complains that there hasn't been enough discussion about UFOs at this convention, and then she asks, "How do you impact the world outside this kind of group?"

Icke answers, "I think we're in a cycle of awakening. It's like a spiritual alarm clock. When I started this personal journey in 1990, I started talking about this stuff a little bit, and I was perceived and promoted as a nutter having a mid-life crisis. As I've wandered through the '90s till now, I have seen the most amazing awakening going on where people who would've laughed in your face at some of this stuff 10 years ago are now looking at it seriously, and there's a reason for that which they can't explain.

"They struggle to rationalize it intellectually sometimes because it's so bizarre compared with their conditioned reality. But at the level of feeling they just *know* there's something in this and they can't often say why. And this feeling change is going on. I feel we're at the start of a fantastic revolution of thought when we are going to enter the mainstream. There comes a point where public interest in the subject is such that even the mainstream media can no longer deny its existence."

A woman who claims to be a victim of mind control asks, "How do you function? How do you deal with manipulation in your personal lives, being individuals that are speaking out? Is there any secure communication? Can the whole body be scanned for implants, inside your teeth or your skull?"

William Lyne replies, "It takes very sensitive equipment. You can't even find those things because they're very low-wattage devices. If they're implants, if you're being targeted with electronic mind control, sometimes it might help just to get out of the house, get in with a bunch of other people somewhere. It will confuse the system, maybe, because they'd be scanning too many people, they could lose track of you. As long as you're at home, they could zero in on you a lot easier, they know where you are."

Icke adds:

"No technology exists in this frequency range more powerful than the human mind in its true power. When disconnected from that, we become open to technical manipulation. Is there any secure communication? I don't give a shit. I say what I think on the Internet. I don't worry about being harmed. If you don't allow the idea of vulnerability into your reality, it cannot manifest. If it's not your reality, you cannot project it. It never occurs to me that these guys can do anything to me.

"Those that were doing this [work] in fear of consequences were getting them. 'I don't know how long they're gonna allow me to do this.' They almost wore their bravery like a war medal. Courage is overcoming fear. If you don't have fear you don't need courage because there's no fear to overcome. You just do it, get on with it, do what you believe to be right without the need for courage because there's nothing to overcome.

"'I'm doing dangerous things, but I keep on going, I'm sure they're gonna do this to me if I keep on.' They will get the consequences, and others who are just *doing* it, won't. And because we create our own reality, what we allow into our field of possibility can manifest. If it doesn't come in, it cannot manifest. I don't worry about defending myself."

Suddenly, as if on cue, an agitated man brandishing a pistol stalks out from the backstage area. Shouting, "The China card will be played big," he aims his gun at Icke, who sits there calmly while the other panelists all duck under the table. A single shot rings out. Panic fills the air, and screams emanate from the audience. But it's the would-be assassin, not Icke, who is the one that falls to the ground. The panel discussion has ended, and the auditorium is cleared.

I show my press credentials to the security guard hovering over the man, who is bleeding fiercely, and they allow me to stay. When a paramedic unbuttons the man's shirt, I can't help but notice that on his chest, just a couple of inches from the gaping wound, there is a patch with an orange-gold liquid inside it. The paramedic pats it gently and says, "What the hell is this?" The man is able only to whisper, "He blew my goddam cover." Then he gasps for breath, and dies.

I had been looking forward all day to a dinner of Colossal Pacific Prawns simmered in Thai curry, but the hotel kitchen had closed early, and besides, I wasn't hungry. I was too preoccupied with what had transpired that evening. I kept asking myself, "Who shot the mad scientist? And why?" I felt like a poker player who's been dealt a hand of all blank cards.

Finally an epiphany came, and I knew exactly what I had to do. I made three calls, then went down to the bar to find David Icke. We selected a corner table, I took out my cell phone, dialed my own number, and when the answering machine started, I dialed the code to get my messages, and handed the phone to Icke. This is what he heard:

"Hi, this is Paul, calling myself. I've already left a message on Nancy's answering machine, asking her to save this tape in case anything happens to me. About the shooting that took place here, my contact in the CIA has informed me that it was a Company job. They killed David Icke's friend before *he* could kill Icke. But why would they be *protecting* Icke? You'd think that they'd *want* him dead because he knows too much. Unless he happens to be one of *them* and they need him to continue spreading *dis*information. So, now that this precaution has been taken, I will go and confront Icke."

He laughed.

"Nice try," he said. "First of all, don't worry, nothing's going to happen to you. But keep that tape as a souvenir, by all means. You're right about one thing, though. I *am* protected by the CIA. Not because I'm one of them, but because I'm *not* one of them. If they wanted me dead, they could kill me anytime they wanted. But they know I'm not spreading disinformation. You have to understand, these guys work strictly on a need-to-know basis. So it's not that I know too much, it's that *they* don't know *enough*.

"Because, if an individual agent knows too much, he may not do what he's been assigned to do. He must have a given order to do something, but if he knows that the end result is that somebody's going to be blown up 12 miles away—and all he's supposed to do is deliver an envelope—he may start thinking about it. So, various agents read my books and check my Web site and show up wherever I speak. It's a safety valve for them, on how far things are going."

"Are you saying that the intelligence community has allowed you to function precisely because *you* know more than any of *them*?"

"Exactly . . . "

The Last Connection

On my return flight the next morning, I found myself reminiscing about the 1987-88 TV season, when I had been a writer and on-air commentator on *The Wilton North Report*, a nightly satirical hour on the Fox network that lasted only 21 shows. Critics blamed the hosts, a pair of disc jockeys who were not untalented but who were deliberately chosen for their inoffensiveness.

I had previously suggested Conan O'Brien, a writer on the show who also did the audience warm-ups. "No," said the producer, "he's not professional enough." Ellen DeGeneres? "Too dykey." Chris Rock? "Too raw." Rosie O'Donnell? "Who wants to look at her every night?" Richard Belzer? "Too reptilian." Belzer is a conspiracy researcher as well as a comedian and actor, but little did he ever dream that ultimately he—his reptilian self—could be the culmination of his own investigation.

Back home, the marketing of conspiracy was on a roll. "Majestic," an interactive computer game revolving around a conspiracy involving corporate intrigue, was available. For $10 a month, tens of thousands of online players would receive screaming phone calls at midnight, faxes, anonymous e-mails and instant messages from mysterious informers directing them to research strange alien conspiracies and nefarious government activities. ["Majestic" was suspended on September 12, 2001.]

I received a call from Andy Klein, a producer of *The Conspiracy Zone*, a new TV show featuring debates about cover-ups, ranging from Freemasons to bar codes to Hollow Earth.

"The frightening thing," he observed, "is that life is so *random*. At least there's something comforting about conspiracies."

He was calling me for recommendations on who might be appropriate to appear on programs about the fix behind professional sports and the fix behind the election of George W. Bush. [The latter topic was discarded after 9/11.] He told me that *The Conspiracy Zone* would also deal with "unexplained" deaths, such as Jimmy Hoffa, Marilyn Monroe and the Kennedys.

"Oh, that's so last century," I said. "Conspiracy research has evolved from 'Who Killed JFK?' to 'Who Fucked a Lizard From Outer Space?'"

One other thing. My visual mantra of the man who urinated and flossed simultaneously had been replaced by a patriotic image of Cathy O'Brien: "I was ushered away from my classmates and taken to an office where Michigan State Senator Guy VanderJagt was waiting with soon-to-be-president Gerald Ford. They laughed as he placed a small American flag in my rectum and instructed me to wave it."

Oh, well, at least she didn't *wrap* herself in the flag.

my cannabis
cup runneth
over

> *"There are 100,000 total marijuana smokers in the U.S., and most are Negroes, Hispanics, Filipinos and entertainers. Their Satanic music, jazz and swing, result from marijuana usage. This marijuana causes white women to seek sexual relations with Negroes, entertainers and any others."*
>
> —*Harry Anslinger, U.S. Commissioner of Narcotics, testifying to Congress in 1937 on why marijuana should be made illegal.*

A Blessing in Disguise

On our way to the airport, I mailed a few letters with the official Porky Pig commemorative stamp. Ironic enough on its own—for here was Porky in the role of a mail carrier buoyantly delivering an envelope at the height of the anthrax scare and saying, "That's all, folks!"—Porky's signature stammer had been politically corrected. No more "Th-th-th-that's all, folks!"

It was Thanksgiving week, 2001, and we were headed for a Looney Tunes cartoon of our own, the 14th annual Cannabis Cup in Amsterdam, where I would be inducted into the Counterculture Hall of Fame. I was accompanied by my wife Nancy and our friend Michael Simmons, who was writing an article about the trip for the *L.A. Weekly*. The whole event was organized by *High Times* and 420 Tours.

In the marijuana subculture, the number 420 has come to represent a time to celebrate—at 4:20 every afternoon—by smoking a joint. Some say 420 is the police code for a pot bust. Others say it's the number of ingredients in the herb. Who knows, maybe it's from that nursery rhyme about 4 and 20 blackbirds. Actually, the 4:20 association originated with the Young Waldos, a group of high-school friends from Marin County, California who shared a joint after class during the summer of '71 every day at the same time.

Anyway, the folks at 420 Tours take pride in being stoners *and* efficient, but in this particular case, they were oxymoronic and goofed on our bookings. I had informed them that Nancy and I would fly from Palm Springs and transfer at Los Angeles, and that Simmons would leave directly from Los Angeles, where he lives—but all three of us were mistakenly booked to depart from Palm Springs.

The day before our scheduled departure, I was told by airline representatives that if Simmons didn't fly from Palm Springs to Los Angeles, he wouldn't be allowed to fly to Amsterdam. Not for reasons of security but because, if he didn't make that one-hour flight first, then American Airlines wouldn't get any money from Northwest Airlines. After an hour on the phone, a supervisor assured me that Simmons had absolutely no choice but to drive to our home that evening and leave with us the next morning. Simmons immediately started looking in the Yellow Pages for the least expensive van service.

In 1994, he was listening to a disc jockey on KPCC, Ann the Raven, who played the blues and talked openly about her own depression between records: "Oh, the Raven is feeling really bad tonight, her boyfriend walked out on her and she's *so* lonely. . . ." One time she felt so unhappy that she spoke on the air of committing suicide. Simmons called and tried to convince her that life was worth living. Seven years later, he recognized her voice as she was driving him in a van from Los Angeles. Which explains why, a couple of hours later, they were embracing goodbye in our driveway.

Coffee Shops and Hotels

In the United States, at a cost of $10 billion, police arrested an estimated 734,498 persons for marijuana violations in 2000. That's the highest figure ever recorded by the FBI, comprising just under half of all drug arrests in the country. Of those charged with marijuana violation, almost 88 percent—that's 646,042 American citizens—were charged with possession of marijuana.

The remaining 88,456 individuals were charged with "sale/manufacture," a category which includes all cultivation offenses, even those where the marijuana was being grown for personal or medical use. Marijuana arrests far exceed the total number of arrests for all violent crimes combined, including murder, manslaughter, rape, robbery and assault. Since 1990, nearly six million Americans have been arrested on marijuana charges.

In contrast, the Health Ministry of Holland decriminalized marijuana in 1976 and, 20 years later, licenses were given out to coffee shops, the same places that had already been selling marijuana and hashish. There are some 800 coffee shops in the country—about 300 in Amsterdam alone—and they are licensed to sell up to five grams of pot or hash to patrons over 18.

Coffee shops have names such as Blue Velvet, The Dolphins, El Guapo, Paradox, Flying Dutchmen and Nirvana. Customers may choose their stash from an actual menu, then sit down at a table and smoke their purchase. They can even buy coffee.

Cup attendees are given "passports" to see who will be the first to have their passport stamped by all the coffee shops where they sample their goods. That adds up to a lot of inhalation. One coffee shop, the Green House, offers a special "energy drink after smoking too much all day." Anyone who gets a stamp from all the coffee shops in the contest is entitled to a free "Official Judge" T-shirt.

In October 2001, a government statement, recognizing that some coffee-shop patrons use marijuana to alleviate pain, said that because "an increasing number of patients suffering illnesses such as cancer, AIDS and multiple sclerosis receive medicinal cannabis," under a new law approved by the Dutch Cabinet, pharmacies would be allowed to fill their marijuana prescriptions, to be paid for by the government, under the nation's public health insurance plan.

In November, the United States Attorney's Office, in order to justify a DEA raid on the Los Angeles Cannabis Resource Cooperative, released a statement that "The United States Supreme Court recently held that, under federal law, marijuana is an illegal drug which Congress has determined has no currently accepted medical use. Proposition 215 is a California state law that has no bearing on the applicability of federal criminal laws."

The Cannabis Cup has become what is essentially an annual music-and-fun-filled Amsterdam trade show. In 1993, there were 52 attendees. This year, there were 1,700. Visitors were warned by 420 Tours:

"Marijuana smoking is not allowed in any of the hotels. Management has advised us that they will be tolerant with *High Times* judges, but keep in mind that hotels are also used by business travelers and other tourists. If you do smoke in your hotel room, open the windows and place a towel under the door to stop the smoke from leaking into the corridor."

However, in the lobby of the funky Quentin Hotel, where the Cup crew and celebrities stay, a gigantic painting of Keith Richards benignly watches over the guests as they sit at wooden tables, cheerfully chatting while they smoke their joints and drink their hot chocolate. This event is a nonstop orgy of pot smoking. There are 22 brands of marijuana to be tested—in a sexist sort of way—11 strains of *indica* to be judged by men and 11 strains of *sativa* to be judged by women.

For many folks, the first joint they smoke automatically becomes the winner, because everything after that one is cumulative and anti-climactic. There is no surcease of euphoria, no time to savor one strain of marijuana or anticipate the next. This is not like wine tasting, where the wine is spit out between samples. At least, in the aromatherapy booth, coffee beans are whiffed between each new fragrance, to neutralize the olfactory sense.

Moments of Sparkle

In Amsterdam, you can visit the Hemp Museum, the Anne Frank House or the Torture Museum. At the Hemp Museum, you learn that the Chinese were making paper from hemp stalks as early as 100 BC, that Queen Victoria smoked marijuana to alleviate menstrual cramps, and that easily grown hemp can save the planet from deforestation.

Folding money (pre-Euro currency) in Amsterdam comes in different sizes in order to accommodate sightless people. There's a McDonald's with a plastic marijuana plant in the window. As we tour the city, there are moments of sparkle that glisten in my memory.

Christmas season is launched with the arrival by steamboat of *Sinterklass*, the equivalent of Santa Claus, wearing the attire of a Catholic bishop. He is accompanied by scores of assistants, *Zwarte Piet* (Black Peter). These are Caucasians in blackface, but—unlike the university students in Kentucky and Alabama who wore blackface and Ku Klux Klan outfits at fraternity Halloween parties—Black Peter's color has nothing to do with race. Rather, it represents the devil, dressed in a 16th-century Spanish costume, though you'd never expect Satan to be leading a white horse with *Sinterklass* on its back, and passing out candies to kids along the parade route, then being given the keys to the city by the mayor at the Dam Square.

The moonlight cruise on the canals isn't usually conducted in this manner, but the passengers are all cannabis judges and they're certainly not being treated the way regular tourists are. Flight attendants bring bingo cards and paper plates of pot to each table. None of us could have imagined that we would be playing bingo on a boat with those stewardesses making sure that we mark the cards properly in case anybody is too stoned to do it right when the numbers are called. Explaining a pause in the action, the captain announces, "There's a small accident with the wheel of fortune," but then it's fixed and the game continues. The prizes, naturally, are fresh buds.

When I was in public school, I got in trouble for drawing a picture of my teacher on the blackboard. She was naked and I gave her a triangle of pubic hair with purple chalk. That was before bikini wax. Now, in Amsterdam, I find myself at the Van Gogh Museum. He was obviously a much better artist than me. Gazing at his rendition of the torso of Venus, I read in the adjoining explanation that "the addition of pubic hair with black chalk suggests that it was a juvenile prank." Standing there in the museum, I suddenly get a rush in retrospect that as a kid I must have been carrying on an ancient tradition of mischief.

The red light district is not just for sex workers. People live and have other jobs in that area. Ah, but the prostitutes, they display themselves, skimpily dressed, seductively sitting or standing in front of their windows, drapes open, serving as instant infomercials to entice pótential customers outside. This, as simultaneously, women in Afghanistan have not been allowed to talk loudly or laugh within their own homes, and they are forbidden to go close enough to the windows to be seen from outside. Nancy and I are standing in back of a small crowd gathered on the sidewalk, watching as a man knocks on the door of a beautiful dark-haired prostitute in the window of a ground-floor apartment. She opens the door to negotiate with him. I ask Nancy, "You want to tape that?" She focuses her video camera on the encounter. The woman stops talking with the man and, leaving the door open, goes back inside. Through the window we see her getting a glass of water and coming back out. Could it be that all the man wants from her is just a glass of water? But, no—she tosses it directly at *us*. Droplets of water splash through the air as the glass breaks near Nancy's foot. This woman may rent her body to strangers, but she doesn't want her privacy invaded or her dignity denied.

As the Vietnam War escalated, I published and distributed a poster that said *Fuck Communism*! The word *Fuck* was in red-white-and-blue lettering emblazoned with stars and stripes; the word *Communism* was in red lettering emblazoned with hammers and sickles. Enough copies were sold to finance reporter Robert Scheer's trip to Southeast Asia. Now, at the Cannabis Cup, I meet science-fiction author Spider Robinson. He had once sent for a *Fuck Communism*! poster that never arrived. But then one day, at the local post office, when all the clerks were in the back, he leaned over the counter and saw a poster—*his* poster—taped to a wall where patrons couldn't ordinarily see it. Employees in their patriotic zeal had committed a federal crime.

The Philosophy Behind the Cup

The impressive thing about the Cannabis Cup is not only all the smoking and the live bands and the sightseeing. It's the sense of camaraderie—intelligent conversations and witty dialogue with old friends and new acquaintances. And the sense of freedom—blithely smoking spleefs at the Cup's two main venues, the Pax Party House and the Melkweg nightclub, which are both adjacent to police stations.

Ironically, the pot-smoke-filled Pax Party House has a sign that says "No Cigarette Smoking." John Sinclair is there. The former chairman of the White Panthers in Detroit and manager of hard-rock band The MC (Motor City) 5, started smoking marijuana in 1963. The cover of his book, *Guitar Army*, featured a photo of him smoking what had been a cigarette but which was altered into a joint because he "didn't want to send the wrong message to kids."

All the strains of marijuana being tested here have their own brand names, such as Sagarmatha Seeds and Homegrown Fantaseeds. The Cannabis Cup provides a respite from Afghanistan, but the war is still on our minds. In fact, while a CNN correspondent is talking about Mazar-i-Sharif, just captured by the Northern Alliance, we are smoking a brand of hashish named Mazar-i-Sharif.

Steve Gaskin, founder of The Farm, an intentional community in Tennessee that left San Francisco in a convoy a few decades ago, started smoking marijuana in 1962. He suggests, "The way to end the war is to legalize pot and hash in America, then give Afghanistan a franchise for the first seven years."

Basically, the war on drugs is a war for control and against pleasure. I ask *High Times* editor Steve Hager for his overview.

"My main focus," he says, "is establishing the counterculture as a legitimate minority group whose basic rights have been denied. A major reason for the drug war is the persecution of our culture. Marijuana is the sacrament of the counterculture. This will never change, and we will never accept the prohibition of our sacrament. How could one expect any legitimate spiritual movement to be forced into surrendering a sacrament? Marijuana has over a 5,000-year-old history of religious use in India.

"Imagine if alcohol was outlawed and a group of Catholics began holding underground mass with real wine. Do you think they would be subjected to mandatory minimum sentences, forfeiture, losing their children? Yet this happens every day to devoted, peaceful members of our culture. Currently these people are being sold into slavery to corporations like Wackenhut, who have turned the privatized prison-industrial complex into the second most profitable industry in America, right behind pharmaceuticals."

The Counterculture Hall of Fame

Previous individuals who have been inducted into the *High Times* Counterculture Hall of Fame: Bob Marley, Louis Armstrong, Mezz Mezzrow, Jack Kerouac, Neal Cassady, Allen Ginsberg, William Burroughs and, at the Cannabis Cup in 2000, Ina May Gaskin, founder of the modern midwife movement.

When her husband Steve challenged Ralph Nader for the Green Party presidential nomination that year, Ina May predicted that she would be "an unruly First Lady." She would turn the Lincoln Bedroom into a birth center for the poor. She would grow hemp in the Rose Garden; all meals at the White House would be vegetarian; and she'd teach a Secret Service agent to braid Steve's hair. When I asked if she had intern concerns, she replied, "No, we'll do the blowjobs in *every* room." Her husband would be left to explain to the media, "I can't control her—you try."

Last year, the emcee was San Francisco stand-up comic Ngaio Bealum, whose parents were both in the Black Panther Party. "You know," he said, "when we were kids, we didn't have bongs. We just had to fill our mouths with water and suck real slowly." He described smoking pot while drinking coffee as "the poor man's speedball." This year, the emcee was Watermelon, who lives in Vancouver, where she sells marijuana-laced gingersnap cookies at a nude beach. She describes herself as "the only nudist, pot-dealing comedienne in the world."

And I'm the only person in the world who has ever received awards from both *Playboy* (for satire) and the Feminist Party Media Workshop (for journalism), but neither presentation took place in front of a huge audience like this one on Thanksgiving night. Ina May is onstage introducing me. We embrace, and then, when the applause simmers down, I begin my acceptance speech:

"Oh, *well*. I've never done this before. And I appreciate getting the Counterculture Hall of Fame Award at the Cannabis Cup, but it's pretty ironic because I've been clean and sober [*looking at watch*]—I'd say for about seven minutes now. When we left the States for Amsterdam, the last thing that George W. Bush said was, 'Let's roll!' And that's all that we've been doing here, is rolling 'em, one after another [*cheering from the audience*]. And of course now in World War III, we here have a secret weapon. And it's the neutron *bong*. The neutron bong—it wipes out the user, but leaves the stash intact.

"So, I truly wanna thank Steve Hager and the whole gang from *High Times* and 420 Tours, proving that efficient stoners is not necessarily an oxymoron. And I wanna thank my wife Nancy, who has never once told me that I was smoking too much pot [*cheering from the audience*]. And it just reminded me that there was once a questionnaire that *High Times* had for the readers, and one of the questions was, 'Is it possible to smoke too much pot?' And some reader wrote in and said, 'I don't understand the question.' And so may we all go on not understanding the question. Thank you."

I start to leave the stage, but Watermelon walks out to present me with a silver cup, a framed plaque—and a three-foot-long bud of marijuana.

"That's for you to tickle your wife with," she says.

"Thank you, Watermelon. Y'know, Watermelon, you have very nice pits. Somebody had to say it."

"And I've got a brain that just won't quit, Paul."

"Well, let's see, this cup will be great for keeping my stash in. This plaque will be great for rolling joints on. And this big giant bud—'It's a French tickler,' and I'm sure that will get me through Customs without any problem."

Then come the awards. It is the ultimate irony of this whole affair that an herb that promotes such a sense of cooperation keeps being inhaled in such an aura of competition. As the new inductee, it's my duty to present the final award—the Cannabis Cup itself—to the coffee shop whose entry got the most votes. Watermelon hands me the envelope, which I open slowly to build the suspense.

"Oh, wait, let me just get this white powder out of the way. You know, at the height of the Anthrax scare, the Postmaster General went on TV and announced that you should now always wash your hands after opening the mail. So I do that and, in fact, I wash my hands *before* opening the mail. I wash my hands after I *mail* a letter. I wash my hands when I make a phone call. But I remember a time when the only people who got paranoid about white powder were the ones who were snorting it... Okay, and the winner of the Cannabis Cup is...B-B-B-Barney's B-B-B-Breakfast B-B-B-Bar for Sweet Tooth!"

I had deliberately stuttered, not merely to increase the tension, but also as a private act of solidarity with Porky Pig, who had been deprived of his natural heritage by a politically correct postage stamp.

"Th-th-th-that's all, folks!"